KAT AMONG THE PIGEONS

BY

LAZETTE GIFFORD

Kat Among the Pigeons
A Conspiracy of Authors Publication
www.aconspiracyofauthors.com
Copyright 2015, Lazette Gifford
ISBN: 978-1-936507-57-3
Cover Art Copyright 2016, Lazette Gifford
Bird silhouettes created with Ron's Birds Photoshop Brushes
http://www.daz3d.com/rons-birds

First Print Edition, June 2016

This novel is dedicated to all my lovely little cat friends who are all Cato and the rest of the kitty-gang in the story.

TABLE OF CONTENTS

CHAPTER ONE

ap, tap, tap.
The incessant drumming of small bird beaks against the bedroom window brought me out of a deep, blissful sleep. I tried not to curse.

Tap, tap, tap.

"Go 'way." I pushed my head under the pillow. Cato, a big lazy lump of an orange tabby cat, made a sound of protest and burrowed his head into the blankets. I started to fall back asleep. . . .

Then I heard the little bird voices.

"Big wings! Big Wings!"

Tap, tap, tap.

"Don't care," I mumbled.

Tap, tap, tap-tap-tap-tap. "Big-big-big wings!"

I rolled over and stared at the ceiling as I contemplated what kind of ecological disaster the earth would suffer if I wiped out the nuthatches.

"Big-big-big-wings-wings-wings!"

Tap tap tap tap tap tap tap tap.

The combination of their tiny high-pitched voices and the pounding of their sharp little beaks sounded like a badly sung round robin and with a drummer out of beat as well.

This was not a sound someone can sleep through. I sat up and focused on the window. I squinted and found a dozen or more panicked nuthatches holding to the wooden frame. A few hung upside down and all of them tapped ceaselessly at the glass. Their voices rose in shrill cries of frantic worry.

Tap-tap-tap-tap.

"Yes, yes, I got the idea. I'm getting up!"

I climbed out of the warm bed and yanked on my robe. Soft light drifted through the window which meant it dawn had barely touched the sky. I muttered things again.

Cato pulled his furry head from under the blankets, blinking sleepily. "What's wrong with the nuts?" he asked and yawned.

"Not nuts," I answered batting at his head as I went past him. I missed as he stretched. "Nuthatches."

"All the same to me." Cato settled into a plump circle, his tail curled around his nose. "Do you think you might quiet them down?"

"Sure. I'll throw you out the window. They'd find that interesting enough to shut up about the eagle or hawk or plane that upset them this morning."

Cato snorted and mumbled something I didn't quite hear. Probably just as well.

Understanding animals is common among the fae. This is part of what makes us good at our work, even on this side of the Edge. I have a problem though since I'm not blessed with the ability to understand all animals the way most of the fae can. No, I got lucky enough to catch only two: birds and cats.

It's not a good combination.

I still work as a border guard like all of my clan. We watch over parts of the human world where the Edge is unstable, which is usually wilderness areas. Magic abhors technology, so wild magic like the Edge stays clear of large settlements. I've been here on the outskirts of Estes Park for the last four years, living in a pretty A-frame house on land which has belonged to my family for generations. Down at the base of the hill is the main road to Rocky Mountain National Park. My location is lovely and peaceful.

Except sometimes things upset little birds, especially with the seasons changing from winter to spring and the migrating birds passing through the area. It's not their fault a big bird came sweeping over the trees and terrified the little guys.

I buried my anger as I cranked the window open. Nuthatches held on to the frame, some of them upside down as they stared in at me.

"Big wings, very very very very big big big wings."

"Everything is okay guys," I said. They stopped tapping on the window, at least. "The big wings aren't here."

Dozens of feathered heads turned, craning around to watch the sky between towering pines where the mountains come down in graceful cliffs behind my house. They scanned left, right and back again.

"What are the guys saying?" Cato asked. He pulled his nose out of the blankets and it twitched a couple times.

"Something big frightened them -- but it's not here." I looked out into the gray light of the yard and found quite a few more nuthatches on the trees. "Something set them off."

"Ah," Cato said and his nose twitched again. "Do invite the little ones in for breakfast, Kat."

"Why? You're so lazy you couldn't catch one if it landed on your head."

"I resent that," he replied with the prissy sound only an

annoyed cat can get. "And I'd like to see you catch one."

"Would you?" I held out my hand. Four swept down to grab hold of my fingers.

"Show off." He curled up and put his tail back over his face.

I spent the next few minutes doing my best to calm the birds. A couple dozen came to my fingers while I stood there. The day brightened into a gorgeous dawn of dark blues, fleeting clouds, and fog. No big wings came around the house and many of the little birds settled onto the trees nearby.

Nuthatches, like most of the tiny birds, panic at *everything*. If I weren't close by they'd fly off in all directions. I'm a beacon to birds. And cats. I spotted three of the local strays lolling near the pine at the edge of the yard and eyeing breakfast on the wing if the birds weren't careful.

"Don't do it, guys," I said to the cats. They'd been hanging around for over a year but I watched them turn my way with a moment of 'dare I pretend I don't understand?' in their eyes. "I'll bring food out for you in a few minutes."

"Some of the canned stuff," a big grey tom called Pawford said with a flick of his tail. "If you expect us to leave the birds alone, I don't want the dry crap."

I leaned out the window and stared at him. Most of the nuthatches headed upwards onto the tree branches, except for two who burrowed into my hair. I plucked them out while I kept my eyes on the cats. Ears flickered and tails twitched. Pawford finally gave a great sigh as he dropped onto the dirt, his head on his paws -- the perfect picture of apparent kitty dejection.

"Food would be nice," he mumbled. "Anything you can spare. Thank you."

I smiled and drew my head back into the room. Cato

had sat up once he heard the other cat and seemed far less interested in the birds. He and Pawford had faced off in a few clashes during the last year and he had two nicks out of his left ear. Cato surprised Pawford when he proved he could hold his own. He may live in the house, but he's not soft.

I'm not even certain how he got to be a house cat. He wandered in one day and I found the company . . . well, nice enough for a cat.

Not lonely here. Nope.

A couple more nuthatches swept down at the window when I pulled myself inside, almost starting another panic.

"Everything is all right." I brushed my finger the tiny heads and used a whisper of magic to settle them. "Everything is fine now. The big wings are gone."

They scanned the sky again, this time including the trees and even the cats, as though they would sprout wings to come after them.

I sent them flying to the trees, watched for a moment to make certain the poor guys remained settled, and then cranked the window shut. I pulled several feathers from my hair and dropped two in front of Cato's nose.

"Tease." He didn't move his tail or open his eyes.

I laughed as I headed for the bathroom and then on to the kitchen where I grabbed the cat food, including a couple cans for the outside guys. They were good for strays, and they behaved around the house. I can't stop them from doing what's natural elsewhere, but here -- where I can understand the screams -- well, they know better than to go after the birds.

The Big Wings didn't worry me, but something seemed odd this morning. I couldn't put my finger on anything out of place and suspected the changing seasons might be affecting me too.

Then, as I leaned down to open the cabinet, a surge of magic spread so quickly and strong through the air that the sensation almost made me ill. I stood and spun, my hands coming up to protect myself, and startling Cato who had followed me into the kitchen.

"What!" His ears went back and his fur fluffed out, making him appear twice his normal size.

"Magic," I whispered, as though afraid a loud noise would bring the power back. The surge had unsettled me. Free magic running through the ether makes me twitchy.

"Is it all right?" he asked, eyes narrowed and ears slanted back still.

"I can't sense anything solid out there. The magic came from far back in the park -- a lot of magic from out of nowhere. I hate it when the Edge acts up!"

Cato made sounds of agreement. He'd noticed the open cabinet and at the sight of cat food he would pretty much agree he was a bird and could fly if that would get me to open one of the coveted cans for him.

I closed my eyes while I reached out with magic, but still found nothing out of place.

I love my job most of the time and I adore living here, meeting tourists and talking with humans. Yes, I miss home. We all have to work this side of the Edge for a few years and there are far worse places to be. This is a relatively stable area. They gave me this location because I'm not the strongest person in my clan. The rest of my cousins were out in the tough areas: The Sahara, the Gobi and a few places that make Antarctica seem like an easily accessible vacation destination.

Free magic can play havoc with the weather, though, and we were already having a stormy April. If the Edge continued having problems, I feared things would get worse for a while.

"Meow?" Cato said, drawing my attention back to the kitchen.

"Very funny." I tried not to smile.

"Hey, you're standing in the magic place." He purred as he rubbed against my legs. "I needed to get your attention before I fell faint from lack of food."

"Oh yeah, you look as though you're going to starve, pudge."

"Huh."

I got the food out and gave him a can of his own because I wanted him to be in a good mood. A happy cat makes me happy. Cato may be a sarcastic furry pain in the ass, but he's a good guy.

"Thanks," he said as I put the plate down on the floor.

Polite, too, which is more than I can say for many humans -- or fae -- these days.

I pulled down more paper plates, spread two cans of food out on them and grabbed a huge dipper full of dry cat food to add to the mix. A quick inventory of the refrigerator found a few things I would not eat before they went bad. I dropped them into the mix, adding a piece of ham to Cato's food.

"Ah, food of the gods!" he said with delight.

I laughed and gathered the plates, using magic to balance them on my left hand. I may not be the strongest with magic, but I am not powerless. There are nice easy things you can do with a bit of reality nudging and that makes life easier on this side of the Edge where there's so little magic in the air to work against you.

I have to be careful going past any electronics. The brush of technology can upset magic and magic can play havoc with technology. If I use any piece of technology, I have to lock my powers down and bury the magic.

Fae to learn these things on this side of the Edge. I wouldn't even have such items in the house except I needed to seem as normal as possible for my neighbors and friends. Besides, avoiding destroying things in my house was good practice for me whenever I went near them in other places.

As I came out of the kitchen I glanced over at Shakespeare, a lovely African Grey parrot I'd acquired a few months ago. There's just one problem with him --

"I have not always been as now, the fever'd diadem on my brow."

That's the problem. Shakespeare doesn't speak parrot. He only speaks human words and those in odd bits of verse. I can talk to any bird in the world . . . except for this one. If he would speak in parrot, I would learn what's bothering him. Well, other than his former owners turning him loose in the Rocky Mountains and Shakespeare not exactly being the type of bird that would do well in the local climate. Rangers found him before he froze to death. They brought him to me.

Shakespeare nodded and preened. He'd been horribly shy the first few weeks and given to shouting things at odd times of the day or night. Lately I thought I'd seen resignation in his eyes.

"Not hell shall make me fear again!" he shouted, startling me.

"Right. Good."

I glanced outside the big plate-glass window where mist wreathed the trees in front of my home. From here I saw no more than a few roofs in Estes Park though I heard the sounds of cars headed towards Rocky Mountain National Park despite the early hour. I didn't blame them:

First light was the best time to watch the valleys come awake. The big horns would rush down to Sheep Lakes this morning; I loved to watch them go bounding down the mountain side. Beautiful animals.

I saw no one nearby, so I scurried out in my robe and bare feet, using magic to brush away the pine needles before I stabbed myself. Pawford stood sniffing as I came closer, and his tail went straight up in the air with delight. He even rubbed against my legs, his matted fur rough. I brushed the burrs out with a quick sweep of magic.

"Thank you!" he said with real enthusiasm as I dropped the several plates on to the ground. Abbie, a small black and white cat and Trouble, a young pure black tom, mumbled *thank you*. They were a little warier than Pawford as they turned their attention to the food. Anywhere else they would have been at each other, but I enforce calm between the cats in my yard.

Quite a few nuthatches had taken to the trees, mingling with house sparrows and dark-eyed juncos. They all acted agitated, which often happens with the smaller birds. It's as though they're psychic or something -- or maybe psychotic. If one gets upset, the panic spreads through every tiny bird brain in the area.

And they come to me. It's just part of the job.

A little magic still lingered in the air. I turned and headed back to the house. The Edge got unsettled now and then. Nothing serious.

CHAPTER TWO

J ust as well I was awake this early since I had an important meeting this morning. I'm not usually worried about first impressions. This time, though, David Carter's reputation as a world class photographer made me uneasy. He is a Professional; yes, with a capital P. He's won awards, has his own studio out in Arizona, and rarely works on assignment. I write travel articles about the area and I never expected a magazine would team me with a photographer of his caliber.

I went back inside and spent extra time getting ready. Magic makes even my mass of golden hair manageable. I tried a few different styles -- the Shirley Temple look was right out, as well as the 'no I'm not hiding antennae under this mass of hydra-esque curls.' I settled for simplicity -- waves down to my shoulders with the top pulled back. Add a touch makeup and nice hiking clothes and I was ready for an adventure.

With a cup of coffee in hand, I sat on the front porch, watching as the sun burnt away the early morning fog. The trees and the encircling arms of the mountain where cliffs, boulders and trees come down on both edges of my lovely piece of land made me feel protected, and that came from more than the wards in place.

I calmed before starting to reach towards the Edge to examine the boundary between here and . . . *elsewhere.*

Every few years, the borders move too close together causing problems, though not often as much as this year's display. Surges like the one earlier had become common which is why someone needs to keep an eye the Edge and make certain the magic remains well-hidden while making certain no magical creature slips through.

I reached far up into the mountains and found several places where the Edge seemed thin. I brushed them with magic, feeding power into the weaker spots. Normally doing magic at a distance would be difficult for any fae, and impossible for me. My father set up a relay system to amplify my weaker powers.

I discovered odd bulges as though something pressed against the other side. Those might be pools of magic and hoped they dispersed on the fae side. Sometimes, though, a powerful gathering of magic can become something. Many of the creatures on the other side are little more than pools of magic within a shell. You don't want them to take shape on this side. Bad things can happen when a newly minted magic creature finds itself in a place with no restraints.

I found nothing wrong this morning. Cato -- having gone out the magic kitty door at the side of the house -- climbed into my lap. He sniffed.

"Perfume? What's the occasion?"

"I am meeting the photographer today." I tried not to sound nervous. "We'll be checking out what we want to work on for the article."

"Today? You're going to be in the park *all day?*" he asked, worried. "You will leave food out, right?"

"I won't be gone more than a few hours. You just ate.

You won't starve."

"Are you sure you won't be gone longer? You don't think the weather will change? Feels like a weather change to me. What if you get trapped and I have no food? I might have to go for the bird --"

"You know what would happen to you if you harmed a single feather on Shakespeare, right?" I stared him straight in the face.

"I don't think I want to know," Cato conceded.

"Good answer."

"Nevertheless --"

"I'll leave food out. Dry."

"You are most kind."

We went inside and I prepared for my day with the Professional. I shoved everything I needed into my weather-worn shoulder bag and I fixed my hair again. I even felt competent when someone knocked.

A shame Cato tripped me as I headed for the door; I hit a bookcase, knocking a stack of magazines onto the floor and they around my feet.

"Sorry," Cato apologized, though he plainly didn't mean it. I heard him snicker.

"You are risking the food," I answered, and swept everything back into place with a touch of magic.

I opened the door and had my first look at David Carter. He didn't strike me as a David. He should have had a more exotic name. This man must have walked in off a beach in Southern California: tan, with long windblown brown hair and bright grass-green eyes.

I blinked. So did he. I don't know what he'd expected, but I know he wasn't my image of a world class photographer with a reputation as impressive as his.

"David Carter?" I asked, hoping I wasn't wrong.

He smiled, looking nervous. "Yes. You must be Katlyn Borders?"

"Kat." I offered my hand. We shook; good hands, long fingered and fine-skinned. He had a camera bag/backpack slung over his shoulder. I'd have to be careful. Magic, cameras, film . . . not a good combination.

"Come in. Would you like coffee?"

"Yes, thank you. I left Loveland far too early this morning." He followed me inside, glancing around the place. I threw a protective shield around the camera bag so any magic in the area wouldn't affect the equipment though I'd still have to be careful if he took anything out.

He nodded as though he approved of the house. "Nice place. What a great cat. What's his name?"

"Cato," I said. Cato did his innocent act, pacing in the kitchen to remind me of my promise to feed him again.

"I bet this is a wonderful area to live in. Expensive, though, right?"

"Pretty much." I tried not to feel guilty. The house came from my family and belonged to the clan long before any human settled at Estes Park. We've gone through the pretense of selling the place sometimes and they'd had the old cabin rebuilt a couple years ago. I didn't have to pay for the place.

I don't need money and I write because I enjoy telling people about the park and the mountains. I also enjoy doing something that requires no magic and I can share with humans on a level where we all connect.

Cato followed me when I went to the kitchen to get David a cup of coffee.

"Try to trip me again, cat and you'll be out hunting food with Pawford."

"I'm trying to remind you of your obligations," Cato

answered.

David laughed. "That's funny. He meowed just like he's talking to you."

"Oh, he is," I said. "I'm sure he has a lot to say, too."

"Good thing you can't understand him," David replied. He took the cup from my hand.

I hoped I didn't turn red or anything. He seemed like a nice guy and I did not want to act like a total loon.

Cato glanced from me to him and back again. He shook his head. "Uh oh. I've seen that look. If you get involved with this one, please try to be a little more discreet than you were the last time. I was mortified to walk in on the two of you doing it --"

I almost batted him on the head which would have been a bad thing to do with David there. He'd followed us to the kitchen, too. "Let me get him some food so he shuts up." I forced a smile.

"He is a nice, talkative cat." David leaned down, scratching Cato behind the ears and down the neck.

"Okay," Cato mumbled, standing still and purring. "You can keep this one. And I don't care what you do with him."

"Well, you're easily won over." Lucky for me the words didn't sound odd. I sometimes forgot myself. It's hard when you can understand cats and birds but others can't. I've drawn a few odd looks.

I gave the cat more food and even found another treat from the fridge for him to keep him busy and away from me for a few minutes. David and I went out to the dining room table and sat down to discuss business while we sipped our coffee.

"I thought we'd take a nice, easy hike today." I hadn't been certain if the photographer would be in shape for a long, difficult trek, but David wouldn't have any trouble on the trails. "That will let you get acclimatized to the elevations while we decide what type of pictures you want to take."

"The publisher wants animals," he said. "Wild Walks Magazine loves those kinds of things."

"Yeah, I've written for them a couple times. I'm not a photographer, though, and they've used stock pictures most of the time."

"I'll do my best to do your work justice."

I blushed this time. I know I did. He sipped his coffee.

"Excuse me, Kat," Cato called from the kitchen. "Might I have some of the nice milk? I believe it's almost out of date."

"Fine, fine," I said. David glanced at me. "He wants milk. Ummm . . . I almost always give him some milk in the morning."

"You shouldn't lie to the human," Cato replied.

"If you want the milk, you better stop now."

David laughed. "He has you trained!"

I did my best not to stalk back out to the kitchen. Cato kept his distance. I poured him some milk. He glanced at me and quickly bowed his head.

"Okay, okay. I'll behave."

"That's better."

I don't mind talking to cats and birds. Just the same, I do enjoy a discussion with humans or fae sometimes.

I gathered a couple Danish rolls and came back to the table. David smiled in appreciation. We sipped coffee while we ate rolls and talked business. He knew little about the writing side and I understood less about photography. We both shared an interest in drawing. I suspected he was far better than me. He talked about shapes, colors and light. I hadn't consciously seen them as separate things in a picture.

He showed me his equipment. I damped down on my powers though I didn't mind this time. I loved seeing his excitement for the work.

"You have a lot of cameras." I nodded to the three camera bodies he placed on the table.

He smiled and sat a larger camera on the table with an odd gentleness. "This is a medium format Hasselblad. I could have bought a car with the money I spent on this camera and it's worth every cent."

"It's lovely."

"Here --" He held the camera towards me.

"Oh, no, no, no. Cameras and I don't get along. I'll admire it from across the table, thank you."

I'd have to be careful of the cameras and phone he carried. People can rarely get reception on the phones anywhere near me. Lucky for me, they blame the location or the weather.

"You must love photography." I watched his face. You can tell a lot about a person by how they react.

He looked at the cameras the way a mother cat watches her new kittens. He even reached out brushing his hand across the Hasselblad and the three others.

"Yeah, I do," he admitted with a wistful sound. He turned my way as though I caught him at some terrible admission. "This is the work I want to do. I want to capture the world and share those views with all the people who cannot come to these lovely places."

"Sounds wonderful," I answered.

"Many people don't understand. My parents want me to get a real job --"

"Even now?" I asked. "You make a lot of money at photography."

"Yeah, well my father is a farmer in Iowa. So were his father and his grandfather." He stopped and gave a quick shrug. "Photography isn't work he can understand and money isn't a factor. How about your family? They approve of your work?"

They didn't know about the writing. "As long as I stay out of trouble, they're happy."

He laughed as he packed away his camera equipment. At least I understood how he got those great arm muscles. Those cameras must have weighed a good amount not to mention the array of lenses and who knew what else in the backpack. He appeared eager to get going.

"I'm ready to leave if you are." I gathered plates and cups to take back to the kitchen. "We can get a good idea of what you might want today, take a short hike, then come back and make plans. I have sketched out part of what I will write about but I want to tailor the rest of the work to the pictures you get so we have a cooperative project."

"Sounds good," he agreed. "This is going to work well for both of us."

"Do you have a rented car?" I asked as I dropped the dishes in the sink.

"Yes."

"We'll take my car. I know how it handles on mountain roads and we don't have to worry about any scratches."

"Sounds great. I pay for the gas though. I'm on the expense sheet."

"Fair enough." I was already enjoying this assignment. I had only worked with one other photographer, a self-absorbed woman who hadn't care about the writing side. She'd done excellent photos, but she wasn't the most pleasant human I'd ever met.

I like humans. I feel closer to them than to fae

sometimes because of the magic -- the fact I don't have as much as most of my family. No one judges a fae by how much power they hold, but it's still a fact, hanging there over me.

Humans judge me for who I am and what I do. I'm easy to get along with, although eccentric.

David stepped into the living room, glancing towards the loft where I have several bookcases, a futon, and a view the gods would have envied, with huge windows on both ends of the house. Maybe we'd go there to talk business after our trip to the park.

"*Dim vanities of dreams by night*" Shakespeare shouted, startling him. He hadn't noticed the bird on his perch in the corner.

"Sorry. I should have mentioned Shakespeare. He's apt to quote poetry at any moment."

"African Gray?" He asked going closer. "I've heard they're smart birds."

"Yes, well, most of them," I answered. Shakespeare gave me a look that could have killed. I almost expected him to say something. Instead he shuffled around on his perch for a moment and turned back to David who carefully approached the bird. Shakespeare let David brush his fingers over his head.

I didn't move for fear of unsettling the parrot. He was . . . well, flighty is a good term. It wasn't only his inability to talk parrot which showed he had problems. He started at every wind and sometimes even the magic I used unsettled him.

He let David pet him and even rubbed against David's hand.

"There are crackers in the drawer to your right, if you want to give him one," I offered.

David opened the drawer -- the one with the claw marks. Shakespeare knew where I kept the treats though he hadn't gotten the knack of pulling against the latch.

He probably thought opening the drawer was magic.

"Well, isn't this interesting?" Cato said, sitting beside me.

I almost answered, but settled for a nod instead. I leaned on the doorframe and watched while David broke off a piece of cracker for to the bird. Shakespeare took it, ate and bobbed his head several times, wanting more.

"That's a good sign," I said, pleased with the reaction. "He's an unsettled bird. The park rangers took four days to find him after some people drove to the highest point of the park before they set the bird free to be in the wilds."

David looked back at me and his eyebrows rose. "This bird. Free in the snowy mountains? Didn't the name *African Grey* mean anything to them?"

"Apparently not." I came over to pet Shakespeare, glad to see the bird so calm.

"*Rendered me mad and deaf and blind!*" Shakespeare shouted and fluffed his chest feathers as he spread his wings.

"He does this often?" David asked.

"Yes. And rarely the same quote twice."

"Incredible! I'd heard African Greys can be extremely smart, but this one might even be exceptional. What possessed those people to throw out such a bird?"

I watched while David gave him the last of the crackers. "Who knows, though having Shakespeare for four months with the odd poetry, I'm tempted to suspect he drove them crazy."

Shakespeare reached over and bit me on the finger. Hard.

I yelped and headed for the bathroom to get my hand cleaned and stop the bleeding. I trusted David would be careful having seen what the bird could do.

Cato followed me and jumped onto the counter. "That bird is a menace, you know," he said.

"He's troubled."

"So are most mass murders and dogs. That doesn't mean you should take them into your house." He shook his head in a very human-like gesture. He might be spending far too much time with me. "There's something just not right about him."

"I know." I patted him on the head. "But Shakespeare stays."

Magic would have healed the wound, but David had seen it. I settled for a magical bandage to dull the pain and stop the bleeding. I wouldn't spend the day wincing at everything I did.

David had finished feeding the bird. He stood by the plate-glass window at the front of the house.

"Finger all right?" he asked.

"Yeah, fine." I waved the bandaged finger.

He nodded to the window. "I bet this is exquisite at nightfall."

"Nightfall, dawn, bright summer days and the middle of winter," I answered. He smiled and grabbed his pack. I found my bag and slung it across my shoulder, giving a last nod to Cato and Shakespeare.

Once outside, I heard the frantic twitters of the small birds still gathered somewhere out behind the house. They grew louder. I hoped we got away before they came to talk to me.

Since David would expect me to lock the door, I foraged around in my purse and pretended to lock the door while I tested out the wards -- just light ones I kept in place because they took little power. I had stronger ones ready, but I had never needed to power them up. The little ones were easy and David didn't even notice.

The morning tasted of pine and wood smoke drifting from a fireplace somewhere down the hill. A nuthatch swept past me, twittering.

"Big wings, big wings, fly, fly, fly!"

I waved the bird away and followed David down the rock-lined path to where his fancy Subaru sat side-by-side with my car, which runs on magic. I sometimes pretend to fill the gas tank just for show. The pieces of the car were all hand-formed by my cousin, who took considerable pains to make everything appear real. Why go to so much trouble rather than buying one off a lot? Because a real car worked with technology so any fae using it -- including me -- must dampen natural powers or risk everything failing. Catastrophically in some cases. This way I can run around town like a human without being powerless. Besides, cutting off our natural powers isn't easy or practical for long stretches of time.

The car is also equipped with magic shields so non-fae can ride with me and not have their fancy tech toys die on them and the baffles made the photography equipment doubly safe from the car and from me. The shield I had put on the backpack would only work if he didn't take something out.

Before we got into the car more nuthatches swept past me, panic growing in their frantic cries. I ignored them, but as I opened the driver side door a flock of nuthatches flew into the air, at least a hundred of them, twittering in panic as they took off down the hillside.

David turned, surprised.

"Bird feeders behind the house," I explained which was, at least, partially true.

"Ah." He opened his door.

Before we got into the car more birds rose into the air, the din of their yells growing louder. A few lifted over the house, and then more, then hundreds -- surely not a thousand! Most were nuthatches who still screamed about big wings. I several other small birds were caught in the panicked swarm as it covered the sky above my home. For a heartbeat they blocked out the sun before the birds turned towards town and flew off to the west.

I watched in shock and dismay and finally turned back to David.

"Must cost you a fortune in bird food," he said.

CHAPTER THREE

T he astonishing flight of the birds had unsettled me. Even I had never seen this odd behavior. For a dozen heartbeats I stared where they had flown, barely noting as David got a tripod from his vehicle. My hands trembled. I hoped he didn't notice.

"How long have you lived here?" he asked as he slid in and pulled the seatbelt into place, reminding me to do the same. Oh yes and start the car. Good plan.

"About five years," I said, trying to keep the sound of normality in my voice. I glanced at the house. Cato, who had come out the magical cat door, looked around as though he'd just missed the chance of a lifetime. Oddly, Pawford, Abbie and Trouble weren't under the trees. They'd even left bits of the food behind. Cato checked the plates out then walked away.

I pulled out of the driveway and turned the car down the narrow winding road that dead-ended at my place. The street sign at the first corner said we were on Fairy Tale Lane. Yeah, my people have been here for a long time.

"This is a nice place to live," I said, knowing I'd been too quiet. "I never want to move. I love the town and the park. Some people find both too touristy."

"I bet this is a great place. I enjoy meeting people and from what I saw of Estes Park, the town has all the amenities you would want anyway."

"Exactly." I shifted down on the narrow straightway which has an incline steep enough to make a good toboggan run. Two kids zipped past on bikes, heading towards school. We had a magnificent view of the city and the mountains across the small valley. David leaned forward, admiring the sight.

"You can't get bored in a place like this . . . well, not unless your idea of fun is the big city life. Denver isn't far away, though," I added.

At the next curve we passed a lovely cottage with a white picket fence -- rather out of place nestled amid the log cabins and a-frames. The house belonged to Mrs. Hale, a petite grey-haired lady who owned half a dozen pure-bred cats. Those included a British Shorthair named Mrs. Miniver, who'd gone astray at one point (so to speak) with a tough old tom. One of their kittens was Cato.

I glanced over to the yard and spotted two of her purebreds and a few of the local strays, including Pawford, Abbie and Trouble. They sat in a circle as though they'd gathered for a morning chat. Cat heads turned my way as I drove by, all with an 'I'm worried' look.

"That's odd," David said. "Did you see those cats?"

"Cats? Oh, at Mrs. Hale's house. She has quite a few cats, including purebreds." I babbled and didn't dare look again. I wanted to park and go ask what was wrong, but I couldn't with David along, so I eased my foot away from the brake, letting us pick up speed. Maybe I should ask someone questions, but I didn't know where to go without David wondering what I was doing.

Or maybe there was one place. I needed to go to the

pigeons.

"I'm going to make a stop at a city park," I said and offered a smile. "To feed the pigeons -- and yes, it gets expensive."

He laughed.

We hit the outskirts of town proper, crossed the bridge over Fish Creek, and headed down to Gully Park. Few people visited the place since the park isn't on the main roads. Locals gathered here in warmer weather. Today mist hung close to the stream at the park's edge and deer darted away at our approach. I parked and got out. David rummaged through his camera bag as I took a bag of bird food from the trunk. I always keep bird food there. Just because I can understand birds doesn't mean they're automatically my friends. Bribes help.

The pigeons roost in an old barn at the corner of the park. I donate a lot of money each year to keep the barn in shape and give them this location. Some of the locals want to chase the pigeons away, but so far I've protected them. Pigeons aren't as stupid as most humans assume. They're staid, sedentary animals who are fixated on where they get their next meal. I've known humans -- and fae -- with much the same attitude.

As soon as I stepped out of the car, pigeons lifted from the roof and head my way. I hurried across to the now dry fountain to talk with them where David wouldn't hear as long as he didn't follow.

He took out a camera which meant I needed to pull in my magic or else I would appear as a big glowing blob on his film which would be hard to explain. The ability to talk to the birds and cats is innate, a part of my brain, not my magic. I held all the magic I needed to attract them in the bag of seed I carried under my arm.

I went to a spot by the fountain. The birds landed at my feet, feathered heads pecking at the cement walkway as though I had already dropped the seed there.

"I need answers guys." I leaned over, dropping grain in semicircle before me and keeping my back to David so he didn't see me talking. "Is there anything going on?"

"Outward, outward, outward," they cried in half a dozen voices. I wondered what they meant. I sprinkled more grain. "Outward, fly, away, get away, get away, get away."

That sounded serious. "Who is trying to get away? Who is flying away?" I whispered.

One bird, a lovely pigeon with spots of almost iridescent purple encircling her neck and scattered across her face, looked up at me. We'd talked more than once. She seemed more intelligent than the others.

"Tell me what's happening, Pretty," I said and leaned closer to her.

"Big wings." She her wings fluttered. "Little wings fear big wings."

"Ah. You're upset because of the nuthatches," I said with a whisper of relief.

"Chickies, jays, little wings."

A chill ran up my arms as I scattered more grain. This was not a case of an eagle or something unsettling the nuthatches. Chickadees scare easily, but jays are more aggressive and harder to chase from their territory.

"Where?" I asked. "Where are the big wings?"

"Fly, fly, fly!" She swept into the air, her and a dozen other pigeons, all circling around me, fluttering in panic they usually only show when something dangerous comes close.

I was sorry I hadn't paid better attention to the

nuthatches because this was not normal behavior for pigeons or cats. I dropped more food hoping they'd stick around, but I feared even the pigeons might consider moving elsewhere, even though they rarely were frightened the way small birds did.

"Where is the trouble?" I asked.

"Big, big, high, cold."

High in the mountains. This might be connected to the fluctuation with the Edge. The smaller birds would have translated something they didn't understand into something hunting them. Instinctive behavior.

I'd have to check the Edge later. I took the grain bag to the car. When I took the driver's seat, David smiled and held out his digital camera. I clamped way down on my powers again and took the camera carefully in my hands.

"The camera is tough; you won't break it."

Ha.

I'd never seen a picture of myself before and this one was . . . magical. The pigeons flew around me, a slight blurring of the wings, while I stood in the middle.

"Very nice."

"I'll print you a copy if you like."

"Yes, I would." I handed the camera to him and glanced at the pigeons.

"Something wrong?"

"They're agitated today." I pulled away, wishing I had better answers. Then I did my best to dismiss the sense of trouble and turned my attention to this job with David. "We'll go to Endovalley today and maybe hike up Old Fall River Road."

He leaned back, watching the scenery. "Wherever you want. I've never been here before."

"Really? I'll have to show you around the park. We're

too early in the spring to go over the high pass but we can take the long drive around to the other side of the mountain before you leave. There's a beautiful area of the park across there. The Coyote Valley Trailhead area usually has elk and sometimes even a moose or two."

"Sounds nice." I heard a hint of excitement in his voice. I suspected he enjoyed nature as much as I did.

We drove past the rows of hotels dotting Highway 34, and we were early enough to miss most of the traffic. Tourists came to the area even at this time of the year, but not in the huge flocks which would appear later. We were past the ski season and too early for the summer tourists.

We headed in the Fall River entrance station. Lily Gibson and Jim Simon were the two on duty. Both stood outside the shack, drinking coffee. They handled the two cars ahead of me and then came over to my window.

"Hey, Kat," Lily said, her southern drawl more pronounced than usual, which meant she was tired. "There's trouble -- who is this?"

I wanted to hear what might be wrong, but Lily stopped and frowned at my companion. Jim Simon, a big burly man who looked like a bear next to little Lily scrunched down and stared in the window to see who else sat in the car.

"This is David Carter. He's a photographer. We're working on an article together."

"Ah," Lily said as she smiled. So did Jim. They're good friends and they know I live alone. "Well, be careful out there today. We got people out tracking though we're not sure what they're after. Something's on the move and even panicked the big horns. There might be a rogue bear or cat in the area."

"We'll be careful." Something panicking the big horns

made me, once again, wish I hadn't ignored the nuthatches.

"I have a tranquilizer gun in my pack," David said. "I used it once in the Amazon and keep the gun with me on field trips."

Jim nodded. "Good."

"Oh and did you hear they cleared out the Stanley last night?" Lily asked. She looked at David. "Is that where you are staying?"

"The Stanley Hotel? No." Her eyebrow lifted and her eyes flicker to me. "I arrived this morning. I'm staying at the Zamond Inn. What happened to the Stanley Hotel?"

"Power outage and they can't seem to figure out why. Everyone's moved to other places." She glanced up as another car pulled in behind us.

"We're heading to Endovalley today and hiking to Chasm Falls," I said. "I don't expect we'll run into any trouble."

"You better get moving before the morning is gone." Lily hit the side of the car as two more vehicles pulled into line. One belonged to a local. "Let me know if you see anything."

I nodded and pulled away, slowing as we entered the park. A chipmunk scurried across the road, a piece of bread he'd found in the trash hanging from his mouth and slowing him in his race to safety. They never understood the danger of this spot.

"The rangers are friendly," David said, already pulling out a camera.

"Yeah, they are. Lots of good people here at the park." The area where we came in wasn't spectacular though lovely boulders crowded down by the road and the rich scent of pine forest filled the air. I loved this drive and enjoyed watching David on his first trip into the park.

I pulled into the lot at Sheep Lakes where other cars had stopped and people stood outside, watching the grassy area in front of them where dozens of big horns stood. The larger males paced around while the others gathered in a small circle munching at the grass though they twitched at any sudden sound.

"Do we have time for pictures?" David asked, getting out as I did.

I smiled. "We have all the time in the world."

"Thanks!" He pulled out the tripod and began to open the leg sections. He grabbed a camera, fished out a big lens and moved away from the car; in a couple moments he began to click pictures. I heard him make appreciative sounds. I left him and walked a little way off and relaxed the hold on my magic.

A couple Brewer's blackbirds paced near the trashcan searching the ground for something to eat. I opened the trunk and grabbed a handful of grain. The rangers frown on feeding the local animals but I needed more answers.

"Good food," the two chorused when I came near and surreptitiously dropped grain at my feet.

"What's got the big horns upset?" I mumbled. "What's everyone upset about?"

The two birds walked in circles around the handful of grain, pecking at a piece here and there, though not answering.

They might know nothing. They didn't appear upset, which helped settle my nerves. I took the moment to reach out to trace the magic in the area. There was something odd a few miles away, but it might have been natural; magic even here gathers into pools sometimes. Most of the magic appeared to be out around Terra Tomah Mountain and Mount Julian. Both were far off from the road. I sensed the Edge even with the sun rose. Usually wild magic is more active at night.

David finished and put the equipment in the car. The birds scattered when I walked back.

"Thanks. I enjoyed photographing them."

"This is a great spot. If we return early in the morning, we might be in time to see the big horns coming down the mountainside. It is spectacular to watch them leaping from spot to spot," I said, pointing to the opposite side of the road. "They look like they'll fall off the side of the mountain, but I've never even seen one of them even trip."

"I'd like to see them."

"Good. Don't worry about us stopping to take pictures, either. If you see something, we'll stop. I'm in no hurry. We have all day. And you're here to get pictures."

"I got some great shots."

"We don't have far to go to the next stop." I got into the car and he took his seat. "Endovalley is a lovely area. We'll probably spot a few elk."

"Great!"

I drove slowly along the road that turned off to the right, heading past the alluvial fan created by the Big Thompson Flood back in 1976. Huge boulders had rushed down the mountain when the high dam broke. I tried not to consider the tragedy and the people who had died in the horrific flood. We had lost fae who tried to stop the disaster, but nature won that round.

We stopped for him to take pictures here, too. I was glad because a set of magpies almost always held court along the trail leading to the platform near the falls. I let David go ahead while I paused by the noisy birds.

"Bad, bad, bad!" they screeched. I winced, trying to urge them to be quiet. Their large black tails flicked left and

right and their wings spread to show flashes of white as
though they intended to take flight at any moment.

"Tell me what --"

"Bad!" The cry came again and again until the sound
drew even David to look our way.

I would not get anything more from them. Worse, I
began to sense more magic in the air -- not enough to
unsettle equipment, but enough to make my skin itch. The
Edge was fluctuating again; a quick check found a slight
pulse of magic. I might have to go look more closely
tonight.

I joined David for the walk to bridge and the view of
the falls. Water dipped and flew, sparkling in the light,
dancing over the rocks and down to the Horseshoe Park
area below us. The weather had warmed enough over the
last week to create high mountain snow melt, which made
the rush of water more powerful than would appear later in
the year. Bits of fog sent tendrils into the chilly morning air.
David pulled his jacket collar closer though he didn't appear
inclined to leave. He took pictures of the falls, the alluvial
fan of rock, and even close-ups of the water. He even
caught a Harrier hawk gliding down toward the marshlands
below us.

David acted like the proverbial kid in a candy shop
who wanted to taste everything. I let him take his time. He
asked questions, and I knew most of the answers. When I
wrote my first articles, I wanted to learn everything about
the area, from the types of birds to the names of the
wildflowers growing through the last tuffs of winter snow.

A pair of tourists arrived and David talked to them for
a couple minutes before we headed to the car. The magpies
screamed at me and half a dozen gray jays had joined them.
Jays don't often gather in groups, and certainly not in the

company of magpies.

"Want to walk from here?" I asked when we reached the car. "The gate isn't too far to the end of the road, then a couple miles up to Chasm Falls. And I do mean *up* in this case."

"Sure, walking would be great!" He put the backpack on and carried the tripod like a walking stick.

"Do you get into the mountains very much?" I asked as we hiked out along the road. Stands of aspen stood to the left past an open grassy area. To the right the mountain sloped down to the road in gentle rolls. Birds flittered about and a few sounded panicked while others seemed all too calm.

"I go hiking in the Appalachians every year and I've spent a few weeks in Yellowstone, too. I kind of expected this to be more like Yellowstone."

"The park has a flavor all its own. The place can get hectic in the summer with all the tourists though."

A couple elk charged down the hillside, dashing into the marsh area as we neared. David didn't even get his camera lifted in time to catch them.

Towards the end of the road, a few rocky walls came down on the right side and brush and bushes grew around puddles of water on the left. We spotted more elk, and he got a couple shots this time. A marmoset waddled by, giving us an evil eye since we disturbed him. We found a car parked by the gate which closed off Old Fall River Road. I'd never seen the road open, despite often walking along this way.

"There's something here to check out first."

I took him off to the left into the picnic area where snow melt brooks ran right to the edge of the tables. The reflection of the trees and dappled light made this one of the prettiest little spots in the park. The water ran high, and we splashed around, surprising a couple raccoons. They raced into the tree and stared while David took more pictures. He would have quite a collection before we even got the first day done.

"This is lovely. Thank you." David smiled.

I smiled in return. I would have thought there was love in the air if I hadn't known it was just far too much magic.

CHAPTER FOUR

We headed to the closed road, went past the blockade and hiked up the steep incline. David re-adjusted his camera bag a couple times though the weight didn't slow him. We made good time along the solitary path with David asking me more about the trees, plants and birds along the way.

We hiked for a couple hours, pausing to take pictures and to discuss the area. When we reached the spectacular Chasm Falls, I realized David would be busy. I regretted not having brought in a picnic lunch. We could have spent all day.

Chasm Falls pours down between two high cliffs with the water splashing straight through the rock and down to the pool below where the stream cascades over more rocks. David immediately took out the Hasselblad and prepared for serious photography. I settled on a log in the open sunlight and jotted a few notes while watching the birds flying around us. These didn't seem as panicked. I even spotted a badger peek out from the shadow of the trees. As soon as he saw me, though, he ducked back into the shadows.

A couple minutes later the badger returned. The

animal moved clumsily through the shadows, and when I stood to get a better look, he glanced my way and moved into the underbrush.

I sat down and discreetly kept watch. A few minutes later the badger returned and began watching us. I even saw his paw tapping the ground in either a nervous or bored reaction.

Son of a bitch. That had to be a fae who had taken over an animal's body. You can always tell because they never get it quite right. This one showed all the signs: besides the behavior improper for a badger, the animal had trouble walking on four legs and sat in a rather human style.

A fae can't use magic in the new form and has to set up a spell to change back ahead of time. There are tales of fae who took animal forms, and when the return spell failed, they never got back out.

As soon as I stood, the badger ran into the shadows once again. Who was playing these games? Taking an animal's body could do the creature harm. They sometimes lose a sense of themselves in the transfer, and I didn't appreciate someone doing something so evil to spy on me.

"What was that?" David asked, watching the woods.

"A badger. Nothing to worry about. I scared the poor guy." I'd be doing more than scare him when I found the person. "Worth the hike?"

"Fantastic," he answered. "You all right?"

"Fine. I'm soaking up the area for my writing. This is a lovely day to be here."

He smiled and continued taking pictures, moving the camera several times as he searched out the perfect light. I kept an eye open for the badger. I wished a hawk or eagle would come by so I could talk to them. They are paranoid, secretive birds, but I've gotten good information from a few.

David shared a candy bar, and bottled water he found down in the bottom of his pack, which seemed to be as good as any magic bag and I wondered what else he might pull out of it. We watched a few deer wander close. Normal deer, I am glad to say.

We headed back down the road in the early afternoon.

And that's when the bobcat sauntered out in front of me.

"Trouble," she hissed in a bare whisper of sound. "Trouble in the --"

She spotted David who had been lagging a few steps behind after the call of nature.

"Human," she growled, and darted into the woods.

Hell.

"Wow. That was -- *wow*." David put down his backpack and pulled out a camera. "I will be ready from now on."

I wished I could say the same.

We hiked back to the Endovalley road in good time. We didn't cross paths with any more bobcats though David got a few other pictures along the way. He still had a 'kid in a candy shop' look.

I pushed away my worries. The flux with the Edge was upsetting everyone. I wondered if something odd had gotten through -- that has happened. I'd return later when I could use my magic to find answers.

I decided to enjoy David's company and stop worrying. We drove around the lower park area, discussing possible picture sites and what I would write about to match the work. The magazine allotted us about three thousand words and four pages. We'd have to limit things before too long.

"Unless we write a guidebook," David suggested, startling me. "I mean after the article. You have a special link for the world of nature. I hope we can consider something later. After the other work."

"Yeah. Later, after everything else is done."

After the Edge settled. Working on something else with him later in the summer might be a lot of fun. Though why not do a section about winter activities, too?

Oh yes, we might spend *a lot of time* together.

We walked through the picnic area again. The sun's position had changed, and the quality of the light altered everything. David took more pictures while I sat atop a table and jotted down more notes.

"This place is different every time I come here; always lovely and always different," I said.

"Yeah. I love exploring a favorite spot at different times of the day and different times of the year. Everything changes, from the light to the sounds. I have a college friend who loves to travel, but he'll never go back to the same place twice: *been there, done that.* I took one trip with him, and never again. We drove each other nuts."

"I imagine so. Come on and I'll treat you an early dinner."

"I can buy. I have expenses paid."

"And I have a stipend for the days I work with you. We can both get our own tickets at dinner. You ready to go?"

"No. I want to see this place in moonlight. I think we better leave anyway."

As we headed back into town, I considered one of the fancy hotel restaurants. Instead, I took David to the Bear Camp, a wonderful out of the way cafe with rustic decor and excellent food.

The restaurant proved a good decision. The waitress, Marylyn, knew me and a couple rangers greeted us. I introduced David. The friendliness of the place enveloped us and we relaxed to a meal of big hamburgers, fries, cokes and a platter of onion rings. We had a nice, wonderful companionable meal.

Although during dinner I noticed David's space cadet side. Twice he didn't answer to his name, and I touched him on the arm to get his attention. He acted chagrined both times.

"Sorry. Guess I'm not used to company. I live by myself, and I spend way too much time inside my head."

"Yeah, I understand."

"You have Cato and Shakespeare. I should get a pet. I've always been partial to cats. They're low maintenance, right?"

"Depends on the cat." We talked about pets and other responsibilities.

We were having a wonderful meal.

And then disaster struck in the form of my cousin Aletta. I didn't even notice her arrival until she stopped right behind my chair and I sensed her magic. I turned around with a start. She wore a mid-calf slinky black dress with more material below the waist than above it. A perfect, brilliant cut emerald pendant rested against her pale chest and the gem glowed with a touch of power from the other side. Pale, thin, with dark-hair styled to perfection: she'd drawn attention, including David's.

"Aletta," I said. She glanced my way and gave one of her imperious little nods. "What are you doing here?"

She slinked her way around the table -- far too overdressed for this crowd and a few of the locals smirked. She slid a chair closer to David before she sat.

"I came to visit you, *cousin*," she said, stressing the last word. "I just knew I would find you here. You are so predictable. When I didn't find you at home I had the taxi driver drop me off at this quaint little place."

Damn. I suspected someone in the family had sent her to help me out during the trouble with the Edge. I did not want Aletta hanging around while I worked with David. She already gave him a steady stare of her dark, almond-shaped eyes. She looked like desire made real . . . ah, of course. A shift of my hand and I touched the power of her glamour spell.

"I suggest, *cousin*, that you turn it off," I said to her.

"Kitty, whatever are you talking about?" she asked with a perfect smile.

I gritted my teeth and didn't snap at her for calling me Kitty. David looked confused, but the reaction came from the glamour she wore, which clouded the mind. Aletta didn't need the spell. She was quite beautiful, at least in the physical sense.

I lifted my hand. I would have used magic to counter her spell, but she sighed and let the glamour fall; all except for a tiny whisper of power which I suspected might be part of her.

I didn't appreciate having Aletta arrive. However, if the others sent her, I would have to deal with her. Maybe I'd already botched things. I sensed something wasn't right in this area. She could help get things sorted out and leave, which would be fine with me.

Aletta, unfortunately, showed no signs of going away right now. She nibbled at David's fries and listened with badly feigned interest to our discussion about work. Mostly, though, she studied David. I found that annoying in a proprietary way I had no right to feel.

But even so. . . .

Dinner turned strained. David didn't act interested in Aletta, despite her attempts to turn the conversation back to her, but he had trouble connecting with me again, too.

"We'll be heading out at about seven in the morning," I said as we finished the meal. He somehow paid for mine before I could stop him. He grinned with delight, too. "We'll take a much longer hike tomorrow now that I know you can handle it."

"Oh, how kind of you to make such judgments," Aletta replied, getting a touch snide. She'd always hated when people ignored her.

"I assume you are not an outdoors person?" David looked her over as though he only now noticed the dress.

She blushed. I'd never seen Aletta embarrassed, which almost made up for her ruining a very nice meal.

"I used to hike sometimes," she finally admitted and her voice lost the usual haughtiness. "I admit I haven't in a long time. I don't get to this area very often."

"There are other trails in the world." I wished very much she would go find one right now.

She sighed. I almost believed the act. "I'm rarely some place where I can get away. I know -- my own fault." She gave a wave of her hand towards me before spoke. Rings glittered in the light and her fingernails looked perfect. I wanted to hide my hands, bandaged finger and all, in my lap.

David nodded and turned to me. We discussed what we needed for the next day.

Aletta got bored and began to tap her finger on the table.

I had seen the same move recently.

Badger.

I suspected I knew who had taken over the poor animal. We would have plenty to talk about later. No one in the family approves of using animals except in dire circumstances. The magic scrambles their brains and some of them can't survive on their own again. I suspected the badger Aletta had doomed the badger she'd used. Aletta possessed considerable power, but she lacked subtlety.

David and I finished our plans for tomorrow despite Aletta's boredom. I'd have tried to prolong the evening if Aletta hadn't arrived. I wanted to deal with her as quickly as possible and enjoy tomorrow without watching every animal for signs of possession.

"Let me take you back to your car and you can head to the hotel." Aletta's eyes widened at my words. She, doubtless, would have lured David into her own bedroom by now.

"Where are you staying David?" she asked with a smile.

Damn, damn, damn. My mistake.

"The Zamond Inn," he answered as his eyes narrowed.

"That's wonderful! So am I! Can I get a ride with you?"

"Sure," he replied. I heard no enthusiasm in the answer. Aletta would use enough magic that by the time the two got to the hotel she'd make it look as though she'd been staying there, too. Damn.

We left, heading out into the late afternoon sunlight. A slight breeze had picked up, and I hoped Aletta felt the cold, though she would use a spell to counter it.

Aletta damped down on all her magic when we reached the car. She didn't know Pela had created the vehicle for me, and I didn't tell her. I didn't mind making her uncomfortable on the ride. Served her right. She sat in the back, looking unhappy. David and I discussed more of what planned for the next day as we drove back to my place.

Once we reached the house, Aletta slinked her way out of my car and over to his, running a finger over the door in obvious pleasure, though she wouldn't be any more comfortable.

"I'll see you in the morning," David said. He smiled. "I'm looking forward to tomorrow."

"Me too." I smiled and felt far better than I had since Aletta arrived. My reaction to her had been childish, born of years of dealing with Aletta's need to get all the attention. Just the same, I realized she wasn't David's type.

He got into the car, unlocked the door for Aletta, and the two of them drove away.

I waited a couple minutes, and then I got back into my car and followed.

The family reunion wasn't quite over yet.

CHAPTER FIVE

I drove to the Zamond Inn, trying to temper my anger before I faced Aletta. I hadn't done well by the time I parked at the far end of the lot and in an area hidden by bushes. I didn't want David to believe I followed them.

Music drifted over from Performance Park and I glimpsed a kayaker working her way down Fall River, which ran right along the edge of the property. A little too cool to be out playing in the water, but the kayak moved swiftly with spring melt and she skirted along without a problem.

I sat on the car hood and waited about ten minutes before I did something I'd never done to anyone, human or fae. I sent a *Summons*.

This is my place of work, assigned to me by the clan which means I have both responsibilities and powers. One of those powers is the Summons -- an ability to call someone to stand before you. When used on a human, the Summons comes as a nagging sensation that makes them want to go somewhere. For a fae, though, it's like a voice shouting in their head, demanding attention. I made this one especially loud and strident.

Aletta stormed out of the hotel, stomping across the lot. She'd kicked off her shoes, let down her hair and changed into a pale gray silk blouse and black pants so tight she probably painted them in place.

I stepped away from the car. No reason to let her realize the car's secret anyway. I wouldn't have been able to use the Summons if I was in or near it.

"What were you doing in the mountains playing badger today?" I demanded and caught her off guard.

"I don't have to tell -- I have no idea what you are talking about. How dare you summon me! You don't have the right --"

"This is my place, Aletta. Unless you're here to replace me? Want to stand guard on the Edge tonight? I'd be glad to give the work over to you."

"I am not here to do your work for you!"

"Then you must be here to work as my assistant," I replied. She still wore the emerald necklace, and when my eyes fell on the gem, she shoved the chain beneath her blouse, as though I would steal it. Petty little child. She had always fixated on the word *mine* from the time. "If the clan didn't' send you as an assistant, I'd have to believe you came for a visit, and I'm not that stupid, Aletta."

"I don't have to tell you anything." Her face flushed and her eyes narrowed in anger. "I'm not answerable to you."

She spun and did something which took me utterly and completely by surprise. She waved her arm, opened a door to the fae world, and blatantly, right there in the parking lot, crossed over.

The door closed. A wind blew through the lot, scattering leaves. I blinked, stunned. She should *never* have used the magic so openly in the human lands.

In fact, she should never have been able to do something so powerful with nothing more than a wave of her arm. Her actions unsettled me more than anything else had today; more so than the nuthatches and pigeons, or the surges of magic in the air.

Did the extra magic help? Maybe she, like nearly every other fae, had better control over the power than I did and the extra magic the Edge was putting out made it easy for her to do something so incredibly powerful with so little effort.

Aletta had gone and I couldn't follow. I got into the car and headed straight home. In the twilight, I saw an occasional cat skulking along their solitary paths. I stopped to talk to a couple, but they didn't want to be bothered tonight.

I checked the mailbox at the end of the driveway. A small recorder sat inside wrapped in a hastily scrawled note -- Richard from The Rookery who had recorded one of his parrots so I could play the sounds for Shakespeare. I had told them I hoped the sound of another bird would help calm him. I damped down my powers and shoved the device into my pocket as I drove the rest of the way up the drive to the house.

My mood was not any better as I stalked to the porch and threw open the door, startling Shakespeare who began to shout various lines of poetry.

"Quiet," I said. The tone got through to him. He settled on his perch, pretending to sleep.

"Bad day?" Cato asked, peering around the corner from the kitchen.

"Aletta is in town."

"Oh." He had met Aletta and shared my feelings towards her. "What does Miss Perfection want here?"

"I'm not sure. I need to contact home to learn if someone sent her. She did something odd. I want to know what brought her here."

"If she shows up at the house, I'm going to go camp down at mom's place," Cato warned.

I nodded with understanding as I sat down on my favorite chair, a big comfortable brown recliner. I leaned back, trying to ease the kinks out of my shoulders while preparing to reach home.

Did I need to cooperate with Aletta? I would for the safety for others. However, I would not stand by while she played games with David. And no, that wasn't my personal interest in David making me react this way. I would be angry if she used her magic to manipulate any human whether using a glamour or anything else.

Now that I knew my reaction wasn't selfish and childish helped me relax enough to get the spell fixed in my mind. I worked my way through the pattern to contact my father or anyone else at the clan house across the Edge. This should not have been hard, even for me.

But tonight getting a connection proved to be impossible. I tried a half dozen times, breaking out in a sweat on the last effort, before I conceded to yet another defeat. The Edge felt odd still, and I sensed the power in the ether as though streamers of magic pierced through the air. I couldn't catch hold of them and they put out interference, adding one more frustration to the day.

I took a warm, relaxing shower, which I consider one of the best inventions mankind has ever made. Oh, I love a long bath sometimes, but a shower with the right temperature and pulse of water can ease any problems out of muscles.

As I dried off again, I sensed Aletta returning to Estes Park, ending the hope she would stay away after I had annoyed her. I had a link to her since I did the Summons though it wouldn't last long.

Ah well. At least my oh-so-perfect cousin didn't impress David.

I pulled on a big, warm robe before I went back to the living room and ferreted the recorder out of my jacket pocket. Deb and Rich kept a number of parrots, macaws and other big birds at The Rookery. They were more than glad to help me out with Shakespeare. I hoped this might trigger his ability to speak parrot again.

I took the device over to Shakespeare. He tilted his head left and right as though he might discern what I was up to by watching me.

"*I spoke to her of power and pride, but mystically -- in such guise,*" he said.

Pretty words. I supposed I should be grateful he didn't shout obscenities all day.

"We're trying something new, Shakespeare." I held the little recorder before I turned it on.

What would have been screeching to most people became the sound of excited bird voices in the background discussing the weather and the shop owner's bad taste in clothing. Just as well people don't understand what they said most times.

"Is this recording?" Richard asked. The loud feedback won a jump from both Shakespeare and me. "Yes. Good. Let's try to get Telora to speak. Come on lovely. Make some nice little birdy sounds for the poor African Gray. Come on my sweet --"

Richard's bird squawked in parrot, which I, unfortunately, understood all too well.

"What are you holding?" Telora demanded, worry in the frantic sound of her voice. "What is that silver thing? Why is he pushing it toward me?"

"Very good, Telora. Nice bird. Say a few more things."

"Oh gods of all feathers! He's going to kill me! Help! Help! I told you they EAT BIRDS! I saw it! Fried BIRDS! He's going to kill me! Help, help, help!"

"Not quite so loud, sweet."

"Oh gods, oh gods, oh gods! They're going to fry me! The humans will kill us all! Someone help me, help me, help me!"

The other birds grew louder, a general mayhem of panic Telora spread through the shop. I shook my head, certain this would not help. I almost stopped the recording, but somewhere in the background, I heard the clear voice of a little cockatiel speaking in badly accented parrot.

"Will you SHUT UP!" he shouted. I heard the rattling of a cage door. "If I have to put up with this damn drama queen bullshit one more time I will squeeze through these bars, break into your cage, and bite off your head! Shut up!"

"I thought they loved me. I thought they cared! They were only interested in food. Help! Help! Help!"

"Shut up! If they don't kill you with the silver thing, I will. I'll shove it so far up your fancy feathered ass they'll be calling you mirror bird every time you open your mouth!"

"Help! Help! Help me!"

"Not so loud, love," Richard said. "Calm down. There's a good bird. You're doing very well! This seems to be going well, Deb!"

"The human woman is coming!" Telora cried. She was almost gasping for breath. "She will bring the knife! Oh help me, help me, help me --"

"I'll help you!" the cockatiel shouted. The cage rattled more. "Give me a chance and I'll help you! Let me out of here! Let me at her! I can't take any more of this crisis-of-the-day crap! Half a year of this is more than you should ask of any bird! Let me kill her! She'd be good fried!"

"Just a little bit more, my sweet."

"I don't want to die! Don't let them kill me! Help! Help! Help!"

"I can't take any more! I can't stand it!" I heard the sound of splashing water followed by a moment of odd, distorted bird sounds. "Oh gods. This pathetic little water dish isn't even enough to drown myself in!"

"Gaylord, you silly little bird, what are you doing? Do you want a bath? Can you say something to the lovely little African Gray?"

"Oh yes, oh yes -- take the silver thing away," Telora said, sounding quite happy. "Kill the cockatiel instead. Yes, much better choice!"

"I'll remember that, sweetie."

I shut off the recording, gasping for breath as I tried not to laugh. Shakespeare didn't seem in the least impressed by what he'd heard but it had improved my mood.

I thought about reading or writing, but I wanted to get past this day and hope that tomorrow would be better if I could get rid of Aletta. I went into the bedroom, pulled on a nightie, and slid under the covers. Cato padded into the room and jumped up on the bed.

"Better?" Cato asked.

"A bit," I said. I rubbed Cato's ears, and he lost all ability to talk as he purred and rolled around a little so I could reach the particularly good spots. "I don't know why she's here, but I think I embarrassed her with David."

"David," Cato mumbled. "Is this all about? David?"

"Maybe so." I hated to admit anything to Cato, but I never lied to a cat. That's just not a good idea. "I'm not going to worry --"

The air changed. The waves of magic hit so strongly I

felt disorientated. Everything seemed to move. Cato yowled as he flattened himself against me. Animals can often sense strong magic. Sometimes even humans do though they think the weather is odd or something.

I caught tight hold of Cato, afraid for him caught in this maelstrom of wild magic with me. This was more powerful than anything I had experienced on this side of the Edge. The power rippled and glided; things appeared to melt, move, swirl, change colors --

Cato buried his head in the crook of my arm. I feared the surge of power would never end.

The magic melted away like a river running dry. I gasped and curled into a ball, Cato nestled between my arms. He made a few mewing sounds, but we both stayed motionless for a few minutes.

I feared something would happen again. I finally sat up, trying not to be ill. Cato did as well though he swayed a little.

"What the hell was that?" he whispered.

"Flux from the Edge."

"It's never done that before!" he protested. Shakespeare shouted in the other room. The word 'hell' seemed to play into a lot of his quotes tonight.

I lifted my trembling hand to survey the area.

"Power outage in part of town," I said. I hadn't suffered one because magic supplied the power to my place. "It should come back on in a couple minutes, though."

"Good. Don't want panicked humans." Cato settled down on the pillow.

I directed my senses toward the Edge. The surface rippled, and it had moved a little, too.

And I found something else.

"Damn! Something got through!"

"What came through?" Cato said, lifting his head.

"I don't know. Something big. I'm going out there. You need to come along."

"Me?" he said, glancing over his shoulder in a comical 'there has to be someone else she's talking to' look.

"You," I said and smiled. "I can't do much magic close to the Edge so I need someone to watch rather than setting a guard spell. I don't trust myself, Cato."

"I trust you. Implicitly. You'll do great. You don't need me --"

"Cato."

"Fine. But don't you think you better get dressed? It will be a bit cold out there."

I was so unsettled that I would have gone out in my nighty. I needed a keeper. Good thing I had the cat.

CHAPTER SIX

C hanging into something warm was easy enough with a little magic. I also added a jacket with enough room for Cato to nestle inside though he still wasn't happy about the idea. Preparing to leave gave me a few more minutes to calm. It didn't help much.

We stepped out into the yard. Clouds obscured the rising moon which meant we might have snow yet tonight. I scared three deer standing in my yard and they darted to the tress and then changed their minds. I sensed no other creatures around tonight.

Cato burrowed in deeper --

"Stop moving! That tickles!"

"You're bony," he complained, but settled against the fleece lining of the jacket. I probably looked pregnant.

Magic easily found the link leading to the Edge and created a conduit of air to lift us.

I walked on the wind.

We'd have to walk on land for part of the trip because it's not safe to do magic near anything as unstable as the Edge. This would get us close though.

"I will not look," Cato said. He'd taken this type of trip before and didn't like it. I remembered the first time he learned we were well off the ground. It had taken me days to heal all the scratches. Cats don't seem to enjoy being off the ground well, despite their love of being up high.

I enjoy flying, though, with the brush of the wind through my hair and against my face. Away from the ties of the ground, I somehow shed all my troubles, and all my responsibilities, up here in the clouds. That's the reason I only fly for work-related problems. This freedom could be too addictive.

"Are we there yet?" Cato asked a little later.

"We're passing over Odessa Falls."

He moved with a little whimper; flying and water were not his favorite things. I tapped Cato on the head and he settled again. This needed all my concentration because I sensed something dark in the air tonight and I didn't want his distractions.

The faint glow of the Edge lighted the ground ahead of us, which meant I had come close enough with magic. Only a quarter mile of the Edge brushed against this world at this spot and it kept hidden in the forest on the east side of Terra Tomah peak. Anything flying overhead, including satellites, wouldn't pick it up because . . . well that magic and technology problem. We also keep a dark mat over the area so no one in the sky -- planes that is -- sees even a hint of glitter.

I settled us on the ground in a small glade where the sun had burnt off most of the snow. Deer, rabbits, and other animals ran for the shadows. I heard no birds -- neither night birds nor anything startled awake by the sudden movement of everyone else. They must have moved on when the Edge became unsettled.

"We're down," I told Cato.

Cato peeked one eye out, gave a quick flick of his head,

and snaked his way out of the jacket. I settle him on the ground and we stood motionless for a moment as we both listened.

"Let's get this done," Cato said with his tail up despite the situation. He did enjoy a little adventure. "I want to get home and sleep. You know, a few shrimp might be in order for tonight's work."

"I'll consider it." Cato is good, loyal, and smart . . . but when it comes to food, I could get him to play drone and fly on his own for the right price.

We headed out of the glade and into the trees, following a path laid down by elk which made it larger than a deer trail and easier to traverse.

The night would have been dark except for the glow of the Edge which permeated everything at ground level like a small aurora borealis. Even when the Edge isn't in a flux period, we need to keep it hidden with repelling spells to keep hikers out of the area.

We hadn't gone far when I found someone to talk with, more or less. Owls are annoying creatures sometimes. They are smart but they only speak in questions. This one almost took off before I got his attention as though he felt a compulsion to fly away from all the magic. Owls are often less susceptible to magic because they've been so long associated with various powers from Athena and on through the ages.

"Is there trouble around here?" I asked. "Did something come through the Edge?"

"What is it? What is it?" the great horned owl asked, leaning down from his perch on a pine tree branch.

"How big is it?" I asked.

"Is it large?" he answered and then turned and flew away.

I hoped to find other animals and ask a few questions. A bobcat would be nice except Cato would take offense for me speaking with one of those wild, uncouth brutes.

The walk itself wasn't so bad though. I love the woods most of the time, day or night. I enjoy going for walks and knowing I'm safe helps. There are few things I fear from this world and little from mine since I have magic enough for protection. I've never seen a reason why a fae would need more. I didn't want to act like Aletta, who uses magic without regard for others.

Why had she arrived at Estes Park and why show up at the restaurant? I had every reason to believe she'd been the badger which meant she had been following me. Why was she playing games in my area? I couldn't do anything to stop her. Not because I didn't have the power, but because I didn't understand her reasons. Legit? Not? Was she in one of her moods and out to prove her superiority? I was an easy target.

"You shouldn't snarl when you're walking," Cato said. "If you want to talk to some birds, you don't want to scare them away."

I almost snapped at him, but caught myself. My moods manifested in more than a look: it was part of my energy and the animals would sense my annoyance. I curbed my irritation towards Miss Perfection and concentrated on what brought me out here in the middle of the night.

"This is too damned cold," Cato said, drawing my attention again. He pranced ahead a few steps and leapt over a pile of snow. "The needles hurt my feet! It's late! What the hell are we doing out here?"

"Keeping the world safe."

"That's not the kind of job you want to give to a cat."

Cato paused by the next stand of trees waiting for me

to catch up with him. The glow became almost sunlight-bright here though the shades shifted in rainbow colors. Up close the Edge looked like water standing on end and holding glowing stars in its depth. If it had been thinner, we would see through to the fae lands.

The magic is beautiful . . . and distracting. I looked away from the shimmering surface and glanced down the length, searching for sign of whatever trouble had pushed into this world. Huge trouble, if I understood the owl.

Too bad I couldn't reach home to ask for help, but you never do magic this close to the Edge. I even *almost* wished I hadn't annoyed Aletta. Maybe she would have come along tonight, though, truthfully, I trusted Cato more.

Cato and I walked along the Edge. Cato kept a few feet from the glowing surface. Sometimes when the colors abruptly changed, Cato's fur would fluff up as he hissed.

"It does no good to hiss at the Edge," I told him, trying not to laugh.

"It's a cat thing," Cato answered, his ears back and his tail remaining twice the normal size. "Now the Edge knows not to mess with me."

"The Edge isn't a thing. It doesn't think."

"It moves. It has shape. You told me the Edge is here because it wants to be here." He looked at me. "What more does it need to be alive?"

I started to speak. Stopped.

"I suppose the Edge might be considered alive," I conceded. "There are creatures on the other side that have less shape and control than this, and we consider them alive."

"Do you have cats in the fae lands?" Cato asked, peering into the Edge.

"Yes. Cats are everywhere. Some of ours have magic."

"Oh? Really?" He sounded hopeful. I suppose after spending a couple years around me, he had grown interested and cats are good at working out possibilities.

"The cats sometimes use magic to go fishing in ponds. They make pretty lures to bring the fish right to their paws."

"Oh, how lovely!"

"Well, it would be if the fish hadn't picked up magic of their own, and are rarely ever caught by those tricks. In fact, they sometimes pull a cat or two into the water. They're lucky not to drown."

"There's always a catch."

We skirted around a tree and past another. I picked up a little speed and passed Cato. I saw a darker spot ahead which might be a tear --

"Watch out!" Cato yelled.

I leapt backwards as something moved from beside a tree and stepped in front of me. The creature growled and lumbered forward -- a shape over two feet taller than me and four times as wide. A bear? A big bear. Two -- no, three of them. All moving in a swaying motion, lumbering toward me --

"Elf meat," one of them grumbled.

Hell. Not bears. *Trolls.* They moved away from the shadowy trees and I saw three big, lumbering ugly trolls with pointed dead-gray horns atop their round heads and long, dark shaggy arms ending in massive hands. Their huge claws caught glints of the rainbow light. They looked as though they'd just woken from a deep, long sleep. I waved Cato away because this was very dangerous. Trolls and fae do not get along. I suppose the crack about 'elf meat' probably gave it away.

"You don't want to be on this side," I said, keeping my

voice steady. I considered calling magic to blast them into small tiny bits. Two things prevented me. First, I'd never held that much power in my life, and second, doing any amount of real magic right here next to the Edge would not be wise.

"Elf meat. Hungry." A second troll came forward. "Said we could eat you."

"Did they?" Trolls rarely make sense. "But you can't eat me, you know. I'm a border guard. You've crossed over."

Heads swung from side-to-side, big wet noses sniffing the air like caricatures of dogs. Trolls are pure legend creatures and they should never have been on this side of the Edge. They absolutely cannot blend in.

I wouldn't hold their attention with nothing more than words much longer. I'd have to use magic. Simple, easy magic. Nothing showy. The opposite, in fact, of a summoning. I prepared the spell in my mind while I stepped forward, almost within reach of those huge, club-like arms.

Fae and trolls have fought long wars over on the other side. Such trouble is inevitable when creatures of such disparate types share the same areas. The trolls didn't help by deciding elf meat one of the best delicacies on their menu.

Which put me in a bad place as I stood before three of the biggest, ugliest trolls I'd ever seen. They seemed dazed, which was all that kept me from already becoming dinner. Anyone arriving finds the transition disorientating at first as though you've lost all sense of direction.

"You want to go home," I said, giving power to the spell I wove, oh so carefully, around the group of them. They moved closer to together, which I wanted -- although hadn't I heard how they mass before they attack? "You want to go through the Edge. This is not a place where you can live."

"Go home," one of them said. "Go after we eat."

"No," I answered, and won a series of growls in return. "No. You need to go now. This is not a good place. You'll die here."

"Why you care?" the leader asked. He stood a little straighter as he recovered his wits. Damn.

"I care because I would have to clean up the mess."

The trolls found that amusing and gave several loud guffaws that sounded more akin to farting. Great: I had made trolls laugh. My day was pretty much complete at this point.

I wove more magic around them using subtle movements of my hands so I didn't draw attention. I glanced beyond them to the hole in the Edge and measured the steps in my mind -- steps for me, steps for them. I nudged them a little. They went backwards one step and didn't seem to notice.

"You come with us, over to the other side," the lead troll said.

"No, thank you." I tried to sound light and happy. "I don't think I'd like to join you as dinner. How did you get here?"

I had asked to keep them concentrating on things other than killing me. I hadn't expected an answer.

"Don't know, don't know," the answer came from two of them. "Sleeping. Tired . . . scent of elf."

I almost lost my hold on the magic. Did I read the answer right? They'd gone to sleep, perhaps not of their own accord, and an elf -- fae -- came along, scooped them up and pushed them into this world?

No. It was probably more flux in the field which made everything odd on both sides. They'd come through about the time as the wave of magic hit this side. Who knows what happened on the other side of the Edge?

I nudged them another step and another. The hole stood at their backs.

The leader glanced towards it, growling. "No. Not go. Not without dinner!"

He swiped huge claws at me. I leapt away and almost lost my hold on them. I used a surge of magic to shove one through but had to counter the flux of magic from the Edge. The last two broke loose. I would have to do something fast.

Sleep?

I didn't have the power to do a real sleep spell. I might make them drowsy . . . but I didn't want more. If they fell over asleep, I'd never get them moved through without even more magic which I wouldn't dare use here at the Edge. The surface already glittered in places. If I managed to make them drowsy --

I called magic and the pretty power danced in the air. I had never seen magic so manifest and lovely.

The trolls must have thought I intended to kill them, which made them manic. They used their primitive magic, but their spells brought a surge of fire from the Edge. I dropped my spell to knock the power away, saving the two trolls and myself.

The troll leader swept his big clawed hand down on my arm. The nails cut into my skin. I hissed in pain and surprise -- sounding, I far too much like Cato just then.

The ground around us had burnt, filling the area with scent of burning pine needles. I coughed, ignoring the pain in my arm. I wanted to have this finished. If the battle went on, they would best of me.

The spell I had created came easier the second time and the troll on the right swayed and went to his knees. The leader -- having an unfortunately clear view of the magic -- avoided the spell. He growled and charged.

I moved aside, and the creature bashed his head against a pine tree. His huge horns raked lines down the trunk and needles rained down all around us.

Any single fae would have had a hard fight against a group of trolls. What made me believe I could beat them? This was impossible for me. Trolls are big, strong, and mean. They like to eat us.

I didn't want to be dinner tonight. I wanted to go meet David tomorrow, have a lovely day in the mountains, wandering around taking pictures and talking about writing a whole book with him.

"I will not be killed." I stared straight into the trolls face. "I have things to do. I am a guardian. Do you understand? Do you know what happens when you kill a guardian?"

"Nothing if not catch us."

He had a point. It wasn't as though it hadn't happened before.

I lifted my hand, sending a wave of magic into the air and heading to the city. "There. Now they will know about you. You want to take the chance?"

He watched the magic move away into the night, shaped into the semblance of a glowing blue bird. He scowled as he looked at me.

"Don't care."

"Yeah, I kind of suspected that would be your answer."

The magic bird circled around and hit him in the back

of the head with the sleep spell. He fell down to his knees, yawning and his big eyes blinking as he tried to fight the compulsion to nap. I didn't want him to fall over asleep just yet, so I grabbed his arm, adding a compulsion to do my bidding. Dangerous work because I drew his attention. I danced away when he growled and reached for my leg. I backed up and by little steps, I lead him to the hole. His companion followed, stumbling along, both of them angry, but unable to do anything other than obey me when I said they wanted to go through the hole to sleep on the other side.

They shuffled forward though the leader stopped before he went through and tried to make one more grab at me. I kept out of range.

"Hungry! Don't want to sleep!"

"Go on through. You'll have better hunting there."

He snarled, but he stepped through and his companion followed.

I leapt forward, grabbing one part of the hole and yanking the pliable substance over the opening where a troll hand tried to reach through to this side. I slapped the hand with a snap of magic more powerful than I had expected. The troll howled as the hand retreated and he didn't try again.

I pulled the hole shut. Red and greens blurred as they tried to tear apart until I realized I needed to get colors to match. I sealed the breach with a last whisper of magic.

Then I slid down to the ground, caught hold of my bleeding arm, and moaned. I had survived an encounter with angry trolls. And I did it mostly by talking, for the love of all the gods. I must have been insane. I should have used magic to kill them all, even if the spell killed me, too. Trolls loose on this side would have been a disaster.

But I'd succeeded. I had sent them back.

I put my head in my hands, willing a little magic down through my arm to heal most of the wound. Nothing fancy, but magic still sparked out from the Edge. I wanted to go home, but first I would have to check the rest of the Edge to make sure there no other problems.

Suddenly I didn't want this job. My little nowhere place on the map of magical hot spots had become far more dangerous than I had ever expected. I loved the area, but I wasn't competent to do a job which included fighting trolls. Even if I managed once, the idea that I might have to try again set me trembling.

And then I realized I hadn't seen Cato since the battle began. I scrambled to my feet, afraid I would find his mangled body. Had I brought him here to --

"Cato!"

"I'm up here," Cato said.

I found a spot of orange fur far up in the branches of a pine tree. He stared down, eyes blinking in the glow of the light.

"A lot of help you were," I answered, trying not to show how incredibly happy I was to see him safe.

"Hey, I gave you the warning and got out of the way before they trampled me. When you talked about not being dinner, I figured I didn't want to be the cat sampler before the fae main course."

I laughed despite myself and felt better knowing he was safe. He wasn't happy though. He watched the Edge, his tail twitching from side-to-side, like a little orange snake.

"You want to come down?" I asked.

"Yeah, sure. You know, I love climbing, but I hate trying to get down. It's always so undignified." He maneuvered himself along the branch.

I was still half ill. I watched ripples and pulses along the Edge while the magic in the air made my skin crawl. Before long my hair would even stand on end -- not a pretty sight.

We needed to finish the work and go home to rest. Tomorrow would be better. No trolls. Any day without trolls talking about having you for dinner was bound to be a better day.

Though I needed to deal with Aletta and for a moment I weighed her against the trolls. It was a toss-up over which one might be more annoying.

Cato had paused at a lower branch and appeared quite content to stay there.

"Come on Cato," I said. "We need to check the rest of The Edge. I suspect the trolls didn't make the hole. Something else might have come through first and sort of dragged the trolls along. They didn't know how they got here."

Cato leaned over and peered at me, about three feet above my head. Why do cats need to be higher than us? "Are you telling me there is something else out there? Something even worse than the trolls?"

"It's possible," I said, a quick glance left and right.

"I'll stay here." He settled on the branch.

I wondered if I dared to use a little magic to knock him to the ground. Then I realized there was a better way to get him to stick with me.

"Yeah, good idea. I'll be back this way in about an hour. Just yell if anything else comes through. I'm not sure the hole is sealed well. With luck, if something comes through, it won't climb."

As I turned, I heard a rather loud plop as several pounds of yellow fur landed at my feet. Cato looked at me, his eyes narrowed.

"Oh, are you going along after all?" I asked.

"You did that on purpose," he accused.

I worked hard to hide my smile. "I told you nothing but the truth."

"Yeah, well. Next time I could wait to make sure before shouting to look out!" He moved ahead of me with his tail fluffed and ears back.

"Well, I did intend to give you half a can of tuna when we get home," I said, following him.

"No lie?" he said. His ears came up and his tail made the funny little question mark shape cats get when they're really happy.

"I never lie to cats. Let's get this done so we can get home."

"Great idea."

Cato would have gone bounding down line of the Edge without me if it would get him the tuna any faster. I didn't rush since I wanted to make certain the place wouldn't erupt in trolls and draw me back again tonight. By tomorrow, I intended to have real help here. My father would send a few fae once he heard about the trolls because everyone knew I didn't have the kind of magic to deal with trouble on this level.

Except I had dealt with something others had trouble handling. When did I start accepting that I couldn't handle magic-related trouble? I had adapted to living in the human world where magic didn't matter, but that didn't mean I had no power at all. My family never judged me, but we all knew my lack of magical ability played into the jobs I got. I wasn't even the only one who didn't have strong magic. We all did our own work according to our best abilities.

This time I exceeded expectations. I grinned, even

though my arm ached.

We found a couple more weak spots on the Edge so I reinforced them. Even Cato pointed out darker, discolored sections where the wall bulged a little.

I'd been lucky when I sealed the big hole closed. The magic hadn't backfired on me and created holes twice the size of the one I sealed.

The realization of how close I came to another disaster sent another chill through me and dampened my good mood. I'd spent years training for this post. I knew all the real tricks of magic although I had trouble handling the fancier stuff. Settling wild magic is hard for me and the work took me twice as long as any of my cousins would have taken, but I did it. I didn't want to leave the Edge weak anywhere along the line. Half done work would mean more work later.

So I paused everywhere the glowing light appeared weak or dark despite Cato's attempts to urge me to quit and head home. At one point I found the Edge so thin I considered pushing through to the fae lands. I might find help there, but it meant abandoning my post for a while. If someone had pushed the trolls through that might not be such a good idea.

I had managed the work so far tonight, though I did get annoyed when I found dozens of small, hand-sized holes at the far end of the Edge where it blurred into the reality of this world. They looked like stress rips caused when the trolls came through the Edge. The work of fixing them was easy, but annoying.

The work took longer than I wanted. We got to the end where the ground sloped down into a ravine and the Edge stuck out in midair for about a foot before it disappeared. It looked fine. On the walk back, I reinforced a couple spots along the way. Cato fell silent on the last round though he twitched whenever something moved in the woods. It always turned out to be something natural to this world. Foxes, raccoons and other small animals sometimes let their curiosity get the better of them.

"It is getting late," Cato said when we reached the far end of the Edge. "Do you intend to walk back and forth along here all night? Because if you do, I'll go climb a pine tree and get some sleep."

"Everything is solid." I glanced down the line one more time. "I considered staying, but it's almost dawn. You're right; we need to get home. I have an appointment with David this morning."

"Yeah," Cato said. He trotted along at my feet, his paws crunching needles.

We headed away from the Edge and walked a few feet. When I stopped, so did he.

"I think there's something more going on, Cato," I admitted. "If something pushed those trolls through on purpose it means a lot of trouble for us."

"Why would someone do that?" he asked. He sat down and cleaned a paw, looking thoughtful.

"I don't know and I'm worried. Maybe pixies were playing games. They have no sense of the trouble they can create when they do stuff. Think of nuthatches with magic."

"Ugh. What an unpleasant image," he said. He rubbed against my leg. "Can we go home now?"

"We will fly you know."

"I know. I want to get back to our nice, quiet house."

"The one with the cans of tuna."

"That would be the one," he agreed.

He made me laugh. I forced myself to move down the

hillside, out of direct view of the Edge. We needed to go at least half a mile before I did more magic or something unfortunate might happen. I'd tempted fate a few too many times already.

We surprised a half dozen elk though not as much as they startled Cato, who leapt, fluffed, hissed and spat as the animals took off at a run.

"Yeah, you're going to scare them," I said with a laugh this time.

"They ran, didn't they?" he said, daring me to tell him it was not because of his bravery.

"Good point. Let's go another half mile and that should be good enough." I glanced back at the glint of unnatural light. Best not to take any chances.

Cato didn't argue. Of course he would agree to anything for half a can of tuna. I don't want to suggest he's easy to bribe, but if you know his price. . . .

We trudged on through another stand of pine with lines of snow in the shadows. Cato cursed under his breath as he bounded through one pile of the dreaded white stuff.

I had reached the point where it would be safe to use magic when something came flapping through the trees at us. Remembering the nuthatches' fear of 'big wings' brought magic to my fingertips until I saw a great horned owl land in the tree before me. The lighter feathers on his chest and wings caught the faint moonlight making them appear silvery while the brown circles of his face seemed darker in the night. His golden eyes shown as his ears twisted back and forth.

"Who is it?" he demanded staring into the night. "Who is it?"

He wasn't looking at me.

I spun and found the ethereal shape of a man on

horseback a few yards behind us. He glowed and not from the moonlight, but rather from pure magic. I almost saw a face in the shape of light --

As the ghostly figured moved closer, I sensed the cold, empty hunger this creature brought into the world. It wanted something . . . and that might be life.

Cato fluffed up, but he didn't hiss this time. He dropped lower to the ground, trying not to draw attention. Wise cat. You didn't want this thing to notice you. I didn't understand quite what stood there before me. This was not a ghost, at least in the conventional sense. He held fae power in the glowing nimbus of magic surrounding him.

This creature did not belong here anymore than the trolls I had already sent back. Neither horse nor rider should have been wandering the woods. They most certainly should not have been following me.

"Who are you?" I asked aloud, sounding far too much like the owl.

Cato made a little shushing sound as though I shouldn't be talking to this creature. I wanted answers. This wasn't akin to the trolls: Sleep would not work on a specter and I had the distinct impression I would not talk this one into crossing over into fae, either.

Purpose. I felt it even above the hunger. This thing possessed purpose.

The horse took two quick steps closer to me. The owl lifted and flew off, drawing the attention of horse and rider, which told me two important things. First, it really was here in this world, not merely a shadow from the other side. Second, the apparition had trouble concentrating. The creature should never have taken his eyes from me.

I lifted my hand and almost let loose a bolt of magic which should have shattered the ephemeral bonds of the shape he held. The rider noticed and hastily pulled the horse to the side. My magic swept past, shattering against a tree in a sparkle of blue and green stars.

I created another bolt, but the horse and rider rushed into the shadowy woods.

I didn't dare let them go, to stay loose on this side where they might be seen -- or where they might do something. I raced after it.

Maybe not wise. . . .

Fae can run easily in the woods, which is a gift of being magical. We are closer to the innate magic of nature.

The horse and rider seemed to have trouble navigating between the trees so they followed the elk trails to a brook and across, making the slightest of sound as horse touched water. Cato howled as we splashed through the water. He tried to keep up with me. Should I stop and grab him? No. The rider slowed a little, and I hoped his reserves were running low. I dared not pause.

"I have to get him!" I said, panting a little as we jogged on through the woods.

"Yeah," Cato answered, more out of breath than me.

We startled more than elk during the mad dash through the woods. We even passed a couple bears. I sent out a pulse of power to make certain nothing raced after us and grabbed Cato who started lagging behind me. Surprising a bear or moose is never a good idea; they'll sometimes charge you out of pure frustration.

We turned towards the Edge. Good. I wanted to chase this one through to the other side. I wanted to go home and not have any more problems tonight.

This thing must have come through with the trolls, wandered around and found me. My magic would be a beacon to anything from fae. I didn't understand what the horse and rider were, but I suspected something connected to mythology. Myths always have magic involved in the tales. If they grow strong enough, the essence of them migrate from the human world to the fae lands. Sometimes the myths want to go back home.

When the horse and rider reached the next opening in the trees, the rider turned to face me. I slowed. I didn't want a confrontation since I didn't understand this thing's powers. He looked like a ghost, but even ghosts can be dangerous.

The horse panted while the rider leaned forward over the neck, patting behind the ears. I saw the odd shape of a helmet on his head, but I couldn't make out the design. I wanted to see more but the moment I took a step forward they fled once more.

"Damn!"

I didn't want to spend all night running through the woods.

"Kat!" Cato protested when I started away.

"Stay here. I'll come back for you!"

"Stay?" I heard him call as I dashed into the shadows of the trees. "Are you crazy?"

Yes, I must be, but I didn't give up the chase. The horse was tiring and I might get them through the Edge before they recovered.

A terrible hunger remained where they passed. They had to leave.

I heard Cato panting behind me. Off to the left the Edge glowed and magic grew stronger in the air. I drew a little to myself, hoping I didn't cause more problems -- and hoped whatever I pursued couldn't do the same.

The ghostly shape stood still in a little opening by the Edge. The horse's head drooped down, and the rider sat slumped in the saddle.

This was almost over.

"Kat!"

Cato threw himself in front of me. I tripped over him and landed face down in the snowbank.

From here I saw the wide, deep ravine between me and the rider. If Cato hadn't tripped me I would have tumbled over the embankment and probably wouldn't have created magic quickly enough to save myself from serious injury -- or from an attack by the rider.

I scrambled away from the ravine on hands and knees with Cato at my side as I stared across to the horse and rider. I saw dark eyes, almost real, glaring at me. We measured each other in a silent moment. I didn't come out the stronger of the two of us.

I panicked, pulling magic from the air despite the Edge; a flash of lightning filled the air as I prepared to cast --

The rider turned to the Edge, the horse prancing forward those few steps --

And they passed through without even opening a door or tearing a hole.

"Oh hell," I whispered. The magic danced in my hands as I stared. "Oh, that can't be good at all."

"Can we go home?" Cato asked plaintively. He nuzzled against my side since I still knelt in the snow. "I think it would be very nice to go home now."

"Yeah," I agreed as I carefully let go of the magic. "Thanks, Cato. You saved my life."

"Least I could do for half a can of tuna," he said.

"Whole can," I replied.

"Let's go."

I wondered if I should stay. What if it came back?

What if --

No, I needed to get home and contact others.

I picked Cato up and carried him away from the Edge. He sat with his paws and head resting on my shoulder and kept watch behind, even when we flew away.

CHAPTER SEVEN

We returned to the house about three in the morning, both of us exhausted. I wouldn't get any rest tonight. After I gave Cato his tuna, I settled in my favorite chair and tried to contact home. Unfortunately, I wasn't calm enough to make the connection. So I made tea and wandered into the living room. I gave crackers to Shakespeare.

"Know thou the secret of the spirit, bow'd from its wild pride into shame."

Spirit? The bird surprises me when he almost echoes real life. Cato and I were talking ghosts when we home. Did he understand or had he chanced on the right connection?

"Talk to me," I said to him.

He tucked his head under his wing and even ignored the crackers.

A quick shower eased the tension from my shoulders. I pulled on my favorite robe and then decided on day clothes instead. I didn't want to call my father and tell him all this wonderful news while lounging around in my robe. I needed to look professional. Competent.

The decision to dress proved wise, because when I did get through, my father wasn't alone. He was at a clan meeting in the keep, and I saw a dozen others in the room with him. Many sat at a long table, with papers and cups spread everywhere so it looked as though they had been at work for a long time. I felt a rush of embarrassment for what I *almost* did and looked down just to make certain I wasn't wearing the robe after all.

"Katlyn," he said with a nod. "Problems, I assume?"

I winced. He lifted his hand, plainly contrite.

"I asked because *everyone* is having trouble. Pieces of the Edge are acting odd everywhere."

"Ah. Yes. Three trolls came through --"

"Gods all," someone said. "We better get right there --"

"No. I sent them back over to fae. Yes, me. Don't get that look."

My father laughed which lightened the mood for both the people on his side and for me. I told them what happened with the trolls and what I did afterwards with the Edge. Nods of approval came all along the table where most of the people sat.

"You did well," Uncle Timber said. He headed the clan and to get approval from him was spectacular.

"Thank you, sir. However, there was another problem."

Then I related the story of my second encounter, including the last part where Cato saved my life.

"I shouldn't have kept racing after him," I admitted. "But I wanted to know what the thing was, and I didn't want him loose on this side."

My tale had drawn all their attention. None of them appeared happy.

"Go check on our side of the Edge." Timber waved a hand towards a couple of my cousins. "See if you can find this thing. Be quick."

"Yes sir," they chorused and left.

Timber moved to stand by my father and nodded to me. I rarely warranted this much of his attention. "You did well, Katlyn. I'm unsure what you faced. This thing should never have been on your side, nor should it pass back through so easily. We have problems. We have problems *everywhere*."

He started to turn away, obviously preoccupied.

"Like mine?" I dared to ask, hoping for a few more clues.

"Not quite. In the Sahara we're having trouble with the Nile gods who are trying to break through and take back their power."

The idea of the Nile gods trying to set up business again bothered me. Gods are tricky beings. They're fae who moved up the ladder somehow. The step affects their powers and their entire thought process. You can no longer guess what they'll do and you can't reason with them.

"Good luck, sir," I said, which sounded entirely inadequate.

"We shall hold the line," he answered with a quick grin. Timber never shied from a fight. "We've contained them before."

"Yes sir, of course."

"You needn't worry over what I think, Katlyn." He looked straight at me. His dark green eyes held power so obvious it's not safe for him to come over to this side and deal with humans. If they peer into his eyes, they believe in magic. They can't deny it exists afterwards. "You have done an exceptional job. You are always quick with your mind, which is something I can't say about many of your cousins. They rely too much on power and sometimes don't consider the full repercussions."

"Thank you, sir." I tried not to remember the couple times tonight when I had grabbed power and not considered what would happen so close to the Edge. My father, standing behind Timber, seemed quite pleased. "Is there anything you can suggest for me to do?"

"The specter bothers me," Timber admitted. "I hope to learn what it is on this side."

I bowed my head in thanks, and Timber returned to his other work. My father stepped forward, still smiling. Timber had praised me for the work I'd done in the past, though this was the first time I felt as though I might deserve his notice.

"I know you have your hands full," I said. "I appreciate you took the time to talk."

"Your problems are important, Kat," he said.

"You guys are battling the Nile Gods! They make even trolls and specters sound like playtime games."

"Trolls are always serious," he disagreed. "And the unknown is worse. I wish I could get free and help you, but right now we're barely holding the line in some places."

"Well, at least Aletta is here," I said.

He looked startled. Paris, Aletta's mother, glanced my way from her spot at the long table. She frowned. I thought she kept track of her precious daughter.

"Aletta is there?" My father frowned. He didn't much care for her either. He turned to the table. "Did someone send Aletta to the area?"

"Not I," Timber said.

"Paris?" my father asked.

"Aletta is a free spirit." Paris gave a wave of her hand, dismissing the question.

"Right." My father rolled his eyes as he glanced at me.

I nearly choked trying not to laugh. The humor brightened my mood though. Aletta had never impressed me. Nice to know I wasn't alone.

"Can you give me any pointers on how to deal with this specter?" I asked, hoping for anything.

"I'll work on the problem, but a spell to shatter the form might be the best bet to try. We'll do the research and find something more. What effect did this creature have on the world?"

"He didn't move through anything solid and he didn't leave death in his tracks, either," I reported. "Which made me suspect this wasn't a real specter. At first I thought he might be an illusion, but he and the horse both noticed things in this world too well. And I sensed a hunger for life in him."

"Excellent points," Timber said from behind my father.

I blushed realizing he still listened and approved of what I noted.

"Yes, good points. I'll see what I can learn. Kat -- you did well tonight."

"He left on his own," I reminded him.

"However, he intended to kill you and failed."

"Because the cat saved her," Paris replied with a smirk.

Several unhappy people turn towards her. Paris wasn't the most popular person in the clan, but she held considerable power.

"She's very lucky the cat was there, since your daughter wasn't. Are you going to tell me Aletta somehow missed the trouble?" my father asked.

I hadn't considered that part. Aletta would have felt the surge of magic that took out power in town and she hadn't tried to contact me, even then. "I wonder what she was doing," I said absently.

"Avoiding trouble and work," my father unexpectedly answered. "Aletta does that very well."

Paris surged to her feet, already protesting. I winced at the sound of her shrill voice and Timber give my father a look of warning.

Though Timber didn't disagree or ask for an apology.

"I need to rest." I drew my father's attention while Paris kept prattling about how no one had the right to say such disparaging things about her daughter.

"Yes, go rest. I'll get back to you as soon as I have something."

"Thanks."

I severed the connection and relaxed, glad to be beyond the range of Paris's voice and rage before she turned her tirade on me. I made a quick check and found Aletta was in the hotel. Maybe the wave of magic frightened her or made her ill. I'd give her the benefit of the doubt. And after all, I hadn't called on her to go with me.

Cato sauntered over and jumped up on the chair arm, burped, and settled down into my lap, circling twice to find a good spot.

"I'm stuffed," he said, contentedly.

"Good. You did an excellent job tonight, Cato. Much better than Aletta ever would have."

"She can't see past her own nose." He already sounded half asleep.

I sat with him for a while. My legs ached from running, and my head still pounded from the trouble and the magic I'd used. However, Timber and my father both said I handled the problem well. Their praise meant something.

Two hits against Aletta in one day. There was no doubt she'd hear what had been said over in fae, too. It almost made up for the trolls.

I relaxed for the first time in almost twenty-four hours. I needed to meet David in a couple hours, so I would use a magical sleep spell and as long as nothing went wrong between now and then --

I almost cursed myself for even thinking such an ill-omened thing. With my eyes closed I did a quick sweep of the Edge and found everything reasonably steady.

Then I found something much closer to home -- from the town, in fact, as though tiny bits of magic kept popping in and out and lingering as traces along the streets. Magic in town? Close to technology? I sat up so fast I won a growl from Cato as he lifted his head.

"Don't tell me there's more trouble." He turned with both ears laid back. Even Shakespeare moved uneasily on his perch, unsettled by my sudden movement.

"Not the Edge. I can feel something odd in town."

"Aletta?" he asked. "She's odd enough, right?"

"I wish this were Aletta." I stood and put Cato into the warm chair. He snuggled down into the cushion.

"You aren't leaving, are you?"

"I'm going to walk a couple blocks. You don't have to go along."

"Good. I'd waddle. I don't want to waddle." He put a paw over his nose and closed his eyes to sleep.

Sleeping cats are always cute, somewhat the same way sleeping baby trolls are cute. He also reminded how I wanted to go to bed. I still went to the door and stepped out into the cold night.

A dog barked down the block, and the wind dashed leaves across the yard. No birds lingered nearby to tell me what they'd seen. I shouldn't have ignored the nuthatches.

I walked through the deserted yard and past my car.

The winding road took me from my house to the next as I moved through the shadows. My steps grew louder in the otherwise silent world. I rarely spook; this time I glanced over my shoulder a few times and wished I'd brought Cato along.

I stepped from the shadow of the trees to a view of Estes Park. Lights shone like little stars down the hillside, those human-made guards against the darkness and the darker things humans didn't even realize existed. I relaxed again seeing the city --

And then, for a brief, very odd moment, everything seemed unreal, as though this place slipped a notch from what it should be.

I blinked, and the city settled back to normal. That moment had been a figment of my imagination brought on by exhaustion and because I kept looking for something else to go wrong. Fae can search too hard for trouble and make problems happen. We're warned all our lives and we still make trouble for ourselves sometimes.

Testing the air brought a partial answer. Bits of magical power drifted sluggishly through town. I sensed Aletta, already awake and moving through her room. I wondered if she'd miss her beauty sleep.

A quick jog down Fairy Tale Lane brought me to Mrs. Hale's house. I hoped neither she nor the neighbors noticed me loitering there.

"Mrs. Miniver? Can we speak?" I whispered.

I waited a couple minutes. Mrs. Miniver is not a cat who does anything quickly. She came out the cat door I had used magic to unlock, tail high and eyes wide.

"Good morning, my dear." She has a cute British accent, which goes with being a British Short Hair. Sometimes a person can hardly understand the Russian

Blues, and American Curls are the surfer dudes of the cat world. "We're certainly having odd days, aren't we now?"

"Yes, we are." I knelt on the walkway in front of the house, half hidden by the picket fence. I didn't want Mrs. Hale to accuse me of trying to steal her prize winning, purebred cats again. "Do you have any information you can tell me?"

"Not nearly enough, I fear," she replied and rubbed against my leg. "The boys came by yesterday -- did you notice them?"

"Yes, when I drove past. I had someone with me, or else I would have stopped and asked what was going on."

"And risked being spotted by the good woman of the house? Not wise at all, my dear, especially since we had nothing much to tell you. The boys say there's odd stuff in town. They're doing a spot of hunting."

"Good for them." I stood slowly. "You will let me know if there's anything else?"

"Oh yes." She started to step away and stopped. "And how is my son these days? A scoundrel just like his father?"

"Cato saved my life twice tonight."

She stared into my face. "Did he, now? Brave after all, is he?"

"Oh yes, quite brave."

"Excellent. I guess blood will tell after all. Give him my regards."

"I will."

She sauntered towards the house with her tail held in a high, happy arc. I watched until she got inside and I could lock the door again. What should I do now? A car drove along the street, the driver jumping out and delivering newspapers at every few houses. I took my newspaper, saving her the drive to my house. The woman gave me a sleepy nod of thanks.

I tucked the paper under my arm and headed towards home. The bits of magic might be left over eddies from the blanket of magic that hit before Cato and I went off on our little troll adventure. I'd felt nothing this strong before and I suppose leftover magic in town shouldn't surprise me. The magic should disappear with the dawn.

By the time I reached the house I had decided that a nice, magically induced super-nap would help me through the coming day.

I jogged to the porch and went inside. Cato momentarily lifted his head. Shakespeare glanced my way and apparently didn't have any handy quote, so he kept quiet.

I tossed the paper down on the shelf by the door and caught the glimpse of the front page. I grabbed it back up and tore the paper open.

New Rodent Species found in Rocky Mountain National Park

And below those headlines I found a rather blurry picture of what could only be a peripix.

"Oh hell!"

"I don't want to know." Cato buried his head in the corner of the chair.

I went to the dining room table and spread the paper to see the article and scanned the words: new animals, believed to be related to chipmunks, extremely friendly towards humans, but difficult to get pictures --

Of course taking pictures of the animal was difficult. If a dozen had gathered for a family portrait, the camera would have exploded. Peripix came from the fae lands. They were magical enough to cause problems with technology and lacked the usual antipathy to keep them away from such objects.

The newspaper reported at least five already in captivity, and someone spotted dozens running along a trail near Bear Lake.

"How the hell did so many peripix get through?"

And then I realized exactly how they'd arrived. I closed my eyes as I remembered the small holes I'd closed in the Edge. I had assumed they'd been made at the same time as the trolls' hole to this world. Now I wondered if they hadn't been there for a day or more already, giving the peripix time to spread. There would have been no way to tell, and I didn't berate myself for making the mistake. I needed to get rid of them quickly though.

Peripix are cute. They're golden furred, slightly larger and rounder than the local chipmunks, with a powder-puff tail and huge dark eyes. They survive in somewhat the same ecological niche as chipmunks. Unfortunately, they carried a hint of magic with them . . . and they get into *everything*.

I understood those lines of magic I'd felt in town: peripix wandering the streets. Soon people would have inexplicable power outages. Cars would fail to start. Anywhere a peripix group nested, technology would soon fail.

I dropped my head on the table and pounded it a couple times.

"That bad, huh?" Cato asked, leaping onto the table and settling on the paper. Just as well I didn't want to read any more.

"Yeah, that bad. Worse than that bad. Not as bad as the trolls in some ways, and worse in others. Peripix are in the area and that means the town will have problems and power outages before too long."

"What can we do?" he asked, sounding unexpectedly worried. "If the fridge died --"

I should have known he was worried about food. "You and I are safe. The peripix could nest here without any trouble since I don't use technology to run the house. This will be a problem elsewhere in town. And the humans are going to put one and one together and realize the failing of technology has to do with the little guys. Eventually they'll even link them to magic."

"I don't care for the sounds of that," Cato admitted. "If technology fails, we won't get any cans of tuna, will we?"

I grinned. "Yeah, lack of tuna would be a problem."

"What can I do?"

"I don't think --" I stopped and reconsidered. "Actually, there is something you can do. You and any other cats you can get in on this. I want you to hunt peripix." I gave him a mental image of the creatures. He would catch one and show them to the others. "Bring them here and I'll send them across to the fae land. Cato, kill them only if you absolutely have to. Don't let them get away."

With those orders, he understood the seriousness of this situation. I *never* give him permission to kill when he works for me. Oh, I know cats are predators and all, and I don't interfere in most cases. I'm fae and we have a link to life, which influences when or why we kill things.

Cato gave a distracted nod, leapt down from the table and headed for the kitty door and went straight to work. Good guy. Better than Aletta who must have realized things were going bad and still hadn't contacted me.

I went to the sofa and forced myself to relax. I set my internal timer for fifteen minutes and used a spell to make those few minutes feel as though I slept for eight hours.

My nightmares featured a full array of trolls, peripix

and specters. And Aletta. I awoke with a start when the spell's metaphorical alarm clock went off. I felt better though no less worried.

David would arrive soon. I'd been letting things go around the house and I realized I desperately needed to get the sweeping done before I also faced an invasion of dust bunnies, which might be a problem with David in the house.

And yes, I mean dust bunnies in a literal sense. Stuff happens around fae who live on this side. The magic we naturally generate affects things sometimes. If the dust bunnies gather enough fluff, they come alive. They also get smart, which makes them difficult to catch.

And they're really damned cute. I even found Cato sleeping with a couple a few months ago. He'd been embarrassed, and then quite upset when I took them away. He thought I was going to kill them.

Instead I opened a tiny door to fae and booted them through to an area where others help resettle them. The dust bunnies have their own island now, filled with other dust bunnies and dust bunny toys. The island has become a popular place to visit.

My father mentioned a growing fear of a dust bunny uprising and maybe a war . . . and you know -- some things are better left unconsidered.

As I swept, I found two small ones. I caught them after a merry chase through the house with Shakespeare shouting. I don't know if he shouted to encourage me or them. Eventually I gathered both in my hands and held on, soothing the poor panting things.

"I'm going to put you in a safe place," I told them. Dark eyes peered from within white fluff. "You'll have much more fun there rather than in this house."

Did the dust bunnies understand me? They stopped fighting. I went to the backyard and opened the door into a holding cell with the stuff they play with and made certain it had remained warm and bright. I dropped them in. As soon as the Edge settled I'd send them off to the island.

This would be a great place to drop the peripix as well, so I made a second compartment and set the magic to make certain the peripix went one way and the dust bunnies the other. The peripix holding cell was larger, and I stocked the place with food, light, and good nesting areas. I didn't want the little guys upset; I just didn't want them in this world. I also pulled the opening down to the ground level and placed another spell so mice or bugs couldn't accidentally fall through. I'd show the spot to Cato and the others and they could drop their catches there.

Not bad at all, I thought.

I heard a car nearing. I brushed a hand through my hair, using magic to clean up and then changed in one quick spell that left my nearly breathless as I headed around the side of the house.

"Ready to go?" David asked. His eyes shone with excitement.

"Let me go get my bag and lock the house. You can put your stuff in my car."

"Great!"

I enjoy being with people who are enthusiastic about their work, especially when the work includes going off into the wilds and wandering around nature. I grabbed my bag and a jacket and jogged to the car as he shoved his own equipment in the back seat.

"Looks like you had a good night's rest," he said as we pulled away.

I caught the hysterical laugh before it escaped. "I did

well. And you?"

"Woke up a couple times feeling odd and disorientated. I slept well before and after though. Did you read the morning paper?"

"The chipmunk-like creatures? Oh yeah." We passed Mrs. Hale's home. Two cats sat in the yard today. They didn't turn my way.

"This is so fantastic, finding something new, right here in our own world!"

"Fantastic, yes," I agreed and still somehow grinned. "We will be in the area today. You might spot one or two."

"Wonderful!"

"We'll grab a quick breakfast and a package lunch from the Bear Camp. They make lunches for me all the time."

We found the cafe already half full of locals. People waved greetings as we took a spot by the window. Dawn grew as a thin line of grey around the buildings.

Lily Gibson, already dressed for work, arrived as we finished the pancakes and coffee. She ordered a cup of coffee, lunch for later, and pulled a chair over to our table when I gave her the nod. She wouldn't have intruded otherwise.

"Be careful today," she said and paused as she sipped her coffee. "The animals are still acting strange. We also found two dead deer and three dead elk, and we aren't sure what killed them. We're lucky this isn't the height of the tourist season."

"Where did you find the animals?" I asked.

"Down by Moraine Park near the Cub Lake Trailhead." She sipped and shook her head then glanced at my companion. "You still have your tranquilizer gun?"

"Yes," David said.

"Good. Don't take chances. Whatever killed those

animals must be big, and there might be more than one. We couldn't find a single clear print. I hate this crap. We'll have everyone in the area shooting at any cat, wolf, or bear they spot."

Trolls might have done the killings . . . though the trolls last night couldn't have gotten all the way to Moraine Park and returned before I got there. Besides, they'd been groggy.

Other trolls? There could have been others. I hadn't looked for prints.

Idiot.

I tried to pay attention to the conversation. Lily and David discussed various tranquilizer guns and what sedation to use for what animals. I left them to their conversation and surreptitiously did a magical check of the area.

I found trails of peripix in the street and used my magic to send them scurrying away. I didn't want a power outage during breakfast. With a small sigh I realized I would be hunting tonight.

"I don't know what we will do," Lily admitted. "We might get trackers in and see if we can hunt them down. Do you think your cousin might be available, Kat?"

"Yeah, probably." I nodded.

"I assume you're not talking about Aletta, right?" David asked with a little smirk.

"Hell, you know Aletta Borders?" Lily asked, her eyes gone wide.

"She showed up here at dinner last night," I said.

"Here?" Both eyebrows went straight up as she glanced around the room. I tried *very hard* not to laugh. I really did, but I couldn't help it. Lily had met Aletta once and my cousin had left a lasting impression. "I didn't think this was her kind of place."

"Yeah, well, if we don't get moving, I fear she might show up --"

Both Lily and David got instantly to their feet.

You know, you couldn't ask for a better reaction from your friends. I was in a much better mood as we left the place. David carried our box with lunch to the car, and Lily waved and went to her car . . . which wouldn't start. I watched a peripix scamper off into the shadows, and as much as I would have loved to hunt the beast down, I offered to take Lily to the park entrance where she worked, instead.

"Thanks. I know Jim won't mind if I'm late while I get the car handled. Still, with everything so strange, I'd rather be there early. Did I mention the weather problem?" she asked, as David slipped into the back with his equipment.

"No." I winced knowing this wouldn't be good.

"Yeah -- more trouble. We have an unusually strong cold front pulling down over the Rockies. We got a warning about the storms late last night. The weather systems are completely screwed up this year."

Magic will affect weather when something as powerful as the Edge throws random currents into the air. I should have been considering the weather. I glanced at the low, gray layer of clouds.

"Snow, you think?" I asked.

"I suspect so. The question is how far down the elevations it gets."

"I've seen spring snows in other mountains." David sounded worried. "I imagine weather gets serious here."

"Very serious, especially if we have to track tourists," Lily agreed. I could see the weather worried her. "This might turn into a full-fledged blizzard so we're warning everyone not to wander too far from their cars today."

"Just one more bit of trouble, huh?" David asked.

"The weather is a good thing if it keeps people away from whatever else we have here. Have either of you noticed there hasn't been many birds around the last couple days?"

"Except for all those nuthatches at Kat's place yesterday," David said.

I nodded, remembering the lack of birds when I walked down to talk to Mrs. Miniver but hadn't considered the wider perspective. I hadn't heard the usual morning bird calls today.

What would scare all the birds away?

Big wings, big wings.

A gargoyle? Many of the gargoyles can fly, despite their rock-like weight, and they could do the killings, too. Not a pleasant thought.

CHAPTER EIGHT

We delivered Lily to work. Jim came over to talk to us and reiterated everything Lily had already said. He even brought a map to show us the two different places where they'd found kills.

"I don't know what the hell is out there, so be extra careful."

"Could the work be done by a human?" David asked.

"I kind of hope it was," Jim admitted as he leaned forward, looking into the car. "We can compare lists of cars and track down people if it happens again. If this is something that moved in from the mountains -- is your cousin going to help us this time?" Jim asked.

"I'm sure he will if I can contact him," I answered and patted David on the arm. "My cousin Cago. He's a really good tracker."

Cago had found three rogue bears, a wounded bobcat, and a lost Doberman in the last four years. He enjoyed working with humans, too. I feared he might be knee deep in the same trouble as the rest of the family and whatever was happening here might not be on the top of the list of things to fix, magical or not.

"I'll try to get in touch with him. He might be off

somewhere, though," I told Jim, and gave Lily a last wave. "See you later!"

"Be careful!"

We drove past the entrance and I slowed for the ubiquitous chipmunk. I swear it was the same one as the day before.

"They're nice people," David said.

"They are. And they're genuinely worried about the weather and what's killing the animals, which means we should be worried, too. We sometimes get nasty storms as winter passes into spring. They start with drizzle, turn to ice, and then add snow, which makes things worse because people don't even realize there's ice beneath the snow pack."

"You've got chains?" he asked.

"I've got excellent all-year tires." And magic. "We can get snow in June."

"I love snow."

"So do I. Still, I take the weather seriously. I planned to go to Endovalley again this morning, but I think we should head straight to Bear Lake in case the weather changes later and we can't get there."

"I leave the decision in your capable hands. Can I ask about your family?"

"My family?" I asked, startled by the question.

"Well, Cago sounds more like you. Aletta doesn't seem to fit in."

"She doesn't. Neither she nor her mother. I don't see her father, Kalin, much. He's usually off patrolling."

"Police man?"

"Yeah," I said, covering the blunder, though in some ways that explained his work. "We're stuck with Paris and Aletta."

"Aletta comes on a little too strong for me."

I didn't smile. I really didn't though I almost choked trying not to.

We took the turn to the left heading to Bear Lake. I spotted a marmoset in the field to the right, so we stopped and he got a couple pictures. I tested the area and found a nest of peripix not far away. Nothing I could do right about them right now. At least they had burrowed in, and if the weather changed, they would stay there.

How many had come through the Edge? I'd call my father tonight and tell him . . . and hope Timber wasn't there because I rather enjoyed the idea that he had faith in me.

We stopped by Glacier Creek where the stream runs close to the road. I loved the location and didn't mind a few minutes there. I drank in the peace while watching the icy water tumble over the rocky stream bed and past the towering pines. David took more pictures. I tested the magic in the area and found odd eddies and a couple more peripix.

We found only one car at Bear Lake lot. This is a popular hike because it's mostly flat around the lake, and the scenery is gorgeous, but we were early and the weather changeable, so few people had come here today. I'd seen the parking lot packed and overflowing with people in the summer. We went past the bulletin board where the rangers posted all the current news and warnings. I saw one note in bright red lettering warning people to beware of a possible rogue animal in the area.

The lake and the surrounding half circle of mountains came into view as we stepped through the arbor of trees. Flattop Mountain and Hallet Peak, with the Tyndall Glacier nestled between them and created a lovely reflection in the lake. There are thousands of pictures of the place, but no one has ever truly captured the real beauty of standing by the lake while the ducks swim past --

Not today. No ducks. No birds. I didn't even see the usual chipmunks and other animals that sometimes come at the sound of humans, hoping for a forbidden handout.

We decided to walk around the lake. I damped down my magic and carried some equipment as we moved from spot-to-spot. David took dozens of pictures of everything. A couple times, I pulled out paper and jotted down a few notes on the scent of the place and the sound of the wind in the trees. Sometimes even I missed those nuances of locations, concentrating so much on the birds and what they are saying.

I didn't have the distraction today.

A jogger went past us. I wondered why he bothered coming clear up here and then going so fast he didn't enjoy the scenery? Might as well jog through Estes Park or downtown Denver.

We took a break half way around the path, sitting on a boulder and watching the lake as the clouds moved in the reflection there.

"Lovely place." David smiled as he looked from lake to sky to mountains and back. "Not as wild as I'm used to, but still pretty. I bet this is a nice place for people who aren't used to hiking in rougher terrain."

"We'll head for one of the other local trails and get to the wilder spots soon. We still have the time today." I watched the clouds with mistrust, not quite believing my own words.

"You know what I enjoy most here?" David grinned when I looked at him. "I love seeing the area through your eyes. You appreciate this place, and you're willing to share your love with others. I'm sorry about the lack of animals, though. I'd have thought we might see a few so early in the morning."

Right then I would have called dozens to him, just to make him happy.

"Since animal pictures are what the magazine wants, I'll have to stick around for a few more days until I get the right shots, I guess." He cast me a quick, almost shy smile.

Or maybe I *wouldn't* call them. David staying didn't seem such a bad idea.

He took spectacular reflection shots of the mountains, the trees, and even of the clouds which appeared increasingly less friendly. David kept an eye on the weather as well, so I didn't warn him. We didn't linger for too long and I suspected we wouldn't be taking any of the longer trails after we left Bear Lake. Maybe tomorrow, instead. I did not want to chance of getting stuck in a storm though I wouldn't have trouble getting clear. I'd have a difficult time explaining how I managed it to David.

I let David get well ahead of me on the far curve around the lake and then used a whisper of magic to search the area to the northwest where Terra Tomah stood. The Edge remained quiescent today although I sensed a few peripix in the woods. What would I need to do to get rid of them? Someone must have peripix trap in the archives. I'd have to ask for a search.

Movement in the wood caught my eye. This might be something I could lure out for David --

Only when I reached with a touch of magic I found . . . nothing.

Jumpy, I told myself. Just jumpy and I needed to stop letting my imagination get away with me. I hurried towards David -- and saw movement. White, soft.

I feared my rider might be back. Hell. I shivered as I made my way to where David worked, setting up the Hasselblad. Perhaps only a hint of errant mist had caught my eye; a touch of fog rising in the morning light.

I had to stop overreacting, both to the threat of danger and to the idea of David staying longer. I had even overreacted to the appearance of Aletta, and to the praise from Timber. Everything seemed out of balance, and I needed to find my center and calm. I faced all kinds of trouble including the peripix and perhaps a gargoyle and needed to get myself under control --

"Are you all right?" David asked, putting a hand on my arm.

And there went my balance right out the door. I grinned at him. "Yeah, I'm fine."

"The weather is changing," he said with obvious reluctance.

And, as if to answer his call, the wind swept through with a sudden fierce gale, sending squalls of water lapping across the lake.

"Good call." I pulled my jacket closer. "I suppose we better leave. We can skip the other hike today. There's always tomorrow."

He stopped long enough to take a couple pictures of the squalls of water. I didn't rush him. We still had time.

David had put the camera away and grabbed the bag when we heard a rushing through the woods. He grabbed a camera back out, put on a smaller lens and started clicking as the first few elk dashed from the trees, found themselves facing the lake, and darted to the right to go around it. It was an incredible sight . . . but not natural. Nor was the rush of smaller animals following: marmots, beavers, raccoons, chipmunks, rabbits, squirrels --

"What the hell?" David asked, grabbing his bag and taking a step backwards, prepared to flee.

"Something spooked them."

I thought about the dead animals and the warnings from the rangers. And here we were, with both the weather changing and what could be something nasty coming our way through the woods. David took out the tranquilizer gun and stuck it into his jacket pocket.

"We can go now," he said but still snapped pictures as the animals turned and disappeared into another area of trees.

I lifted my hand testing for magic, but found nothing except the cold bite of the wind. Had the wind startled the elk, and they panicked the other animals around them?

Except I saw a white movement in the forest again. Oh damn.

David started away and didn't slow for more pictures as we headed towards the lot. He glanced over his shoulder every couple steps as though to make certain I was still there. He almost tripped twice, so I jogged up beside him, and then pressed ahead so he would keep his eyes on where he was going.

I rushed past the trail entrance sign with all the warning posters. The wood groaned as the wind pounded it, promising a dangerous storm before too long. In the parking lot I found something that gave me hope. On the hood of my car sat a huge golden eagle, his head bent against the wind, his feathers ruffled and his wings held close to the body.

Waiting for me.

I hurried to the car which was the only one in the lot. No one remained on the trails. I hadn't crossed halfway when the bird looked at me -- and then past me.

"Human! Traitor! Human!" the eagle screamed, spread his wings and took to the air, fighting against the wind, and then curving around to glide away.

Eagles and hawks have this big conspiracy thing going, and they don't trust humans at all. I hadn't considered what reaction the sight of David would bring and silently cursed as I watched the bird disappear over the stands of pine.

"I think I got some great pictures!" David said as he joined me. He still had the camera in hand.

I smiled anyway. Hard to be annoyed around someone so happy.

Drizzle fell, and remembering my talk about drizzle, ice, and snow from earlier, I decided we shouldn't waste any more time.

A few flakes of snow already fell as we left the parking lot. I'd driven down to the entrance when a ranger truck pulled up. I rolled down my window.

"This is cutting things close there, Kat," Jordan Fuller said, his dark face breaking into a smile.

"Yeah. We were about half way around the lake when the wind changed. I think the weather spooked the animals too. They were on the move. How is the weather doing?"

"Snowing like hell at the pass. I can't tell if we will get anything down this way or not." A snowflake fell between us, and then another, and another.

"I'd say we have a sign," I replied, still smiling.

"Go. I need to lock the road behind you. You're the last ones here?"

"The last car in the lot so we're it unless you have someone in on foot."

"If they are, they'll have to hike down to wherever they left their car anyway. Go on."

I rolled the window up and eased the car along the

already slick road. Jordan turned around, got out and locked the gate, and followed us. I felt oddly safer with him at our backs.

"Seems as though you know everyone here at the park," David said.

"I spend a lot of time here and call on them for answers to questions."

The wind buffeted the car as we wound our way down from Bear Lake. The rough wind had brought down couple branches across the road, but we made our way around them. Jordan stopped to lock the lower gate, but he remained on the other side, probably intending to clear the branches away. I wondered if I should warn him . . . but about what? I decided the sudden weather change might have spooked the animals.

I honked and waved. He waved as we drove away.

We stopped down by Moraine Park and ate an early lunch in the car, watching the icy rain and discussing the possibilities for future hikes, as long as the weather didn't turn worse. I feared a lot of things were going to be worse before they were better though.

The rest of the drive to Estes Park wasn't too bad. The rain fell harder, but I didn't care. We'd gotten away from the park, and for some reason I couldn't even name, leaving the park behind made me feel as though we accomplished something difficult and evaded danger.

As we pulled over to David's car he put a hand on my arm. The touch sent a thrill from my arm and straight to my heart.

"I want to have dinner with you tonight. Me, buying. Bear Camp would be fine, or anywhere else nice and cozy. Do you think we can avoid Aletta?"

"Oh, I can make certain she doesn't show up," I

replied with so bright a smile I feared my mouth would hurt afterwards. I would make certain she stayed away, too. I knew a nice repelling spell to send her in the opposite direction. Or if she showed up all I could suggest she do some work, which would prove as effective.

"Good. I'll come back sometime between five and six after I call the publisher and talk pictures. I'm not sure how long this will take me."

"Don't worry, I'll be here."

"Good. See you later."

He scurried over to his own car, tossing the equipment in out of the rain. He waited while I hurried to the house. I should have invited him in for coffee or hot cocoa or something.

As he drove away I got better control of my swirling emotions. This was damned bad timing, to be honest. Yeah, I liked the guy, but there were things I had to do, and I had trouble doing the work with him around. I was letting his presence interfere with my job. At normal times, I wouldn't care. Now . . . just damned bad timing.

I stepped into the house. Shakespeare flapped his wings a couple times and Cato lifted his head from the chair where he probably spent all day sleeping after our long, rough night.

"You don't look happy."

"I have to get him to leave," I admitted aloud. "Maybe if I do this nicely enough, he'll return at a better time."

"Ah. We're talking about David, are we?"

"Yes, of course."

"Of course." Cato buried his nose under his tail, and this time I had the distinct impression he might be snickering.

"This is so typical of my life. Not only does Aletta

arrive at the wrong time, but I find someone I'm interested in and work gets in the way. Work I can't even mention to him!"

"Life's rough," Cato agreed as I went past heading for the bathroom.

I changed clothes and spent time staring at the mirror and trying to figure out how to handle tonight. I wanted to impress David, to make him remember me after I sent him away. I tried different things with my hair and making it fancy the way Aletta did hers.

Only David didn't want to have dinner with Aletta. He wanted to see me tonight. Aletta had overdone her *fem fatale* act and found a guy who wasn't interested.

He was interested in me.

The trouble with the Edge would go away soon. The problems never lasted more than a few weeks. I'd still have to deal with the peripix, though I suspected the cats might handle them in town and I would round up the rest in the woods. I had things in hand.

As long as I ignored the ghost riders in the forest.

I came back to the living room and knew I needed to calm. I felt like a raving lunatic, worrying over everything and I wanted to enjoy tonight.

"Let me have the chair, Cato. I Anything on the peripix?"

"Fast little buggers."

I grinned as he stood, stretched and got down in his own good time. "I have a hole open in the backyard to drop them through. I can even set the spot to kick out a treat each time."

"Do you think you can bribe us?"

"Absolutely."

"Good. Yeah, bribes will help, especially with all the

work it takes to catch them. If you don't want peripix disappearing inside Pawford's tummy, then make certain the cats get something better for dropping the catches down the hole."

I nodded, pretending the same bribe didn't apply to him. What I would never say is that I didn't want the cats eating the peripix because they would acquire magic. Not a problem I wanted to deal with along with everything else.

I relaxed before dinner with David. We would discuss *future* projects, and I'd nudge him into the idea of returning later.

I had time to contact home and learn where Cago might be right now. Yes, time to concentrate on work and not David, at least for a few minutes!

I closed my eyes . . . and almost immediately caught the surge of a message from fae. I lifted my hand and opened the view.

The message came through garbled and fuzzy, reminding me of something on a television with bad reception. My father stood in the same room where I'd last seen him. Others moved frantically behind him. Timber waved his arms in a very un-Timber-like gesture of frustration.

The sound proved worse. "I can't hear you!" I shouted. He spread his arms in much the same gesture as Timber. For a moment the sound cleared.

"All hell is breaking loose!"

And then the picture and sound faded away.

"*Halo of hell, and with a pain -- not hell shall make me fear again!*"

I glanced over at Shakespeare and shook my head. "Thank you so much for the commentary. Very helpful."

The bird nodded several times.

A cold pit of worry opened in my soul. Things were bad on the other side. Was my father trying to warn me about something specific or if he'd been letting me know I was on my own?

And that meant nothing good for my corner of the world if I didn't figure the problem out fast. I wanted answers.

I tried to reach him again and then tried my mother off at court. Nothing was going through. That ruined any thought of sitting and resting.

"You can have the chair, Cato." I stood, heading towards the door.

"You're going out already?"

"Just on the porch. Did you see the stuff on the link?"

"Yeah. Looked tense."

The rain fell harder outside. I stood on the porch, letting the breeze blow dampness over me like a cold shower. My heart still pounded too hard since the contact with my father. I wanted everything to settle: my nerves, the trouble here, and whatever problem my father and the others in fae faced.

At least Aletta was in town. I tried not to wince at the thought. Aletta might not be my favorite person in the world -- or two worlds, for that matter -- but she was here, and she was a powerful fae.

Taking a deeper breath, I turned and reached for the door to go inside. White, filmy movement at the line of the trees caught my attention, and I saw the shape of a horse and rider.

Something from over the Edge should never have been this close to the city and the technology in the area. To live here is hard enough for fae and should be impossible for almost anything else.

I blinked, wishing the creature to disappear. The horse and rider stood in the rain watching me. I put my hand on the door and lifted the other to create magic, but he turned and fled into the rain.

He feared my magic which gave me what little hope I had. He didn't return, and eventually I went into the house, trembling with fear, rage and worry.

CHAPTER NINE

The storm grew in intensity at sunset. The sky brightened with flashes of lightning and thunder shook the house. Cato scurried off to sleep in the closet for the night and Shakespeare danced along his perch, nervously glancing through the window. I gave him several crackers, hoping he'd be content. He kept quiet.

David arrived and ran to the porch, laughing like a kid in a summer storm. Damn, why couldn't he have shown up at a better time? Humans so rarely enjoy the world the way the fae do and I so wanted to share this with him!

"I thought we'd go for a ride before dinner," he said with a smile. "But the weather seems to be against us tonight."

"Oh, a short drive sounds nice." I glanced towards the trees. No ghost riders there, at least. "I love rain storms."

"So do I --"

I stepped forward when something rushed from the woods and onto the porch. I lifted my hand and almost did something very bad with a human present. Lucky or me, I suddenly recognized the group of cats.

Pawford had led the way to the porch. He shook, splattering my pants, and when the lightning flashed, he dashed under the porch swing. The others found various spots, safe from the storm, all of them cursing and complaining about the weather.

David shook his head with a grin. "I get the idea they're used to taking refuge here."

"Yeah. Let me get them some food before we leave. I'll meet you down at the car."

I added the slightest nudge of magic to the words to hurry him off the porch. He went to the car, and I went inside to get the food. Cato appeared as soon as he heard me opening the cabinet. I gave him food, too. He happily munched while I loaded up a couple paper plates.

"The strays are on the porch. I'll check if they have anything to tell me, then I'm going to go spend the night . . . the *evening* with David."

Cato nearly choked on his food at my blunder. He gave me one of those really evil cat smiles, too. "Don't do anything I wouldn't do."

"You have no morals."

"Exactly."

He snickered while I headed for the porch. Pawford came from under the swing when I put the plates down for them. He didn't look happy.

"Catch any of them?" I asked.

"Those damned peripix are fast and slippery." He gulped down a mouth full of food. "But I'll get the little bastards."

"There's a hole in back where you can drop them. I set a spell to kick out a piece of fish each time you put a live one in." I sent an image of what they needed to do to all the cats. They moved uneasily at having pictures shoved into their heads, but none of them complained. "Will the fish help?"

He glanced at me, green eyes blinking. "It's a game now, you know. Catching them has gone beyond food. But I'll bring them *here* for the fish."

"They have to be alive."

"That will make the game . . . more interesting."

"Good." I almost patted him on the head, but Pawford is a real stray, and he doesn't appreciate the touchy-feely stuff. I stood and nodded to the others. "You heard the deal. Good luck."

The others gave tentative agreements. I'd have to monitor them for magic levels but I suspected my fish-treat plan would work.

I hurried to the car while lightning flashed overhead. David opened the door, and I slid inside, grateful to be out of the storm. I feared there might already be a touch of ice in the cold drops. Tonight might be a rough night for the area. A good thing the strays showed up, so I didn't worry about them.

Before I changed my mind I began the first nudge of a spell to start David thinking about finishing the work here and leaving. I hated to, but I needed to get him away for both of our sakes. He was in danger while he spent time around with me and he distracted me from my work.

I didn't intend for him to go away forever though. So I planned to have a nice dinner and talk about the future.

"Shall we drive for a while?" David asked. He laughed. "It's a guy thing. I have this fancy car -- much better than my own -- and I wouldn't mind having the feel of the car in this weather."

"Sounds fine." Relaxing proved to be harder than I expected since I started seeing the shape of ghost riders -- yes, more than one -- in every flash of lightning. A good thing David drove tonight because I would have had an accident. When one crossed right in front of us I even lost hold of my magic for a moment. The car coughed and almost died before I got control

"Must be the rain," David said. "Seems okay now. Where do you want to go?"

I directed him away from town so I could see if the riders were elsewhere. He wasn't seeing them, at least. We drove down Highway 66 and left the riders behind at the edge of the city. Except for peripix, I couldn't name any magical constructs that congregated around technology but these were staying in the town. I wanted to reach home to ask about them.

The storm sent waterfalls cascading down the side of hills wherever we passed, glittering light in the headlights David stopped and stood in the rain while he took pictures of a couple, the camera's flash brightening the area. He leapt into the car and apologized, but I laughed.

"You should take advantage of this while you're here," I said.

"That's one of the things I enjoy about being with you. You understand about stuff like this."

"I also understand the weather, and I fear this is going to change on us real soon. We should head back and go to dinner before we lose our chance."

"True enough. I think I saw a couple flakes of snow," he admitted. He even kicked the heat on in the car. "I've enjoyed being in this area. There's a lot more opportunities for pictures than I expected to find. I want to come back again and do more work here."

Those words made the night seem better. I smiled, and we talked about future projects. I even gave him several ideas for things we might do in the summer. And winter. And any time but *right now*.

We drove through town and I again noted the lack of birds, and of cats as well tonight, though they would take refuge from the rain like Pawford and the others. Even the peripix seemed to have disappeared, no doubt nesting some place warm, dry, and where they shouldn't be. The deluge hadn't stopped and water rushed down the side streets, making them close to impassable. If the weather turned cold enough to ice, I might have trouble getting home, even with magic. Nature has a way of working against fae powers sometimes and often when its most inconvenient for the fae.

We drove through areas of town without power, and I wondered if this was a result of the storm or the peripix. I directed David and soon we parked at the Don Marco Restaurant. I made a quick sweep of the area and found peripix in the trees nearby . . . and in the trashcans and under cars. I made sure they wouldn't nest in our car. I needed to enlist far more cats if I wanted to get this in hand. Peripix can have four or five litters a year. The thought won another shiver from me.

A check towards the Edge settled my nerves, though, since I found only a slight disturbance which wasn't unusual during a storm. I hadn't seen the riders since we returned to town. I hoped they'd give me a little peace tonight and by the time I got home, I could contact someone who could help me.

I let myself believe everything would be fine because I had no clue what else to do.

We hurried into the entrance alcove, shaking water from our clothing. A waitress met us at the door, holding it open as we came into the building.

"We have a power outage," she warned with a wave towards the candle lit room. "We can still provide most of the items on our menu, but I'm afraid with the power out we cannot accept credit cards."

"I have cash," we chorused.

The woman laughed and showed us to a table by the window. The moment I stepped inside, I knew I wasn't leaving without something to eat; and yes, I would have used magic to coerce the food from them. The scents of a dozen Italian dishes were heavenly.

We shared a lovely meal of manicotti and veal parmesan. Over a decadent chocolate dessert, we discussed projects for the future and things we'd done in the past.

Others came in, many of them from houses without power. I tried to get an idea of where the most trouble might be. I might need to send cats tonight or tomorrow to get the peripix out of the worst hit areas. We faced a major job, but I didn't fear getting it done. That came from the company tonight. David made me feel competent.

I remembered I hadn't blocked Aletta from interfering with tonight's meal. I went to the Ladies Room -- lit with candles -- and set a spell blocking us from view. Subtly, though, so the spell didn't have a 'black hole, that's where they are' effect. I found her in town, and I still wanted to learn what brought her here . . . but not tonight.

I wanted nothing to ruin this meal with David. I had planted my seeds, and he'd be leaving soon, but I hoped he had established enough of a natural tug -- to this area and to me -- to draw him back again.

"Are there many magazines interested in work from around here?" he asked, worried.

"Some." I named a few, and he grabbed a napkin to jot them down since he'd left his bag and phone in the car. We talked about business again. I enjoyed staying right there, nestled in the quiet corner of the world with the storm raging outside and good company at the table.

The rain let up, but neither of us suggested leaving yet. We talked for a long while about many important and inconsequential things. We discussed our other interests in life. Neither of us watched much television, but he spent a lot of time with music. My musical tastes ran to court musicians on the fae side -- people he absolutely never would have heard about, so I only nodded now and then until we moved on to another subject.

On books we hit common ground though. He enjoyed reading fantasy, as oddly, so did I.

"Tolkien, of course," he said, and I nodded agreement. "But Pratchett at the other end of the spectrum."

"Yeah. I love to read Pratchett," I agreed. We compared a few books.

I sipped my coffee and glanced out the window.

And that was when I realized I was living in a comic book.

There, standing by the car, was Cato. And I mean *standing*. He was on his hind legs and frantically waving his front paws back and forth to draw my attention.

I choked and sputtered. I also sent a whisper of a 'time to go' spell to David, almost making it too strong in my panic. Whatever sent Cato hunting me down in this weather had to be serious.

"I guess we better leave before the weather turns any worse." David couldn't see Cato from his position though I almost yelped when he turned to the window.

He got up and paid the bill, and I walked outside into the alcove. Cato darted in beside me, shaking water out of his fur. The poor guy looked drenched, so I used a spell to dry most of his fur.

"T-trouble." He still shivered from the cold.

"Something is trying to break into the house. Something -- doesn't feel right at all."

"Damn. We'll be there in a couple minutes --"

Cato darted away as David stepped up to the doorway. I wished I could slip the cat into the car with us, but I didn't have time to do any magic that would hide him and protect the car. As we drove away I watched him huddling beside the restaurant, looking miserable.

This would be another tuna night.

"Yeah, it's starting to turn to ice," David said as we took one turn and the tires didn't quite catch. We slid a little until he corrected. "Are we going to get snow?"

"We might," I answered, trying to focus the conversation. I didn't dare use magic while I sat in the car, and I desperately wanted to learn what was going on at the house. I feared I could sense tendrils of magic from the direction of home.

Forcing myself to calm, I turned to turn to David and smile. "I had a wonderful evening."

"I hope we get a chance to have dinner again soon."

"Me, too." After everything else is settled. I even reinforced my spell with the tiniest bit of magic and the car lights dimmed for a moment.

"Must be getting water in the engine block. Not a surprise, all the puddles we've splashed through. You all right?"

"Yes." I tried to bury worries. "Just tired, I guess. This has been a long, and wonderful, day."

"I agree. I will hate to leave. And there are things. . . . Well, I'll get them straightened out later. There's this problem I haven't told you --"

"You're married," I said, and then clamped my mouth shut over what had to have been the most stupid thing I had ever said in my entire life.

He gave me a quick startled look and then laughed, stopping at what appeared to be one of the few working lights in town. Water rushed down the windshield, hardly deterred by the wipers. I stared at the storm as my face went red with embarrassment.

"Sorry, shouldn't have laughed." David eased the car into the street which was lucky. A pickup charged through the red light and cut in front of us, no more than a foot away. At another time I would have cursed them. Really. Those people need to stop driving for a while, and I can make certain the car didn't work. "But I'm not married, no. The problem has more to do with who I am and what I'm doing." He glanced my way, frowning this time. "I don't want to lie to you."

I didn't understand where this conversation was going, but I didn't much like the tone of his words. This wasn't a good time for something serious, either. I sensed trouble ahead, even before we reached Mrs. Hale's house. The rain eased, but the lightning got worse and a strong wind whipped down the hillside. David concentrated on driving. I stared ahead straining to see my house through the curve of the road, the towering pines and the boulders blocking the view.

As we came around the last curve of the road I saw . . . things moving off into the trees; white and filmy and the sight made me shiver watching them drift away.

The door to the house stood open which meant something had battered through my wards. I leapt from the car and headed toward the door, but even from here I felt nothing out of place in there.

But outside. . . .

"What the hell," David whispered as we started to the

house where Pawford lay on the steps, his neck crooked to the right at a bad angle. Dead. So was Abbie, who lay just outside my door.

"Oh hell." Tears came to my eyes, lost in the rain. I found two more dead cats in the yard, all of them with their necks broken.

"What did this?" David whispered.

"Something from the --" I stopped what I almost said. "A bear or one of the big cats. Sometimes they get crazy, especially this time of year. Hell. Poor little guys."

Nothing normal had killed them. I sensed the taint of darker magic everywhere, and when I looked towards the woods where at least one rider still lingered, hidden among the trees.

David stood by me in the rain, shaking his head with sorrow for creatures he'd never met. But I knew them. Pawford and Abbie, had names. I stopped at the step and touched old Pawford, hoping he found a place with all the tuna he could eat. And the same for Abbie. I started towards the house when David caught my arm.

"Something might be in there," he warned. "Let me get the tranquilizer gun, at least."

He dashed away, trusting me to wait. And I did, but only because I didn't have the will to go on. I had left the little guys here, and they'd faced this danger while I was having a nice dinner. This wasn't right.

Part of me geared up for a rage that would take something -- or someone -- by surprise. I let the sorrow hold me and waited for David to return. I didn't want to be alone.

The rider still hovered there, at the edge of my sight. I intended to get the bastard.

David touched my arm and led me up the steps past

Pawford and Abbie, and into the house. I found no sign of Shakespeare except for a few feathers scattered by his perch. No blood, which made me suspect he had flown away.

"You can stay here," David said, but when I shook my head he didn't argue.

Something wild and magical had entered the house, but there came with it -- with one of the riders, I thought -- someone solid. The specters hadn't broken the necks of the cats, or knocked down the books on the shelves. There didn't seem to be anything else wrong. We walked through the house, checking each room, and started up the stairs to the loft. There I found Shakespeare very much alive. He had wedged himself into the corner by the window and the bookcase, hidden down near the floor.

"Poor guy," David whispered softy. He put the gun aside and knelt beside me. "Can I help?"

"I think I can get him." I held out my hand, urging the bird to come out of hiding. He bobbed his head and squirmed so I used magic to help and he popped out and fell into my hands, quivering with fear.

I wished he would tell me what had happened here. I even considered using magic to slip into his mind, but I would probably have driven him to madness, if not death. I wanted no other dead friends tonight.

We took the poor bird to the futon and the three of us sat there in sorrowful silence. David let me lean my head on his shoulder while I held the bird. Both of us needed the comfort.

Shakespeare pushed his head against my chest, the closest he had come to showing affection. He'd been quiet, too. I thought he might be whispering things, but they sounded like the usual quotes. I brushed my hand over his feathered head.

When I took Shakespeare down to his perch, I brushed away the feathers and gave him a treat which he took with one set of talons, but didn't eat.

"The rain is easing," David said. "Do you have a shovel? I can bury them."

"I have shovels in the shed." My voice had gone to neutral mode, a good middle ground between the sorrow and rage battling inside me. "I appreciate the help."

I truly appreciated his being here. I kept a shield of magic around us while David and I dug the little graves by the trees. We buried the cats, and I wept for them again; at the futility of their deaths and at my inability to protect them when they needed me. I would have wished them back to life if I'd had the power, but some things are beyond even the strongest magic.

We found stones and laid them over the graves to protect them from the predators in the area. I stood over them and wished them well one more time.

As we walked to the house I made another magical sweep of the town. Other magic still played along the streets. I took a moment and sensed the Edge, far away in the mountains. It had grown restless with the night and the storm, but nothing seemed out of the ordinary.

David and I went back to the house in silence.

"I haven't seen Cato," he whispered, his voice filled with worry. "Do you have a flashlight? I can go look."

I liked him all the more because he worried over a cat he'd barely ever seen.

"He'll be all right. If he wasn't here on the porch, he went down to Mrs. Hale's place. I'm sure he will be fine." But I worried. I'd seen Cato in town, but he might not stay safe. I tried to search for him with magic, but with so much power in the air I couldn't locate something as small as a wet cat.

But he would come home soon. I knew he would.

I glanced at David and took hold of his hand. His fingers felt warm and strong, curling around my own. "Thank you for being here tonight. I'm sorry the evening ended so badly."

"I hate to see this. And I hate to see you upset. I knew they were more than just strays. You treated them like friends."

I blinked back tears one more time and took a deeper breath. "Thank you. You should go to your hotel. I'll be fine for the rest of the night."

He stared into my face, and for a moment I wondered if he would offer to stay with me for the night. I don't know what I would have said. He had more wisdom than me because he finally gave a loud sigh.

"You'll be all right?" he asked, his fingers curling around mine.

I nodded.

He pulled me closer, and we hugged, there in the chill of the night by my door. His arms were strong, warm, and safe. Pretended safety: David was no match for my troubles. I had taken care of the trolls and I could handle this.

I just didn't want to do it alone.

But I couldn't take David with me.

I turned my head and gently kissed him on the lips.

Only the kiss lasted longer than I had intended. Warmth spread through my body in the kind of magic you don't find anywhere else. His breath caught, and his lips parted . . . and the kiss became far more intense than the chaste 'thank you and good night' I first intended.

His body pressed against mine and mine answered despite what my mind said. I didn't want the kiss to end. He tasted of chocolate dessert and spring in the mountains, and I sensed his love of everything I loved; I tasted everything in the magic that came from two people who are kindred spirits, no matter if they were both fae or not.

And I wanted . . . but knew we shouldn't. Wanted the kiss to never end -- and I'm not sure which one of us pulled away from the other.

David took a quick step back, his face flushed. The cold damp breeze swept between us and I shivered.

"Kat." His voice sounded husky as he took another step away. I stood there, speechless, but knowing he made the right choice, even if he didn't know why.

"I'll see you tomorrow," I whispered.

"Yes. Definitely."

He turned and hurried down the path. I stayed on the porch and waited while he started the car. He sat there for a moment longer. I wondered what he considered, and why he told himself we shouldn't be together tonight. I had trouble convincing myself I had a good reason to let him go.

He pulled away. I waved, and he honked, and disappeared down around the curve of the road.

And I waited on the porch feeling very much alone.

CHAPTER TEN

I took several deep breaths as David's car disappeared and I searched for my peaceful center. I tried to ignore the memory of our parting kiss so it wouldn't distract me while I did the next bit of work.

When he was well away, I reached out to the yard and traced the spots of dark magic I had noticed there. The storm which carried wild magic from the Edge, had imbued every raindrop with a whisper of power, and those had wiped away nearly all the tracks in the yard, both real and metaphysical. I barely found the spot where David had passed only moments earlier.

I tried to read the areas where Pawford and Abbie had died and gained little, except a sense of their bravery as they faced the enemy. The end, at least, had been quick.

I blinked back tears as I stared out into the night. The rain had picked up, and the wind blew in my face. Maybe Cato had stopped to stay with his mother or found refuge from the storm somewhere else . . . or had something hunted him, and he was no better able to defend himself than the others?

I paced along the porch and stared into the night; if I went out there, I wouldn't find him and he might come home and be no safer without me here.

Movement in the trees and a hint of luminous white light caught my attention.

"Come on, you bastard!" I shouted, welcoming the rage growing inside me. Magic played at my fingertips. "Come on. You and whoever helped you --"

Saying the words aloud made me stop and consider what had happened. Someone corporal had helped the ghost riders get into the house. They were not strong enough to open a door. I had sensed the presence of someone inside. Besides, the specters didn't have the ability to kill the cats -- at least not in the way they had done it.

I lifted my hands and searched out the area in the woods around my house. Something solid moved there. Something more than the ghosts that were little more than cold spots in the night. More than one, perhaps but they blurred in the rain and before I reacted, they'd slipped out of range. I almost ran out after them, but something like better judgment caught hold of me and I went back to pacing the porch.

Finally, I saw the shape of a cat hurtling his way across the yard. I stopped, my breath held and my hand up, ready for any trouble.

"You could have come back from me!" Cato shouted as he dashed up the steps and into the light. He looked wet and muddy and miserable. "I had to swim -- *swim!* -- across a couple streets and I almost got sucked down into a drain. Why the hell --"

But he had hit the spot where I had found Pawford, and even with the rain he must have caught the scent of death there.

"Who?" he asked, blinking up at me.

I didn't want to answer him. I gave a little bow of my

head. "Pawford, Abbie and two others."

He didn't move as the shock and dismay showed in his face. "Four? Oh hell. I came out through the magic cat door to find out what was going on when the fuss started. Pawford yelled and told me to find you since I would have the best chance of scenting you out. As I ran I saw shadows, but nothing that looked substantial enough to hurt them. I couldn't make out much in the storm. Damn."

"Come on in out of the rain. I'm sorry I didn't go get you, but in this storm -- so much magic -- I couldn't even find a trace of you."

"Yeah, I suppose so." He took the last couple steps, his head bowed, and didn't even try to shake the water from his fur.

I leaned over and picked him up, using magic at the same time to dry and clean him. We remained on the porch, both of us staring out into a night full of dangers, and Cato didn't even purr.

"David and I buried the others in the back. The attackers got into the house, but I found nothing wrong except a few things knocked over. Shakespeare is upset though."

"Poor guy," he said and sounded as though he even meant the words this time.

"There." I brushed the last of the water and mud from the tip of his tail. He gave a little contented sigh.

"Thanks." He lifted his head to glance out at the yard, but he turned to where the strays usually came to eat. "We had our spats, the boys and I, but Pawford stood his ground when it counted. Abbie -- Abbie was okay, and the others weren't bad cats at all. I don't understand why they're all dead."

"Neither do I unless someone meant to upset me. If

so, someone will be in for a hell of a surprise -- because they *did* upset me, and someone will pay for this."

"Good."

"I'm glad you're safe," I said, and even held him a little tighter. He butted his head against my chin. "Let's go in. I'll get you a can of tuna --"

"No tuna. Not tonight. This isn't a time to celebrate."

I understood. Even my dinner with David felt wrong now. "I found no problems inside, but be careful anyway," I warned as I turned and reached for the door.

And magic hit though not from inside the house. Power lashed out towards me from the yard and I dropped Cato as I turned; something slapped me across the back and I hit the porch floor hard as a tendril curled around both of my legs, like a tentacle from a land-roving octopus. The magic burnt into the cloth and my skin, and when I tried to turn, another tentacle caught my arm.

I panicked and grabbed hold of the door frame with the other hand and refused to let go, even when another tendril slapped at my fingers. The stings and slaps of pain distracted me from my magic, and every time I started a spell, I lost the power in the next breath. I needed focus!

The tentacles tugged relentlessly at me, and I started to lose my hold. Once I did, the thing would yank me right off the porch. Focus --

I found my focus in an unexpected way. Cato yowled, and from the corner of my eye I saw him fluff up to three times his normal size and hurl himself at the enemy -- the same one that had probably killed four cats already tonight.

He attacked to save me.

I found my magic. Power came first to my fingers holding the door frame. I anchored myself there, and even if I released the wood, my magic wouldn't let go. More magic surged through my left arm, burning away the tendril holding me in a burst of bright blue light. Another two came to take its place, but I brushed them aside with enough magic to scorch the wood of the porch. I heard something hiss in pain. Good. This thing felt pain, and by every God of every world, I would make sure this monster felt a lot of pain tonight.

Cato yowled once more as he charged towards the stand of trees to the right. I also heard a muffled curse which meant someone real stood out there. I twisted around and swept my hand down over one set of tentacles holding my legs, my blue fire shriveling one limb while the other retreated, though I didn't know where they went, out there in the dark yard. All I heard was Cato growling and snarling. I had to help him!

My legs had circles of burns and ached to move, but I got to my feet -- and I heard Cato give a startled cry. Something hurled through the air --

I reached up with magic and caught Cato before he hit the house and broke bones. The enemy rushed away in the dark of the storm and in a flash of lighting I saw the shapes of things disappearing into the woods and down the road.

"Damn --"

"You know, I don't like flying," Cato said, still sounding shaken. His claws had hooked into my shirt and nicked the skin. "I don't know what birds see in it."

"I need to go after them, Cato --"

"Do you really think that's a good idea?"

"I need --" But I stopped. Leaving wasn't wise. I felt shaken, and my legs wouldn't hold me for long. I'd need magic to heal my own wounds and more magic to make the house safe. "I need to make certain trouble isn't heading for town and others. That's my job. But I can do the work from here."

"Yeah, good. This has been a hell of a night. I want to go to bed now."

"In a couple minutes. What did you see out there?"

"Something, but hidden, you know? I sensed it, but couldn't see anything. I got close -- and then I was flying."

He gave a little shudder. I held him closer again.

I reached out and tried to follow the trail of dark magic. Someone powerful had brought the creature, fully realized, into being, and done it in a heartbeat. The magic had disappeared. I couldn't sense anything more heading for the streets of Estes Park. I tested a couple times because I didn't trust my own powers. By now my legs trembled so much I feared trying to walk back to the door. I put Cato down to make certain I didn't fall and hurt him.

"Those burns are nasty," Cato said, getting a look at them from his level. "You better do something or you'll have trouble walking all the way to your shower."

I nodded, gritting my teeth to do the work. The magic tried to slip away from my grasp, making me weak. I had fought a couple battles and won and though I regretted the loss of my little friends, I hadn't fallen. I reached down and gently brushed a little magic over my right leg, pulling aside burnt pant material and sealing the wounds to ease the pain and get me into the house and then did the same with the other leg. We needed to get inside and out of the open.

"Go in," I said, waving Cato ahead of me.

"Not until you do."

"I want ward behind me. Nothing will get into the house tonight."

"Good. I'm tired." He took a step past the doorframe and waited for me while he watched my back.

Fearless little lion.

I turned to watch and made the step backwards while making certain nothing in the yard to popped up and grabbed me again. I warded the door as I came through, and spread magic over the rest of the house, triggering stronger spells already in place which I rarely used. I closed the door and turned the lock.

"Nothing is going to get in," I said. "Not, at least, without making a considerable amount of show."

"Then we should be safe," Cato said, but he paced around the pile of fallen books and out toward the kitchen and back, as on edge as me.

I went to my chair and tried to get a link to fae and my father. Nothing would even catch hold, and I worried there might be more trouble. Nile Gods? Far worse than what I faced. I would have to try later after the last of the storm dissipated and less wild magic raced through the air. Besides, my father already knew about the trouble I faced earlier, so he'd likely try to reach me.

Like he had already, to tell me all hell was breaking loose. I wondered how true his words might be tonight.

I'd never felt as worn as I did now. I hadn't enough energy to go take a shower, even though I desperately wanted one. I sat in the chair and stared at my hands, as though the answer, or at least some energy, lingered in them.

"Bed," Cato said, coming to stand before me. Even he limped. "Come on. You'll sleep better on a nice mattress. You go to sleep there and you're going to fall and hit your head on the floor. And I'll laugh at you, too."

I remembered him, a few years younger, sitting on the arm of the chair and swaying back and forth while I read, and finally tumbling off to the floor. I had tried so hard not to laugh.

He made me smile. I stood, joints popping and muscles protesting. A little wave of my hand put the fallen books and other things back into their places. I wanted a sense of normality to help my state of mind.

Shakespeare rustled on his perch, and bobbed his head, when I limped over to him. His water dish was dry, so I filled it and put out more bird food. He let me pet his head a few times, welcoming the contact, though he started when the wind blew against the house.

"Poor guy," I said softly. "I wish you would talk to me. What happened here? You might help."

"*The more than beauty of a face,*" Shakespeare whispered, as though afraid something would hear him. "*The more than beauty of a face.*"

I petted him and considered delving into his mind to find the answers. I couldn't do something so terrible, not when I had buried four other small friends tonight.

Not ever. I would never be so inconsiderate of another life.

There are fae who use their magic with careless ease and regret problems they created afterward and fix those with another wave of their hands. I wished I held such power tonight.

But even they can't fix a problem with an animal after they've swept through their brains. I would not risk hurting Shakespeare no matter how maddening the inability to talk to him became.

"Bed?" Cato asked again, and this time with a frustrated sigh and his tail twitching back and forth.

"Yeah. Okay. I'll take a quick shower and be there in a couple --"

I stopped talking, seeing something sitting on the table by Shakespeare. I carefully picked up the recorder, afraid my unsteady powers would ruin the device.

Cato made a frustrated sound.

"You can go to bed without me," I said, glancing down at him.

"No I can't. I don't trust you. You might do something weird tonight. Come on." He nudged at my leg, but I was still so weak I nearly fell. I waved him back away.

"I have an idea which might help get Shakespeare to talk. He might give us some idea of what happened here. But. . . ." I sat the recorder down on the table. "No, I can't do it."

"You are going to drive me crazy. You really are. And I think you're doing it on purpose."

"What? Oh, sorry. No, you can go to bed. I'll be there in a minute." I looked at Shakespeare.

Cato limped back over and sat at my feet. "Okay, what's this plan you want to do but fear you shouldn't?"

"There's a bird at The Rookery --"

"You're right, you shouldn't do it," Cato said emphatically.

"He's only a little bird. A cockatiel, but he speaks pretty good parrot."

"Your parrot only speaks human and you want to add a cockatiel who speaks parrot. What a great combination."

I grinned, glad to see him back to himself. "I wonder if Shakespeare might open up to another bird, especially one who is kind of outgoing and --"

"Obnoxious?"

"Well yes. But don't worry. I won't get him."

"Why not?" Cato asked, wincing as though he regretted having to ask the question.

"This is no place to bring another animal. It's not safe for the two of you, and I can't justify --"

"Kat, as far as I can tell, with the trouble going on here and in town, there isn't anywhere safe. And I suspect things will get worse out there. Here, at least, we have you and a lovely ward to keep us safe *to sleep in our own warm bed tonight.*"

I hadn't thought of it that way. The trouble, though directed at me for the moment, would not be just my trouble for too long. The magic was getting stronger, and even the peripix --never mind the specters -- would give the city all kinds of problems. Something was behind all of this. Something attacked me and that made me leery of bringing others here. But still --

"Kat, I'm going to bite you on the ankle if you don't get moving. There's nothing more you can do tonight."

I really hate when the cat is thinking far clearer than I am. I also hate when he bites me on the ankle. So I went off to the bathroom and took a shower, lacing the water with a little healing magic. Little magic . . . I was good at little magic and my inability to do the big stuff worried me more than it ever had.

I came to bed a few minutes later to find Cato already curled up and asleep. I settled in beside him. He twitched every time the storm rattled the window.

So did I.

CHAPTER ELEVEN

A t dawn, I swept up dust bunnies and dropped a couple more into the holding cell out back. I glanced over at the little graves and got tears in my eyes, but I went back into the house feeling calmer than I had in days. Real sleep had helped. I sat down at the table with a cup of tea, watched Shakespeare for a moment, and tried to get my thoughts in order for the day and pull some sort of plan together.

I tried contacting my father but with no better luck than I'd had yesterday.

Outside, a storm built into towering clouds as the sun rose and heated the atmosphere, creating another round of thunderstorms. I listened to the distant roar of thunder and wondered how long before the rains reached us.

The phone rang.

I jumped. So did Cato and Shakespeare. The phone does not ring often in my house; I almost cursed, with the possibility of turning the device into something I might have to chase down later.

Phones are iffy for me, even with my powers damped. I walked to the wall and gingerly put the receiver to my ear. I heard a lot of static.

"Hello?" I said, tentative and worried.

"Good morning, Kat," David said, his voice a little quieter than usual. "How are you doing this morning?"

I felt better hearing the caring tone of his voice.

"I'll be fine. Are you ready to get going? Breakfast?"

"I want to jog to Bear Camp this morning since I haven't been doing my morning jogs since I got here, and I think I can do this before the rain hits. I'll meet you there, okay?"

"Sounds good. I'll see you there."

I dressed in good hiking clothes, a warm jacket, and my hair pulled back in a tie. When I left the house a few minutes later, I promised Cato and Shakespeare I would be back before dark. I double warded everything on my way out and made certain I would know if anyone tested the wards.

A single cat sat by the trees: Trouble, who seemed worn but unhurt. I went back in and got him food. He glanced around as though he expected to see his friends.

"I went across town last night." He shook his head, his bright golden eyes blinking. "I heard the news from Mrs. Miniver. There's talk around town. Something bad is going on."

"Yes, it is."

Trouble nodded and nibbled at his food. I left him there and considered stopping to talk to Cato's mother on my way to breakfast. Unfortunately, I saw Mrs. Hale out in the yard with the cats so I didn't even slow for fear she'd believe I would leap out and grab a couple.

Lily's car still sat in the parking lot along with two others that looked as though they'd been there for a few hours. I wondered what people thought -- and I found out as soon as I went in and Marylyn brought me coffee.

"I hope you can see your car from here." She peered out the window and nodded. "Good. There's vandalism going on. They've hit dozens of cars all over town. The police are suggesting it's a teen prank, but they haven't caught them yet."

"I'll keep an eye on the car," I said. Humans always came up with reasonable, non-magical answers to troubles.

Lily and Jordan entered and crossed straight to my table.

"We may not need Cago. We have something tracked to the Odessa Lake area," Jordan said as he dropped into a chair, nodding when Marilyn brought two more coffee cups and a full pot to sit in front of us. "There's been several kills in the area last night, so we're hiking in today. If you're going to the park, stay clear of there, okay? And watch this damned weather."

"I will," I said, in answer to the second part. I didn't, actually, answer the first part because I would have had to lie.

If there was something killing things up by Odessa Lake, I had feeling whatever they found would be dangerous -- and not anything they could handle. My bet was still on a gargoyle, and one in an extremely bad mood.

I had to get there ahead of them and deal with this problem because they would not survive an encounter with a gargoyle. Gargoyles are bad-tempered, fast and some species can fly. By the time you're close enough to shoot one, you're in a damned lot of trouble: They have skin like stone, and the bullets would just bounce off and annoy them even more.

I needed an excuse to give David. I didn't want to make the rangers suspicious, and I didn't have time to work up something magical to take everyone's attention. The rangers all ordered more coffee to go and headed back out. Damn. Only one person left to help me.

I Summoned Aletta. Not as strongly as I had the other night, but I let her know I wanted her to arrive right now.

She showed up five minutes later, her dark pants and grey sweater more suited to the place. She scowled.

"Don't start," I said and waved her to a seat at the table. She took it, giving me a sullen glare. "The Park Rangers are heading up to corner something in the wild. I fear there's a rogue gargoyle out there --"

"Gargoyle," she said in surprise though the wide-eyed expression looked faked. I needed to stop making snide judgments and get over my loathing of her. "How could a gargoyle get here?"

"Things are coming through the Edge. Trolls, peripix, who knows what else."

"You aren't going to send me after a gargoyle!"

"No." I hadn't even considered the possibility. She would never stand up to a gargoyle, and she wouldn't do her best to protect the humans heading there. "I want you to stay here and wait for David. Tell him -- tell him I am trying to reach the rangers to tell them something from Cago. I'll be back as soon as I can. The two of you should wait at my house. I have the place warded, so be careful going in. I'll set the wards to open for you."

She smiled and nodded agreement. Oh yes, this played right into her hands. She'd have time with David. I wasn't happy about the reaction but concentrated and keyed the ward for her so the two of them to go inside the house and *not* back to the hotel. I felt sorry for Cato and Shakespeare, but I trusted David to watch out for them.

"This won't take me long," I said, and hurried out because I didn't dare be there when David showed arrived for breakfast. I doubt I could have lied to him.

I got into the car and headed for the next block, turning away from the direction where David would be jogging. Everything outside felt damp, muted, and dangerous. I drove close to the park and pulled off on a dirt road where I hid the car behind an illusion. If I went farther the rangers would spot me. I had to get to the area well ahead of them and --

And when I lifted my hand to test for magic I discovered something that scared the hell out of me.

The Edge had moved farther than I had ever heard of a barrier moving. I found the magic settled near Odessa Lake, where the Rangers headed, and where the gargoyle -- or whatever other creature might be out there -- waited.

"Damn!" Frustration brought tears to my eyes. No one had ever talked about barriers leaping miles of wilderness to move closer to towns. I didn't know what to do!

I had to keep the rangers safe. That took priority and afterwards I would go home and contact someone on the other side to find out what the hell else to do. People hiked in this area, even in winter. If they found the Edge, I didn't want to consider the consequences.

Do the first job. I thought of Jordan, Lily and Jim facing a gargoyle. The creature could blend into the scree of the mountains and become another boulder among many -- until it was too late.

I ran rather than fly. I couldn't risk someone spotting me in the air on this bright morning. The clouds were still holding off, but I sensed the storm building, not helped by the extra magic from the Edge. I didn't dare waste power on being invisible, so I darted up over the rocks and down through the gullies, knowing I could out distance the rangers who would stick to the trails. I didn't know how to deal with the gargoyle. None at all. Sometimes they can be quite reasonable. Other times --

And this would be an 'other time' because everything else was going bad.

Even I slowed going up the incline to Bear Lake and stopped when I reached Nymph Lake. I had seen no sign of people on the trails I had crossed -- still too early, and besides the weather felt dangerously changeable. Thunder rolled somewhere off in the distance and I sensed snow in the clouds above me.

For the first time in a couple days I even spotted birds. Three stellar jays, their bright blue plumage standing out against the gray world, came hurtling down at me so quickly I stumbled back and landed on my ass. Lucky for me only the birds noticed, and they appeared too frantic to laugh today.

"Trouble, trouble!" they cried in unison.

"Can you show me where?" I asked.

"No, no, no -- kills everything. Trouble, trouble!"

And they flew away into the woods.

I marked the direction of their flight. After making certain no one was around, I lifted over the lake, hit Flattop Mountain Trail for a short distance of easy running, and made a difficult transition to Fern Lake Trail.

Along the way I found increasingly frantic birds. I almost tripped over a couple blue grouse sprinting along in the underbrush, racing from one cover to the next. Owls flocked about by day, unusual behavior in both ways, since they are solitary nocturnal creatures. From them I got better directions.

"Is he near Notchtop?" a long-eared owl said when I asked where the creature might be.

Notchtop would be perfect terrain for a gargoyle, with

lots of rocky areas where he could blend into the scenery. I headed in that direction, and managed not to curse as a light snow began to fall, the hint of white swirling in the air. I feared I saw something else white in the woods, but I didn't stop check for another of the damned riders. I had other problems to deal with today.

Magpies and Flickers flew past, and I took my new bearings from them. Not long afterwards a Northern Harrier hawk swept down from a tree and kept pace with me.

"Trouble," she said. "Bad trouble. Something has set a monster in the woods to destroy us."

Hawks and their conspiracy mentality . . . but I nodded, somewhat breathless.

"The monster is closer than you think."

Those words brought me up short, stopping with my hands on my knees, breathless and unable to ask questions. She landed in a tree to my right, her head flicking to me and ahead, as though she expected the trouble to burst out of the woods a few feet away.

Watching her made me nervous. Magic almost tingled along my hands, but I held back, trying to control both my fears and my body. I would need the power later. I dared not waste any.

When something moved in the woods I spun as a bear gambled out of the trees. He gave me one distraught glance and took off down the opposite side of the trail. You know, it's never good when something worries a bear that much.

I went forward though I moved slower.

And heard something troubling, but not a gargoyle. Distant growl of a sound --

The rangers had come up on dirt bikes and even with all my running, I had barely reached here ahead of them! I thought about the bear and used my magic to keep the more dangerous creatures out of the way of the rangers. They were apt to kill a hapless bear or big cat that was running and trying to escape something worse. They wouldn't realize the mistake, seeing only something acting oddly.

I looked up at the hawk, surprised to find she had stayed with me.

"You need to fly away," I told her. "Escape. This place is dangerous."

"Help you," she said, her head bending low to stare into my face. "Help set the woods right. *Trust you.*"

My breath caught. I had *never* known a hawk or an eagle to trust anyone. Her words sent a shiver of surprise through me, but coupled with a surge of pride. I bowed my head to her.

"Thank you. I need help. Can you find the monster for me? But carefully. This creature might fly." And I remembered the little nuthatches and their *big wings*. Poor little guys must have been scared out of their minds -- and I'd ignored them.

"Carefully," she agreed, and took to the air, flying off to the right. I watched her long, brown wings glide up over the top of trees, passing an owl heading in the opposite direction. They barely even acknowledged each other.

I needed to move off the trail. The rangers sounded far too close and I could never explain how I had gotten here ahead of them.

I found an easy answer to hold them back for a while yet. We'd had a few storms lately. I found a huge dead branch clinging tenaciously to a Douglas fir and pulled it gently down to make the trail difficult to traverse. To make certain they didn't take the dirt bikes around, I brought ground water up near the surface and created huge, muddy flats on both sides of the trail.

Then I rushed to follow my hawk companion. I barely got out of sight before the dirt bikes roared up the trail and came to a sputtering stop. As the silence filled the woods I heard Jordan's voice, clear and strong.

"We might as well leave the bikes here," Jordan said. "We need to get in on foot anyway. Don't want to scare it off."

"Yes," Lily agreed and her voice grew a little softer. "I assume you guys saw the bobcat running full out back there? What the hell set him running?"

"I don't know," Jordan answered. "Make sure you have your rifle ready. Whatever is up here has to be damned dangerous."

They were right, and they took reasonable precautions for what they expected to find. I still had to outrace them to the danger.

I saw one little rabbit rushing down the hillside, but nothing else moved except the wind in the branches. My hawk companion circled around and landed on a branch a few yards ahead of me. I jogged up to her and stopped, catching my breath again.

"I found the monster. Up and up," she said, her head lifting.

"Is it flying?" I asked, worried. If my friends spotted a gargoyle in the air --

"No. Up the hillside. Noisy. Those other humans will find it and it will find them."

My worst fear.

"Up and up," she repeated. "By the rocks. The monster leaves a trail of bones and dead things."

I rushed forward, wondering if I should bring the

rangers in on the secret and get help to destroy this thing. Few humans know about the fae, but I trusted Jordan and Lily, though I wasn't certain who else had come up with them. If they showed up at a bad time, I would tell the group everything and live with the results.

The decision calmed me, giving me one less thing to fret over. Under the circumstances, I wouldn't have a problem with the rest of the fae world if I had to give away our secret.

As I stepped past the tree line, something moved along the shadow and rock; a hulking shape of magic almost blending into the natural magic of the world. I found him, lost him . . . and found him moving along the line of scree toward the trail where the rangers would appear. I was right. We had a gargoyle.

I suspected he caught the scent of them coming since gargoyles are damned good hunters and predators. There is something about the un-magical nature of humans which draws such predators their way, probably because they're much easier to kill than something with magic.

I had an idea which might help keep my friends away and my secret safe. I sent a sprite breeze off down the hillside, having it make enough noise to draw the rangers in a different direction, and I even added the bellowing sound of a bear to get their attention. I hoped no real bears remained in the area. If one did . . . well, the loss of a bear would be bad, but not as bad as the deaths of several rangers. Sometimes you have to make those choices, but I still did my best to avoid the possibility of any animal needlessly dying.

I remained still and tested the area with a hint of magic, making certain they had gone chasing after my phantom while I got my breath back and calmed before I faced the real problem. I was about to take on one of the most dangerous creatures from my world; I didn't dare charge in, and I wouldn't talk this one into going back. I needed a plan and a way to get closer without the gargoyle killing me.

The hawk landed beside me, patiently waiting.

And there was an answer.

"I can't," I whispered. She tilted her head. "I can't take your form. I've never done the magic before. Others of my kind do, but I can't --"

I was babbling, and the hawk remained silent, though she knew what I suggested. She could have flown away. She should have.

"I need to get there," I whispered, feeling chill in the morning light and I watched either a ghost rider or morning mist moving off to the left. "I must get where I can catch the gargoyle off guard."

"I understand," she said.

"I could hurt you."

"But you will not do so on purpose. There is danger in these woods, fae. There is trouble others make. I have fought to be here because you can end this trouble. I wish to see this monster gone."

"Thank you," I said. I set the release spell in my mind, ready to trigger at a thought. I reached up to rest my hand on her willing head and considered about what I must do --

And I slipped into her body.

The change came too easily and startled me. I fought to keep control of myself; I didn't want to take over the hawk, only ride on her wings. I didn't know how to fly and I needed her to do the work. Besides, this was too strange, confined to this body without hands and arms. I wanted --

I shoved my wants and needs into the tiny corner of

my being and let the hawk do what she needed. Other fae don't like the loss of full control and they don't enjoy sharing thoughts with something which isn't akin to them.

I found the link fascinating. She could see little mice trying to run away, and she wanted to pluck them up, such tasty little tidbits there for the taking. Instead, she lifted upwards, sweeping into the cold, cloud-covered sky.

Flying. Truly flying -- not just the race across the sky as I had done with Cato the other night. The wind brushed against our feathers as we skimmed over the trees. We saw Grace Falls, the clarity amazing. We wanted to sail on the winds, slip off into the wilderness, away from the others --

Others. The memory of friends in danger drew my thoughts back from hers. Gargoyle.

She found the gargoyle -- I don't know how. I didn't spot the great hulking rock-like creature until he moved. We swept through the sky above him and the gargoyle's wings unfurled. I didn't want to face the creature in the air, so the hawk and I slipped straight down to the ground and we landed in a tumble of boulders and broken trees.

Out!

I came out of the hawk in a flash of power -- like the heat of fire and the cold of a wind all at the same time. I stood shivering for a moment at the transition. Confused, I looked down and found I was myself. The magic had worked.

The hawk, however, walked in circles, obviously dazed. I'd been careful, and I hoped she would recover soon. I carefully put her up in a nearby tree, but she fell off the branch. She panicked when I started to leave her and came after me, rushing forward on foot.

I couldn't abandon her. I wrapped her in a blanket of soothing magic and put her in the cradle of my arm before

I started after the gargoyle. Having been in the brain of the hawk had given me a plan. What I needed was prey for the gargoyle to chase back to the Edge. I created a herd of ten phantom deer, putting considerable reality into them. I almost went down to my knees, lightheaded and weak with the loss of power, but my creations stood by the tree line, away from the trail.

The gargoyle spotted the animals, which I had placed out of range of scent, I hoped, or else he would smell magic all over them. Or maybe not since this area near the Edge held so much magic already.

I held the hawk in one arm and directed my simulations with the other. The gargoyle went after them and I followed behind both the hunter and the prey as we moved closer to the Edge. The easiest answer would be to send the gargoyle back to the fae lands rather than kill it. I wouldn't have much chance going one-on-one with this thing.

Easiest being a relative term.

The gargoyle danced along the debris at the bottom of Notchtop, moving with no appreciable difficulty. So did my simulations. I, on the other hand, had a lot of trouble holding onto the hawk and not falling. I would use magic, but I had already pressed my limit with the creations and I needed to conserve what I had left.

Directing the deer back to the edge which wasn't far away, proved difficult and by the end I panted and gasped, while my sight had flickers of odd lights and dark spots. We kept moving: me, pretend deer and the gargoyle. The rainbow light of the Edge touched the shadows now, and I hoped no one came this way.

Almost done. The gargoyle charged the simulation standing close to this side of the Edge.

I dropped the hawk with an apology and sent a spear of magic into the Edge right where the gargoyle charged, his huge legs thumping against the ground. Trees shook and shale skidded down the mountainside nearby.

I forced a door open in the Edge and the pretend deer and real gargoyle charged right through after them.

"Yes!"

And he bounced right back out.

The elation of a moment before turned to anger and frustration -- and I went a little crazy.

No -- I went *a lot* crazy.

I ran towards the gargoyle. This was the closest, in fact, I'd ever been to one. I noticed the gray and black veins of his skin, creating granite pattern. The body looked as though a boulder had grown a head and sprouted stocky arms and legs. I had trouble seeing the wings where they folded over the carapace. Beneath the shell would be softer skin -- at least softer in comparison. Most daggers would break rather than cut through it. Even a fae needed a lot of magic -- which I didn't have -- to kill one of these things.

He turned icy blue eyes my way, and the thin mouth beneath his nub of a nose drew back showing a row of obsidian-like teeth in an obvious show of threat. I didn't care. I grabbed him up in a web of magic and threw him at the door -- and this time I kept shoving.

Something shoved back from the other side. Another fae? Something else? I didn't know. Whatever was there, it didn't want the gargoyle in his area, but I sure as hell wasn't leaving him on this side!

The gargoyle grew frantic as he found himself caught between two forces. He thrashed out at me as I shoved his head into the Edge. A stone-clad arm connected with my shoulder and I staggered back and went to my knees in pain and barely held the gargoyle in place with my magic. I might not have much power, but I'm stubborn as hell. Aletta probably could have shoved the creature through and closed the door with a flick of her perfect little fingers.

The thought annoyed me more.

Annoyance is good sometimes. So is the fear for the safety of friends who might see this show. I shoved harder.

The gargoyle tumbled and then stood on the other side. I saw other movement; something getting out of the way very fast. Good luck to them, I thought, and scrambled back to my feet. I sealed the door in the Edge closed -- easier than repairing a hole, but I trembled with exertion.

I paused with the door nearly sealed and considered checking things on the fae side. Something was wrong. I could imagine all kinds of trouble beyond the Edge and leaking through to my side.

There had been wars in the distant past, often between one fae clan and another. Boredom had led to many of the old feuds, or the taste for certain magic prizes which can only be taken from another fae. Clans had disappeared in the smoke and blood of war, and not even the legends brought them back.

Or the fae might face something worse on the other side.

The Nile Gods? The fae had dealt with them before and won. Demons might be making trouble, but why would they start a war here? We had nothing in common, and there are enough realities to go around. Infinite places, some close to this, others farther away and unlike this world. We could spread out anywhere, but we generally kept close to this reality because we love this place. The humans here had been kind to us with legends and stories.

If there was trouble on the other side, wasn't my place

there, fighting with my people over such a danger?

I stood there, trying to reason my way through a pounding headache, an arm that twitched with pain from the blow to the shoulder and my tumbling rage and fear.

My place --

Was here. I am a border guard, and my job is to stand on this side of the Edge and keep things safe, like I had just done. Now wasn't the time to walk away and ignore peripix and specters. I wouldn't leave this place unprotected from whatever else might still come through to this side.

I carefully sealed the Edge completely closed. Then I sat down on the cold, hard ground and cried. I wanted to go home. I had never been meant to hold a position where I had to work this hard.

That pathetic thought gave me a mental slap in the face. I wanted to go home because the work got too hard? I had managed the work. When had I become this lazy?

I took a few breaths as the hawk walked. She stared into my face and shook her head. She even spread her wings twice.

"I'm sorry," I told her softly. "I hope you'll be all right soon."

She gave a little nod of her head. With a little tendril of magic, I located the rangers who remained some distance off, but heading this way. So I wasn't done yet.

I desperately wanted to stretch out and sleep, right here in the cold wet morning. A mist lay over the lake beneath Topnotch, and clouds hung across the mountains, waiting to descend on me. Rain would fall before too long, and then snow.

But the lake, the mist, and clouds turned out to be breathtakingly beautiful, and I drank in the unexpected peace. Somewhere a chickadee called out a greeting with a soft whistle that held little more than 'safe, safe, safe' in the sound. I smiled. I'd done a good job.

How could I dissuade the rangers from continuing their hunt? Even though I had dealt with the danger, I still didn't want them anywhere near the Edge. Who knew what might come through next!

I ran a spell line all across the Edge and created the equivalent of a trip wire. If anything tore its way through I would hear little bells ringing in my head. I wanted no more surprises, big or small.

The spell should also let me know if the Edge made another great leaping move. It had already moved too close to civilization and might draw attention. I couldn't make the Edge go away and trying to force it back to the wilderness . . . well, even I wasn't that brave or stupid.

The spell line magic appeared solid and calm despite my state of mind. I took another deep breath and checked the area, pulling a little more physical cover over to hide the slight glow. I had gotten used to using magic near the Edge, it appeared, and hardly got any reaction from it at all. My focus was good.

I needed to reach my father. I had to believe even if they fought a war on the other side they'd still be able to help me. The rangers would soon find the trail of bones leading up the mountainside. I did my best to erase the tracks the gargoyle had left in the soft soil heading after the pretend-deer. I had control of both my rage and the scared witless mode. Good.

And a ghost rider came through the Edge; the thing didn't make a hole in the wall of the Edge and didn't set off my trip wire. The horse simply galloped through and headed straight for me.

The horse and rider seemed more ice rather than mist

this time. The chiseled shape of the rider's face held a hint of darkness where the eyes would be. The horse slowed and pranced, head down, and I heard the sound of leaves crunching beneath his feet. This thing was becoming more real.

I backed up a step. This could not be a specter or ghost of any sort. Those types of creatures remained incorporeal, and this thing had taken on solid, substantial form. Details where clearly etched on the rider's helmet, and the slight upturn of his eyes seemed to hint at something Eastern.

He stared at me. His white lips curled back in a smile that showed no friendliness. Across his saddle, he held a sword, glittering as though light lived inside the blade - but when he lifted the weapon, I felt as though darkness itself had reached out.

Death sword. They are swords with the magic to undue life, to kill with a single blow, even though they leave no visible wound. They take centuries to forge.

I tore my eyes away from the crystalline blade and backed up, afraid.

"What do you want?" I asked softly.

The man gave a kick, sending the horse galloping straight towards me. And I knew now what he wanted: he wanted me dead.

I stepped back -- and the hawk found her wings and leapt up into the air --

"Evil!" she cried. "Run Kat!"

And she dived at the man.

"No!"

The sword swept up and neatly ran her through, like water through air. No blood, no gore. But she flapped once and tumbled dead to the side of the horse.

Enraged beyond anything rational, I yelled and called magic to my hands, throwing a bolt straight at the rider as he brought the sword around towards me. I startled the horse, and the blade missed me by bare inches --

And the storm hit. The massive magic I'd used, unchecked, and so close to the Edge, finally pushed the balance over to something dangerous. Wind tore through the trees and lightning rent the sky with a power brighter than the sun. Thunder shook the world and rain came in a sudden torrent. If the man had truly been made of ice, he would have melted.

He didn't. The storm took him by surprise, though, and he glanced up at the sky. I threw myself at his horse and used more magic to startle the beast backwards. Not a fae horse -- magic didn't startle them -- and I wondered what he and the rider were and how they passed back and forth between fae and here with an ease most of my family would have found amazing.

The rider got the horse in hand and turned his attention back towards me. The sword swept downwards, and I danced out of the way, rain drenching my face and making it difficult to see around me. Or maybe that came from the tears. I dared not look at the fallen hawk who had shared her joy of flight with me.

Lightning flashed across the sky with powerful, natural magic. I grabbed the lighting and dragged the power down towards the rider. He lifted his arm, the sword in hand, ready to strike me.

The lightning found the sword, and drove down through the blade, illuminating the world with an unnatural green glow as it burned through the weapon. I did not let it go, holding the lightning in place with more will-power than magical power. Fae children learn never to mix natural magic with created magic because they are incompatible in most cases. Dangerous.

I had nothing else to use. I didn't let go.

The sword exploded, sending me tumbling as the power ripped branches from nearby trees. Pieces of the shattered sword flew in all directions, and far too many of them hitting the Edge in a spectacular array of fireworks. I thought I would die, but the pieces held no power to kill. They didn't even cut -- just hit me and dropped and disappeared.

But impacting the Edge only made the weather worse. The rain turned to snow in a heartbeat and laid white about us and stung my face with cold.

The rider held his arm to his chest. Felt pain, did he? Good. Anything which can feel can be destroyed, and by the Gods, I intended to take this one down. No one should have brought such a deadly, magical sword to this side of the Edge where such a power would always attract the wrong people. If the weapon had fallen into human hands, civilization itself would have been in danger.

That would not happen this time. I'd destroyed a death sword. I worried what problems even the shards might cause, but nothing remained except the final whisper of a display beside the Edge, where a last little piece melted away into the ground.

"Not here," I told the rider as I looked back at him. "You are not welcome here. I don't know what you are, and I don't know what you want -- other than me dead -- but you are not coming through my part of the Edge."

Had he come here because he knew I was weaker than the others, and this would be an easy way entrance into the world? I hoped I had dissuaded him and his companions of the idea.

I stepped towards him. He held his ground and pulled another sword. For a moment my breath caught, but then I realized this one had no special powers beyond whatever made him.

I looked up into his face. "Go ahead and try."

The horse took a dancing step away as I lifted my hand and the rider didn't fight the retreat. I could see more of his face -- Eastern beyond a doubt, and with the hint of a scraggly beard. But I didn't know the face and put no name to this man or myth.

I stepped closer. The sword swung in my direction, and I batted the weapon away with a little magic, even though I felt nearly depleted.

The storm returned with a rush of wind while thunder shook the world and the snow fell harder. Snow storms within thunderstorms can produce the heaviest snowfall of all and this one proved the point. I don't think the magic even contributed much. Snow blanketed everything within a few heartbeats. The horse shook the flakes from his mane, unhappy with the weather. He backed up yet again, this time with the rider's agreement.

We had reached the Edge once more. Rainbow light cast an odd glow through the icy bodies of the rider and the horse.

"Go back," I said to him. "Go back and don't come through again."

But he tried for me one more time. Out of desperation -- which I suspected fueled my strongest powers -- I pulled a broken branch to me with magic and hit the horse firmly across the chest. The animal reared this time. I hated the hurt any creature, but I swung again.

The horse fought the rider's commands, and I helped by throwing a circle of magical light into the horse's face, trying to keep the animal off balance.

I got careless and took a bad cut in the same shoulder where the gargoyle had hit me. I almost dropped the branch as pain lanced through the arm, but I grabbed it in my left hand instead, swung around and nearly unseated the rider. The sword caught in the branch and broke.

As I stood there gasping, I started to pull another lightning strike from the sky --

The rider turned and lunged back through the Edge and once more without making a door, without tripping my magic, and without more than a ripple in the surface.

But for a moment I saw through to where he had gone.

A shimmering city sat on the other side, filled with domes and the light of a desert sun; a large city of age, wealth, and power.

Such a place of obvious magic should never have been this close to the Edge. Nothing solid should have been able to withstand the twists and turns which came as the Edge moved from place to place. This had to be an illusion. I reached through with magic, even though the wind blew harder on this side. I tried to make the illusion go away.

Instead I found the solid brick, dirt paved streets and palms of a very real city. The place felt . . . as though the city waited to come through -- but that couldn't be possible! Nothing could --

I drew my hand back, preparing to turn and run, when something else caught my eye. There to the left of the city, on a plain of withered grass and golden sands stood horses and riders, all poised to come through the Edge.

Thousands of them.

Chapter Twelve

No! This couldn't be real! I stumbled back from the Edge, sick with fear as the ripple disappeared and I no longer saw through the rainbow-like surface. What I saw must have been an illusion and nothing real.

I wanted help and the only person I had would be Aletta. I needed to go to her and hope she could reach home. I didn't care -- I would swallow my pride and admit to any weakness, as long as I didn't stand alone against . . . this.

I went to my knees, shivering from far more than the cold of the storm. Blood ran warm down my arm, dripping into the snow as I stared, unable to think. I couldn't find any answers. The city, the riders -- none of them should have been there. The gargoyle, peripix, trolls hadn't appeared on this side by chance. Something -- very many somethings -- wanted through, and I suspected the others were a test or to weaken me . . . or for other reasons I didn't understand either, but they were not coming through by chance.

Should I sit here and wait and watch? What would I do if they rode into this world? I needed help. I *needed* Aletta.

I tried to stand, cursing softly, and without any power to make the curse real. Pain lashed through my arm when I moved, and everything went dangerously dark for a moment. I took deep breaths, knowing I had to heal my arm before I went anywhere. I drew little tiny tendrils of magic from the air, but the storm still swirled with a new harsh wind.

The work on my arm took too long, but I didn't dare rush. I fixed torn muscles and blood vessels, ligaments and flesh, and the thin skin over everything. Not a perfect fix. I drew a little more and repaired and cleaned my clothing before I headed back to Estes Park and hopefully get there ahead of the others.

Damn. I'd have to make certain my friends reached safety, too. With the sudden power of this storm, even the best trained hikers might find themselves in trouble. I had saved them from the gargoyle and wouldn't let them die in the snow.

I stayed kneeling in the nearly four inches of snow and tested out the area until I located the park rangers. They had found the kill site, but they wouldn't continue searching for a crazed animal in this weather. They would come back later. No matter. She had chased the gargoyle away and as long as nothing else came through, they could hunt all the wanted.

If the army came through the Edge, what the rangers saw would be the last thing I needed to worry about.

I gently, gently, oh so carefully, got them back down to the trail and to their dirt bikes. They might have been able reach safety on their own, but I couldn't trust such a thing to happen today. I gave them more safety in a wave of magic.

I crawled forward about a yard to a small white mound

and gently brushed the snow from the hawk's dead body and picked her up from the ground.

"I'm sorry," I said. "If I hadn't --"

I stopped the words. She deserved better. If I hadn't accepted her gift, I might not have gotten to the gargoyle in time. I belittled her memory to think anything else. She had willingly joined in the fight, and from the cry she gave at the end, she realized the danger when she tried to attack the rider.

Tears froze on my cheeks. Too many had died in the last couple days. I feared to go back to the house and find there might be worse waiting for me there.

But I was a border guard. Damn the Edge and whatever worked on the other side against me. I wanted all the trouble to go away and things to return to normal. My wishes wouldn't bring back the cats or the hawk though.

I watched the sparkle of light through the falling snow, so deceptively pretty. I couldn't close the Edge down and I couldn't stop anything happening on the other side.

I had to go back and get help.

I stumbled to my feet and made my way towards the trail, moving a little faster with each step. I carried my dead companion in one hand, and beside the lake I made a little cairn for her, and wished her soft winds and cloudless skies where she had gone.

The rangers had gotten away well ahead of me, pushing the bikes through the snow, anxious to get back to the lower elevations. I heard the distant sound of their laughter, which seemed a strange, alien sound.

Once I thought I saw a ghost rider charging off through the snow, but he didn't stop to harass me if that's what he'd been and I was glad enough to let him go. This time.

He did not head towards the rangers, either. I followed their path, about a half mile behind my friends. When they slowed, I purposely sent a little more power into the storm, pulling the snow and winds along with me, and encouraging my friends not only to hurry but also to shut off access to most of the park for a day or two. Better to close this area rather than to risk endangering people if something else came through the Edge.

And I kept glancing over my shoulder, expecting an army of those riders to be following me. The fear made me ill. No matter how hard I thought, I had no idea how to stop them. I had fought one-on-one with a single rider and barely survived. Thousands?

He had been more solid than the riders I had seen on the drive with David. I tried to call back the image beyond the Edge -- an army on horseback, perhaps a banner waving in the wind . . . but nothing came clearly. I had seen nothing like them on the other side. I had an odd impression that they belonged to this world as though a human army had gotten lost and ended up in the fae lands. Such things had happened in the past when the Edge had spread wider than now. I would do some study at the library tonight if I got the chance. If I learned more about them and found they belonged to this world, I would gain more power over them.

Knowledge is power is really a fae saying.

The rangers reached the Bear Lake parking lot and their trucks where they loaded the dirt bikes. I stood by the sign, clothed in the white of snow, and watched as they piled into the vehicles and began the laborious work of heading down the mountain in the storm. I laid a little more magic into their tires and made certain they would get back down without any trouble.

Oh how I wanted to climb into one of those nice warm trucks with them. I had a long, long ways to go back to my hidden car. As they drove away, I stood there in the snow, listening to the silence of a winter storm where only the wind moved the trees. The moment would have been exquisite at another time.

I stepped out from the little shelter provided by the sign when I heard something high above me: the flap of huge wings. I stared upward, terrified as I caught the barest outline of something gigantic, gliding through the snow.

Gods don't let there be a dragon on this side! Dragons rarely showed themselves, even in the fae lands, and they hadn't been in the human world for thousands of years. Besides being inherently dangerous, they were the harbingers of trouble and change, and things I didn't want to consider.

I stared up into the sky and followed the hint of movement in the snow; a long shadow moving and then gone.

"Big wings," I said softly. "*Damned* big wings."

I tried to find animals on the way down, but spotted only a couple rabbits and the single fox. They scattered at the sight of me. Most animals can sense a fae, and even if I can't directly communicate with rabbits and foxes, they aren't afraid of me. Watching them run bothered me.

I found no birds at all and I wanted them back, realizing how much I needed their eyes to watch things up here.

I also needed to make certain the rangers backed my story later. I reached out and found them in their cars and planted a little thought: I had been somewhere in the park, trying to reach Cago. Hell, if I could, I would have called Cago here. I would have called *everyone* to come here.

By the time I reached my car the snow, even down at this level, had reached six inches on the ground. I sat in the car for a moment, letting the heater kick in and defrost both the window and me. I trembled and this time I couldn't decide if that came from the cold, the wounds, or the natural cold fae suffer after the use of so much magic. Or perhaps I felt just plain fear.

Suddenly all those problems melded together, and I trembled more than I had in my life. I made my hands hold tight to the steering wheel to keep them from shaking, and I inched the car out of my hidden spot and down the dirt path to the main road. I found tracks there already, and I levered the car into those ruts and headed for home.

But a whisper of magic swept past me, and I had the feeling the *big wings* were not far away. I didn't want any dragons involved in this trouble.

But if one were here, the car wouldn't be much more than a plaything. A dragon could scoop the vehicle up and carry me off without a problem. I rolled down the window and watched the sky, almost shouting a dare to whatever might be up there. *Yeah, come and get me. I don't care anymore!*

But I did care, if not for myself, at least for all my friends. I pulled my head back in, twisted the steering wheel until I found the ruts once more, and forced the car forward and through town. Hours had passed since I left the Edge and when I turned up the road to home.

I had never been so happy to see my place. I sat in the car for a moment, made certain my clothing showed no tears or blood. David's car sat next to mine. I smiled as I hurried up to the house and stopped on the porch long enough to brush the snow off.

Aletta and David sat up in the loft which was, after all, a nice place watch the snow. I had rather wished I had been there with David rather than Aletta taking the spot. I sighed when she came down the steps in slinky ski clothing that had never seen the slopes and fitting every curve perfectly.

David followed her, frowning. I felt guilty about sticking him with her. I wanted to make this up to him. He even moved with an angry, heavy step I'd never seen before.

"About time you got back," he said, frowning at me.

Aletta put a hand on his arm. He sighed and nodded as though she had reminded him of something.

I didn't like it.

"Did the work go well?" Aletta asked with a bright smile. "Did you get a hold of Cago?"

"No, I didn't." The words sounded short and bad tempered, but I felt as though I had intruded where I shouldn't be.

"Ah, too bad," she said with a wave of her hand.

"Well, since we can't go out in this weather, Aletta and I are going back to the hotel," David said as he walked past me, limping a little.

The words struck me like physical a blow. I couldn't breathe for a moment, and I feared I would cry. He headed to the door with Aletta. I lifted a hand, to test what spell Aletta had put on him.

But she hadn't. I did find a wash of magic over him, and something repulsed me --

Oh hell. I had done this myself! This had to be the spell I had made to get him to leave. I wasn't used to such delicate magic, and obviously I had pushed a little too hard, and shoved him right into my cousin's willing arms. He had moved over to a new path and I had pointed him there.

The situation shouldn't upset me. In the scheme of things -- hell, I had to get him away from me so I could do my work anyway. With him around, I couldn't even talk to Cato or test for magic, or try to reach home.

But it still hurt. Aletta had done this on purpose, stepping in and taking advantage of the spell meant to protect David and help settle the problem.

There are things you don't forgive. She saw that truth in my face as she went over to grab her jacket from the dining room chair. Shakespeare flapped his wings and made a clicking noise at her with his beak as though he had every intention of biting her. She backed away with a yelp.

Good bird.

"I don't understand why you keep that evil thing," she said, glaring back at the bird. I almost expected her to cast a spell, but she didn't. Instead she fought with her jacket until David came over and helped her.

And Shakespeare snapped at him too. I remembered the first day they met, and how much the bird had liked him. Now he acted as though David was no better than Aletta.

"There are things we need to talk about later, Aletta," I said, trying to keep my voice even. If I hadn't needed her, I would have pushed her out the door, sealed the ward and never let her near me again.

"Sure, whatever." She put her arm in David's and she almost laughed -- but what she saw in my face drained the humor from her. "Call me later, if you can get through."

"I will," I said, and the promise in those words made her worry.

What had she done to win David? I didn't think David would be the kind who would fall so easily for her. I sensed no glamour, and the magic around David was my spell.

I should have had him stay at the cafe. I should have used magic to make him believe we would meet later. I thought of a half dozen things I could have done rather than putting him with Aletta.

I shouldn't have been blaming her. She happened along at the right time and slipped into the void where my spell pushed him away.

I'm a fool. I know it.

Shakespeare still flapped about, more unsettled than usual. I went over to him and petted his head. He rubbed up against me and glanced into my face.

"*And a proud sprit which hath striven, triumphantly with human kind*," he barely whispered

"What did he say?" David demanded sounding oddly strident.

"Nothing important. More of his poetry."

David made a dismissive noise as he hurried to the door ready to leave. My breath catch as a pain settled in my chest. I didn't deserve this. I didn't --

Shakespeare reached over and bit my finger. Not as hard as before, but with enough force to draw my attention. David had stopped and stared out the big window. I watched the hint of his reflection, and how for a moment, something changed in his face.

"Don't trust me," he said, almost as softly as Shakespeare.

"What?" I stepped closer, testing for magic again. I found nothing but the same repulsion spell. What --

Aletta came and took his arm. He smiled at her. "Don't trust me on the walkway. I'm apt to pull you down, love."

My heart would break. Aletta laughed, and they went out the door. David hadn't even remembered to pick up his camera equipment on the way out.

And damned if I would let the pack sit there and remind me of how miserable I felt. I threw the door open to find them starting down the steps from the porch. They both almost slipped.

"You forgot your camera equipment, David."

He glanced back; his eyes narrowed, and he gave a quick nod to Aletta. She came back to the door.

"Are you going to let me get his stuff or not?" she asked.

I stepped aside. The weight surprised her as she slung the pack over her shoulder, banging it against the door. I thought of all the nice equipment and how much care David took of the cameras, but he kept heading toward the car and didn't take notice.

She followed and tossed the pack into the back seat and opened the driver's side. He took the other seat. In a moment they pulled away, lost in the fall of snow. I listened to the car heading down the hill.

"Son of a bitch!" I stepped back and threw the door closed so hard the windows shook. I stood there, panting as though I had run a long race. Tears ran down my face. "I did this myself. I drove him away with my damned spell. But Aletta -- Aletta stepped in on purpose!"

Cato made a careful appearance, with his tail down and his ears back.

"They're gone, right?" he asked.

"Yeah. Gone. What went on?"

"Nothing. They showed up about an hour ago. David kept pacing back and forth, back and forth. The bird got upset every time Aletta would come near him so they went up to the loft and sat down and talked."

"About what?"

"I don't know. They stayed quiet. Aletta chased me out the front door. I came back in my cat door, but she didn't realize it. I went to sleep back in the closet."

"Aletta knows I can talk to you, so she didn't want you to tell me anything afterwards. How did David act? Aside from the pacing?"

"I expected him to protest when Aletta chased me out, but he didn't," Cato admitted. "I really thought he liked me. I thought he liked *you*."

"Well, I screwed that up." I threw myself down in my chair. He leapt up on the arm and rubbed his head against my shoulder, trying to be nice. I didn't wince, even though the shoulder still hurt. "I was trying to get him to leave for a while -- not long. Just while I got this mess cleaned up. And we have a true mess, Cato. A bad one. I intended to ask Aletta to help me --"

"You must be desperate."

"Yes. I am. I need back up. But now . . . now I feel as though I can't trust her. I have to trust the person I work with. Why did she do this? David isn't even her type!"

"I could bite her on the nose. Nothing looks good with a swollen nose."

He made me laugh a little. I reached up and rubbed his ears, and Cato jumped into my lap and settled there with happy pussyfoots. A happy cat always helps me to relax and having him here meant a great deal today.

I glanced at Shakespeare.

"*Thine image and a name -- a name! Two separate -- yet most intimate things.*"

I sighed. This was my world, with a cat as my best friend and a crazed bird as my only other companion. I leaned back in the chair and forced myself to relax. I accepted I had lost David. Maybe, after I got through the rest of this mess, I could somehow work things out, but I had far more important worries than my romantic future.

"I think there might be dragons," I said very softly, as

though I didn't even want to admit such a thing aloud.

"Like you think dragons might really exist, right?" Cato said, his head coming up, his large eyes blinking. "Not like *I think there might be dragons here on this side of the Edge.* Because if there are dragons out there, I'm never leaving the house again."

"I'll have cases of food delivered for you."

"Oh." He lowered his head and tried to bury it in the crook of my arm. "I don't want to know."

I wanted to bury my head as well and hope everything went away. Instead, I spent a fruitless hour trying to reach someone at home. Twice I saw my father -- a relief, at least, in a day where everything else had gone wrong -- but I couldn't contact him, and he didn't even glance my way.

I wondered if the others still had troubles though I believed no one had problems worse than mine.

I got back up, letting Cato have the warm spot on the chair, and went to the kitchen to find something to eat. My shoulder ached and my head pounded, and every time I thought about Aletta and David the headache tripled. If I'd a spell to erase them both from my memory, I would have done so. I needed clear thoughts.

Over a bowl of soup, I watched the snow slow and stop, and even start to melting as the clouds parted and sunlight spread over the world.

"I'm going to talk to the pigeons," I said. "They might have heard something. I'll ward the house and this time I'm not giving any kind of key to Aletta."

"Good," Cato said. His nose twitched. "Vegetable beef?"

I laughed and poured the remainder into his bowl and put good bird food out for Shakespeare, who at least didn't try to bite me this time. I couldn't say I blamed him for being upset about Aletta and David.

Then I left the house, sloshing through the wet snow. Any other time I would have loved this weather. Late spring storms are wonderful if for no other reason than the snow won't last for long.

I drove down the slippery streets and headed for the park. No cats sat outside at Mrs. Hale's house -- not in this weather. A few people scooped sidewalks, and kids made a snowman though he melted even as they patted him together. I'm unsure why, but I gave their creation a little whisper of magic to hold together, which wasn't hard with the amount of magic in the air -- and the snow. I wanted them to have fun and bring laugher back in the world.

Not a single pigeon showed up at the park, and in the scheme of things that didn't shock me at all. They hadn't been gone long though; feathers sat atop the snow by their barn. I opened the bag of bird seed and spread a good amount inside the door. At least the bag felt lighter on the way back to the car.

What more could I do? I got in the car and drove away, but turned abruptly at the next corner when I realized I had been heading towards David's hotel. I didn't want to go anywhere near there -- or the Bear Camp and remember the meals with David, though I'd have to get over the aversion to the last one or starve. I ate more meals there than I did at home.

There was one other place to go this morning. I headed towards the outskirts of town and found the sign to The Rookery. Birds flew away as I approached the building, and I felt better already for seeing them, though I couldn't quite catch what they said.

I slipped inside the building's door, tapping snow from my boots, and glancing around at the tall cages holding parrots, cockatoos and macaws, all of whom watched me with interest. Several cages of cockatiels sat scattered through the large room. This wasn't going to be easy.

"Kat!" Deb said, coming into the room. "Did the recording work?"

I crossed to her and spoke quietly because I didn't want every bird in the place realizing they understood me. That had happened before and the reaction had unsettled Deb and Richard.

"No. I want to try something different. I want to adopt -- buy -- another bird. Something smaller than Shakespeare so he doesn't feel threatened."

"Hmmm . . . yes, I can see where something like that might work," she agreed.

Birds stood in a dozen cages, and a tank of lovely fish sat against the left wall. Neither of the two shop cats were around, but they were indoor cats and I couldn't have learned anything new from them anyway.

As we walked through the cages, I listened to the birds babbling away, but most of what they said concerned their next meal.

"I think a cockatiel. A friendly one."

"Oh, I have several of those!"

I needed to find one in particular which proved impossible with Deb following me around and showing me each bird. The talkative little cockatiel who spoke parrot didn't show himself. I hoped they hadn't sold him. The little guy on the recording might be the companion I needed for Shakespeare.

So I made a little disaster with a few falling boxes for Deb to go handle in the back room. Nothing serious. Once she was out of range I moved to the middle of the shop and glanced around.

"Okay," I said. "I'm looking for Gaylord."

"Now there is a neat trick," a bird said from behind me. I recognized the voice and turned to find a cockatiel clinging to the side of a cage, the yellow feathers on top of his head standing high as he tilted his head back and forth. "I didn't know humans could speak a bird tongue."

"I'm not human. How did you learn parrot? I heard you talking to Telora on the recording they made for me."

"Is that what they were doing? Huh. I half hoped they really planned to kill the feather brained princess." He shifted his hold, his head tilted to the side. "You try spending all your adult life in a cage next to something you can't communicate with. I was bored. I'm still bored."

"How would you like to go home with me?"

His little feet did a quick nervous dance, and then he stopped and stared. "What's the hitch?"

Smart bird. Just what I wanted. "I have an African Gray who only speaks in human quotes. I'm hoping you might get him to talk about some things going on. Bad things. It could be dangerous to go with me."

"Danger is my . . . well, it would be my game if I weren't stuck here," he said with a dramatic sigh. I suspected Telora wasn't the only drama queen in the shop. "Another damned parrot, huh?"

"Afraid so. And a cat."

"Both? So you want to take me from the limbo of purgatory and lead me straight to hell?"

"Do you want out of here?" I asked.

A dark blue hyacinth macaw came over to the side of the cage beside us and leaned out, trying to pluck at my sleeve.

"Nice person. Lovely person. Take me. I'm such a pretty bird." Telora fluffed up her feathers and preened.

"Wouldn't you want a pretty bird? See all my lovely feathers? You don't want such a scrawny little thing. Such a little thing is hardly worthy to be called a bird --"

Gaylord tried to reach out and bite her. She pulled back with a little squeak of dismay. He looked up at me. "Take me out of here. A cat has to be better company than this fluffed up feather duster."

Deb came back. Her eyes went wide when she found me standing by the cage with Gaylord and she shook her head in worry before she even got to us.

"This one is . . . well, he has an attitude, Kat," she said, tapping the cage. Gaylord tried to bite her, and she drew her finger back in haste.

"Yes, I can see," I said. I laughed and put my hand out.

She made a sound of warning, but Gaylord came over and rubbed against my fingers.

"Well," she said. She shook her head as though to dislodge a vision that couldn't possibly be true. "I've never seen Gaylord act so politely."

"Well, you know me. I seem to attract odd, troubled birds."

Gaylord looked up at me, and I knew he considered biting -- and thought better of it.

"Well, let's get you set up."

We worked our way through the shop. Gaylord gave me hints -- very loud ones -- on the type of food and toys he wanted. I gave in. After all, I was taking him into danger and to be the companion to a parrot. I figured I owed him something for the problems he would face.

Richard arrived and looked equally shocked when he learned I intended to take Gaylord. I felt sorry for the little guy, but he had brought most of this on himself.

I took Gaylord out of the cage and put him into the

smaller one I had bought for him. He wouldn't be in it for long, but I had to make a show for the humans. I had ways of making even recalcitrant birds behave at home without a visible cage, and he'd have a perch like Shakespeare's.

"If you have any problems you can bring him back," Richard said as he helped gather up the supplies to take out to the car. "It's our normal policy and goes double this time. Gaylord has been a problem since the day he hatched. He seems to have taken to you though. Maybe this is a good match."

From the look Gaylord gave him I suspected the little cockatiel understood not only parrot but a good amount of human as well. Very smart bird.

"We'll be fine," I said. "Thanks."

Richard went out ahead of us, and Deb went back to the other room, shaking her head in obvious wonder. As we headed out the door we passed a cage with four lovely little female cockatiels, all of them fluttering around and giving Gaylord a few 'come-on' whistles.

"Buy me one of those?" Gaylord asked as we passed.

"Maybe later, if things work out."

"Huzza! Things are looking up!"

When I had driven a block away from the shop I opened the cage and let Gaylord come and sit on my shoulder. He looked around, nodding.

"So this is the real world, huh? Doesn't seem so bad. What's the white stuff?"

"Snow. Water so cold it's frozen."

"Gah." He did a little mock shiver and jumped down on the steering wheel, holding on tight as I turned left and right.

"The snow will go away soon. But you'll be in a nice warm house, anyway. The world's not safe outside for small birds."

"I'm tough. I can --"

A semi-truck and trailer went through the intersection in front of us. Gaylord screamed, threw himself backwards off the steering wheel and tried to dig his way into my jacket. I fought very, very hard not to laugh.

"You can come back out," I said. "The truck is gone. But those are some of the things you'll find out in the real world."

"I'll stick to a cage," he said, his voice muffled.

But he came back out later and cautiously held to my shoulder. I drove at a nice, sedate pace, enjoying the calm.

As we went past Mrs. Hale's house he saw cats and made some rather rude sounds.

"Be nice. Those are some of my friends."

"Friends? You have a pet cat and cat friends? What kind of weirdo are you?"

"The kind who can speak to cats and birds."

"Oh, that's got to be great," he said. "I can imagine what the cats have to say: *Could you please hand me that cute little bird there, if you don't mind? It's just far too much trouble to leap up and grab him.*"

Well, he had that remarkably right.

We started up the hill and headed towards my house, and as the place came in view I found David's car parked in front, and David sitting on the porch swing, reading the paper.

He'd come back!

"Into the cage. The human doesn't know about me and birds and cats."

"Ah. Okay. Cover me up, will you? I was cold going from the shop to the car."

"No problem."

I got him into the cage and put blanket over the top. Then I grabbed the cage, the food and the toys and headed toward the house, smiling --

"Where the hell have you been?" David demanded as he stood, throwing the newspaper down on the swing. He took a slight limping step towards me. "We were going hiking today. I have work to do."

He didn't even look like the David I had known. He'd pulled his hair back and stood with his legs slightly apart and his hands on his hips and appeared belligerent and angry. Part of me wanted to tell him to go to hell.

David must have seen the emotions in my face and something changed, but I couldn't say the new look was for the better, though not quite as belligerent.

"I want to get this job done," he said, but in a tone which made him sound as though the job was the last thing he cared to do.

He wanted the job done and to get away from me. Fine. As much as being with him hurt, we'd get his damned pictures so he would leave. Maybe the spell I had used would wear off once he got away.

"Let me put Gaylord in the house. I know a couple quick hikes we can make, even in this weather."

He nodded and stalked away, slipping a little on the steps as he lost his footing. I wondered about drugs, but a magical check showed nothing but the same repulsion spell -- stronger than I normally would have been able to create. All the magic in the air helped, no doubt.

The wind blew, and I grabbed the newspaper before it blew off the swing. He'd been reading the arts section about a museum display in Denver. The color pictures showed gold and gems. I wished I could have read the paper with David -- the David I had first met. History fascinated me, and I knew nothing about the Golden Horde and the Far East.

"Hey, you with the hands. It's friggin' cold out here, you know."

"Sorry."

I opened the door, glad I'd kept David out. I hated those feelings, but I did not trust the way he had begun acting and --

And I had to stop obsessing over David. My relationship -- or actually the lack of one at this point -- was the last thing I needed to be worried about in the midst of this mess.

I watched as David fumbled to get his car door open. Something had him upset. This had to be my fault because of the damned stupid spell I had set. I would have to live with the results.

I took the blanket off the top of the cage and carried Gaylord across the room to where Shakespeare sat. The larger bird stared when I brought Gaylord out of the cage and put him on the perch next to him. He even sidled away a little.

"Ah come on, big guy. I took a bath today," Gaylord said in parrot.

Well, Gaylord had Shakespeare's attention at least.

Outside David hit the horn several times.

"So what's wrong with the creep?" Gaylord said shaking his head.

"He's not --" I almost said he wasn't a creep. But actually, at the moment, he was. "He won't be around for much longer."

"Yeah, whatever. Just make sure he doesn't mess with me," Gaylord said, clicking his beak several times. "The guy is odd, you know?"

"I know," I said. "Don't worry. Can I trust you two not to get into trouble if I leave you out?"

"Hey, I'll be a perfect angel," Gaylord said.

Should I believe him? I ignored the occasional horn blasts and worked hard at curbing my anger. At least he hadn't brought Aletta along, which cheered me up a little. I put food and water out for both birds, smiling when Shakespeare checked out what I had given to the smaller bird.

"Hey, how about a little food for me, too," Cato said, walking into the room and jumping up on the chair nearby.

Gaylord landed on my arm and leaned down over Cato's face. He fluffed out his feathers and half raised his wings.

"So, you're the cat, huh? Think you're hot stuff do you, Mr. Fuzzy? Well don't mess with me, cat. I'm faster than you'll ever be and you're never going to fly, butterball. So don't even think about trying for me."

Cato watched the little bird twittering away, his head tilted as he listened. Gaylord snapped his beak a few times and stopped. Cato glanced back at me.

"So this is him, huh? Cute little guy," Cato said.

"What did he say?" Gaylord demanded staring the cat in the face.

"He said you look very dangerous," I answered.

"Good."

Content that he ruled the roost, so to speak, Gaylord went back up on the perch with Shakespeare, who still eyed him with open speculation. I trusted them both, but I whispered a little spell to keep them from going at each other if something upset them.

The horn honked, long and loud. I gritted my teeth.

"Food?" Cato asked, hopefully.

I almost waved him off, but David could wait a few minutes longer while I got my temper under control. I gave Cato his food and got myself a glass of water and aspirin.

When I stepped out of the house he had started to honk but he stopped as I stalked down to the car. He, wisely, said nothing at all when I got inside the car. We drove away in silence.

CHAPTER THIRTEEN

David said nothing as we left Estes Park and headed to the place I had so loved sharing with him just yesterday. He had trouble keeping the car under control, and I feared my emotions were affecting the vehicle. I tried to clamp back down when it almost died for a third time. I wanted this finished.

The ranger at the gate -- Tom something, a new guy -- warned us to be careful of the weather and said most of the park was closed.

David drove to Deer Mountain Trailhead. Maybe he thought the name would be a good omen, and we'd spot animals, which might be true since we were far away from where the gargoyle had been.

My arm ached as I remembered the dawn encounter. I'd had a lousy day, from start to . . . well, I couldn't say to finish because it wasn't even quite noon yet. I dreaded the whole rest of the day. Things might actually get worse.

I glanced towards the sky, fearing I sensed magic moving through the low, gray clouds. As soon as we got out of the car, David stalked up the trail, the pack slung carelessly over his shoulder. The weight must have put him off balance because he kept slipping, even on the easy part of the climb. I wondered why he had me go along since he moved out of my line of sight. I didn't mind. Being alone on the trail gave me unexpected peace.

I love the wilds and the trees, which looked gorgeous in snow. The place made me wish I could do photography and take the pictures home to treasure forever. If I bought a camera and wrapped it in a close fitting anti-magic shield, I might be able to take some shots. I could do the same with a small printer. I'd never considered something of the sort before, but I would enjoy photography as a new way to share all I loved with others.

The idea cheered me and I turned my attention to what I wanted to write for this article. I spotted fresh deer prints and almost called David back but changed my mind when he stomped over a little rise ahead of me. I slowed and continued to enjoy this lovely walk. What had happened before -- and what would happen later -- didn't mean I shouldn't appreciate this pretty little area any less.

The first strong brush of a breeze brought a fall of snow though not as heavily as earlier in the day. I almost yelled to tell David saying we should turn back.

Not yet. This was only a little snow, and nothing dangerous. I figured if the snow grew worse or it got too cold, he would come back and we could leave. The snow came down in a beautiful veil of white and the breeze died down almost immediately. I stopped and breathed in the calm of the place. Though I lived in town, I belonged in the wild. I didn't spend enough time here anymore.

I closed my eyes and stood in the snow, listening to the whisper of the breeze through the trees. The sound is lovely as long as you don't mind the cold. I enjoyed the moment. Calm. I needed calm to face the battle to which I must return soon. I needed to remember my place in the world which was not chasing after a handsome human male.

Timber had praised me for using my head and thinking my way through problems. David was a problem on far too many levels. I had to get away from him.

Okay. I accepted the truth.

I opened my eyes and blinked --

Something moved in the falling snow to my right; something misty and horse-shaped.

I held my place and my breath, watching with a slow turn of my head. This wasn't a 'nearly ice' type of horse and rider like I had faced earlier today, praise all the gods, but rather one of the misty ones drifting through the storm as though circling me.

I found another -- and yet another at my back. I turned and marked the three closest to me, and a few a little farther away in the snow. Though aware of me, they came none closer.

Time to get David and get back to town.

Unfortunately, I couldn't see David at all now.

"Hey! David!" I shouted. The sound echoed through the silence, and he should have heard me, but I got no answer. Oh hell. I'd been a fool to let him go wandering off alone, especially when there were dangers here in the woods!

I hurried up the trail, watching his prints in the snow, searching for any signs of trouble with the horses and riders trailing along with me. The snow fell harder, and the wind grew sharp and cold. The calm and serenity of a few moments ago disappeared, and I feared I had made another stupid mistake.

If he had been hurt because --

The tree beside me moved.

I ducked as something swept over the top of my head. I dropped and rolled in the snow and came back up to my feet, spinning to find a hag of a tree sprite swinging at me with long, clawed fingers. Her desiccated skin hung like dead bark on her body, and her hair had long since lost the green of spring and turned to a dirty gray. The eyes staring at me flashed with red magic and she swung with a speed and strength I hadn't expected.

Damn! Another thing that shouldn't have gotten through to this reality! I began feeling put upon by the constant attention of creatures who wanted to do me harm. This time I acted quickly and decisively. I pulled the power up inside me and focused the magic in my hand, sending a wave of magic to immobilize her.

The spell bounced off her dead, bark-like skin and almost got me instead. I ducked as she laughed -- a sound reminiscent of twigs breaking. Not pleasant.

She leapt at me.

Slow, at least. Something in my favor. What should I do? She had shrugged off my magic. I might outrun her -- but I had nowhere to get help.

She swung as I backed out of her range.

The riders closed in on me. I decided to shove one of the mist horses to see if I could move the creature aside, but I hit a wall before I got close. Magic, of course, and this ward had a tag aimed right at me, so they could move in and out of the circle, but I couldn't. Someone had set the spell to keep me in place. If I didn't get through the circle, I wouldn't be able to escape the tree sprite. Even if I called to David, he had no way to fight her.

Hell, hell, hell!

A rider reached for me, but he wasn't corporeal enough and I only experienced a cold pass of his hand through my head. Not pleasant but it could have been worse.

I heard an unexpected growl over my right shoulder and a large, and very rare, mountain lion bounded through the snow.

They're beautiful animals and almost hunted to extinction. She appeared to have run far, and she came to a panting stop as she navigated her way past the horses. The ward didn't stop her. She laid her ears back and growled at the tree hag.

"Careful," I said. "She's dangerous. And she's not from this world."

"I know," the big cat answered. She stalked forward, putting herself between me and the creature. "We've been noticing a lot of things not right lately. They seem to be aimed at you."

"Yes, I noticed that part," I said, keeping a wary eye on everything around me. "I can't use magic on this one."

"Well let's see if claws and teeth work better."

I almost warned her to stay back, but the cat made a leap straight at the neck of the tree sprite. She didn't seem to have any trouble sinking her teeth into the creature and bearing her to the ground. The sprite got in a couple cuts and I leapt forward, grabbing one arm, risking wounds as the cat bit harder. The sprite bellowed, and I jabbed my fist right into her face when she twisted around and tried to bite me.

There was something satisfactory about using brute force when you're already having a lousy day and creatures keep trying to kill you. I hit her once and her head snapped back. She grunted in surprise. The cat had almost bitten through one arm and the sprite looked worried.

So I hit her again.

The wind kicked up in a fierce wave of cold that my fingers almost froze to her arm. I lifted my other hand to shield my eyes. The riders galloped off, but not in the direction David had gone.

The tree sprite yelled, bucked and got free of both of us. She scrambled off, lost almost against the bark of other trees and the veil of snow. I started to follow --

"I'll get her. You get out of here," my cat savior said. She stopped to lick a wound on her side, which I healed with a touch of my fingers. Great golden eyes stared up at me. "Thank you. But go."

"She's dangerous. I should --"

"There's worse than her in the woods right now. Get the human and get out of here. Don't come back until you're ready to fight the real battle."

Wisdom. Why had I come here, knowing the danger? Why did I bring David, who not only couldn't protect himself from my enemies, but also kept me from using my powers?

"Thank you. I'll get David and leave." I healed the wound on my arm, straightened my clothing, and even sent a rush of snow over the area where we'd fought, covering the marks and the blood.

The mountain lion took off, bounding through the snow after her prey. I wished her luck and watched until she disappeared into the snow. The riders hadn't followed them. The big cat would have a chance.

I took stock of myself once more, making certain I showed no outward signs of the battle before I hurried up the trail. David was closer than I expected, which almost put him in danger. I had been stupid to let my anger overcome my good sense!

He hadn't gotten out a camera, and he stood on the

trail as though he didn't have a clue what to do now.

Fine.

"Let's go," I said. "The weather is changing, and it's not safe to stay out here any longer."

"A little snow is going to scare you off?"

"Oh stop with the damned macho crap," I said and startled him this time. He must not have realized he could push me so far that I lost my temper. "Come on. You obviously aren't going to take any pictures anyway."

He tapped the backpack, frowning, as though he intended to argue with me. A rider arrived not far behind him, a faint shape in the falling snow. I feared they might make another attack, and I considered leaving David to go take care of the trouble.

I took a deep breath and prepared to cast a quick spell to compel him to go with me. I didn't want to, especially considering how much the last spell had backfired, but we needed to get away.

As I lifted my hand to use magic, David moved, going past me with a slight snarl.

"Fine. We'll go back."

I dropped the spell and turned to follow him. He moved as though something made him angry as he limped unsteadily down the trail. I wondered when he had hurt his leg and wondered if I should help, even now. We reached the car without trouble, even though the wind had kicked up and the snow fell harder. Riders moved in the trees, but David saw nothing out of place.

He drove back towards town, silent and sullen, and still having trouble with the vehicle. I found a touch of magic on the car, something no doubt left in place to protect it from Aletta when she rode with him, but apparently not enough to shield it from my continuing bad mood.

I gave a wave to Tom as we went past and headed out. Almost immediately I spotted movement at the side of the car. A rider kept pace with us, and another took a spot on the other side and heading into town didn't seem to deter them at all.

More of them paced the streets as we came back into Estes Park. I shivered, my breath catching at the sight of such blatant magic right there in the heart of technology and during the day. Too many, everywhere. The army I had seen on the other side of the Edge must have come through while I did other work. Damn, damn, damn.

David didn't notice. He seemed oblivious to everything, in fact. Maybe he had a headache. I couldn't feel sorry for him or call up the energy to care.

A couple riders were close by the house, but they galloped away as we pulled up. As the car came to a stop David looked at me and the glare remained. So did mine.

"I'm going back to the hotel and have lunch with Aletta."

"Have a nice time." I didn't care; I wanted him away from me.

He snarled something I didn't quite understand as I got out of his car and he drove away without crashing into my car or a tree. I watched him go, a couple riders trailing after him, which worried me -- and didn't. They were everywhere. I worried about everyone at this point. Besides, he did have Aletta.

I trudged up to the house and threw the door open.

"*Oh human love! Thou spirit given, on Earth of all we hope in Heaven!*"

I sighed when I saw the cockatiel shaking his head in disbelief. "No luck, huh?" I asked.

"Not so you'd notice," Gaylord said. "Sorry."

"I expect this might take some time. You've barely had a couple hours." I threw my jacket on the chair and went to the kitchen, pulling open the refrigerator. Cato showed up at the sound.

"I can just look at you and know this is a chocolate day," the cat said. "Things did not go well?"

"Oh, everything went swell. The riders hemmed me in while a tree sprite tried to kill me. I got away with the help of a mountain lion. Then I had to deal with David, who seems to believe the world revolves around him."

I reached for the fudge I had stuck back in the corner of a shelf where the temptation wouldn't draw my immediate attention. Fudge -- chocolate in general -- is humanities greatest gift to the universe. I also pulled out a piece of cheese for Cato. I hate wallowing alone.

"The riders are those guys on horses, right? Not something new?" Animals notice things humans are too logical to see which makes them good companions for fae. "We've been seeing a lot of them out in the yard today. They make me nervous."

"They're not good news, that's for sure."

I sat down at the table. Cato leapt up beside me. I broke up a piece of cheese for him. Then I stood and got the birds some fancy crackers. Like I said, I don't like to wallow alone. I'd be a pathetic drunk.

"What are you going to do now?" Cato asked as I sat again.

"I haven't a clue. Try to reach home, I suppose." A rider went by at the edge my property. They seemed to keep some distance away. That might be the work of the ward. Glad it worked for something.

I also felt out the Edge. The damned thing had moved again, and this time even closer to the town. Everywhere I turned something hit me in the gut and I wanted to go curl up in a ball until all the trouble went away.

I wanted -- needed -- help, and I wouldn't get any from the only other fae within the area. I had to take care of this myself, and I didn't know what to do.

So I ate my fudge in silence while thoughts crowded their way through my head. Cato ate his cheese. Then he leaned over and rubbed his head against my shoulder. I petted him and he purred for a moment before he sat back.

"You'll do all right, Kat. You really will. I know it."

"Cato, I don't --"

"You don't have answers. You'll find them. Don't let David get you down. You know humans are fickle."

"Yeah." I sighed and ate the last piece of my fudge. I'd have to make more, and soon the way this week was going. "I need answers. You're right."

"Where are you going to get them?"

"I'll try to reach home." I stood and headed for the chair. "Afterwards, I'll go talk to the pigeons if they're around."

"I haven't talked to any of the cats for a couple days. As soon as the storm dies down, I'll go ask around," Cato said, though he watched the window with disgust. "Despite how I dislike the snow."

"I don't want you out there, Cato. It's dangerous --"

"There are dangers everywhere," he said, a statement of fact. "I'll be careful and I expect you to do the same."

I nodded agreement.

"I'll go nap now since this will be a long night," he said and headed back to the bedroom.

I spent the next hour in a futile attempt to reach home. The connection seemed to have gotten worse instead of better. I wondered if this problem also came as a backlash of my own unsteady powers. Everything had been going wrong after all.

"You don't look happy," Gaylord said, coming to sit on the side of the chair. "I know things are bad. I mean, I don't understand the ramifications of what you were saying to the fuzz ball, but I could tell from the tone that you talked about some dire stuff. And those big white things out there, the half human things -- man, I ain't never seen anything like them. I about laid an egg when I saw one riding past."

"They aren't good. But they're so much the real problem as a manifestation of worse things. They'll be a true problem when they get completely into this world, but right now they're still half illusion. And those are men riding on horses."

"I've heard of horses." Gaylord turned to the window and shook his head so hard his entire body followed the action. "Never thought they'd be so big. Damned dangerous things, aren't they?"

I almost told him I'd seen far worse, but why should I worry the little guy? "Yeah, they are dangerous. Especially when the people riding them are not friendly."

"And they're after you?"

"Yes. You want to return to the nice safe bird store now?"

"Are you joking?" he asked, startled. "Yeah, those things are dangerous. But here I am in a nice warm house, free to fly around, with a parrot who doesn't jabber about how pretty she is all day and even the cat sleeps most of the time. I'd be an idiot to go back after coming here."

"This place isn't safe. What would you do if you had to face down one of those horses?"

"Jab it right in the eye. And the rider, too."

Really, that sounded like a good plan. I nodded and petted him on the head. Cato had been right about there being nowhere safe anyway. This house had wards. Gaylord might be safer in here than anywhere else in town considering I had seen the horse and riders everywhere.

"I've got to go out. I'll be back before sunset, if I can. If I'm not, stay inside and keep out of reach of anything if it breaks in. If Cato tries to urge you to do something, follow his lead."

"You want me to follow the orders of a cat."

"Yes."

"I'm supposed to trust him, am I?"

"Yes."

"You keep him well fed, do you?"

"Very well fed."

"Okay then, but I have to tell you, if he tries anything funny, I'll take a chunk of out of his cute little furry ass."

"Next time I see him, I'll warn him."

"Good." I stood and Gaylord fluttered up to stand on my shoulder. "Be careful out there. Things don't feel right. I'm worried."

"I'll be careful." I felt all soft inside, thinking about the warning from both the cat and the bird.

"My breast her shield in wintry weather," Shakespeare said and bobbed his head several times.

"Thank you," I replied, believing he had said much the same thing as Gaylord. I had good friends.

I put my jacket back on and stepped out onto the porch. The riders closed in a little. I sent a wave of magic towards them, and the horses bucked as they hit the wall that hadn't been there until now. The wind kicked up as well, which meant there was too much magic in the air. What a surprise.

I got to the car without a problem, and drove down to the park with the riders tagging after me, but at a good distance. I watched them in my rear view mirror, a trail of oddly shaped white smoke following me.

There were not many other cars on the road and the riders avoided moving vehicles by prodigious leaps and bounds. If there had been no other people out, I would have tried my luck at running at a few of them.

I had lost a lot of my 'don't hurt others' feeling in the last day. I hoped I got it back after this trouble ended.

At the park, I spotted a flutter of pigeon wings at the barn and grabbed the bag of food, heading there. However, when I arrived and stepped into the building I couldn't find a single bird.

"What the hell is going on?"

Riders had trailed in behind me. I sent them off with an angry wave of my hand and a flash of magic, thought getting rid of them wouldn't be as easy when they got more solid. I wanted answers from the pigeons -- or from any other bird. I reached out to find them --

And I touched the hint of a spell purposely keeping things away from me. I found a magical shell about four yards beyond my physical reach. The only birds and cats who had come near me were either my own, the ones in the shop who couldn't be repelled before they came within my shell, and the hawk -- who had said she'd fought to be near me.

I'd been an idiot. *Again.* I tried to learn who had made the spell. Aletta? I truly didn't believe she had that kind of finesse. Someone else might be here. I couldn't grasp the key that would have told me about the spell maker, and I had to concentrate on destroying the magic instead.

The spell came apart in strands -- birds here, cats there,

and a more general touch for everything else. No wonder animals had run from me when I approached them in the wilds. The work had been intricate and fae-made, beyond a doubt. The world changed around me as I tore the spell apart, a subtle shift. I hadn't realized how deaf I'd been until I heard bright, bird voices.

"Kat, Kat, Kat!" The pigeons cooed as they flocked down around me. I poured out handfuls of grain, but they seemed more interested in me than the food.

"Dark things," Pretty said, stopping by my shoes and staring up at me. "Dark times and creatures wandering the night that should not be here."

I wasn't particularly surprised to find there might be more trouble. I would have been far more shocked if the pigeons hadn't given me news of something else gone wrong. It had been that kind of week.

"Where do they go in the daylight?" I asked, leaning down to her.

"Into the sewers. Back to the mountains. At night they wander everywhere. They look at things."

"They are planning something," I said.

She bobbed her head and took interest in the grain. I let her eat and listened to the others -- fragments of descriptions liberally mixed with pleasure at having me back. Their happiness filled me with joy and I held the emotion even when a horseman came to the barn door.

"Be gone," I ordered. The rider spied on me to take the news back to someone. I reached with a quick spell and tried to make him go and when it didn't work, I struck the ghost rider with a bolt of magical energy. The power had come of pure frustration, and the careless expenditure put me down to my knees, panting and dizzy.

"Careful Kat!" Pretty warned, her wings flapping in

distress.

I watched with grim satisfaction as small pieces of the rider scatter on the breeze, tendrils pulled away in waves of mist until he disappeared.

I wish I had such power to attack all of them. Despite the extra magic in the air, I had trouble pulling enough in to recover from the loss. I had so little natural magic left that my skin had gone pale and my body translucent. More loss too soon and I'd no longer be me. I might reform after a while, but I'd have lost this life along with the memories of who I am.

I was still quite sane enough to think life as a spirit on the wind didn't sound like an interesting adventure.

I sat in the cold with the pigeons dancing around me. They ate the grain I offered and sang happy songs about me. Not everything in the world had gone bad.

The extra magic in the air finally helped me recover. When I could stand without feeling ill, I bade farewell to the pigeons and walked back out into the snow-filled day. The riders had moved out of my immediate range so I guess my show at least had done some good.

Pretty came to the door behind me and stopped as a dusting of snow covered her feathers. "Careful Kat," she cooed and shifted from one foot to the other. "Careful."

"I will be," I promised, happy for the warning from a friend who cared.

A flock of chickadees flittered around the limbs of a tree nearby and shouted greetings as I headed for my car. They had nothing to add to what the pigeons had said, but I didn't mind. Having them nearby soothed me.

I drove straight home. Birds had gathered in the trees outside my place and I had the suspicion I now had more guards than I could feed. I would have to go back to The

Rookery or one of the co-ops and pick up more bird food.

I smiled as I went up the porch steps and opened the door -- then looked back with a start as half a dozen cats charged across the yard. I stepped inside and held the door open for them as they ran straight into the house with Trouble in the lead.

"Holy shit!" Gaylord shouted. He leapt from the perch to the top of Shakespeare's head and from the startled parrot to the top of my china cabinet.

"They won't hurt you," I told him.

He didn't believe me, no doubt because some of the cats watched him with what could only be a hint of hunger and the lust for a hunt.

"Yeah, right. I'll just stay up here."

Trouble rubbed against my leg, which he'd never done before. The others stood back and waited. I had never met two of them.

"We tried to reach you," Trouble said, his voice a loud rumble, deep and strong. "But something kept pushing us away. Some cats wanted to stay clear of you after what happened to Pawford and the others, but I knew their deaths weren't your fault. And you always done right by us. You gave us fish, and we never starved. I figure we owe you."

"Thank you," I said. They would get plenty of food today. "What --"

Cato stepped into the room, yawning and stretching. Fur fluffed up all around the room and hisses filled the air -- normal cat greetings. Cato's tail fluffed out and his ears went back, but before I gave a warning to either side, he shook his head and took a step backwards.

"I'll just go to go nap in the closet again."

He turned around and walked away.

Trouble watched Cato retreat, his head to the side, plainly perplexed. He looked back up at me.

"We're still trying to catch those little creatures," Trouble said. He gave an impatient flick of his tail. The peripix must have been frustrating them all. "We get a few on the street, but they've taken up nesting in places where I suspect they shouldn't be. The power plant, the cable and computer buildings --"

"Oh hell," I said with another of those rollercoaster surges of adrenaline. "They'll cut the power to everything before too long!"

"Maybe it's what they want," Trouble suggested. The other cats nodded agreement.

"I don't think peripix have the intelligence to plan --" I stopped, remembering what the pigeons had told me. "They have help."

"Yeah. We seen things at night," a little gray cat spoke at last. She shivered. "Big things and they eat cats. We stay clear of them. But sometimes the little things go wandering around with them."

"Stay clear of them. Don't risk yourselves," I said. Green, gold and blue eyes turn my way with a little disdain. Cats never like to hear that they're small and weak. I quickly rethought my statement. "I need you guys to keep watch places where I can't go. Someone purposely made certain you couldn't talk to me because you're important. I need you."

Those words suited them better. Trouble rubbed my legs again.

"I know you've seen the riders," Trouble said. "The humans don't notice them yet, but they will soon."

"That's what I fear."

"We'll keep watch." He turned and headed back out

the door. Outside the birds flittered around, and I heard groups heading off on recon work. Things appeared well organized.

The riders hovered, just beyond the yard. There would be more problems from them soon. We were running out of daylight and I feared the problems we would face tonight.

CHAPTER FOURTEEN

I didn't expect Aletta to show up at my house. She walked along the street, looking like a fashion model who had lost her way from a magazine cover. She paused and glanced into the trees, frowning at the birds. With a wave of her hand, she sent them all scattering.

I was not in the mood for her games, so I met her on the porch, hoping to get her away all the faster.

"Kitty." She took a step forward as though she expected me to invite her in for tea. I didn't. She gave a petulant little frown that probably melted men's hearts, but the look did nothing at all for me.

"I'm working, Aletta. Or haven't you noticed the problems?"

"Problems?" she asked and then gave a little wave of her perfect fingers. "Oh, the Edge moving. I talked to my mother. She told me it moved all over the world, but everything is stable now."

She had talked to her mother? I couldn't get through -- but I said nothing. "I meant the riders, Aletta."

"What riders?" she asked.

They weren't here. None in sight. Hell. I didn't need more pressure, so I didn't even pursue it with her. She wouldn't be any more help than she had been so far anyway.

"What are you doing here?" I asked.

"I thought David might be here, working," she said with a bright predatory smile. "We need to make plans for tonight."

Somehow I kept my hands from rising and smacking her with a nice good, ugly spell like a big wart on the end of her nose to make people realized what kind of bitch . . . um, witch she was.

"As you can tell, he's not here. Nor is his car." I kept my voice calm. I felt obligated, I don't know why, to say more. "He's been acting strangely, Aletta."

"He's a human." She gave a wave of her perfect hand again and dismissed my concerns.

Fine. I had given her the warming. "I have work to do. David will turn up at the hotel."

"Well you don't have to be rude. Honestly, I don't understand how any of your family got to hold so many posts. You're all so bad tempered."

"You want to take over for me?" I asked.

She made a little noise of disgust. "Can't even be bothered to do the work? Well I have better things to do."

She turned and stomped her way across the yard. I watched until she disappeared around the curve of the road. What the hell had brought her here?

"Don't like her, don't like her!" a pair of ruby-crowned kinglets shouted as they swept into the tree.

"Well, you're not alone there."

I went into the house annoyed and bad tempered, which aggravated me more since Aletta had already accused me of such behavior. Even Gaylord took one look at me and decided meticulously examining one of his new toys might be a really good idea right now.

I did the dishes . . . by hand and without magic. I still needed time to recover my powers before I faced the enemy tonight. I needed to keep busy. Cato came out, lapped at the water in his dish and nibbled the dry food I'd put in the other one. He said nothing either. We were all waiting for something to happen.

I found two dust bunnies when I swept. I cuddled the little things for a couple minutes and then put them in the holding cell. I considered following them like Alice down the hole.

Since Aletta had talked to her mother I tried contacting my father. I settled into the comfortable brown chair and closed my eyes. Cato settled in my lap, purring when I petted him. Better. Much better.

I still couldn't reach home, though and gave up after a few minutes, knowing I shouldn't waste any more magic.

I wanted help. I wanted to talk to someone for advice because this was way over my head. There was no one but Aletta, and she was no help at all.

I sat in the chair and closed my eyes, but the calm didn't return. The night would fall soon, and I feared that sunset would bring far too much trouble for me to handle. What should I do about the peripix? Why were they purposely nesting in places where they would do the most damage? Why was someone directing them there?

Why did they want the city powerless?

No technology.

This time I shivered. Nothing from the other side would purposely mess with humans like this unless they planned to do something big and powerful, and very much against all the rules, laws, and covenants.

I still had no idea what to do, so I decided everything

needed dusting. Busy work sometimes helped in an odd way.

I dusted the china cabinet, straightened things by the birds, with both of them quiescent and uncomplaining. I moved on to the bookshelves. Those needed more work since I hadn't straightened them after someone had broken in and knocked everything down. I pulled books and put them in order and then stacked magazines in their little spot.

The top was a nature magazine where I had an article published. I flipped through the pages to my page and remembered how wonderful and simple everything had seemed. I wanted to return to writing and not watch the gathering of disaster right outside my window.

Yes, the riders were back, and they appeared more solid. Darkness was less than an hour away and then the other things would hit the streets.

I started to close the magazine when something caught my eye: An article on the Mojave Desert, with pictures by David Carter. My heart thumped, and I flipped the page open, staring at the lovely shots. He had talent. I wanted to work with the man who had taken those pictures and who loved the world. I wanted *that* David back.

On the last page, at the bottom of the article, I found a picture of David Carter standing beside a tripod, the camera ready.

An age-lined face and slate gray hair. Glasses.

Not the David Carter I had met.

Something caught in my throat. Someone must have mixed up the pictures. No, the writer was not David Carter either. I grabbed a handful of magazines and went to the table, using magic to locate the David Carter articles. Two more had photos of him. One was from an entirely different magazine.

All of them showed the same, older man. None of them were my David.

I sat on the chair and stared while an entirely new fear made a little hollow in my stomach. The man here in town -- the one who had spent time with me, whom I had even kissed -- was not David Carter the photographer. I swallowed the sour taste in my mouth and shivered.

If he wasn't David Carter, who was he?

Aletta needed to be told. As much as I disliked Aletta, I would not leave her with this imposter without a warning. I tried to reach her by magic but failed. Of course I did -- but she might have blocked me.

"I'm going out." I stood and glanced at Cato, still in the chair. "David isn't -- he's not who he pretends to be, and I have to go warn Aletta."

"Are you sure?" Cato asked. "You really have to tell her?"

"Yeah, I do. I don't like her either, but I can't ignore this."

"I guess that's what makes you better than her," he said with a sigh. He stood and stretched as I headed for my jacket. "I'm coming with you."

"This might be dangerous --"

"Well *duh*." He looked at me with a little frustration this time as the tip of his tail twitched. "In case you haven't noticed, staying here isn't safe, either. Nothing is right now."

"I'm going in the car."

"Good. We don't have time for a nice leisurely walk and I sure don't want to fly in this weather."

I almost argued because I didn't want one of my friends with me in case I ran into trouble. But hell, he'd done well to watch my back. I needed help. He was willing.

"Come on."

We left the house. I asked the birds outside to keep an eye on things and find me if there was any trouble. Then I gave Cato one more chance to go back inside the house. He climbed into the car ahead of me.

When I pulled out of the parking spot, he stood up with his paws on the dashboard and stared.

"The riders seem more -- I don't know --" he said, shaking his head.

"Solid?" I offered as I started the car.

"Anxious."

While I had been noting the riders, I hadn't studied them. The horses pranced more, and the riders sat straighter and glanced towards the sun as though to measure the time until sundown.

Damn.

I headed down the hill. Cato turned to watch behind the car. "Yeah, we have a parade following us. Can you lead them out of town?"

"Worth a try."

I drove to Highway 34 but near Lake Estes the riders stopped, milled, and turned around and I had the odd feeling I'd been the one run out of town. I turned around at the first cabin driveway without high snow drifts -- the stuff was melting but not fast enough -- and headed back into the city.

We soon had our tails again, and I shrugged at the same time Cato did. He'd picked up far too many of my mannerisms.

With a little magic I hunted down Aletta. She appeared to be at the hotel. I wanted to peek in on what she was doing, but she'd notice such an intrusion. Instead, I followed the magical trail.

The shadows grew longer as the sky darkened behind the inevitable clouds. I wondered what to do when sunset came. Maybe the news I was bringing would shock Aletta into realizing something dangerous was happening and she would help me.

Right. And pigs would fly.

Actually, I could make pigs fly. I couldn't make Aletta do any work.

I left Cato in the car and jogged across the slush-filled parking lot to the front door of the hotel. Riders galloped through the lot, avoiding cars and leaping bushes. I wondered why they hadn't gone into the buildings. Ah, of course -- though they were creatures of magic, they remained tied to what they did by the shape they took. Real horses didn't charge through walls into buildings. While these might leap higher and run farther and faster, that extended what a horse could do, and was not a complete change.

Which meant they wanted to be real horses. What would happen if the riders ever got down from the saddles?

A hint of the magic led me towards the restaurant where I spotted the two lingering over an early dinner, both apparently pleased with life.

I almost backed away, deciding to wait for Aletta somewhere else. Unfortunately, David -- Not-David -- spotted me.

Since they were the only two in the dining room I went ahead to confront them both rather than slinking away. I walked straight over before either spoke and leaned both hands on the table and stared the man in the face.

"Who are you -- and don't lie, because I know you're

not David."

He sat back, startled. "How did you figure it out?" he asked.

I had secretly hoped for a denial. I hoped I kept the hurt from my face.

"I found articles you'd worked on and the pictures of the real David Carter."

Shock came to his face, but a moment later I saw amusement. I stepped away from the table. He must be some sort of madman: a stalker who had assumed David Carter's identity. I worried about what might have happened to the real photographer. The magazine people had said he would be the one to meet me.

Had this man adapted to the persona Aletta would like when he went with her? It made an odd, twisted sense of everything that had happened.

Aletta appeared confused, glancing from her dinner companion to me. This stranger reached over and patted her on the hand. I wanted to slap those fingers aside and snatch her to safety from whatever danger he represented.

"Aletta, he's lying about who he is --"

The realization seemed to amuse her. "I guess that makes him a little mysterious."

"Aletta --"

"Do go about your business." She waved her fingers in dismissal and I saw beyond her usual facade to the hatred this time. "Just go. Don't bother me anymore."

"You are an idiot." I turned and walked out.

They laughed. The sound hit me in the gut and made me ill. I stumbled at the door, even waving away a hotel worker who asked if I was all right.

I stepped out, looking at the ghost riders, willing to face them. Even though I didn't know what or who they were, they had never lied to me. They had never *laughed* at me.

I stumbled across to the car and slid in, then leaned my head on the steering wheel and shivered, remembering David in this car, sitting next to me. I remembered the lies of the nice person I'd liked -- the one who had never been real.

"Hey." Cato put a paw gently on my arm.

"Sorry." I lifted my head and sniffed. Tears still rolled down my cheeks. I felt stupid and weak for the reaction, especially when one of those damned ghost horsemen stopped right in front of us and stared.

So I turned the car on, hit the gas and rammed him. Oh yes, he felt the impact. The horse limped away, half maimed. And didn't that make me feel better, taking out my frustration on an animal?

I couldn't win.

I couldn't win.

"I don't know what you're thinking, Kat, but I've never seen you look so bleak. It scares me," Cato said.

I said nothing as I maneuvered my way out of the parking lot and didn't try to hit any more horse and riders. I should have and been trying anything to lessen the number of enemy I would face later.

"Kat?"

"I can't do this, Cato," I said, stopping at the edge of the lot. Cars passed in front of us, sloshing muck and dirty snow everywhere. "I can't fight this one. I don't have the power to handle a major battle, and the only other fae --"

"Would have been more trouble than help."

"Yeah." Someone honked behind me, and I pulled out. Horses and riders swarmed in around us. A dog in a car ahead looked back and barked, banging his head against the window.

"Hey, this is fun!" Cato snickered as the dog fell when the driver turned the corner. "The riders are good for something, I guess."

"Cato --"

"I understand things are tough, Katlyn, and you think this is more than you can handle, but I don't believe it's true."

"I lost Aletta's help --"

"You never had her help," he replied with a snort of disdain. He was right, of course. "Look, I'm not stupid. A bunch of cats and birds are not the best help in the world, but we're all you've got. And you're not alone as long as you have us."

I stopped at a light and turned to him. Tears had come to my eyes, but they were a different kind this time. Not alone. And not helpless.

"You guys count for a lot." The light changed, and I eased forward. The horses stayed with us. I scared a couple by making a sudden lane change. One leapt to the left and knocked against a van which swerved and bounced against the curb before the driver got control. He would think he hit ice. I'd have to be more careful, though. "You've helped me out more than I give you credit for, Cato."

"We aren't --"

"You are important." Something settled within me and calm came next. "You're *very* important. And we both have proof. Someone tried to stop the cats and birds from helping me. If you weren't important, the person never would have gone to the trouble."

"Oh." His ears came up as he sat straighter. "Yeah, I guess so. Why didn't the magic keep me away?"

"That would have been too obvious," I said. "Whoever

is doing this didn't want me to figure out why I wasn't seeing birds and cats. They wanted me off balance."

"Was this something Aletta and the guy did?"

I mistrusted Aletta, but I never sensed her presence in the magic. "I've known Aletta for a while. She's always been sloppy with her magic. This stuff was fancy. I could be wrong, but I can't find any hint of her in the spells. And David -- whoever he is -- doesn't have magic at all. The two of them are only added nuisances when I least need them."

"Where are we going? You're not heading to the house."

"To the grocery store. We're almost out of cat food and tuna."

"Ah. Good plan. Yes. We need supplies." He nodded enthusiastically.

Everything seemed almost too normal at the store, even with the spectral riders milling around in the parking lot. Birds gathered on the light posts and screamed at them. Humans barely noted the loud birds and remained oblivious to the dangers although the ghost horses knocked a couple people down on the ice.

My enemies were becoming dangerous to everyone.

CHAPTER FIFTEEN

Sunset arrived with a sharp, winter wind and a stream of ice-white clouds. Snow followed before the last light of day had gone. Most of the birds found shelters since they were unable to navigate far in this weather. Cats slinked in and out of the door which I left open, but shielded to all but them. I made certain they had plenty of food and let them rest inside as long as they wanted. Even Gaylord got used to them though he still kept his distance.

The cats brought me word about dark things wandering the streets though even those creatures didn't appreciate the weather and were taking cover. For the moment, they seemed to be less trouble than the town's usual human tourists.

Power soon went out in part of town. The peripix were doing their job, I feared.

The Edge became more active as darkness fell, so Aletta's mother had been wrong. What a shock. I didn't know why the magic seemed drawn towards the city and wondered if the creatures roaming the streets worked as magical magnets. Had something sent them in and used them as conduits? Could magic work that way?

Why would someone purposely want magic in Estes Park?

I wanted answers, and instead, all I got was another tendril of magic trying to curl down out of the mountainside and into town. I grabbed the power --

And experienced the same horrible rolling magic like Cato and I had suffered through in the bedroom. I went to my knees but held onto the magic. It seemed to pass more quickly this time. When I recovered, I discovered the Edge stood a couple miles from the city limits, nestled somewhere near Rams Horn Mountain, beyond Marys Lake and it poised there, as though ready to sweep right down on the city.

A little later some of the cats came to the house. None of them had liked the wild magic, but they stayed at their work.

"Not much to report," Jules said, scratching at his ear where something had bitten him. I reached out and did a quick repair job. "Wow. Thanks, lady. My ear feels much better. Can you make all the teeth fall out of every dog in town?"

"I'll think about it," I said. "I'm a bit tapped right now."

He snorted. "Yeah. I can see you're weak and all. The northern part of town lost all power while I was out there scouting around. I think the little peripix creatures are working their way down through the rest of town. Power crews out were out, but they haven't found the trouble yet."

Those words drew all my attention. "They haven't spotted the nests of peripix?" I asked.

"Nope. I keep thinking they should. But they don't see anything at all."

"Hidden. Magic," I said, which once more pointed to

someone directing the little creatures. I needed to find a trail to whoever was doing this.

Cato had been standing by the door. He growled and backed away. I crossed to the door, knowing there had to be trouble.

Aletta arrived on the porch, breathless and startled by the cats rushing past her. I stepped outside. She lifted a hand and gasped for a moment before she spoke.

"Okay, you're right," she said, her eyes wide -- the look still seemed far too fake. "Something odd is going on out there. I did my own checking, Kitty. Things are out of hand. What's the Edge doing so close to town?"

"I don't know," I said. I wished I had an answer and sounded wise. At least she'd come to me, though.

"I tried to go look around," she said. " but I couldn't get close. There is something in the hills -- something big and dark. I realized I had better get you. The thing is near the Edge, and I think the creature was casting magic."

"Can you take me there?"

"Yes."

"Let me get my coat and we'll go."

She nodded and appeared relieved.

"I'm going with Aletta," I said to Cato and the other cats as I stepped into the house. Cato gave her a wary glare. "She found something which might be what's causing the trouble."

"Kat --" Cato began.

"I have to go. Keep things calm here, okay?"

"Yeah."

I walked over to the birds and told them the same thing. Gaylord glanced over my shoulder and shook his head.

"She looks like trouble, boss," he said, his voice softer

than usual.

"She is trouble. But at least she's trouble I understand," I answered.

Shakespeare nudged my hand with his beak, which was as friendly as he had ever gotten. "*With loitering eye, till I have felt, the letters -- with their meaning -- melt, to fantasies - with none.*"

Was he trying to say something? He stared into my face with more earnestness than I had expected, almost as though he would speak at any moment --

"Kitty," Aletta said from outside, impatient.

I went to the door, grabbed my coat and went with her out into the cold night.

"We'll take my car as far as we can," I said. The riders had once more disappeared. Did they fear Aletta, knowing she had stronger magic than I did?

"I don't understand how you can stand these things," she said, damping down magic as she got inside the car. I almost told her she didn't have to, but you know . . . some small part of me, even now, wanted a little revenge over David. Or whomever he might be.

We headed along Highway 7, skirting along the mountains. I saw riders far behind us but the night had grown dark, and the wind kicked up snow covering our path and obscuring everything within a few feet of the car. I didn't enjoy driving in this weather, even with magical powers, but it still took less magic than if we had gone on foot. We'd need that power later. I went slowly, and Aletta sat, silent with her hands glued to the car seat, afraid of my driving and the weather. We skidded on the turns a couple times. Petty stuff, but I enjoyed her reaction.

I sensed the Edge out on the right side of the road, still in the wilderness, but glowing with flashes of bright blue and green that I could sometimes see from the road. I drove the car as close as I dared and pulled to the side even though no one else was out tonight.

I also sensed something else magical but made out nothing more than a large dark mass of power. Worry crept in to my mind. What would we face?

"This way!" Aletta scrambled out of the door, anxious to get away from car. Some fae never get the knack of living in this world. I sometimes wondered why they came here though with Aletta I made a good guess. Even without using overt magic, she still had beauty here, and they made her important. In the fae lands she had never been much more than a dilettante and a spoiled child.

And didn't that make me feel better about having Aletta as my only ally?

I didn't have trouble keeping pace with Aletta as we climbed the snowy hillside, pushing through brush and scrambling over dead wood. I soon reached a cliff and stood with the road down to my right. The Edge sat to my left, glowing with all its usual beguiling rainbow beauty. I wished I could share the splendor with humans --

I heard the distant call of an eagle shouting a warning about something behind me and I turned --

Aletta swung a branch at my head, her face set in a grimace of hatred and anger, transforming her into something truly ugly. I would have noticed magic coming, but by using the wood I wouldn't have known she was about to attack without the warning. I raised my right arm as the wood hit. Pain shot from my elbow to my wrist and then up to my shoulder, but she would have hit me across the back of the head if I hadn't moved. She might have killed me.

I yelled something -- not polite -- and lost my balance on the icy rock. My right arm felt as though fire raced through the nerves every time I moved. I grabbed hold of a scraggly, snow-covered bush with my left hand, making certain I didn't slide off the side of cliff.

"Son of a bitch!" Aletta yelled. "Help me! I didn't get her!"

Movement came at me from the shadows of the nearby trees. I couldn't see quite who yet, but I knew anyway.

"Give me some light!" he ordered gruffly.

Aletta cast a ball of light into the air, showing me. I scrambled away from the cliff and got to my feet, shouting magic, born of anger, pain . . . and loss. A wave of force hit Not-David and shoved him into Aletta, who had started to cast her own spell.

Aletta must have rolled every bit of power she had into the spell, and it would have killed me if I hadn't deflected some of the spell with Not-David's inadvertent help. The lightning struck to the right of me, and I gasped at the heat and leapt aside out of instinct. The next bolt shattered a huge spruce tree. I swept the flying splinters and magic away from me and watched as the remnants of the spell rebounded -- far weaker -- to hit both Aletta and Not-David.

The result was both spectacular and illuminating in a way I hadn't expected.

The strike staggered Aletta, and she went to her knees with a gasp of pain. However, the power encircled Not-David -- and for a moment I saw another shape overlaying his: the silvery white of a ghost rider without his horse. Something had taken over his body, just as a fae can take over the body of another animal.

I'd been an idiot.

And I still was. The sight of Not-David (in so many

ways *Not-David* at the moment) took my attention when I should have attacked Aletta. She snarled obscenities as she got to her feet. I sent a wave of power knocking Not-David down on his ass and spun to face her.

I had never experienced such rage in my life. The wave of power I sent at her filled the night with a bright green magic. She screamed and nearly didn't shield in time. I hurt her, but not enough -- and I had almost depleted all my reserves. How fast I could get to the road and my car?

She began to cast. Anger helped her, and she'd always been more powerful than me --

The golden eagle very nearly evened the odds though.

He swept down out of the trees behind her and grabbed at her shoulder, leaving a long ragged wound as he dragged her a few feet before he let go. Her spell went astray and the backlash hit Not-David yet again. This time the power drove the thing out of his body by a couple feet.

"Kat," he whispered, frightened, lost. "Kat -- I don't understand -- don't let her --"

The ghost thing reached for Not-David again.

I did not want this creature to have him. The evil thing had taken away my friend, had gone to Aletta and had *laughed* at me -- and had tried to kill me here in this ambush.

I hit it with a bolt of force, driving the ghost rider away by at least a yard. I would have destroyed the thing if Aletta hadn't leapt over to save him. I rushed forward and awkwardly grabbed Not-David. He came with me, unsteady, his eyes wide and his skin pale and cold shock more than the weather. I didn't do anything for him because I had to use all the power I could to heal my wounds and get us away.

I glanced back as a ghost horse came for his rider. They both appeared to be pale and insubstantial, but I didn't think the weakness would last for long.

Aletta, though, was substantial enough. A cut bled across the side of her face, and her shoulder was drenched in blood where the eagle had grabbed her. She lifted her hand, but Not-David and I slid down the side of the trail and out of sight.

The eagle swept over me.

"Thank you!" I shouted at him. "Go!"

"Get clear! Get away from her!" the eagle shouted and disappeared into the dark.

I heard other wings-- something larger but farther away to the north. I worried for a moment about the dragon and then I didn't care. Whatever flew out there wasn't attacking me. I had real problems to consider.

I expected Aletta to come after us: Aletta, her friend and all the ghost riders. I slipped, dragging Not-David down with me and had a hard time getting him back to his feet and moving, but we finally reached the car. I had seen no sign of the others.

Cold and frightened, I shoved him into the car. His head fell to the side, his face almost snow white, but he blinked at me as I pulled the seatbelt into place and I saw reasoning returning. Good. I wanted answers, and he might have them.

Any answers.

I rushed to the other side and climbed in, hitting the car on and moving so quickly, I almost buried us in a snow drift as we skidded off to the side. I needed to get us to my house and inside the safety of the wards, which would be the best protection we could find.

This time I was smart enough to spread a thin wedge of magic in front of the car like a snow plow. If anyone noticed later, they'd believe someone with a pickup plow had been done the work. Though worrying about anything so trivial seemed silly when they were likely to spot the Edge itself before too long.

"Kat?" Not-David whispered.

"I'm here," I said and reached out to touch his shoulder. He turned, his eyes gone half wild as he shivered beneath my fingertips, though not from the cold. "We're going to my place. You'll be safe there --"

We came into view of Estes Park. The storm parted, and I stopped the car and gasped with shock and fear.

The shimmering outline of the city I had last seen on the other side of the Edge now stood as a ghostly shape overlying Estes Park. The high towers, spires and domes were unmistakable, even though they weren't entirely here. Ghost riders moved along streets, which, between one blink and the next, appeared covered with either sand or with snow.

I eased the car forward, holding my breath for fear I would cry out in dismay. Not-David had his eyes closed. I didn't want him to look because I feared, even though a human, he would see the golden city, too.

And if he saw this illusion, so could others. I spotted no one at all on the streets -- no one real, at least. As I drew closer to the buildings, the veil of snow brushed over us, obscuring the wider view. I caught only glimpses of the desert city as I neared and I drove slowly as I entered the illusion, trying to find a weakness. I wanted to destroy the phantom city before. . . .

Before what? A ghost city took over Estes Park? We were in the real world and this came from the fae side. Nothing could --

But this illusion shouldn't have been here at all. The Edge had moved, the city had slipped over, and the ghost riders seemed more solid. I wondered if they intended to take over humans, the way one had taken over Not-David.

The idea angered me. I purposely swerved into one and hit with a thump, startling my companion awake.

"We're safe," I said, trying to keep my voice soft and bury the worry. "Rest."

I added a touch of magic to the word, and he turned to me, his eyes blinking. "Strawberries and sugar," he said. "I'm glad I like strawberries."

He closed his eyes. At least I had gotten him free, and he seemed better already, even if a bit incoherent. I would learn more later, but I knew the most important part though: Aletta was part of the trouble. Why hadn't I considered it when she showed up right as things went bad? She would pay for this one. We have laws and she had gone far over the line.

Even on the streets of town, no one appeared to be out around except an occasional ghost horse and rider. There might be something in the air -- besides the fae city -- keeping everyone in their homes. It would be easy to do magic with so much available from the storm and the Edge.

Everything appeared normal back at Fairy Tale Lane. I even spotted a couple cats prowling around, and as soon as they saw me they headed towards the house.

My house stood untouched by the ghost city. No shadow of anything else overlaid the exterior though I had still seen such things as I turned up the road. The lights inside glowed bright and welcoming. Cato came from the side of the house and bounded through the snow as soon as I got out.

"You all right?"

"Yeah, barely." I went around to the other side and pulled Not-David out.

"So you left with Aletta and return with this one? What a glutton for punishment."

"Something had taken him over, Cato," I said, grunting as I kicked the car door closed and used magic to get him to the house. "He wasn't himself."

"And who would *himself* be?" Cato asked.

"I'm not sure yet, but I'll find out. For now, though, he stays with me. Aletta wanted him, so we want him away from her."

"Ah." Cato got to the door and went inside first -- cats always manage that -- and stopped to wait for me. "Does this means Aletta is no longer allowed inside?"

"I'd love to see her try. I'd like to see her show her face at all, in fact," I said.

Cato purred.

I brought Not-David in and settled him on the comfortable chair. Cato sat on the arm of the chair watching him intently, as though he didn't trust the man, even unconscious. I went to the kitchen and made two cups of hot tea with honey. I pulled a chair over from the dining room table and settled beside him, watching his face much the same way as Cato was doing.

He came awake a moment later. Cato and I staring at him had to be disconcerting, and he gave a little start. He turned to me, his eyes focusing. He smiled a little.

"Kat," he said, a soft whisper. Cato jumped, as though he hadn't expected any words. David looked worried, and the smile faded. "I -- I don't understand what happened. I felt -- odd. Like something had me. I couldn't --"

"Something did have you," I said. I held out a cup of tea. He accepted with shaking hands. "You know things are not as normal, right?"

"Yeah," he said. He sipped and sipped again while

trying to come to grips with his own fears. I gave him time to get control. "Yeah. I realized things . . . weren't right. Aletta -- what is she?"

"The same as me," I said. "Fae. Only I'm a border guard and she's a bitch."

He laughed softly, a good sound, stronger and more himself. Even Cato appeared less worried.

"Can you tell me anything of what happened? Who was it that held you?" I asked.

"I don't know. When he took control everything went blank. I only had glimpses. Sometimes, when he -- we -- looked into mirrors, I saw myself and knew what had happened. But he stayed clear of them most times. I really don't remember much else. I think there were ghosts and horses."

"The control of your body would depend a great deal on believing he is you, but every time he saw a reflection, he would see the truth, and you'd be a little stronger. Something even happened here once, when you saw your reflection in the window, but I was too stupid to realize. I'm sorry. I should have been paying better attention."

"You better ask him about the other stuff," Cato said.

Not-David gave a startled yelp and splashed tea over himself, me and Cato. He turned frantically to me. "I didn't know he could talk!"

"Oh my," I said and gave a grin. Cato nodded -- he obviously had understood what Not-David had been saying, too. "He can't talk. You understand him, which I have always been able to do. Gaylord -- say something, will you?"

"Oh, I've got plenty to say," he said, but went silent when I waved my hand.

"No, I only hear bird sounds. You can understand

them, too?"

"Yes."

"Birds and cats," he said, glancing from me to Cato and Gaylord.

"Afraid so."

"Well your life has to be interesting." He tilted his head and smiled. "You are strawberries and sugar. I can taste them whenever you come near me. And your house is filled with vanilla."

I understood that part now. "You've lived closely with magic," I said and smiled. I remembered what he had said in the car about how he liked strawberries. "Sometimes, for a non-magical being, the power creates links in the brain to something that is already understood. You sense magic as a scent now."

"And you are magic," he said, his hand reaching over to touch my fingers as though to see if I were real.

"I'm fae. We are very much magic. Not many humans ever know about us. I'm sorry this happened to you. You must be frightened."

"Being with you isn't frightening," he said. He ignored Cato's little snort. "But being taken over by something else -- did I do anything horrible?"

I wasn't sure laughing at me and being rude counted for horrible. Trying to kill me did, but he remembered enough of the incident and I didn't have to say more.

"You didn't have a chance. The real changes out there seem to be starting tonight."

"Why can he understand me?" Cato asked. "And why can I understand him?"

"I used a lot of magic to get him free and some of my power washed over him. I suspect it might stay since he's already made the scent/magic connection in his brain."

"Okay. Fine." Cato leaned over and stared him straight in the face. Not-David drew back, worried. "Tell us who the hell you *really* are."

"Pardon?"

Cato's claws came out and rested on his hand, little needles right against the skin.

"I was looking through a magazine and found a picture of the real David Carter," I explained, a hand on Cato's shoulder. "You are not him."

"Oh." He turned red and bowed his head over the empty cup. "No, I'm not; I'm his apprentice, Adrian Caine. David's been trying to get me a chance to break into the big time, but none of the name magazines would take a chance. It made him mad. So he gave me an assignment they had given to him. He wanted to prove them wrong and so did I. Where's my equipment?"

"In your car or at the hotel," I said. He sounded almost reasonable.

"Here." He gave me his cup and stood, though he swayed as he pulled a billfold from his pocket. He dropped in to the chair as though standing had taken all the energy he had. "Glad the billfold is still here. You'll find all my IDs and among the pictures, you'll find one of David Carter and me."

The driver's license confirmed the name, and I found the picture showing the real David Carter and him, both with cameras, both smiling and that was confirmation enough for me. Even Cato nodded.

"I'm sorry Kat," he whispered and looked stricken. "I really am. I hadn't expected this to be any more than a quick assignment, prove myself as a photographer, and later let you know what had happened. I hoped there would be no bad feelings. But . . . but even before this madness . . . I felt badly. I should have told you --"

"It's all right," I said. In the scheme of everything else, this was really a little thing. Besides, his face had paled, and he looked upset. "You not being David Carter made all of this seem worse. I didn't know what to believe, and that made me grab at Aletta for help."

"I should have told you right away, as soon as I . . . as soon as I began to trust you."

"We've both made mistakes. Mine was to trust Aletta at all. And I'm sorry, David -- *Adrian*. I should have known from the moment she arrived that she intended something."

"Can you stop her? What is she doing?"

"I don't know the answer to either since I haven't pieced enough together. She might be trying to bring some of the fae world across to this reality, but nothing from my world will last once the Edge settles down."

"The Edge?"

"The area where my world touches upon yours. Most of the time the Edge stays calm, quiet and hardly noticeable, but sometimes the thing kicks up a fuss. This is one of those times, and it is worse than usual all over the world."

"Could Aletta have something to do with the Edge being so unstable?" Cato asked.

"Well, she's irritating, but I don't think she could irritate an inanimate object."

"If anyone could, she would be the one," Cato mumbled.

Both Adrian and I nodded. Odd. I had never considered sharing this ability with anyone. Most Fae understood cats of course, but they didn't share my life and work. I didn't mind. Neither, apparently, did Cato. The other cats would likely be upset though. I wondered how Timber and my father would take the news . . . if I ever got in touch with them again.

Adrian stood and walked around a little. He didn't limp, which meant it must have been a part of the ghost. I filed that away as one more fact I hoped would add up to something useful.

Gaylord and Shakespeare still watched him warily though even Shakespeare didn't seem as upset. Adrian wandered and obviously still weak and shaken. He listened as cats came in and reported what they had found. He said nothing, which I appreciated. These were the wilder strays, and they came in slinking with their tails down and their eyes darting everywhere. I felt sorry because they feared bright lights and warm houses.

Four in a row brought the same news: Whatever had been happening when I brought Adrian through town had faded, even though the power should have gotten stronger during the night. The riders had disappeared from the streets, and even the dark things had taken refuge. Had they suffered a defeat when I survived and they went to regroup? Why didn't I feel as though I'd had a win?

"We're okay for the night," I said at last. Snow fell in a light but steady curtain of white blocking off most of the world. Magic drifted down in every flake. There was far too much magic in this area and that would affect everything here for a while, no matter what else happened. I would have to deal with it . . . later.

Adrian leaned against a chair, his head bowed, plainly too worn to even stay to his feet much longer.

"Come on," I crossed and took hold of his arm. "You need rest. We all do."

"But --" he said, waving his other arm toward the door.

"Things are calm tonight. I've used all the magic I can. I need rest. Aletta and her allies do as well. So let's take advantage of this time. If anything happens, the cats or the birds will come to tell me. But right now . . . come on."

He didn't argue. I sent him in for a shower, and he didn't take much time, coming out in his jeans, but shirtless. He had a few bruises, but so did I. We'd both had a damned rough couple days and we hadn't even started to fight the war yet.

He sat on the bed by me, looking uncertain, worried -- afraid, though he hid that well.

"Lie down," I said to him. "Go ahead. The bed is large. We'll both do better if we're here, together."

He didn't argue. When I started to take off my shirt, he reached to help, though fumbling with the buttons. Whenever his fingers brushed my skin, it sent a shiver through me. This was not the time. We were tired, worn, worried --

"You've gone through hell," he whispered as he helped pull the shirt off my shoulders. I nodded and turned, tossing the shirt aside.

He rubbed my neck, fingers kneading sore muscles. I leaned into his touch despite myself and even made a little purring sound. He gave a short laugh. I don't even remember how I went from leaning into the soothing motion of his fingers to lying down and letting him work his fingers down my back. I needed this tonight.

He leaned closer and kissed the back of my neck.

I turned to wrap my arms around his neck and pull him down closer, our lips meeting -- sweet melting, warmth -- even better than the first kiss. His bare chest brushed against my bare skin. I shivered at the touch of his hands in my hair, turning my head. I pressed against him.

"Strawberries," he whispered, his voice panting softly as our mouths parted. "Strawberries."

Movement -- the flap of wings. I pulled my head away, and he turned. Shakespeare had come into the room -- Shakespeare who never left the area of his perch. He landed on the table beside the bed, and looked at the two of us, shaking his head.

"*Hath not the same fierce heirdom given, Rome to Caesar, this to me?*"

And something clicked finally. *Strawberries.*

"I get it! I understand. Shakespeare can't speak parrot because he's gone through what you have! He's been trying to tell me -- something. I don't know what yet -- but I know he's trying to give me answers."

Shakespeare nodded several times. He came closer and brushed against my hand. I understood. He had answers though I still had to find out what they meant. This was the first real break we had.

I sent him to his perch and used a little magic to close the door before I fell back into Adrian's arms.

CHAPTER SIXTEEN

When I woke the next morning, I was far calmer than I had since this insanity began. *I'm not alone.* I felt languid, relaxed, and I smiled at where Adrian slept, his face turned a little into the pillow in Cato's usual spot. He even smiled in his sleep and didn't wake as I slid out of bed and stretched. Snow fell outside the window. Good? Bad? I didn't know: The snow existed, nothing more.

After a quick shower, I found Adrian had pulled a pillow over his head, obviously trying to block out the sunlight. He looked cute.

Yeah, I know -- the new love stuff can drive a person crazy. I'd have to try to curb all this sweetness and get back to work soon. Really.

I realized there had been a buildup of magic overnight. At least nothing hit in one of those horrible, overpowering waves I'd suffered through when this mess started. The day even felt calmer, despite the weather and the magic. I didn't believe that feeling came entirely from me.

I dressed and walked out to the living room where I found Gaylord on a chair by the window and making kissy sounds. On a branch the other side sat a startling blue

Steller's jay.

"What are you doing?" I asked, standing beside him.

"Are you kidding? Look at her! She's gorgeous. Look at those wings! Man, I'd love to nest in those wings. And those tail feathers!" He gave a cockatiel version of a wolf whistle.

"She's not even your species."

"Hey," he said, jabbing at my arm. "Do I say anything about you and the human?"

I couldn't argue that point.

I went to the kitchen and made tea and toast, sent a little magical nudge to get David . . . *Adrian* out of bed and into the shower. I had breakfast waiting on the table when arrived though I used a little magic to get everything done and in place in time.

He appeared startled at first and then pleased when I waved him towards the chair. I had already settled into mine and sipped my tea as though I hadn't rushed through the kitchen like a crazed pixie. Oxymoron there, I know.

"Thank you! This is great!" He smiled as he took the chair across from me. "Do you think this snow is going to continue all day?"

"I think we're going to have snow until this mess clears up. This much magic in the area is bound to interact with the weather."

He sipped his tea and watched me over the cup. "What are we going to do?"

I thought about saying I didn't want him involved, but I try not to say the kinds of stupid lines I wince at in the movies. He was as involved as me at this point. Tell him he couldn't help because he didn't have magic? Neither did Cato, but he helped me.

And this was his world.

"I'm not certain what Aletta is doing, except --"

I stopped and lifted my hand, carefully searching the world outside my safe home. I found something different out there, and the touch worried me in the light of day. Adrian said nothing, waiting patiently as he sipped his tea. He distracted me, just sitting there, but I made myself get over it, which was the far better choice than sending him away.

The strangeness was nor far out of town.

"I found something odd. Some kind of magic shield has encircled the whole area around us. I don't think Aletta wants anything in or out of town. The ward goes all the way into the park. And the Edge has moved though no closer to town at least. Damn. I don't understand what any of this means."

Adrian reached over and put a hand atop of mine. I smiled.

And Cato, walking over from the chair where he had slept, snorted. Gaylord did much the same.

"You two might find yourself playing in the snow," I said.

"Sure," Cato answered with a dramatic sigh. "You get a human male and you kick your faithful companions out into the winter weather --"

Adrian laughed. He apparently found Cato more amusing than I did. Shakespeare at least stayed quiet.

"We will have to check things," I warned and sipped my tea, trying to figure out what would be best to do. "We need to go out during the daylight, when most of the wild magic isn't as strong. Sunlight holds powerful natural magic and counteracts most unfocused magic."

He nodded as though what I said made sense. We ate our breakfast, neither of us in any real hurry to go. I hadn't forgotten about the danger or how much of the human world depended on me. Sitting here for a few minutes to gather my wits helped. I needed to think about the situation. I had spent too much time rushing around, half-crazed with worry. There would be no outside help unless I somehow reached my father. Aletta had probably made a spell to stop me from reaching home, but I found nothing specific in the miasmic magic around us.

I had to do this alone . . . or at least without any other fae help. In fact, I had an odd feeling Aletta, and whoever worked with her, would be surprised by the help I had.

When we got ready to go out, I made certain our clothing would keep us warm. Right after I placed the spell we had to step outside to keep from sweating. Adrian gave a little laugh despite my distress.

"The magic is working, and this is wonderful!" He wrapped his arm in mine and we leapt off the porch into a knee-deep drift on the other side.

A Steller's jay sat in the tree and laughed at us. "You're like a couple kids playing hooky from school!"

She was right. I felt like a kid shirking duty and having a snow day. Real danger lurked not far away. I felt the power, both in the odd pulses emanating from the Edge and out to the solid sphere of magic which had closed off the area. But even so, the snow-filled landscape was gorgeous. Birds flittered around us reporting nothing new and horrible, and the few cats daring the snow only grumbled about the weather as they headed to my house where they would find warmth and food.

Adrian watched as each cat passed and smiled in wonder as he understood what they said. I had talked to birds and cats all my life and I enjoyed his reactions although I warned him not to speak to the strays since some had a hard time dealing with even me. I didn't know how they would handle a human talking to them.

We went past Mrs. Hale's house. Mrs. Miniver stood in the window and head butted the glass in greeting. I waved and ducked my hand and bowed my head when the gray haired woman came to the window. She might not recognize me, walking with a companion and all.

"Problem?" Adrian asked, glancing at the house.

"She believes I'm trying to steal her cats because I talk to them," I said. "The one in the window is Cato's mother. Lovely British Short Hair. Pure bred -- won a few awards, too."

"Ah. You know a lot about cats? Should I get a book or something?"

"I have some books on cats in the loft. We can go over them together."

"Sounds nice."

Yes, I thought so, too.

We walked to Fish Creek Road and along the curve of Lake Estes. I couldn't see across even the narrow edge through the snow fall. As we reached the outskirts of town, we found cars abandoned in the storm, though everyone seemed to have found shelter.

Eventually, we reached Highway 36 and started east. The crews hadn't cleared the roads and left behind the drifts that stood waist high and were growing as the wind blew across the empty expanse of land and road. The storm stretched out over the mountains, even beyond the shield of magic. In fact, the size of the shield and amount of magic would be part of what created such a huge storm and pulled the weather in on itself -- and on us.

About half a mile out of town, we found a young couple struggling through the snow. They turned to us with open hope and trudged our way. I gave them a little boost of strength and warmth as they came closer which helped ease the growing panic they'd been suffering.

"Good to see you!" the girl said. Purple and black spiked hair stood out from the sides of her knit cap, and the little bobble inserted in her eyebrow had frosted over and had a tiny icicle hanging from it. I tried very hard not to stare.

"We got caught in a drift last night." The guy had a shaved head and piercings in various places. I wondered why his head didn't freeze since he'd given his knit cap to the girl. She had pulled the covering down nearly to her eyebrows. "I'd just gassed up the car, so we stayed warm and we waited for light and the storm to ease."

"You're close to a place where you can take shelter," I said, and searched out such a location with other young people, so they would fit in and have a nice adventure. I gave them quick directions, but mixed a liberal amount of magic in with the words so they'd get there.

They hurried off, laughing and kicking snow at each other, their mood changed. They would be fine.

"You know, that's the first good thing I've seen magic do. Well, and staying warm out here," he said with a grin.

My mood improved knowing I'd helped him realize not all magic is dark and horrible. We often use our powers to help correct problems, not only for ourselves, but for others. If we didn't care about anyone else, we would abandon the Edge, and leave this world (and the others) to whatever fate had in store. Sometimes we do big things, but often we use magic in little ways, like to help the lost people find safety in the storm.

We found another car off the road along Highway 36, but I used magic and tracked the people to a cabin not far away. Most of the people in this area knew when to get in out of the weather, and they'd taken to their homes, waiting for spring to come again. They wouldn't have to wait long.

Everything seemed normal, despite the magical shield which wasn't far away. I saw nothing out of place through the falling snow, so I needed to get closer. Adrian didn't complain about walking, but we weren't far out of town when I lost the road and found we had headed off into a field.

"Damn. I need to pay better attention." I reached out with magic and located the road. We returned to the flat surface hidden below snow.

And a few minutes later I lost the road again.

The third time I realized this wasn't either chance or an effect of being love-smitten.

"What's going on?" Adrian asked. He frowned and glanced towards the sky. "I swore we were heading a little south of east, but. . . ."

I glanced up, too. Hard to mark the sun behind all those clouds, but the sun had slipped off direction. Or we had, which was damned hard for a fae to do. We have a superb sense of direction once we settle into a place.

I went back and found the road yet again. Everything around us slipped into place, including the direction of the sun. A few steps away and the world changed once more.

I lifted my hand and searched out the area before and behind us. The shield stood less than twenty yards away though I couldn't see the magic through the snow storm. I touched the power though, and I found something else decidedly unsettling.

"This is bad." I backed up and made certain I had the road firmly under my feet, for all the good it would do. Adrian glanced at me, worry etched in his face. "Let me check again."

I moved slower this time, searching out not only the shield, but also what was on both sides of the magical wall. I shook my head.

"We have a new problem?" he asked.

"A new part of the old problem," I said trying not to give way to despair. "We aren't losing our direction, Adrian. The direction changes."

"Changes." He didn't say the word with any doubt. At this point I supposed he believed anything possible.

"Yes. The shield is inching inward, and what is on the other side isn't Colorado." I took his hand and started forward, moving a yard and another. I wanted a close look - -

And through the blowing snow we saw the ward, a glowing bubble of translucent power. I felt as though I lived inside a snow globe someone had shaken. Brown and gold stood outside the shield, and sand blew across the ground.

"No, not Colorado," Adrian agreed. He shook his head and held tighter to my hand. "And the snow is changing to sand there at the edge."

I stared at the ground and watched the shield inch towards us while the glittering white of snow transformed to golden sand where the magic passed. If people came this way and saw this -- I don't know what they would think. Anyone could walk out into the desert and escape the snow storm but I didn't know if the desert would be better. The shield was permeable on this side. I backed away.

I sensed a hint of the fae world in those blowing sands on the other side -- and yet the desert didn't seem a part of the fae lands at all. I searched until I found another shield overlaying this one, and beyond the second wall I found snowy Colorado again. A circle within a circle, and the inner one contracting, filling the area with desert sand.

"What are you thinking?" Adrian asked.

"Sorry. I'm used to working these things through on my own," I admitted. "I could walk through the wall and go out there. We both could. But I don't know where 'out there' is. Even if thought it safe, I have to stay here, Adrian. I'm a border guard. This is my place, and I have to do what I can to fix this problem. Running away to some place warmer -- calmer -- isn't an answer for me, though I located Colorado again in the distance. But . . . I don't dare walk away and hope I can come back and fix the problem. I have to face it here."

He smiled, bent closer, and kissed me. I guess I had given the right answer.

We studied the shield for a few more minutes. This was a massive, intricate spell, and I'd never seen anything like it. How did the shield remain powerful in the daylight? I finally found a link to . . . to a night place? Fueled from somewhere else? What would happen tonight?

We walked away in silence, heading back towards town. The road became steady beneath my feet, and Adrian's arm around my waist seemed to make the journey easier, though I had plenty to worry about -- as though I hadn't been worried enough already.

A little junco found us, the grey and black bird gliding in through the snow flakes to land on my collar. He tangled in my hair and I pulled him into my hands, shedding a little warmth to stop him shivering.

"Thank you, thank you, thank you," he said, chattering away. "Trouble, trouble. Pretty lights, eagle place. Trouble. Bad things, all there."

He flew off into the snow.

"We've got another problem, I think. It's hard to tell with little birds, but I believe he told me there's trouble near the Edge. I need to check. You don't have to go with me."

"Of course I do," he said. He gave a little sheepish shrug. "I want to go with you and learn what's going on. I want to help where I can."

"Thank you." I meant those words. I didn't want to face this alone. Besides, every time I felt Adrian's hand in mine, I remembered my job was to protect *his* world. I might not be the most powerful fae, but I was far from helpless. Having someone who cared helped. There are powers other than magic in both worlds.

I reached out and found the Edge within the sphere, close to Highway 7. At least we didn't have to hike out to the middle of nowhere, I told myself, even though that was exactly where I fervently wished the Edge to go. I wanted it away from the town instead of coming closer and closer to Estes Park.

Did the sphere draw the Edge in closer? I didn't understand the connections. Not understanding annoyed me. I glanced towards the street leading to home, but kept going a few more blocks to Brodie Avenue. We crossed over the bridge, both of us glancing into the water, but seeing nothing. A few ducks had taken refuge in the underpinning of the bridge and I gave them words of hope, but we didn't linger.

"Did I mention the peripix problem?" I asked, waving towards dark buildings as we passed. Wood stoves and fireplaces kicked smoke into the air everywhere in town. A few people stared out windows, but mostly we passed without notice.

"Peripix?"

"Annoying little creatures -- you saw the picture of one in the newspaper. They're from the other side, and they have a bad habit of finding the worst places to nest -- which is what they've been doing here, and why so much of the town has been losing power. Magic and technology don't mix. The cats say they're nesting in the power plant, cable company -- anywhere they will cut power to the humans."

"They're choosing those spots on purpose."

"Not them. Something is directing the peripix, though."

"What can you do? If these people have no power --"

"The people in this area are prepared for winter storms." I waved toward the houses where curls of smoke drifted upward from chimneys. "And I long ago made certain the hospital's generator wouldn't fail --"

He stopped and caught my arm, drawing me into a big, warm embrace.

"Hey," I said into his chest.

"You are a wonderful person. Or whatever."

I laughed. We kept walking, magic helping us as we headed out of town again. Before long, we found the Edge. The wall glowed and would attract far too much attention tonight. How could I hide or disguise the glow in this place where most everywhere else would be dark? I feared everyone would see --

I rethought the problem.

"I need to stop worrying about the Edge drawing attention, and concentrate on saving people," I said aloud.

Adrian nodded --

And we both heard the sound rushing toward us through the snow. Four riders appeared, all of them silver ice and not misty as they had been at first. They rode straight at us with swords drawn and for a moment I almost panicked, fearing those were death swords -- but no. Just ice swords.

Deadly enough.

I created magic fueled by fear and anger and tossed a ball of fire right into the face of the first rider.

He and the horse melted. Not like ice melting, but more like plastic; a loss of shape, pulled downward by gravity. The next rider rushed at us before I created a second ball of fire.

Another went for Adrian, but he ducked under the blade and swatted the horse on the rump. The animal was solid enough to feel the hit and shied away while the rider -- almost a face, and dark-eyed -- fought for control.

I stopped watching Adrian and dealt with the two who came for me. They had different faces, I realized. Individuals and not clones of some sort. I ducked one swing and hit the horse in much the same way as Adrian had, but with far more power. The blow sent the horse tumbling with the rider underneath the animal. I was glad they didn't have voices when I saw him screaming.

The other rider nicked my upraised hand with the blade, but not a bad cut, lucky for me. I cursed and backpedaled out of reach, but then I charged straight in while the horse and rider tried to change direction. They were real enough to notice the snow and ice, and not as sure footed as I was with my magic. I got past, found the rider still under his struggling horse, and grabbed the sword out of his hand and when the magic started to waver, I infused the blade with my own power and kept it real enough to use.

I found a whisper of metal in the blade, like a memory of what it had once been. I brought the sword up, parried a

blow which might have cut half way through my head --
not a pleasant thought -- and swung at the rider. The blade
tore through the man's arm and struck the horse, and they
disappeared into a gust of wind and snow. I thought there
might be a white blood on my blade, but I didn't check too
closely.

Instead, I killed the horse and rider who were still
down. I went after the other one Adrian had managed to
keep busy during my battle. This last rider proved a little
quicker with the sword, but I met his blows and cut his arm
and the horse's head, half blinding the creature. They spun
and disappeared into the snow as well -- disappeared
entirely in a few steps. They existed here anymore.

"You're damned good with a sword," Adrian said with
a little surprise.

"Comes with being fae." I healed my wounds and the
cut on his forehead, shushing him when he protested. "This
is easy stuff, healing little wounds. And now we won't have
to explain them to anyone one we meet. But the sword --
fae use bladed weapons. Technology doesn't work well with
us. Even flintlocks tend to fail around us."

"Your car --"

"Magic built. I use more magic so we can drive over
the top of the snow, but I don't want to draw attention and
the humans to start panicking."

He said nothing as we headed into the hills. Yes, we
were still heading for more trouble. I should have run the
other way, but I needed to know why the junco had been
worried.

I found out soon enough. The magic-laden snow
didn't fall near the Edge, but instead sublimated into the
other powers nearby. The Edge sat in a little hollow, at least
hiding some of the glow. Magic crackled through the air

and magical creatures of all sorts had gathered to bask there. I realized they must be the ones roaming the streets at night. A few even wore human clothing as though they would blend in on the streets. More came through even as I watched. There were at least fifty already, of varying sizes, intelligence and belligerence.

"Oh no. We don't need more," I said.

The Edge's free magic helped me, too, and I'd gotten used to working magic near the Edge over the last few days. Better yet, not one of these newcomers was fae or a higher being, so I had the advantage on them in power and -- I hoped -- intelligence. I checked the surrounding area, gathered my power, and waited until they were pulling something large though, which might have been a troll. I didn't want another one here.

So I patted Adrian on the arm, handed him the sword, and signaled him to stay put. He gave an emphatic nod. Not stupid.

I stood and let out a scream, startling Adrian, the creatures by the Edge, and probably half of Estes Park. I ran headlong down the hill side, using a magic scoop to capture everything in sight and funnel them through the hole they had open in the Edge.

They met resistance trying to go back through, but I didn't care. I shoved harder, and I sensed something, as though a bubble burst, and they tumbled over one another into the fae lands. A couple tried to rush out again, but I reached the Edge and shoved them through before I pulled the strands of magic together and sealed the hole shut. I had gotten good at the work.

This time I definitely sensed something trying to counter me on the other side. Maybe fae, maybe not -- but intelligent and magical. Rage and frustration came through the Edge in the form of a wind and almost drove me to my knees. I didn't let go of the magic I was using, and I reinforcing weak parts in the area. I realized my warning system still sat out by Terra Tomah so I found it, and brought it here, for all the good it had done.

"We're safe," I called to Adrian. "Well, safe being a relative word."

He cautiously came closer, watching the Edge, which appeared quite impressive, even in the bright sunlight.

"It feels like I'm standing too near electricity," he said and stepped away. "My skin tingles -- not unpleasant, but not right. And the tastes mingle and are overpowering as though everything mixes together."

"We won't be here long." I began to sooth the Edge with gentle magic, sealing over more rough spots. "Can you keep watch behind us? I'm almost done."

He watched the woods. I used little magics for this job. I didn't want to risk any more dangerous work here. My magical scoop had not started any massive reaction. I would not risk --

"Rider," Adrian suddenly said.

I turned in time to see one fleeing into the snow and trees.

"Time to go," I decided. "I can't do much else, and we don't want to stick around and find out what he brings back."

We hurried to the road. I spotted riders on the trails, but we slipped past and headed into the city. We moved as quickly as my magic would allow, rushing tirelessly through the snow drifts. I wanted to get home --

More riders blocked the road to my house. The two of us moved off in another direction and tried to go around them, but the riders kept coming between me and home. I almost panicked, but Adrian kept hold of me, and we headed back into town. I hoped the others were safe: Cato, Gaylord and Shakespeare, and any of the strays who had taken refuge there. The ward seemed intact, but I thought something tried to get inside the house.

We soon realized the riders were hunting us.

"We need to get behind some walls," I said to him. "The horses won't go inside buildings."

"Why not? They aren't real horses."

"They aren't real *yet*," I corrected. "But they are the essence of horses, and act in accordance to what they appear to be. The ghost horses, believing themselves horses, can't walk through walls and won't go inside a building without directions from their riders. Whoever is setting this up has to keep them believing they are horses so they'll become solid. So far the riders don't seem to want to be inside either. Outside they can soak up all the free magic and inside they can't."

"Free magic?" Adrian asked as we reached the business district. A few people even walked around. "Is that why I keep tasting vanilla?"

"The storm is laden with magic and it's helping me," I admitted. "But the magic helps them as well."

I used a little power to send the few curious people to their places of safety. This was not a time to be out admiring the weather. Someone had even tried to plow the street, but abandoned the truck right in the middle of an intersection. A snow drift half covered the cab door.

"Things will be worse tonight," I said. "We need to find some place to rest for a while before sunset."

"My hotel?" Adrian asked.

"Good plan."

The hotel wasn't far away. We turned, fighting our way

against the howling wind. I feared the storm would soon grow worse, and the weather had been bad already.

As soon as the hotel came in sight I pulled Adrian to a stop. "I need to make certain Aletta isn't there, waiting for us."

"Will there be a time when I'm safe from her?" he asked with obvious worry.

"Yes. I'll make certain you're safe, and so will most of the others in the fae lands. I don't think even her parents will stand by her this time. She's been . . . well, kind of like one of those spoiled little rich princesses you see running around. Until now, her parents thought she could do no wrong, and we only misunderstood her."

"Ick," he said and which about summed up everything. "I guess fae are like humans in a lot of ways."

I used magic to search the hotel and found no sign of Aletta though I located something interesting in the stairwell. She had expected me to visit Adrian at some point. The trap had been sitting there for a couple days, ready to spring on any unwary fae who happened along.

The trap might have killed me if I hadn't been careful.

"We can't take the stairs," I said.

"There is an elevator."

"Elevators are pretty techie for a fae to risk," I replied and then shrugged. "I can hold my magic down. I'm used to doing it here in town. There's a trap on the stairs, obviously intended for me. Aletta's work. Sloppy as always."

We crossed the street, fighting our way through the drifts. I spotted a rider a block away, but he didn't spot us as we hurried into the hotel lobby.

I almost threw the magic sword away, but if I did -- or tried to destroy it, Aletta might pick up the magic and trace us to the one place I hoped she wouldn't expect us to be if we got past her trap. There was no reason to take the chance, so I hid the weapon in an invisible scabbard which I hung over my shoulder. We might need a weapon anyway.

People milled around, all of them worried and unhappy. They appeared to be tourists and a few business men. Many were worried about being trapped here for along; I caught a touch of their emotions, almost palpable in this magic-laden day.

The tall, dark skinned doorman -- who also worked as a bouncer at a local bar -- came towards us when we entered. He was an imposing man with muscles bulging beneath his company uniform, and he managed a no-nonsense scowl which kept most people in line.

"I'm afraid the hotel is out of rooms, but people are welcome to stay in the lobby if they need to."

"I have a room," Adrian said, and fetched his electronic key out. "We had a hell of a time getting back here, though. I hope no one has let my room out."

"I believe the already occupied rooms are still assigned to the original person," he said, and then grinned. "Kat!"

"Hi Tommy. We were working on an assignment and the weather even caught me by surprise."

"Yeah, same for most everyone." He walked with us towards the elevator and waved away other workers. I suspected they'd called in everyone who could get there to help deal with the influx of stranded people. "Damnedest storm I've ever seen. Posey-poo had kittens last week. You must stop by and see them."

Adrian hardly concealed his grin.

"I will." I promised and began to pull in my powers as we neared the elevator. I didn't tell Adrian I had never dared ride in an elevator.

"I left her plenty of food and water before I came to

work," he said, but frowned. "I hope she and the little ones will be all right. They're on the porch and they should be warm enough. I made certain she had plenty of blankets."

"She'll be fine," I said and with a touch of authority -- and a little power -- so he didn't worry. "Mother cats are very strong."

"True. Thanks." He looked from me to Adrian and back again. "Have fun."

I turned red. The elevator door opened and disgorged a family with kids heading for the restaurant. Adrian and I slipped in and he hit the 4th floor button. The door closed.

The experience of moving upward kept my mind off of other things. I held my magic close, and I enjoyed the moment, watching the numbers click away, the bell chiming at each floor. I almost regretted reaching the destination. It isn't often a person has a chance to experience something new in life.

We stepped out into a wide hall. The wall at the right side of elevator had a huge window, and I supposed the view of the mountains would be wonderful on days when the snow didn't fall as thick as a blanket.

I followed Adrian around the curve and to room 426.

And stopped him before he put the key into the slot.

"Trap," I said, softly. Magic pulsed from the door. "As sloppy as the one on the stairs. She might not have expected me to reach this far, but she wanted to know when you arrived."

"What do we do?" he asked.

"I can get past this one. If I can open the door, and the trap doesn't go off, she won't realize we're here. Better yet."

He smiled. I carefully slid my hand over the door, found the threads of magic and pulled them apart.

"Open the door. Slowly. Then get inside."

He slipped past me and I carefully moved away from the front of the door to the back, the magic passing from my right-to-left hand. I nudged the door shut with my foot and let go. The trap slid into place, undisturbed.

Perfect.

Adrian crossed to the side of the room and lifted his camera bag, looking inside and nodding with relief. I felt better knowing the pack hadn't been lost.

"I put a little shield around your equipment the first day," I said as I walked past him to lift an edge of the curtains and peer out the window. "Everything should be all right, even with Aletta and her companion around."

"Thank you."

I sat on the bed, exhausted after all we'd done. He sat as well and pulled me close.

There were far worse ways to spend a cold snowy day.

CHAPTER SEVENTEEN

Sunset came too soon. I didn't want to go outside knowing we faced a dangerous night. More magic gathered in the air, like a hurricane about to break over us. Adrian tasted the power which laced vanilla with other flavors now. I wondered if we wouldn't be wiser to stay in the room, content with each other's company.

No. The time resting -- more or less -- was done. I needed to see what I could still do to help.

When we left, I wore one of Adrian's sweaters and felt warm and comforted. Protected, in an odd, emotional way.

Not alone.

Adrian put his digital camera into a smaller bag along with batteries. He even put his cell phone in, which I suspected might be habit more than anything. I smiled as I warded the bag to keep it all safe.

"Lighter stuff," he said as he closed the bag. "I can't go out there without any camera. Crazy huh?"

"No, not crazy. Just holding on to something normal and hoping we go back to the safer world soon."

He nodded agreement. I brushed my hand over the still invisible sword, but shook my head. "I'll leave the sword here in case Aletta and her people can trace it. If they do, I want them to find it here and not with us."

He didn't argue. Trusted me. I wasn't certain why.

Down in the lobby someone had managed to get a Wi-Fi link -- technology winning through the magic -- and everyone crowded around to watch the news. Massive storms still grew over the area and ski fanatics lined up in Denver, but no one could get the roads plowed fast enough to reach the slopes or the town.

While Adrian went to see if he could get us a sandwich or two to go, I read a handout the hotel had on the counter. The management had everything covered: Plenty of food, generators running well and enough fuel since they had an entire fuel delivery truck sitting behind the building, trapped by the storm. They were buying what they needed straight from the company. They asked people to conserve as they could, but not to worry about being cold or trapped in the hotel.

Tommy came to us when we started toward the door, shaking his head with worry.

"You aren't going out there tonight?" he said, looking at the growing dark as a brisk wind plastered more white against the door.

"Don't worry." I patted him on the arm and reinforcing the words with some magic. "We'll be fine."

"If you go near my place, can you check in on Posey-Poo and the kittens?" he asked. "There's a key under the flower pot to the right of the door. If you could, would you get her and the little ones inside where they might be warmer? I never expected I'd be gone for days, but the manger asked me specifically to stick around. We've dealt with some frayed tempers and I've kind of helped keep things settled."

"I'll take care of her and the kittens," I promised. He

didn't live very far away and often rode his bike to work every day. I didn't mind a little detour to help.

As Adrian and I went out, I sent whisper of magic behind me, making certain no one else wondered about people walking out into the worst storm of the century.

No one else was out on the street. Both the storm and the innate sense humans get when something is out of place had sent them all indoors. They didn't have to see or believe in magic to feel something wrong tonight.

We'd taken a couple steps from the door when something moved to the left, coming out from beside a heating unit at the side of the building. I spun and stared in shock as Cato, Gaylord and Shakespeare appeared.

"About time you two came out," Cato said. He stepped into the snow and grimaced while the two birds flew over and took refuge in my arms.

"What are you doing here?" I asked, glancing warily around.

"No longer safe at the house," Cato replied as Adrian picked him up. "Thanks. I hate snow, especially snow I can't even see over."

Gaylord had slipped between the collar of my coat and the sweater. He peeked his head out again. "You smell like the human."

"It's because I'm wearing his sweater."

"Yeah, right." And he disappeared into the warmth once more. Shakespeare contented himself with nestling into the crook of my arm much as Cato did with Adrian. I gave the big bird a little warmth of his own, and he nodded enthusiastically.

"What happened at the house?" I asked.

"Aletta and some of her ghost companions are there. She's determined to get inside because she thinks both of you are hanging out in there. We kind of helped keep the illusion going by playing the tape of the birds and turning on the TV a couple times. You know, you fae are sometimes really easy to fool. She heard voices and apparently never considered anything tech-related."

"I wouldn't fall for that trick," I said, then thought about it for a moment. "Maybe."

"Maybe," he agreed. "Anyway, I realized she was getting closer to taking down the ward. She almost got the door open once. So I led the other two to the cat door and carried them out. That big damned bird needs to get his claws clipped. And if little beaky here doesn't stop running up and down my back, he's going to be lunch."

I smiled and reached over to give Cato a kiss on the top of his big furry head. "You're a good guy, Cato."

"And pretty damned smart," Adrian added. "I'm not going to kiss you, though."

Cato laughed with a soft whisper of a purr.

"What we doing, boss?" Gaylord asked from somewhere in the folds of the jacket. He tickled when he moved.

"Sit still," I said, squirming a little. "I'm not sure what we're doing yet. Have you seen any riders nearby?"

"A couple, I think, before you came out," Cato said. He glanced down the street. "Hard to tell in this storm. I talked to a couple strays on the way down here -- and wasn't that just wonderful, explaining how the birds were my companions and not there for a late lunch. But anyway, the peripix have stopped roaming the streets. And the big dark things disappeared this afternoon."

"I sent most of them back to the fae lands." I patted Shakespeare and gave him more protection from the weather since he still shivered. A bird like him should never be out in the snow.

"*The rain came down upon my head, unsheltere'd - and the heavy wind rendered me mad and deaf and blind.*"

"He's a smart bird and I wonder what he's been trying to say to you in those quotes," Adrian said watching Shakespeare intently. "I think they're important, somehow."

"I think so, too." I stopped. "The library. We might find an answer there."

Adrian agreed and at least we had a destination and one not too far from Tommy's house. I pointed the library out and then turned down a side street to Tommy's place. Adrian smiled at me.

"I didn't think you told Tom you'd do this without intending to."

"Do what?" Cato asked.

"Move a mother cat and her kittens inside. You behave, Cato. She'll be nervous enough."

I told Gaylord the same thing. He said he wasn't coming out of the jacket anyway. Shakespeare nodded several times.

Posey-Poo peered out of the blankets when I opened the door. She gave a great sigh of relief, even when I sat Shakespeare on a shelf.

"Kat," she said. "I'm so glad to see you!"

She slipped out of a cocoon of blankets, a thin calico with bright green eyes. Four little kittens streamed out after her; one a miniature of her mother and the other three variations of bright yellow marmalade stripes. "Mommy, mommy, cold, cold, cold."

I gathered them into my arms as Adrian got the key. Cato eyed the little ones as I held them and shook his head in dismay, but he said nothing.

"Cato, lover," Posey-Poo said, looking at him. "I told

you they'd be adorable. You should have visited your little ones before now."

I glanced at Cato. He stared at something absolutely fascinating on the ceiling. Adrian tried very hard not to laugh.

We quickly got everyone inside the house though it wasn't much warmer. At least the wind didn't blow through the cracks. I made her a new bed, charged the blankets with a little extra warmth, found her food and water and a litter box. She settled next to the kittens, obviously relieved.

"Thank you for coming by," she said and stopped to clean the head of one of the little yellow and white kittens. "I worried, with the storm. Is Tommy Bear all right?"

Adrian choked a little.

"Water in the kitchen," I said. "Tommy is fine. He's worried about you and the little ones. I'll tell him you're okay."

"The storm can't last much longer, right?" she asked, looking toward the window. "I hope he can come home soon. He'll have such fun with the kittens."

"The snow should be over before too long," I said, hoping so for my own sake.

"Do be careful, Kat. All of you. I've seen some strange things out there. It's not safe."

I petted her and then nodded to Adrian. We left the house. Shakespeare settled in my arm, though he peered around the corner at the cat and kittens as I pulled the door closed, plainly intrigued.

I had to use more magic to keep a path open for us. We couldn't simply trudge through the snow which had drifted higher than my waist in a couple places.

"I know humans have odd silly nicknames for their

pets," Adrian said. "I never considered how they might have the same sort of names for us."

"You don't want to know what we call Kat," Cato offered.

"What?" I asked.

"Oh no," he said. "You won't hear them from me."

"Hey boss," Gaylord said, peeking out. "Where are we going?"

"The library." I eyed Cato, but this probably wasn't the time to badger him about such trivial things.

"Library? Got any cute birds there?"

"No, afraid not. Might find pictures of a few for you, though," I said when he sighed.

"Thanks, boss."

We slipped past Town Hall and hurried to the library, only a block away. They had alarm systems at every opening, and powered by an independent generator, but the alarm on the main door was easy for me to bypass.

"Technology and magic . . ." I said, putting my hand on the door. Something fizzled and sparked for a moment. ". . . don't mesh."

I pushed the door open, and we slipped inside the dark building. As soon as I closed the door, I created a quick illusion which would make the place look dark and deserted. Adrian gave a yelp when I sat a magic light in the air.

"Sorry. I thought that would help. No one can see us from the outside." The room was cold, but we were warm from my magic, so I didn't waste more power to make heat.

"What are we searching for?" Adrian asked, glancing around.

"Poetry, I suppose. Shakespeare --"

"Oh, is that why you gave him the name? He's not

quoting Shakespeare," Adrian said, shaking his head. "I studied English Lit in college and I had a passion for Shakespeare and I know he's not quoting The Bard. This would be easy with a computer. I could type in a couple lines of what he said, and we'd have an answer." Then he smiled at me. "I guess computers are right out with you around, though."

"I've seen them. I can dampen my powers and probably use one, but there's no power here, anyway."

"There might be a poetry codex of some sort. Some of his quotes sounded familiar, but it's just not works I know very well."

Adrian knew his way around libraries, which helped. He found what he wanted and searched through the book while I tried to recall some of the lines Shakespeare (maybe not the best name) had said. The bird did not help at all by quoting anything.

But we found something.

"Tamerlane. Edgar Allan Poe."

"The 'Nevermore' guy, right?" I asked.

"Yeah, him. Not the type of poetry I would have associated with Poe." Adrian disappeared into the shelves and then came out with a book in hand. He sat at the table and flipped the pages open. "Tamerlane is from some of his early work. He went odd later in life. Damned good writer though."

"I thought all writers go odd, which is why I chose to write for a profession. I hoped I would fit in better."

He laughed and leaned over the book.

I read the poem over his shoulder. It was longer than I expected and I heard echoes of my bird in every few lines. "Interesting. Nice stuff, but I don't see how this fits in with our trouble. These creatures are from fae, and the poem isn't so well known it would create a myth strong enough to live there."

"Tamerlane was a real person."

"Oh, well, that makes a *big damned difference*," I said, startled and leaning closer. "Sorry. I don't know enough human history. If he was real, then this isn't the only story about him, right? There were myths and legends along with history?"

"Yes. He's not one of the better known figures in history, but he isn't forgotten." Adrian stood. "We might not find much on him."

He returned to the shelves of books and I took the poem to read more carefully this time. A historical person made sense of a lot of what I had seen. I sought clues in the lines -- *Kind solace in a dying hour* -- but I couldn't quite put everything together.

Adrian placed two encyclopedia volumes to the table. I opened the first and read through the material, little though I found: born in the north, an Islamic conqueror known both for his cruelty and his spread of culture. The combination seemed to be quite an achievement.

"I'd say this is who we're dealing with," I said. Adrian frowned, but not in disagreement. I guessed what bothered him. "And yes, I believe he is the one who had hold of you, since I can't imagine Aletta would bother with anyone else. This gives us a chance to figure out what's going on. The city I saw -- the one on the other side of the Edge, which seems to be slipping through -- might be a mythical version of Samarkand."

"Are you telling me Timur is fae?"

"No. The real Timur, the one who died hundreds of years ago, was human, and the history of him is mostly true. But his life generated myths, and those often drift over to

the fae world and take on a life of their own. When they're
myths based on a real person, they sometimes have
exceptional strength as well as a stronger tie back to your
world. We're not dealing with the real Timur the Lame --
which explains the limp you had! Anyway, not the real
Timur, but the essence of his legends and myths."

"That sounds worse," Adrian said.

"Yes, something made of the myths and legends could
be worse. They leave their humanity behind." I read more
material and found something else. "He conquered The
Golden Horde. When you were -- when he had you, I
found him reading the newspaper on my porch. It was an
article about treasure from the Golden Horde that they
have on display in Denver. I suspect a fae manipulated
things so the treasure would be here, close to where he
intended to come through. This is something real, part of
the Tamerlane history, and would help make him real if he
got his hands on it. There would literally be power if he can
touch the things that the real Tamerlane once held."

"How can we use this?" Adrian asked, glancing at me
and then over at Shakespeare. "How does knowing these
things help?"

"We have *named* it," I said. He looked startled. "Yes,
names can be important in magic, especially in case where
the thing is tied to something specific. We know, for
instance, that we do not want him to get to those items in
Denver, no matter what else happens. Before this, I did not
understand what I was facing; a fae, a ghost, specter, or
something new I'd never heard of before this encounter. I
now know we're dealing with a myth come to life and one
which should never have gained this much power, since the
story isn't well known here. You don't want to run into
Arthur, but he's happy with his fae realm, so I don't see him

trying to return."

"Hell," Adrian said, a little worried and no doubt considering lot of things he wouldn't want to turn up in the human world. I didn't mention the trouble with the Nile Gods. He had enough worrying him right now.

"Tamerlane never should have been this powerful," I repeated. "Someone is helping him along."

"Aletta?"

"She's part of what's going on but she's not running the show. She never had much control, ambition, or such control of her powers. We're dealing with someone who has a considerable power and can manipulate the Edge and create magic to move Tamerlane's mythological world over to this reality. Why, though, is the other big question?"

I stood and paced for a moment. I had clues, but I still didn't have an answer.

"Why would someone bring a fae-made city to this side?" Adrian asked.

"I don't know. Bringing even a few minor things over is extremely dangerous, but a whole. . . ." I stopped and stared at him, my mind leaping ahead several steps. "Making a myth real in this world and forcing a breach between fae and the human world would start the fall technology. And from this place, his stronghold, he can ride out and conquer the world."

"*On mountain soil I first drew life*," Adrian quoted, nodding at my words. "He's come here, because this place is something he understands, something he can control."

"And a place where the border guard isn't as strong as some of the other locations." I waved away his start of a protest. "As fae go, I'm not strong. Even so, I've foiled several plans. Aletta likely chose you to be his host just to bother me because she's petty. She would have done much better not to draw my attention too soon. And that's why she's not in charge."

"No one else has been taken over, have they?" he asked softly.

"Not as far as I can tell. I think Tamerlane wanted a more direct contact with the world while the magic drawing him and the city here grew stronger. Once he grew strong enough on his own, he would have abandoned your body."

"What are we going to do?" Adrian asked.

"We're going to go find more answers," I said looking back out at the cold, wintry night. "But at least now I know what we're searching for."

CHAPTER EIGHTEEN

I considered leaving Cato and the birds at the library, but I didn't know when we could return, and there was no easy way for them to get out if they needed to escape. I considered another magic cat door, but that would only lead into a deadly storm. At least if they stayed with me I could protect them from some harm. Besides, they were my allies, and we had to work together to end this invasion.

Me, a human, two birds and a cat.

I tried very hard not to think the world was doomed.

The night had gone dark, and the wind howled through the streets, sending snow in cascades from buildings. As we left the library I saw the glitter of magic as the shape of a different building overlaid the outline of the library. The ghost city had come back and appeared far more powerful this time.

"Everything tastes like licorice," Adrian said, shaking his head. "Licorice everywhere."

"A lot of magic around us." I brushed my hand over the ghost wall. It felt a little warmer than the real one. "And a lot more in the air."

"Are people going to see this?" He waved towards a wall which already seemed more desert brick than mountain wood.

"I fear they will soon. Then we have more problems. I want humans to remain calm and sane and not worry about magic. If there was anything I could do --" I considered something that might help. I lifted my hand into the air. "Magic in every snowflake." I spread a whisper of a spell out through the storm, dancing on the winds. "Little spells, little whispers. Sleep, sleep, sleep -- all the people in the city sleep through the long night, go somewhere safe and warm and sleep peacefully --"

Adrian swayed and almost say in the snow since he was already safe and warm in the magically heated clothing. I caught hold of his arm and brought him awake with a little shake and a surge of magic to counteract the spell.

"Whoa. The magic really worked!" He looked half-wired now. Maybe I'd used a little too much power to awaken him.

"The spell should keep the humans quiet for the night -- most of them anyway. There's always a few who are resistant to magic, but we might get lucky. If they're at home, they might not notice anything."

"Riders," Cato warned with a little hiss.

We hurried into the shadows behind a snow drift and I sent a little breeze to cover our prints. The two riders didn't spot us. I had feared my magic drew them here, but they seemed to be on a patrol of the streets.

I had hoped the magic might send them to sleep, but apparently they were not human enough yet.

They had color tonight, and while they were not quite solid, they were still far more real than I wanted them to be. I heard the whisper of words as they passed.

We waited until they were well away. When we stood, Cato had draped himself around Adrian's neck. He looked huge and heavy -- but warm. A live fur collar.

"I heard them talking," Adrian whispered.

"They're gaining reality here. A shame they're not more so. My spell might have put them to sleep, too."

"Where do you want to go?"

"Let's check out some of the town. If Tamerlane is bringing his Samarkand here, we might learn something about the places he's targeting."

Adrian nodded as though I had said something wise. I put a little broom spell in behind us, whisking away our prints. I didn't dare use any stronger magic. I didn't want to glow and draw Aletta, or anyone else, to us and find myself in a fight before I found answers.

The white streets glittered with magic which still looked lovely even though I wanted it to go away. I tested the sphere and found both circles in places I wished they weren't. Tamerlane would have this city before too much longer -- another night or two at the most. I had to stop him.

I had no clue what to do. None at all. I made people sleep tonight, but in a few days those phantom buildings would be real even in the daylight. In a few days, the people of Estes Park would find themselves in a whole new world, and one they didn't understand.

Humans don't do well with those kinds of changes. They want their world solid, the rules of physics set in stone -- and in their world, cities do not morph into other places and magic does not exist.

I had to keep that world safe for them.

Adrian held my arm as we walked as though to let me know I didn't stand alone. Gaylord had gone to sleep in my jacket and Shakespeare held to my shoulder, a slight weight and a brush of his feathers whenever he shook a little snow off. Cato dozed, and I used a touch of magic to ease the weight so Adrian's shoulders didn't ache.

I did little things to help us, but nothing which would end this trouble. We avoided riders. Not all of them had acquired color yet, but none remained the misty ghosts I had first seen.

At least I knew who and what I dealt with, but I had no idea what to do *with* them. Adrian asked no questions and must have seen the growing despair in my face, even though I saw trust in his eyes.

Building after building had a magic covering from Samarkand. We walked inside a couple, and the interiors appeared normal, though the magic started invading even there. At the grocery store we ate the sandwiches Adrian had gotten from the hotel and I found treats for the other three. We sat in the corner of the little cafe on hard red benches, eating in silence.

I felt horrible.

"I don't know what to do," I admitted aloud. "I have no idea how they are doing this. Should I cross over the Edge and try to find an answer there, or would going take me away from the one place I might really be needed."

"Stay here, Kat. Surely the others on the fae side must realize something odd is happening by now, right?" Adrian asked.

"Yes, I would hope so. But the last time I heard from my father, he said all hell is breaking loose, so they have problems, too. I guess that means going there wouldn't get me help either, right? Okay, so we're alone here for this fight. I need to find something I can grab hold of -- something to give me an edge over the rest of these things."

"Something linked to Tamerlane?"

"Maybe. Or maybe I should concentrate on the riders. They must represent the army he used to conquer the world. If he had no army, it might be enough to stop him. But I don't understand how to deal with them either."

"What about Aletta? Where does she fit in?"

Shakespeare glanced up from his piece of fruit. "*I have no words -- alas! -- to tell, the loveliness of loving well!*"

"Oh, so that's why she's involved?" I asked. He nodded vigorously. "In love with her, huh? He's an idiot. Thank you."

He nodded several more times and went back to his slice of apple.

"Can knowing he's in love with her help?" Adrian asked, though the question appeared to worry him.

"Maybe. Love holds an odd magic, and mixed in with the rest of this, could make it tricky."

The words troubled him and Adrian must be worried about someone using his love against me. Love is a dire thing, tying us to another, providing a weakness for enemies -- which Aletta had already exploited. However, love gives us strength when all else fails.

"It's always the dame that's the problem," Gaylord said when I explained everything to him.

At least he made me laugh.

I had grown tired of wandering from place-to-place without a plan. We had to stop wasting energy and time. I'd examined everything. I needed to sit and still gather new information.

"Cato, are any strays around who might have more news?"

He licked up the last tidbit of Fancy Feast with resignation in his eyes. "I knew this was too good to be true. I suppose you want me to go out there in the *snow*."

"Just long enough to find a couple cats so they can spread the news to come here, not home."

"Yeah, good idea. Can you make a door for us? I don't want to stand around outside howling until you -- or something else -- notices us."

"Good idea." I went with him to the wall and carefully made a magical cat door. I'd have to remember to close it later, or else the store would have all kinds of odd problems. I also made certain Cato had protection against the storm and wouldn't get too cold. He still made a disgusted sound when he stepped into the snow.

"You don't think she'll find us here? Aletta or her companions?" Adrian asked when I came back to the table.

"There's too much magic around." I waved towards the world beyond our little refuge. The shield I'd put on the windows dulled the view, but I still caught the glitter of buildings nearby. "And I'm not doing anything big and messy to draw her attention. We should be okay, but I'll be careful."

"You don't think we should keep moving?" I saw fear he hadn't shown before now.

I reached across the little table and took both his hands in mine. "I'll protect you," I promised. "In the ways only I can. Aletta won't get past me. I trusted her before, but never again."

He gave a tentative smile; not disbelief in my promise, but trying to accept there could be safety in the world. He moved his hands a little, his fingers wrapping around mine. I leaned forward.

And Gaylord made a loud cockatiel kissy sound.

"Gaylord!" I laughed.

"I don't know what he said --"

"A kissing sound. The bird is incorrigible."

He had lightened the mood. I gave Gaylord more food and made a place for him and Shakespeare to sleep for a while. Adrian and I wandered through the store and I grabbed more cat food. We discussed favorite vegetables. The way my life was going, this was as close to a date as I was likely to get.

Cato returned after a couple hours. He hurried in with two strays at his back, the first a young gray tom and the other an almost pure white blue-eyed female with a notched ear, a spot of black on her forehead, and a regal attitude.

"I worried about you, Cato," I said as the three walked over to the table.

"Things are getting rough out there. The snow is a mountain high in some places, and the riders are doing more than ride aimlessly around. They chased me twice. I suspect they're searching for you." He flicked snow off his tail and leapt onto the table, putting him above the other two cats and on level with the humans. It was a good strategic move. "But there's a good side. The more real they become, the more trouble they have with the snow, too. The horses don't like it much at all."

"Good! And these two are?"

"Smoke and Snow," Cato introduced the two with a quick nod of his head.

"We've been trying to find you," Snow said. She sounded annoyed. "Smoke and I live by the big house. The one on the hill where all the people come and go."

"Stanley Hotel," I guessed.

"Yes, whatever the humans call the place," she said with an annoyed flick of her tail. "It turned strange today."

"Strange?"

"Everything . . . changed," Smoke whispered and gave

a little shiver. He had a softer voice than Snow. "The building glowed and things changed, and people moved in and out who didn't belong there and who weren't real."

"Sounds as though this is more than the illusions we've been seeing," Adrian noted.

Both cats started, leaping backward with their backs arched and their ears back as they hissed.

"Sorry." Adrian lifted his hands in apology.

"He speaks." Snow's eyes narrowed in mistrust. "How is it he speaks?"

"Some of my magic slipped into him."

"Humans should not speak." She glared at Adrian and still kept her distance. Adrian bowed his head and said nothing more though his silence might have annoyed her as well. Sometimes you can't please cats no matter what you do.

"He is right, though," Cato intervened. "This sounds more serious."

"I suppose we should go take a look," I said, though going out didn't appeal to me. I'd finally decided to stay put for a while. I should have known better.

Adrian got his jacket. Cato muttered something about fae who never take enough naps.

Shakespeare blinked, half asleep. Gaylord didn't even wake. I decided to risk leaving them here for a while and covered the two birds with a magical blanket to keep them safe from any cats wandering in from the cold.

I put two plates of food on the floor. Even Snow showed a little wonder at the feast.

"You two should sleep here tonight, where you'll stay warm. If humans arrive before we return, go out the magic cat door. We don't want to give our secrets away."

"We will." Snow promised as her eyes moved from the

food to me. "I'll tell anyone else who shows up as well."

"Good." They'd obey her, too. She had that *I am in charge* attitude. I trusted her. Cats are surprisingly good about keeping their word once you pry it out of them. I didn't worry about those two. I blocked off the rest of the store though.

Adrian draped Cato across his shoulders. The cat appeared to be quite comfortable, and Adrian looked warm.

"You're going to spoil him, you know," I said.

"I know," they chorused.

I shook my head as they both laughed and glanced at the clock as we slipped out of the building. Nearly midnight, the point where magic would be strongest. Well fine; I could use the power, too.

The glittering shells around the buildings appeared almost real. I sometimes saw latticed windows and ornamented doors. The riders were more real too, and I heard them speak to each other sometimes. The horses even left prints in the snow.

We moved silently through town. The snow had stopped falling, but clouds obscured the sky and I suspected the storm would turn worse before sunrise. Because the riders were closer to real they proved easier to avoid. We heard them coming, and while we had a couple close calls, we avoided getting caught. We worked our way around the curve of Highway 34 towards the hotel --

And there we stopped.

"You know, they might have mentioned the problem with the riders," I said very, very softly.

The riders we'd seen in town were doing their rounds, but now we found the full army encampment. They covered the hillside leading up to the distant hotel -- or where the hotel should have been. Instead, we found a tall building with graceful arches and even a minaret that rose into the snow-filled sky. I saw the Stanley hotel's concert hall, looking normal, but the hotel had disappeared behind the eastern facade. Even desert sand had replaced snow around it.

Adrian and I backed away to a stand of pines, and Cato tried to bury himself in Adrian's jacket collar to go unnoticed.

"What are we going to do?" Adrian whispered.

I peeked out from our cover. Snow and Smoke had been right: whatever building had morphed itself over the hotel appeared to be close to solid. The walls didn't even glow as much as the others had, which meant more reality and less magic.

I also noted that the riders -- some of them off their horses -- did not go inside the building. In fact, they seemed to have made a wide corridor between their encampment and the ornate front door.

"We need to get in there," I decided. Both Cato and Adrian made sounds of distress, but they didn't argue the point. "I could use magic, but I'm afraid too much will draw attention. No flying."

"Praise Bast and Sekhmet," Cato replied. "I've flown with Kat before and it is not something you want to do unless you have absolutely no choice."

"Disguises," I said, ignoring him. "I can make them see us as two more of the soldiers and they'll see what they expect us to be. That won't take much magic and should be lost in all the other power out there."

"So, as long as they don't expect us to come here and walk in the front door, we should be fine, right?" Adrian asked. He looked towards the building again. "But if they expect you, they'll have some a spell to detect you."

"True."

"We might as well try."

"You two are crazy. All two legs are crazy. I knew this, but I didn't realize how much so --"

"You can stay here." I patted Cato on the head. "I understand. You don't have to go with us."

"Oh, let's just go," he said, but he buried his head in the collar of Adrian's jacket again.

Adrian trusted me too much. I feared doing something wrong . . . no, I would not. This wasn't much magic, I told myself. Child's play, in a literal sense since we learned this trick to play hide and seek when we were kids. A fae could see through the spells if she knew where to look, but these were not fae. The more solid they became, the more human as well. There were a few of the guard walking around the road on foot so we would not stand out.

I cast the spell, tapped Adrian on the arm, and headed for road and the men on guard there. Cato made mewing noises until I tapped him on the head.

Snow crunched beneath our feet. Too loud, I thought. The riders weren't this loud, they weren't this real, they weren't --

The guards bowed their head, and we walked past.

Horses with riders moved along the path, going past us with shouts and salutes. No one stopped us. I had started feeling giddy by the time we reached the open area by the building and feared I would lose the spell.

Three of the hotel's vans sat at the top of the road, incongruous with the army of horse soldiers and the ancient building settling itself nearby. The vehicles held too much technology, and they were holding out against the encroaching magic. They provided cover. We got to the side of the building without incident. I feared we wouldn't have as much luck slipping back out, but I didn't say so.

The sunbaked brick still held the warmth from a desert day where there should have been winter-cold wood.

I headed for the door before I lost my nerve. Adrian moved with me as we walked into the building . . . and into *somewhere* else. The interior had not fully materialized, but it was still more than we'd seen in other buildings. I could barely see through parts of the illusion.

A woman clad in veils walked around a corner and came towards us. Adrian and I both froze until she walked through me as though I didn't exist.

Which I didn't, in her world and even less so than she didn't quite exist in mine.

"We can talk," I said aloud. Adrian glanced around, frantic and expecting trouble to leap out at my words. Cato buried his head a little farther into the jacket. "They can't see or hear us. They're not really here yet. We're seeing myths coming to life, and they have enough trouble maintaining shape and form. They're concentrating on that and not on where they are."

"I wish I understood how this worked." Adrian watched with worry when two men appeared at the end of the corridor, but they didn't turn our way.

"I'm not entirely certain how this works either," I admitted. "This doesn't happen every day. In fact, I've never heard of it before now. We're watching both whispers of history and the overlaying of a myth mixed with fae magic. It won't matter which is which if this becomes real."

We hurried down the corridor. The place seemed to be a labyrinth of passages and I kept track of our path so we knew the way back out. The people continued to pass through us. Odd how you could get used to something so quickly. The walls became almost solid as we walked farther into the building. Buildings might be easier to make real than people. At any rate, I didn't intend to stay and study the process.

Adrian nodded to one of the side corridors. "It looks dark that way, almost as though there isn't anything there."

"I don't think there is anything yet. The building is still in the process of becoming real. Some of the sections must be more important than others."

A group of men passed at the next intersection. A few moments later another group followed them. We headed the same way.

Cato uncurled from Adrian's neck and got down, walking a few steps ahead of us and staying well in sight. Like most cats, he often let his curiosity overcome his worries. He seemed to find the place more interesting than I did.

The moment we entered another corridor I sensed a difference. Mosaics with intricate patterns lined the walls and sconces with bright flames lit the way at every few feet. The light flickered and cast shadows, even of the shadow people, though not of us. I almost heard the murmur of voices, like the distant drone of bees.

We didn't have far to go before the corridor opened into a huge room, blazing with the light of a thousand candles, and scented with incense so nearly real I almost sneezed. Cato had stopped at the entrance to the room, his tail twitching.

On a raised dais at the far end sat a man on a throne, veiled women at his feet, and a great, golden-eyed tiger chained to the left of the throne. The tiger turned her head and stared at us. Oh yes, she saw us, even if the humans didn't yet. I bowed my head and silently wished her well.

The man on the throne was Timur the Lame, our Tamerlane of the poem. The few portraits I'd seen in the books at the library had been true enough likenesses so I didn't doubt his identity. He had the eyes of a tiger, darting everywhere, noting, no doubt, who stood with whom, who bowed their heads quickly and who did not.

A man knelt close by, scribbling away at things I would love to have read. I wanted to understand everything here and to find answers before we headed back into the snowy night to run like rabbits to our hiding places again. This might be a place of answers if I could discern them from the ghosts and the myths.

I glanced around at the men. Some might be commanders in the army Timur had used to sweep through the Muslim world in the late 1300's and conquer everything in sight.

The women, I noted, were less substantial than the men, and even less important than the tiger. Only one seemed to have any substance, and I wondered what unrecorded part she had played in history.

Another group of men passed through us and into the room. I didn't even notice until a brief film came over my eyes and disappeared as they stepped forward. This group proved to be guards and a prisoner -- and behind them came more guards carrying trunks.

The prisoner knelt before Timur though not willingly. I wondered who he might be since Timur appeared pleased. Timur spoke, though not long, but the words struck the prisoner like a blow. The guards took him away, and he fought more than he had when they brought him to this room. I didn't want to know what had become of him.

Timur stood from the throne. The others in the room bowed their heads, and I found myself half bowing as well.

Power gathered in this man; not magic, but strength of a human kind.

He crossed to the first trunk, and the guard opened the lid. His eyes gleamed as he smiled with a brief flash of white behind a mustache. Timur lifted something glittering from the trunk.

I leaned closer to Adrian, speaking softly despite knowing they couldn't hear us. "I saw a picture of the golden bowl he's holding. It's part of the exhibit from Denver. It belonged to the Golden Horde."

The glitter of the golden bowl drew my attention. I saw the shape of the handles, made into intricate water dragons. The golden light filled the room, and I lifted my hand to shield my eyes. The glitter died away slowly.

And then the guards brought in the prisoner, and the scene started over again.

"This is important," I said aloud. The tiger moved and her head tilted. I stayed and watched a second time, and a third. Cato had backed up until he pressed against me, and he watched the tiger with both fascination and worry.

"The bowl is important?" Adrian asked as we watched him lift it once more.

"Yes. He needs to have the real one -- or something else he owned -- to help become real, but this bowl has some special meaning."

The cycle started once more. I backed away this time, the other two coming with me. The tiger watched us go, and I knew how a mouse must feel, slipping quietly into the shadows.

"Can we get the bowl from Denver?" Adrian asked as we hurried away through the corridors.

"We can't even find Denver right now, let alone the treasure. I think this part will come after everything here is settled, but whoever is trying to make it real is ingraining the scene into this reality so that when they get the bowl, it will be locked into place. I wish I could find a way to disrupt this place." I put a hand on the wall and whispered a trickle of magic --

Not a good idea. My power sent a tiny charge of lightning through the wall, a flash of power as I yelped. We hurried away before anyone arrived to find out what had happened.

Adrian and I came to a gasping stop, only a turn from the exit. I had not dropped our disguise yet, so I reinforced the spell again. He had already grabbed Cato and held him in his arms this time rather than over his shoulders.

"I wanted to change something here," I whispered. I feared even my voice might bring trouble. "This is the center of the spell. The conquering of the Golden Horde might have begun the myth part of his life, even though he had already gained mortal power."

"We can't do anything here?"

I shook my head. "I fear anything I do would be spectacular and messy, and might not help."

"Could he send Aletta to get the bowl?"

"Might not wise to do so yet, before his power base is set. Being real before he is ready to take over would make him vulnerable."

"Why don't the riders come in here?" Cato asked. We had reached the door and watched them outside.

"Commoners? They wouldn't be allowed into the presence of their ruler," Adrian explained.

"True. We're lucky we were invisible inside, then. That's just because they expect nothing from out here to walk in. They're also working with a delicate balance. What's inside this shell is what they want to be real and creating reality from a myth will take more power. Things kind of work the same way in fae when a legend comes over though they don't usually have to contend with real world stuff as well. Graceland took quite a while to settle though --"

"Graceland? Elvis?" Adrian eyes went wide.

"Yes, Elvis."

"I want to hear more. Later."

We moved away from the building, skirting along the cars, staying mostly out of direct sight until we were well away from the door.

I trembled from exertion. The spell wasn't difficult, but the stress had played havoc with my nerves. I wanted to take hold of Adrian's hand, and I refrained when I thought about how holding hands might look to the others.

We had a long, silent walk towards the road. Only a few yards left to go --

Aletta rode in with Timur the Lame. Damn. The one in the building was historical, and this one mythical, and this one was a bit taller, stronger and plainly tied to magic. The two would merge at some point -- but not yet.

"Oh hell," Adrian whispered.

I glanced around, frantic for somewhere to hide --

The riders bowed. I grabbed Adrian by the arm and pulled him to the side of the road, closer to the others than I wanted to be, but he understood. He held Cato tight, and we bowed with the rest of the soldiers.

Aletta turned to look out over the army.

"A problem?" Timur asked.

"I -- this magic makes me crazy," she said. "I feel her everywhere."

"But surely not here," he replied, and waved a hand which seemed to point directly at the three of us.

"The fae have powers to deceive," she said, but turned away and kicked her horse into a faster trot. "But not Kitty. She never had the ability to do any real magic."

Oh how tempting to drop a lightning bolt right on her pretty little head right then. Instead, I used her words to strengthen the power of our disguise. Aletta glanced back frowning, no doubt wondering about the little spark of power. The two rode to the top of the hill, but they didn't go into the building. We milled about with the others for a moment until I was certain everyone watched their ruler and his companion. Would she become as insubstantial as the women inside the building?

We headed down the road and into the shadows. No one stopped us or asked questions. I realized they were still mostly show and not enough *here* to understand what happened around them.

I made certain we were well out of sight before I dropped the spell. Adrian caught hold of my arm when I almost fell.

"Your cousin is going to be in for a shock when this is all done," Adrian said and even grinned at the idea. How could you not like a guy who offered such sweet words at a time when you began to believe she might be right?

"I suspect we don't have much time left," I admitted, glancing back at the building. "Tamerlane's palace is too real already. I hope the magic hasn't done irreparable damage to the Stanley Hotel. They must have jinxed the power early on -- that's why the hotel was cleared out. I hope nothing damages it."

"The hotel survived The Shining. It will survive this."

I laughed agreement. He put his arm across my shoulder and we walked on, listening for the sound of horses. Cato walked ahead, far more silent than usual.

"I understand your worry, Kat. We need to stop this from going any farther and worry about the damage they've already done afterwards. You need to concentrate on what to do to end this."

"Concentrate." I needed a few more answers. Knowledge is power. "Cato, I need to find out where Aletta and Timur are when they're not here. I can't see them bedding down with the troops. Not Aletta, at least."

"I'll go find a few friends and we'll see what we can learn." He came closer and reached out to bat at my leg. "They have done nothing to stop us so far, Kat. Timur is relying on Aletta and her magic, and he doesn't know she's not very strong."

"She's stronger than I am."

"Is she? What has she done so far that you haven't been able to counteract? Not this show with the riders and the buildings -- we both know this isn't her."

"I --" I stopped and bent to rub his ears. "Thank you. Be careful."

"We'll find the answers, Kat." Cato brushed against me and then turned to go.

And stopped.

We all did. I heard the flap of very big wings, high in the clouds, where saw only the movement they made in the mists. We stood still, all three of us. Something circled, and I could almost make out the shape of a wing and a long, sinewy neck.

Silence filled the night.

Snow began to fall again.

And as Cato walked away I could hear him whispering.

"There are no dragons, there are no dragons, there are no dragons."

CHAPTER NINETEEN

J ust after dawn the next morning, a scrawny half-grown
black kitten with huge golden eyes came to tell us he'd
tracked Aletta to her hiding place. I don't know how he
survived out there in the snow and the storm. The wind
alone should have blown him off into Kansas. But he gave
Cato detailed directions on where to find Aletta and finally
nibbled a little food, almost too weak to eat more. I petted
him and gave him strength and a place to rest. He already
looked better before we left.

Cato, Shakespeare and Gaylord came with us this time.
I wasn't certain how long we'd be gone or if humans would
arrive at the store today, so I couldn't leave them behind.
The stray cats would slip out through the cat door, and
while the two birds could have followed, this was not good
weather either of them should be out flying around.
Besides, I wanted them with us. I needed my allies and my
friends.

Aletta had taken a condo out by Marys Lake; a fancy,
expensive place and damned near impossible to get close to
because of protection spells. We found refuge in a partially
finished condo with line of sight to where Aletta stayed.
The storm wasn't as bad now, and the winds had swept the

snow off her balcony. I watched her briefly step out onto as
the wind and snow blew around her. I feared she might
spot us, sitting on the plain wood floor behind sliding glass
windows.

Adrian watched and gave a little shudder. "She acts like
a queen surveying her world."

Aletta went inside again. I carefully tested the magic,
but I found no way to get to her.

"The spells are too strong," I admitted, checking over
the rolling yards and the frozen lake to the left while I tried
to find a weakness. All I saw was white on white
everywhere. I longed for spring which had been so close
and now seemed lost in winter again. "Even these spells
can't be her work. Someone wants to make certain she's
safe. We'll never get in."

"But we can watch her." Adrian sounded optimistic for
some reason I couldn't fathom. Maybe staying in a half-
finished building appealed to him more than wandering
around the snowy streets.

"True." I settled on the floor and he moved closer and
I leaned against his chest. He wrapped his arms around me.
Suddenly the idea of sitting here didn't seem so bad. Cato
even came and nestled into my lap and Shakespeare found
a beam to sit on and appeared content. He'd been quieter
since we figured out the poem, and seemed less crazed, too.

I wanted to know what had happened to him and how
he happened on the Tamerlane poem. I had gotten him
before the trouble started . . . no, only before I *noticed* the
trouble. Had something tried to give me warning? I should
have been paying more attention to him and to the
nuthatches.

I found Gaylord on the floor staring through the
sliding glass door towards Aletta's condo. He tilted his head

and finally nodded a few times before he turned to me.

"I can get in."

"I don't think that's a good idea, Gaylord," I replied.

"Come on, boss! Do you want to know what she's doing or not? Is she there alone? I can get in and out."

"She knows not to trust birds. She may have set a trap --"

"So tell me if she has, boss." Gaylord stared straight into my face. "And then tell me some more why I can't help."

I wanted to say it wasn't safe for a little bird to go out there, but he wasn't a nuthatch who wouldn't have been able to tell me anything useful and who would have gotten distracted and caught anyway.

"Sit still for a few minutes. I will do a very careful search before you go anywhere near the condo."

He settled beside me, watching the building with the same intensity I did.

Aletta's hideaway had all the spells paranoia could provide, making seals around the doors, the windows. And even the chimney. I started to shake my head --

And I found the chink in the armor.

"The spells only work if she has the place sealed closed. Every time she steps out on the balcony she breaks the seal until she goes back in."

"So I need to get in while she's out," Gaylord said. He tilted his head. "We need one of them little spycams from TV. I can tell you what's going on, but it would be better if you saw yourself."

"Spycam." I managed not to laugh. Gaylord had plainly watched too much television. "I don't have any spycams. And she'd detect any spell."

"I guess it's up to me, boss," he answered.

"I will need to strip all the magic away from you, Gaylord. You're going to be cold out there."

"It isn't far." He tapped at the glass. "And now's the time. There she is again."

"I don't know if you'll find anything, Gaylord --"

"And you won't know until I try. Open the window, boss."

Against my gut feeling and every worry which sprang to mind, I pulled the magic from him and inched the door open. Gaylord scooted out before I changed my mind and I slid the door closed with a sigh of worry.

Adrian's arms tightened around me and Cato lifted his head to watch. Shakespeare came from his roost and pressed his beak against the window.

Gaylord swept in low under Aletta's line of sight, and I lost track of him in the gentle fall of snow. At the last moment I saw him flap twice, glide upward and land on the balcony behind Aletta. He walked inside.

I held my breath, hoping he'd scurry out but Aletta went inside and closed the door behind her.

"Let's hope she continues to be restless." I learned forward to watch, forcing myself to stay calm.

"I think she's waiting for someone," Cato said.

That possibility hadn't occurred to me. I feared he might be right. "Why didn't you say anything?"

"I didn't know he was going inside. I thought he'd fly around and look in the windows. Don't worry, Kat. I could be wrong."

"I don't think so." A little bell went off in my head. Literally. My spell finally worked! "Something came through the Edge and is heading straight for us! Down!"

I shoved Adrian backwards so fast his head thumped against the floor. I grabbed Shakespeare and Cato leapt close to us as I leaned over and threw a big *blanket of nothing* over of us.

"We're nothing. We're nothing."

It's difficult to create nothing out of a world filled with somethings. I saw where my magical blanket frayed along the edges, and Adrian's boot stuck out. I hastily threw more nothing over us.

Aletta's guest arrived.

I sensed the fae coming because he cast spells searching for others everywhere. The wards around Aletta's hideaway showed a little more than usual paranoia but this proved to be ten times worse. He checked the buildings around the townhouse, and in a moment the air above us filled with the magic light of detecting spells.

"We are nothing, we are nothing, we are nothing."

The spells lingered as my heart pounded, and I kept whispering my mantra, holding on to the spell, holding tight to my friends, waiting for discovery --

The light died as the detection spell slipped away. I held a moment longer, and another, but I slowly lifted my head and watched where Aletta stepped out again. A man in a long dark cape pulled her into an embrace before they walked into the building.

"Oh hell," I whispered, my voice shaky. I caught hold of Adrian's arm as he sat up. "Sorry --"

"We weren't found. You did fine." Adrian wrapped his arms around me. Shakespeare and Cato snuggled close. I had shivered.

"Gaylord." I whispered.

"Gaylord is an inventive little guy," Adrian answered, a soft whisper at my ear. "Wait and see what happens."

"Be ready if the fae leaves," I warned, taking deep breaths. I tried to pull more magic in from the air, but I had

to do so carefully and not draw attention. I would need the
magic to cover us again or else we had to get out of the area
--

And leave Gaylord?

I took another deep breath and forced calm. I would
not abandon him.

The visitor stayed for a long time which helped me
gather magical strength. I did nothing to draw attention
because whoever visited Aletta had far more power than
me.

Calm. Wait.

The door slid open. I tried to glimpse the person who
stood there with the hallo of light around him, but I didn't
dare take the time to study. Adrian already flattened
himself, probably to avoid another bump on the head. Cato
and Shakespeare leaned in close to me as I leaned over
them again.

Calmer this time. "We are nothing, we are nothing."

The spell didn't work until I panicked and frantically
grabbed at strands of the magic, trying to keep us unnoticed
as I spread the shield of nothing over us again.

I feared he must have sensed my frantic magic, but he
passed over without pause. I dared to lift my head and
watched Aletta standing on the balcony.

Behind her, Gaylord scurried out, dropped over the
side of the balcony and into a snow covered bush. I almost
laughed with joy, but I held most of the magic in place,
waiting.

Aletta finally went inside and slid the door closed.

I dropped the spell and reached for the door. Gaylord,
with a frantic flap of his wings, headed our way.

"Thank God he's safe," Adrian whispered. The words
made me love him more if that were possible.

I opened the door enough for Gaylord to get inside the room. He arrived with his beak chattering from the cold and threw himself into my lap. Both Shakespeare and Cato snuggled in beside him, and in a moment he pushed his head out from between the larger bird's wing and Cato's fur.

"Hey, this ain't half bad. The big fur ball is kind of warm and he rumbles like a vibrator --"

"He's purring, Gaylord," I said, stopping him from going any farther with that analogy. I gave him a little magic to help get warm.

"I didn't expect the fae guy." Gaylord shimmied his way out from between the two and began to talk, his wings fluttering in obvious agitation. "I'm sorry I couldn't hear much -- I didn't dare get close to either of them. Right before he arrived, though, she talked to someone using a necklace with a big bright green stone she wears around her neck. I think it was the same guy."

"That might explain how she can reach across the Edge and I can't. The stone must have a spell embedded, and she triggers it for contact. The magic wouldn't be easy to track in the rest of this mess. Do you think she called the person to come over?"

"I don't know what she told him, but she seemed a little upset. When he arrived I hid behind the television and kept an eye on them. I figured I would be safe behind something techie, but it scared the shit out of me to be so close to two fae. I hope they don't find it."

"You were very wise." I patted his head. He rubbed against my fingers and fluffed his crown up, preening for a moment. Then he nestled next to Cato, obviously still cold. "Okay, when the big guy comes in, he hugs her and kisses her on the forehead. I feared things would get out of hand, but they broke the clinch and she goes to the sofa and he settles in the chair. They talk. And they kept laughing. I think. . . ." He stopped and shook his little head. "I think they kept saying a name, one you guys say sometimes."

"Tamerlane?" I asked.

"Yeah, I think so." He bobbed his head several times. "Tamerlane. And then they'd laugh."

Oh, now that sounded interesting. I repeated his story for Cato, Shakespeare, and Adrian.

"Sounds as though things aren't as tight between Aletta and Tamerlane as he believes," Adrian said and shrugged. "But we can't really know."

"The necklace, though --" I stopped and explained about the stone. "I want the necklace. The stone should be a direct link to someone on the other end and that's our real power in all of this."

"You couldn't tell when he flew over?" Cato asked.

"No. I didn't dare try to test out his magic or he would have found us. What did he look like, Gaylord?"

"Tall, dark haired, mustache, dressed-funny --"

"Someone who doesn't come to this side often. They all dress odd over there," I explained. His description fitted half the fae males I knew. A powerful one? Most are more powerful than me, so I didn't know how to judge.

We stayed for a while longer, and the lights dimmed in the other condo so Aletta must have gone to bed. I tested out the magic once more, hoping to find another chink -- but she remained safe behind the wards and I found no way to get to her. I considered staying around and trying to catch her after she came out, but she might not be alone. Sitting here would waste time.

Time to move on.

"Cato, can you get a few cats to keep an eye on the

area and tell me when she comes out and where she goes? But carefully -- really carefully, because she won't hesitate to kill any of you."

"Like she probably killed Pawford, Abbie and the others." Cato's eyes went dark and anger came to his face. "Don't worry. We already understand what kind of person she is, Kat."

I walked with him down the stairs to the door to let him out. "Meet us at the grocery store, Cato. Don't stay out too long, either. I worry about you."

He had started to step out, but came back to rub against my leg, his tail curling up and brushing my knee. I bent and gave him an extra scritch behind the ears and he left with a rumble of a purr even as he darted out into the damned snow which fell harder again. The magic the fae had used triggered more bad weather, of course, but no worse than we'd been seeing before this.

I climbed the stairs and found Adrian had shared crackers with the birds. They sat staring at the dark condo and munching away like kids watching a movie on TV. They made me laugh a little and brightened the mood.

"Come on. We'll head to the store for the rest of the night and check on word from any of the other cats. Staying here won't help, and this place isn't very safe."

Adrian grabbed his jacket and pack. The two birds both sighed with resignation, neither happy about going out into the snow even with my fae powers to keep them safe and warm.

I didn't blame them. I wanted to rest, but not here, so close to Aletta and where the other fae might arrive, and catch us by surprise.

We'd barely left the area of the condo when a group of magpies arrived. They were a strange sight in the middle of a snowy night. They swept onto the bare branch of a tree, knocking snow off as they paced back and forth, more nervous than cold.

"Found you!" they shouted, almost in unison. "Riders, many riders, in the hills. Not real and suddenly very real -- faster than before. Many!"

"Thank you," I replied, adding this information to my vast array of tidbits. I hoped something made sense soon.

They took to the air, heading away from the city as I told Adrian what they'd reported.

"Everything is gaining momentum." I worried what this new information meant but gave an unexpected shrug. "If they're getting stronger, I guess it means this mess will be over soon."

We walked to the store, avoiding the riders who appeared to be as unhappy with the weather as Adrian and me. They might not be working as hard as they had been when they were more ghost than real.

At the store, I found a half dozen sleeping cats, happy to be in out of the weather. Gaylord took one look around and buried himself back into my jacket.

"I'll just stay nice and close to you, boss," he decided. His muffled voice drew a few cat eyes blinking in my direction.

I drew him out and put him on a high shelf with Shakespeare. They nestled in close to each other, Shakespeare giving the cats a stare which apparently stopped a few of them from considering a little dinner on the wing.

I got the cats more food, just in case.

Caring for them was a way to pass the time. Adrian settled at a table with a magazine on backpacking. I found a spot near the wall and sat on the floor with a couple of the cats and let my eyes close for a little while. We were as safe here as anywhere. I even napped though not for long.

When Adrian found me awake he went into the store and came back with everything, including a tablecloth, to make a little picnic for the two of us.

"I felt guilty about taking the stuff," he admitted. "But I can pay them later. Hell -- you, me, the birds and the cats -- we're saving the world. I figure it cuts us a little slack."

"Yeah, I guess so," I agreed. We had a nice little meal, and I wished for a real picnic with him, somewhere out in a field, with flowers and birds, and maybe a few chipmunks coming by to steal food from our basket. I looked forward to such a day.

And in accepting the thought, I also accepted we would win.

"Thank you." I slid over to hug Adrian. "You did just the right thing."

"I'm glad." He pulled me closer, and we kissed.

And I heard Cato snigger. Nothing can kill a romantic mood faster than a cat laughing at you. Well, maybe a bird making kissy sounds is right up there, too.

"I don't have a lot to report," Cato said. His nose twitched a little as he stepped closer to the food. "Two cats went out into the desert. No one's seen them since, so we assume they can't return."

I silently wished them luck wherever they went. At least they would be warmer.

"Tamerlane is camped with his troops -- do I smell roast beef?"

I dug a piece out of the packet Adrian had brought. Cato practically inhaled the first bite and sedately ate the second.

"Almost as good as tuna." He gave me a hopeful

glance.

"Maybe later," I promised. "Anything else?"

"Before she came to the condo, Aletta broke through the ward at our house. Don't worry. She didn't have time to do more than knock over some books and yell a lot. Wish I had seen her reaction when she found we weren't there."

I smiled at the little bit of vengeance, forcing her to spend time and energy to break into the house. "We'll have to be careful when we go home though. She might have left a trap."

Cato nodded and settled into the middle of the tablecloth, paws tucked in, tail curled up to his chest. He appeared quite sphinxlike.

Sunrise would come too soon. What would we do today? I feared by midnight tomorrow there would be considerable more trouble. We might even face the true battle.

I didn't have an army to fight Tamerlane's.

"We need to find a weakness with the riders," I said. "Their numbers will win over us, if nothing else."

"I wasn't going to tell you this yet, but. . . ." Cato stopped and looked up at me, his eyes narrowed. "A few of the cats have been attacking the horses and riders. Some haven't survived. But they learned something important. The riders have a string tied around their wrists. If you tear it off, they melt away and their horses disappear with them."

I remembered attacking the riders and watching the one melt. I had hit the arms and probably accidentally cut the strings. With this added information, I had a weakness. A true, real weakness to use against them. "That's very good to know. Tell the cats not to attack any others though. I don't want the enemy to realize I know the secret."

Cato nodded his eyes bright.

"What do you think the string is?" Adrian asked.

I didn't have to disappoint him since I'd seen the magic before, though not quite the same way. "The string is a line to draw magic to them and keep them whole. They might not need the magic after they've been real for a while. Cato, do you Tamerlane and Aletta know we learned about the strings?"

"Probably not. The cats have been finding riders alone. Chances are they believe you killed the soldiers like you did the others in battle. We think the attacks might also keep Aletta confused about where you are."

"Damned smart cats," Adrian said with a smile.

Cato gave him a regal bow of his head. I hadn't considered Cato's work until now. He must be a general for my cat army out there. I didn't doubt he'd set the others to find out if they could kill the riders. He made certain cats reported to me, and he created relays of cats to pass information our way. I hadn't realized how much I relied on him.

"Thank you, Cato, for everything you're doing and keeping things going out there."

He gave a little snort. "Me? I'm just a pudgy little house cat."

I gave him another piece of roast beef.

Contrary to how things should work, magic grew stronger as dawn approached. I sensed the power moving in a wave washing over us. All the cats leapt to their feet, fur bristling. Adrian, who had been reading, dropped the magazine with a start.

"Honey," he said, startled. "The world is suddenly filled with honey."

"Yeah, we all sensed something. I'm not sure what

happened, but --" I reached out and found a trail of magic. "Something is definitely out there and moving."

"And we need to find out where and why," Adrian said.

I stood. He quickly took the magazine back to the rack and grabbed his little pack, shoving food in with the camera. I picked up all the debris we had scattered around and cleaned the place before we left.

"The cats can stay here unless a human arrives," I told them and saw relief in their faces. "Don't get caught going in and out, guys."

They agreed. Shakespeare came and rested on my shoulder and Gaylord slipped inside my jacket, squirming a little. I wished I weren't so ticklish. He settled quickly. Adrian had Cato in the crook of his arm.

As I opened the door to the store, the brisk cold wind blew snow in our faces. I closed and locked the place. The alarm no longer worked but everything else would reset when power came back and the world returned to normal.

I had to believe *normal* would happen.

I followed the trail of magic though a town where the facade of Samarkand had started to fade. We saw no horses and riders out today and I suspected they worried the local populace would spot them. Good. It meant they weren't ready to move yet.

Oddly, the magic trail led us straight to the Zamond Inn. I hurried towards the door, Adrian saying nothing until we got inside the lobby. He put a hand on my arm and shook his head.

"Honey," he whispered. "I can taste honey again. Can a person put on weight this way? Cause I think I'm going gain a lot of weight before this is over."

"Even if you did, you'd be walking it all off with me," I

said.

He gave an amused nod of agreement as I moved forward. People slept on the lobby sofas, leaning against the walls, and stretched out where they could. The only clear space was by the door and the huge front window, which must have been cold.

No one noticed our entrance. My sleep spell still held, but would fade in the light of day. I detected an incredible amount of magic somewhere nearby. Maybe I had tracked a fae here, and I only hoped this wasn't the one who had met with Aletta.

Adrian put Cato down and drew the digital camera out of his pack. "CNN loves this stuff, if I can upload to a picture or two," he said softly.

I moved aside, making certain I kept my power in check. Where was the magic we had followed here? The power was too strong it overwhelmed everything.

I glanced at Adrian as he moved to the side, careful not to disturb anyone, and took the picture. He glanced at the camera screen --

"What the hell?" he said, and more loudly than I expected.

I crossed, dampening my magic even more and took the camera.

A bright blue spot glowed in the middle of the picture. Magic. Something magic right there --

I turned in time to see someone stand, a dark cloak wrapped around her so only part of her face remained visible: eyes of emerald green, slanted and wild --

She spread her cloak and everything blurred. A wind hit us, knocking Adrian and me down as she swept over us and headed out so fast she broke the huge front window.

Everyone awoke at the sound -- children crying and

men cursing. Jordan Fuller from the park came out of a back corner, wiping sleep from his eyes as he walked to the window with a shake of his head, as though he couldn't believe something else had gone wrong. If they had all stayed asleep, I would have fixed the glass with magic. Now I didn't dare do anything except make sure none of the children charged into the shards.

"Kat -- and David, right?" he said.

"Adrian," he corrected.

Jordan looked startled. "I don't know why I thought David." I almost laughed. "I didn't see you two come in last night."

"You were busy," Adrian replied. He turned to the window. "Someone better get the glass swept up."

"Damn weather -- wind and the cold must have been too much for the glass." Jordan shook his head. Nice, the way humans can always find such easy, logical answers for the inexplicable.

"What are we going to do about the window itself?" a tall woman asked. I realized she was the hotel manager. She glanced at the bird on my shoulder, started to say something -- no doubt about hotel policy -- and then changed her mind. She turned to the window with a little despair and shivered as a sudden wind blew snow through the opening. "This will sap what little heat we have."

"We need something to make snow bricks," Adrian said. He walked over to the window, glass crunching under his boots. "And a ladder for the higher levels as we build the wall."

"Will snow bricks work?" Jordan asked, following him.

"Should help. I was part of a team in Siberia a couple years ago where we made a huge snow palace. The place was surprisingly warm as long as you got enough snow to make sure you have a good insulation."

"Yeah. Okay. We need something to make the bricks." Jordan and the manager went in search of such things and Adrian organized people to help. Others cleaned the area of glass.

Good people, all of them.

Cato let children pet him and Shakespeare sat on a fake tree, letting everyone admire him while he quoted bits of Tamerlane to them.

I undid my jacket, realizing we would stay for a while. Gaylord tumbled out and barely righted himself before he hit the floor.

"A little warning, you know?" he said sleepily and fluttered up to sit on my shoulder. "Small humans. There are *small humans* here. I'll stay out of reach."

"Good plan," I agreed.

At least one of us had a good plan. I fretted over the imagine of the woman with the green almond eyes, wondering what the hell we had in the game now. The magic hadn't seemed fae-like when she swept over us. There were other magical beings, of course, but this one had powers I didn't recognize.

Happily, Adrian hadn't asked about her yet so I didn't have to admit I had no answers again. We had enough problems I already couldn't solve. I didn't want to consider another one . . . but the image of the jade-eyed woman stayed in my mind.

CHAPTER TWENTY

I reinforced the haphazard pile of icy bricks with more magic which was easy since there was so much magic in the snow itself. I even made the area on the interior a little warmer. These people didn't need to be cold when I could do this so easily.

Many of the people here were starting to get antsy, and a few had moved on to bad tempered. Cell phones no longer worked, even if they had power. The hotel's generators were fine, though I gave the machine a little reinforcement as well -- difficult to do, matching technology with magic. I had done the same for the hospital generators a few years ago, so I understood how to help. I also put up a ward against peripix, though they seemed to have stopped wandering thought town.

"Some of the guests are suggesting we're at the start of a nuclear winter or something equally dire," Abigail, the manager said. She sat at her desk and I was in a chair across from her. She'd given me a nice cup of hot cocoa. "Your pets are well trained. We had a yapping little dog in here last night and we finally had to stick it in a closet with his owner. I didn't think birds and cats could be so well behaved, especially together. And they're entertaining the children, bless them."

"They're an exceptional group," I said, and tore off a little piece of marshmallow for Gaylord to try.

"Tastes good, but too gooey," he said with a shake of his head.

I smiled.

"He acts as though he's talking to you," she said and watched Gaylord with a little wonder. "That's kind of neat."

Voices rose in the outer room. She stood, but everyone quieted, and she sat once more, looking exhausted and nearly hopeless.

"Food will run low soon," she admitted. "I hope we can get some brought in today. We have several hundred guests plus all the people who wandered in out of the storm. I've been here for ten years and never seen weather like this, though I haven't said so to anyone else."

"The storm will break soon," I said. I even meant those words. Realizing the trouble she faced, I knew I'd have to bring this insanity to an end as soon as possible. "Another day, maybe. Things will be better soon."

The peripix would come out again when the snow went away. Even if I settled this trouble and get rid of Aletta and her friends, I suspected the peripix would continue to be a problem for a while.

Abigail didn't seem to notice my preoccupation, and I was glad to leave her to her thoughts and work. Gaylord settled into my lap and I leaned back in the chair, letting my head rest against the back.

I napped.

"Kat?" I blinked and looked at Adrian who frowned, his face a little red with anger, which had to mean trouble. What had gone wrong this time? "Aletta is at the door."

Not at all what I expected. I stood, frowning as much

as he was now. Abigail glanced from Adrian to me and started getting worried as well.

"It's all right. Aletta is my cousin and a pain in the ass -- but it's a personal problem. I don't know what she's doing here." I stood and stretched, grabbing my jacket from the chair, and putting Gaylord in the inside pocket this time.

"Hey, a nest! I didn't know this thing had a nest!"

He made me smile, but the pleasure passed as we walked out into the lobby.

Aletta stood there in all her dark, fae-bred and magic-made beauty. She had the attention of everyone. The glance she gave Adrian held more than a hint of worry though. Oh yes, she might be upset to meet with the man she tried to destroy by giving his body to someone else.

"Kat, we need to talk," she said. "Alone for a minute."

"Not without Adrian," I said.

She looked around --

"I'm Adrian."

"Oh. Uh. I thought --" But she stopped and shook her head. "All right. Out here. There are things you need to know."

"We know a good deal already," I said. "About you and Tamerlane, for instance."

She snarled, but spun and headed out into the cold. Adrian and I followed though I did a check to make certain nothing worse waited out there. Aletta stopped, just outside the door, in the alcove where the wind didn't hit so hard. Snow fell in the same white veil I had gotten far too used to seeing.

"Yeah," she said. "I have been with Tamerlane. My mother sent me to find out what he was doing."

"After what you did to Adrian, do you expect --?"

"I didn't do anything. I don't have that kind of power.

I stuck with him because I knew Tamerlane had gotten into him somehow. When you came to the hotel I thought you'd figured it out. I thought you were there to help."

"And how about when you attacked me?" I asked, wondering how she would talk her way out of that one.

"Are you an idiot?" she said, sounding angry this time. "If I had seriously attacked you, do you think I wouldn't have won? I was trying to gain Tamerlane's trust. And the trick worked better than I hoped because Tamerlane lost his hold on David --"

"Adrian," I corrected.

"Whoever. His hold on the human." She waved in a dismissive gesture towards *the human* in question. "You got him back and Tamerlane had to rely on me to help him reach safety. The bird attacking me was uncalled for. Have I complained to you though?"

I didn't believe her, but I held my tongue this time. Adrian said nothing either, but the nervous glance she gave him made me wonder if she feared he knew the truth. I didn't doubt there'd been a lot said between the two while Tamerlane held him.

"Tamerlane is up to something. He has an army up by the place they call Sheep Lakes. I can't reach my mother, and this is serious, Kitty. We need to get there and do something!"

"You can't reach across to fae either?"

"No, not at all. Not for a couple days. I haven't been able to talk to anyone."

And I knew she lied beyond a doubt now, but I nodded.

"Okay. I'll meet you there at noon. Don't be late."

"Noon? Why not now? Where are you going?"

"I need to study the Edge and make certain there won't

be any more surprises. And I need things from my house. Aletta, you need to find out everything you can about what's there and what they're preparing. Can you do that? Carefully?"

"Yes," she said. Her eyes gleamed a little. "Yes, I can do it."

"Good." I patted her on the arm. I considered slugging her instead, but I'd play her the way she had played me, luring me into a trap. "I'll see you there at noon."

She turned and headed away, into the storm. The snow parted around her so she went untouched by the cold and the wind.

Adrian watched her and then turned to me with another frown. I held up my hand, and he kept quiet as we headed into the building and well behind the little barrier of snow and magic which would help shield anything I said.

Cato met us inside the door.

"If I could have gotten the door open, I would have gone out and bitten her on the ankle," he said.

I gave him a little smile. Shakespeare came and landed on Adrian's shoulder, startling him. I spread a little more magic to keep others away for a couple minutes, sending even the small humans charging off in other directions. How could children have so much energy?

"I intend to meet Aletta at noon in the park," I said.

"You know she's lying to you," Adrian replied, and he looked more intrigued rather than angry now. "How are you going to use this against her?"

"She's setting a trap. We need to be trickier than she is." I let the worry come to my face. There was no use hiding it from my allies. "I don't know quite what we will do, but we have a couple hours to figure something out. I have to do this, Adrian. This is my job, and right now I fear many humans will die if I don't get control here. He has an army for a reason, you know."

Adrian glanced around the lobby and turned back at me. He nodded, worried as well.

"I'm open to ideas, guys."

"I take it you're really desperate, right?" Cato asked looking up at me.

And I knew I would not like what he said . . . but I listened anyway.

CHAPTER TWENTY-ONE

I wanted to go to the park alone, but Adrian wouldn't let me. With a little magic, I could have made him stay behind at the hotel.

I didn't.

Adrian adjusted the pack he wore which carried food and other supplies in case we needed them. I hoped we had a chance to take some pictures soon. I wanted normality to return.

We hurried along the road, careful and quiet, because I didn't know what Aletta had in mind or where she might attack. Sheep Lakes seemed the most likely spot though. She wanted me there.

The wind blew through the trees sending cascades of snow tumbling to the ground. Snow drifted high in places, and evened out the dips elsewhere, giving the land a deceptively uniform appearance. Adrian and I walked on top of the snow, my magic creating a trail that made certain we didn't slip into a crevice -- or a trap.

Adrian kept pace beside me, silent and ready. I felt odd not having the birds and Cato with us. When, I heard the rustling of wings to the right, I stopped and shook my head.

"Stay back."

I watched a flash of black and white wings as a magpie flew off, the bird unusually silent.

We reached Sheep Lakes, the place where I had taken Adrian the first day and we'd watched the bighorns in the meadows. Nothing moved today, and the stretch of land, glittering in the faint sunlight, looked peaceful.

Lies, all of it. Especially the welcoming smile Aletta gave us as she stepped away from the shadow of a tree -- practically the only landmark visible to indicate the location.

"Licorice everywhere," Adrian warned softly.

I glanced into the sky: high noon. I doubted Aletta paid enough attention to any human culture to understand the symbolic significance.

"Where is the trouble, Aletta?" I asked as she came a little closer. I sensed the little whisper of a shield wrapped around her. Paranoid and worried.

"Oh, the trouble is very close." I caught the glitter of excitement in her eyes.

She lifted her hand.

Tamerlane showed himself first, stepping through the veil of snow which should not have hidden him. Strong magic there, and not hers, either.

"You were far too easy to play," Aletta said, gloating over every word. Tamerlane came close enough to put a hand on her shoulder though his fingers glittered. Not entirely real yet.

The horses and riders coming behind him looked solid enough to be trouble though. Aletta watched me staring towards them and her smile grew.

"Let me show you, Kitty, what you really face." Her long perfectly manicured fingers flashed with red nail polish in the light. Magic moved and the entire veil dissolved. That helped -- in an 'oh shit' sort of way.

"One question." I tore my eyes away from the army. A thousand? More? Aletta gave me an imperious little nod and Tamerlane grunted agreement. "Why did you need Adrian? They all become real anyway."

"To hurry some of the processes along." She turned her pretentious smirk my way. "And I loved seeing you so upset about your little human friend."

"Enough talk with this *woman*," Tamerlane growled.

"Charming," I said.

Aletta blushed. Tamerlane growled words in another language and gave a wave of his hand.

The riders gave a shout and the horses bent to the gallop. The snow didn't slow them. More magic.

"You never had the power for any real battles," Aletta replied with a haughty lift of her head.

"True," I agreed. "However I do have the one thing you never did." I said and lifted my own hand. She looked startled. "I have friends."

The eagles and hawks came first, rising out of the trees all around the area. They swept down on the army with screams of defiance, startling both horses and riders. Behind them came magpies, jays and a mixture of smaller birds, all of them screaming in attack as they flew from the heights where they had been gathering for hours. They came in such numbers that the wind moved at the flapping of their wings.

Take that you stupid hurricane-spawning South American butterfly!

And then the cats arrived, following the path where I had left magic to make the snow hard for them. Bobcats, cougars, and smaller cats of every breed and size raced to join the battle.

Cats can run very quickly. They were hardly more than a minute behind the birds as they leapt at horses and men.

Panic came to Aletta's face. Even Tamerlane backed away, unsettled.

"I don't have much magic. But I'm not stupid, Aletta."

A merlin swept at her and raked talons across her raised hand as she screamed in pain. Behind her, the nearest horseman disappeared as two magpies slashed at his face and a black tom held to his pant leg with all claws and used his teeth to rip the magical string from the rider's arm.

"Take her!" Tamerlane ordered waving towards me. "Take her and we must be gone!"

"Just birds and cats! Your army can handle --" But Aletta made a strangled sound of dismay as she watched the men disappearing under the combined attacks of my friends.

Cats and birds had been lost as well, their bodies falling beneath horses' hooves. I couldn't watch.

Aletta had panicked but hadn't moved. Tamerlane spoke; a curse, though I didn't understand the words. He swatted aside a crow as someone else might swat at a mosquito and reached for me.

Wanted me -- not dead, just *wanted* me. I stepped away in haste while Adrian moved to my side and pulled out the sword we'd grabbed from the hotel room. I had kept the weapon hidden until he pulled the shining sword up. Adrian swung quickly, the blade hitting Tamerlane's shoulder, and he backed away in haste.

Tamerlane shouted something. The horsemen turned and rode full out away from the battlefield and heading for the distant woods.

Tamerlane had faltered. Aletta cast a healing spell to save him. Sloppy as ever; the magic even helped me.

Tamerlane, his shoulder almost healed, gave a shout of triumph and grabbed the hilt of his own weapon.

Cato leapt and sank teeth and claws into the hand while Shakespeare lunged at his face. He screamed in rage and fear and Aletta began to cast --

Adrian took another swing at Tamerlane to help the bird and cat while I went after Aletta and not with magic, either. I kicked her in the knee and she dropped, howling --

Adrian stumbled, a hand on his bleeding arm. He rushed forward at a horse that nearly trampled Cato and startled the larger animal back.

Some of the riders had already reached the woods. One group of horsemen had not gone with the others. They charged in and I barely had time to get out of the way. Tamerlane leapt up with one while another grabbed Aletta by the arm and swung her unceremoniously in front of him. I tried to grab her back, but the horse knocked me aside --

Gaylord swept past me and straight into Aletta's face. She screamed and lifted her hands in protection -- and he grabbed the chain at her neck and ripped the necklace free.

"No!"

She cast in panic; so did I, and I deflected most of the spell, but Gaylord still tumbled to the ground and I couldn't cast fast enough to keep him from being trampled --

Shakespeare flew straight at the horse, startling the creature aside once more before the larger bird swept towards the ground and grabbed Gaylord out of danger. The little bird still held tight to his prize.

Aletta, screamed in protest as they rode away.

I took Gaylord into my hold and healed broken bones. He gave a shuddering sigh of relief and held the chain out for me.

"You shouldn't have done something so dangerous!"

"You said you wanted the stone, boss. I figured I had the best chance."

I didn't berate him. Instead, I took the gift with a nod of thanks and settled him in the nest pocket inside my jacket. I held the stone, remembering how Aletta had tried to hide the pretty bauble from me. I had been stupid to think she had been simply petty at the time.

I had the stone now but I couldn't do anything yet. If I found out who was on the other end of the link, I wanted to make certain someone was there to grab him.

I worked at healing the others instead -- first Adrian and then the birds and cats who came limping to me or the ones others brought. I dragged magic out of the air and even out of the snow until it melted and left me in a puddle of icy water. I couldn't save them all.

My hands appeared translucent. I hadn't the strength left to stand. Adrian wrapped me in his arms as he lifted me. He did not let me see the battlefield as he carried me away.

We had won the battle, but not the war. And this ploy wouldn't work a second time. Good. I could never stand to put my companions in such danger again.

CHAPTER TWENTY-TWO

Adrian must have realized how dangerous using so much magic had been for me. I could barely talk as he carried me away. My arms wouldn't move. Cato walked with us, and Shakespeare stayed on Adrian's shoulder, looking at me with worry. I hoped my magic held for him and Gaylord and they didn't get too cold.

"The Edge," I whispered. "I need -- the Edge. Magic there."

Magic that I wouldn't have to convert from the snow. Magic I could drink in like water. I needed to get there.

Adrian stopped and glanced frantically around the empty, snowy countryside. "How do we find it?"

"Close," I whispered and lifted my trembling hand to touch the magic. The Edge had come closer though not in the direction Tamerlane and his people had ridden. "About a mile." I pointed off to the left. "Find the Lawn Lake Trailhead. Just get me there."

He'd do everything in his ability to get me up the hillside. I spent a little more magic to help us because if we didn't reach the Edge, I would not have enough to save us from any other trouble, even if I survived. Adrian panted as he hurried. Birds flew around us, and few cats came with

Cato. I watched a bobcat run ahead as a scout.

We reached the Edge, the glow bright and beautiful even in the daylight. Adrian took me so close I could kneel before the swirling colors and put my hand right on the magic of the wall. The area darkened as I drew out the power more quickly than I ever had. Power sparked around me, but nothing drastic happened.

I had never pulled in power quite this way. I'd accepted magic passively from the snow and even from being close to the Edge, but I had not directly tapped the source until this time. This was not my power, but I could use it to survive. My blood seemed to tingle, but my sight cleared and the world came clearer. My thoughts began to race.

And I realized I'd made a bad mistake.

"We need to get away from here." I stood so suddenly that even Cato leapt up, startled. Adrian must have seen my desperation. "We need to go --"

Magic swirled in around us in a huge suffocating mass, sending a powerful wind gust blowing through the area. Adrian and I grabbed at each other while birds and cats floundered and tumbled away. I watched Cato sliding over the snow howling as he went.

Horses and riders arrived in a heartbeat and from the mass came Tamerlane, his face red with anger, and Aletta smiling gleefully, despite a scratch across the side of her face.

I shoved the necklace into Adrian's pocket -- and I let go of him. He shouted in dismay, and tumbled backwards, caught off guard, and was swept out into the snow with the others.

I anchored myself with magic and stayed.

Tamerlane rode forward with the wind at his back, almost flying those last few feet to reach me. He grabbed me by the shoulder, and I didn't fight this time. I pulled more magic to me, waiting for Aletta's flamboyant -- and rather messy -- arrival spell to die.

She even panted this time, leaning over the neck of the horse. The wind died, and I hoped all my friends had the wisdom to stay away. I had forgotten Gaylord in my pocket, but he kept still. I would think of something --

"Finally. Right where we want you." Aletta slipped from the horse, her hand brushing against the Edge. The colors moved with patterns and gathered beneath her fingers. I didn't have that much power, and I resented her for the show.

"Do this magic of yours," Tamerlane demanded, shoving me into Aletta's hold. She almost lost me, too, but Tamerlane blocked the way when I turned, and Aletta grabbed me, her claw-like fingernails digging into my arm. Talons: I thought they might draw blood, despite the cloth of my jacket.

She shoved me against the Edge and held me there as she pulled out strands of magic and wrapped them around me -- reminding me that we came from the same clan, and she had the same powers over the Edge that I did.

Only better.

I tried to send magic against her. She laughed and brushed a spell away with a little flick of her fingers.

I couldn't breathe or figure out why she trapped me here --

Then I understood. Understood it all.

She was trying to open a door to the fae lands with me as the key. The door would trap me between both worlds, and because of my power as a border guard, I would keep the door open for as long as I stayed there -- and I feared her spell would keep me there forever.

They would bring more of the fae lands into this world. They would spread and take control because nothing on this side would have power over them and the fae would be too late to stop this once it started.

I fought desperately, keeping the area closed while magic danced all around us. I wished for someone on the other side to sense this trouble -- but they wouldn't. They hadn't even noticed the magical Samarkand, which meant someone used a lot of magic to make sure they didn't look here. I searched for a way to escape as she tried to push me harder into the Edge. If she won, I would change both worlds --

I almost got a hand free, for whatever good it might do. I tried to grab Aletta to pull her in as well. I wouldn't leave her behind to survive this win and to change things to suit her --

She shoved my hand aside with another laugh.

I glimpsed movement before I heard them. The birds and cats arrived with a cacophony of sound, drawing all our attention. They rushed towards us, but Aletta and her companions were ready this time. Tamerlane's riders rushed out to stop them. Aletta cast a quick ball of fire at the birds. I almost closed my eyes, afraid to see them die, and knowing I wouldn't be able to help them this time. I couldn't even cry out a warning, the breath gone from me, the ties holding me, dragging me away --

At the last moment the creatures scattered, and both riders and magic didn't seem to catch them.

Adrian came for me. He ran from the side of the Edge, leaping towards Aletta and knocking her down before he reached and grabbed me by the arms. When Aletta moved Cato leapt on her and did what he had always wanted to do: he bit her nose. She screamed.

I tried to yell at Adrian to get away. He didn't have magic to free me anyway.

He had something better.

Adrian pulled the cell phone from the pocket in his pack, turned it on -- and shoved the device into the opening Aletta had made. He wrapped his arms around me --

The explosion sent us flying. I gasped for breath, and all that saved us from broken bones was a high snowdrift.

Tamerlane and Aletta were sprawled on the ground, and horses were scattering, and magic lashing out in all directions, unstable as hell. I smiled.

"Good . . . *damned* good work!" I said to Adrian. He wrapped his arms around me, and we got to our feet. The birds and cats were gone, except for one bobcat which remained close. Even Cato had taken off to get clear of Aletta who still howled and held her nose.

I started to go back after Aletta and Tamerlane. I wanted to end this, but the riders got in the way. I almost dared magic, but it might backfire in this miasmic mess. We had to get away.

"This way, this way, this way," the bobcat hissed and even came to nudge us.

"I should try to --"

"This way, this way." The big cat glanced upward at the sky and shuddered. "Big wings. Big wings come!"

Dragons? I thought I might hear their wing beats.

I grabbed Adrian's arm and began to move away as quickly as we dared. We both limped, but we made good time. By now a new storm had sprung up. All the damned magic in the air sent peals of thunder and flashes of lighting every other heartbeat. The storm would get much worse tonight. Snow fell, thicker with each step we took.

I glanced back once and saw Tamerlane staring at the sky and with a show of fear I hadn't seen before now.

The big wings were not his friends, but I couldn't count them as my allies. Dragons made their own choices. I didn't understand the reason these dragons might be here, but this wasn't the time to stop and try to talk to them.

Tamerlane shouted and his riders abandoned hunting us to surround him -- a very worried man, looking for protection in numbers. Someone threw Aletta over a saddle. She still had a hand to her nose.

Good.

We disappeared over a hillock, and into a ravine. I was too rattled to keep the snow solid, and we left tracks a blind Pekingese could follow. The wind and the storm helped us. The others had troubles of their own. I could still hear shouts and cries of fear back by the Edge.

The beat of wings moved somewhere over us. Definitely more than one creature. Adrian glanced up, his eyes gone wide as two enormous shapes glided through the snow trailing magic where they passed.

"Honey," he whispered. "I taste honey again."

Hell. Had we seen a transformed dragon at the hotel? Hell. Hell. Hell.

The dragons didn't come for us.

The bobcat sat at the top of the next rise, waiting impatiently while we struggled upwards through the snow and ice. I stopped, took several deep breaths, and spread magic behind us. I tried to find Cato and Shakespeare, but I sensed nothing but Tamerlane and his people and the huge pools of magic gliding down at them.

Maybe the dragons would solve my problem. I'd read a lot about dragons, and even their fae allies took precautions when meeting them. Dragons held a logic all their own.

I might understand some of the problems I'd been having, too. Those massive waves of rolling magic could well have been dragons coming through the Edge. They might even be part of the reason it kept moving. They held powers fae never fully understood.

Adrian and I followed the bobcat, sliding into another ravine and rushing across a stream that sat frozen beneath the covering of snow. We followed no trail, and we weren't heading to town. I thought I should protest, but at least the bobcat led us away from the trouble.

We climbed another hillside which proved difficult though near the top we found a wide ledge blown free of snow and a small-mouthed cave. The bobcat urged us inside, batting her head against my legs.

"Go, go!" She cast a wary glance at the sky. "Go in. Warm. Safe."

Adrian said nothing -- probably so he wouldn't upset the large cat the way he had Snow. I nodded. Getting out of the cold, and out of sight, would be a good idea. I would have preferred to be in town but no one would find me here.

Adrian pushed his pack in and crawled in first and I followed, with the bobcat at my feet, making anxious sounds. I soon found out why. Two little ones hissed and growled when they saw us, but settled as soon as their mother appeared. Adrian and I went to the far side opposite them, Adrian moving the sword so I could lean close to him.

"My human friend can speak cat," I told her as Adrian and I leaned against the wall. "I hope this will not bother you, my friend."

"A human who speaks?" Her head lifted and stared at him, her eyes catching the light of the open cavern. "How interesting."

"I hope I don't offend you," Adrian said, bowing his head to her.

"You behave well for a human."

Adrian gave her another polite nod, and the corner of his mouth twitched in a little smile.

We had survived.

I considered what had almost happened. My hand found Adrian's, and I probably held on too tightly.

"You saved not just me, but everything, Adrian. They were using me to open a door to the fae lands. The door would have stayed open forever with me trapped in the middle."

"I didn't know what they were doing and Cato -- Cato said you'd rather be dead than let them use you for something evil."

"He was right," I answered. I laid my head on his shoulder. "But I'm glad I didn't die. I'm glad to be here with you."

"I had to think fast. I remembered how you had shorted the alarms at the library, and how magic and technology didn't mix. We can't let Tamerlane take you again." Adrian took my chin in his fingers and lifted my face so I looked into his eyes. "You can't be at risk --"

"I can't hide. If I hide, they'll just find another way to get what they want. They might lure another fae here. I know what they plan, Adrian. And this is my work. This is why I'm here. I have to do what I can to stop them."

He nodded and let my head rest against his shoulder.

"Sleep for a while. We won't have a chance to rest again soon."

I nodded and lowered my head. He wrapped his arm around me, and I felt movement in my jacket, followed by the inevitable tickle as Gaylord worked his way up to the collar.

"Hey where are we? Did I miss something?"

I almost choked trying not to laugh.

The bobcat turned our way. Her ears flickered and her eyes narrowed to golden spots of light in the dark.

"Nice little bird," she said in a soft, near purr.

Gaylord spotted her and ducked back into the jacket, burrowing deep into the pocket.

A very nice and *wise* little bird.

CHAPTER TWENTY-THREE

The storm didn't last for as long as I expected, given the amount of magic we had used. The snow fell in fits and starts, and the wind dropped to a gentle breeze long before the sun disappeared over the mountains. Perhaps there wasn't enough moisture left in the air to create more snow. I hoped for such a simple, natural answer, and not find that the magic had pooled somewhere and all hell would break lose at the worst possible time.

Perhaps I was getting too pessimistic.

Or maybe I was finally becoming a realist.

I sat, still nestled in Adrian's hold as he kept watch. We had shared food from the pack with the bobcat and her kittens. The night remained deceptively calm and quiet. I thought everything was coming together . . . though it might be preparing for the end of the world.

I fell asleep and awoke to the sound of a hiss, and the whisper of snow moving on the ledge outside, as though with a sudden breeze. I sat up, blinking, and touched Adrian's arm. Something --

I heard the steady beat of wings. One, two, one two -- and shadows passed over the ledge.

And returned.

The dragon landed with a scratch of claws on stone and the tumble of rock shifting under the huge weight. Magic swept over me so fast my head swam. The tip of a wing, sky blue and glowing like water and ice, settled at the edge of the opening. A talon moved, the tail wrapped forward -- and the shape changed to a human in a long cloak. Now I knew, beyond a doubt, what we had seen in the hotel.

"I would speak with you this time." A woman's voice said, lovely and compelling; the words sounded like music in the chill night air.

I pulled away from Adrian and signaled him to stay put. He wanted to argue, but he obeyed.

I crawled out of the cave and stood. The night had fallen, but the dragon glowed with power, even in this form. A person cannot help feeling dowdy and dirty in the face of something so magnificent. Even in human form, she held grace and beauty, diamonds and magic, and the world sang around her. I bowed my head to her.

"Look upon me, fae." Magic sang in her voice. I obeyed. I might not have had a choice but I don't like to consider those things. "You are the one who must win this battle."

"I'm doing my best." I feared it sounded as though I was whining.

She tilted her head and her long hair moved. The strands were as dark as the cloak she wore, and I couldn't tell where one ended and the other began. Her jade green eyes caught the light of the moon -- or did they glow with their own power? Her glance looked through a soul, I thought. I might have preferred her in dragon form.

"Who are you?" I dared to ask.

"We are the East and the West, and the ones who

ruled the world before the usurpers came. Timur the Lame is not the first such human, but he took something precious we had put in the hands of others who served us well --"

"The Golden Horde." I remembered watching him lift the small golden bowl with the dragon handles. Of course the moment started a legend, linking him back to real dragons. There had been magic in that moment.

"We do not wish for him to have such a myth again, not in this mock form. We sent you such warning as we could through the fine gray bird and only dared come closer after technology began to fail. We gave the bird the words of a myth about this Tamerlane."

And that explained Shakespeare. It made sense they used a poem -- Dragons loved such things. "Thank you. Once I realized he was telling me about a myth and a man, I found find the link." I didn't say how long I had taken to figure out the problem, but she probably knew already. She didn't berate me.

"We have done what we can to unsettle Timur the Lame and his army. We have tried to remove the fae, Aletta, but she is protected by greater magics than come from her own powers."

"Why did you go to the hotel?"

"To lead you there and watch this human for myself, the one you keep hidden in the cave. I wanted to see him and judge his actions -- but he found me out too soon. He walked with the soul of the other, and we did not trust him. I saw his soul though and found him free of the hold. With him, you will defeat Aletta and Tamerlane."

"I'll do my best to stop him. I want him to go back where he can live as a myth and do no harm to this world."

"So it should be."

"Why are you here?"

"If you fail, we shall make certain he cannot survive to do harm here."

I thought that might not be so bad . . . and then I thought again. Dragons rarely did things in delicate measures. The work they had done with Shakespeare had been extraordinary. Dragons were big and expansive and they did not act by small measures.

I worried about what they would do to end this trouble. An action which stopped Tamerlane might mean pulling down the mountains and burying us all.

"You understand quite well," she said. I shivered, both because she read my mind and because she didn't disagree with my assessment of the problem. "This is our nature. We are big in body and magic, and we do not act in the same delicacy as the fae. We settle things *permanently*. I do not wish to do so here, but we will act, rather than have this link made between the two worlds which would change and destroy both in time. He cannot succeed. Go now. Fix this, and quickly. Another day will be too long."

She spread her arms out, and the cloak grew. I leapt to the opening and flattened myself there as I watched her change from beautiful human to exquisite dragon. She looked at me with the same jade green eyes and blinked, nodded, and reached out with a huge talon to touch me over the heart.

Magic.

Magic like I had never known before coursed through my body. The power healed, gave me strength and gave me the chance to do this right. I bowed my head with tears of gratitude. We had a chance. We might yet survive this. Along with the magic, she gave me hope I had not had until now.

She turned and pushed off from the ledge and glided

out over the trees below our retreat. Her companion swept down and joined her -- a golden dragon, glittering in the moonlight.

Adrian came out of the cave and stood beside me, watching as they flew away. I took Adrian's hand, listening long after the big wings disappeared.

"We have to go now," I said, my voice calm and certain. I would not let the dragons make the final choice on what happened. They had given me fair warning. She had also given me strength. I had to do the rest.

Adrian didn't argue. He crawled back in and grabbed his pack. We said farewell to the bobcat and her kittens. I wished them well in the world and hoped the world would still be there by this time tomorrow.

We started down the hillside. Far off in the distance I saw a lovely glow of blues and greens. "We're going back to the Edge," I told Adrian.

"I always knew we would." He seemed serene and calm. I didn't think a human who had seen such a creature as the dragon would react that way, but Adrian had seen a lot of magical things lately.

I savored this hike tonight. We didn't rush off to fight another battle for which I was not prepared. The world would end tonight -- though I knew the two of us might never see the dawn. We were coming closer to midnight, and I accepted the peace of the moment and prepared to face whatever trouble came next.

"I understand why some of the oriental philosophers were always so sedate and their words so calming," I said at last. "The dragons were always closer to them."

Adrian nodded and frowned a little. "Should we be more . . . I don't know . . ."

"Panicked?" I laughed at his emphatic nod. "I don't

think panic would help now, Adrian. We will either win or we won't. We need clear thoughts."

"And what are you thinking?" he finally asked.

That was a good question. I'd been going through everything I had done before now. I was also measuring the magic the dragon gave me. Could I take on Aletta, Tamerlane and all his men? If I failed, what would happen?

I had to give us the best chance to survive because we didn't dare let the dragons act.

"I need help because I will never have the power to defeat an entire army and Aletta. I can't use the cats and birds again because Aletta will have a spell ready to use against them."

"So what will we do?" he asked.

"You'll stand guard, and I'll open a door through the Edge and call for help."

Adrian stopped and looked at me, worried this time. "But opening a door might help Aletta, right?"

"It might. Adrian, I do not have the ability to stop her, even with the magic the dragon gave me, I'm limited in what I can do. However, I have friends and relatives who can help if I can force a call through to them, and that, is the best way to use the magic the dragon gave me. I don't understand what's going on in the fae world, but if they knew the seriousness of this trouble, they would come running."

"I heard the dragon. We have little choice in what we do now, don't we?"

"Very little. I have to act as quickly as possible. I have to get us what help I can so that there is a chance of survival if I fail to stop Tamerlane."

He nodded and didn't argue with me.

I loved this human who stood by my side, who

understood the weight of my decisions, and who accepted my answers. I'd known others who would have wanted to argue with me -- fae and human, men and women -- just prove themselves. I was lucky to have such a companion.

I hoped Cato and Shakespeare were well and that I found somewhere safe for Gaylord.

We climbed one hill, and I saw the double sphere off in the distance, slightly glowing in the night. The expanse of golden sand had grown wide between one wall and the next.

Most of a mountain had disappeared, turning from snowcapped and high, to a wide desolate waste of weed and sand. I feared the sphere moved inward more quickly now.

"Not much time," Adrian whispered.

So we walked faster.

TWENTY-FOUR

We found Tamerlane's army camped before the Edge. Timur and Aletta were seated around a campfire -- a normal one, no magic there -- with the magic glittering and dangerous at their back.

Too close. I had expected them to move away again in hopes of luring me closer.

I would never reach the Edge and open a door before they stopped me. The plan I had worked out in detail during the long hike dissolved at the sight of those below.

The usual panic didn't follow. Instead, I took hold of Adrian's arm and we both slid into the shadows. I feared Aletta might detect me this close, but the overpowering magic of the Edge no doubt blinded her to my presence.

Riders moved here and there watching for trouble, so we moved into a little ravine and took shelter below a fallen pine. Animals had lived here for a while, but they'd probably gone as soon as the magic came so close.

"What can we do?" Adrian whispered.

"I can scare them," I replied. He looked surprised, but pleased. We had little time for me to plan anything elaborate. "I'm not sure it's wise, what I plan do -- but we haven't the time to search for wisdom."

"What do you need from me?"

"To watch and guard while I get the door open. I'll give you a shield against Aletta's magic, but my power might not hold her back for long. I want to know if they get too close though."

He didn't ask for more.

A few quiet moments settled the spell in my mind and there I formed the image I wanted and feed magic into and let it take shape until I thought the spell would burst from my head. I didn't let go as I took Adrian's hand as we returned to the hill overlooking the camp.

I turned towards the moon, a glow of light behind the clouds, and I let the magic slip from me and up and up -- and the magic formed into a shape dancing in the light . . . flapped huge, blue wings --

Shouts of fear spread the scene by the Edge. I knelt in the snow by Adrian and watched the army abandon their camp and race for horses and weapons. Chaos erupted as the image of the dragon glided towards them. I forced the semblance low -- but not too low, then the dragon went back up and curved around through the clouds.

Tamerlane and Aletta scrambled to a horse and prepared to ride. He grabbed a crossbow from behind him on the saddle and shoved Aletta forward over the horse's neck while he took aim. If he tried to shoot the dragon, he'd realize the secret. The horses had taken up the fear of the humans, moving so erratically that he hadn't a chance to aim.

I patted Adrian on the hand and gave him a shield of magic just before we slipped over the hillock and across the snow. We had no shadows to hide us in the bright glow of the Edge but no one looked as they watched the dragon, expecting an attack.

I reached the area where the Edge tapered off into the real world but had to go farther along the line to find a stable spot to begin my work. Aletta gave a cry of anger and I glanced back and saw her waving towards me. Tamerlane shouted, and horsemen turned and galloped our way. Adrian drew his sword --

And cats rushed from the woods nearby, yowling like banshees as they attacked. Cato ran in the lead, along with Snow, Smoke -- and even Mrs. Miniver.

The birds followed. Gaylord squirmed out of my jacket and launched himself over Adrian's shoulder and at an oncoming horse and rider.

My breath caught.

And then I turned away again.

I opened the door with little trouble, but I needed something to draw attention and give Timber, my father and everyone else a reason to come running to help us. I had to be flashy and loud --

"The dragon is not real!" Aletta yelled in anger and frustration. "Get your bastard soldiers back here and stop her!"

I had run out of time, so I grabbed at the magic and tried not to remember Aletta's touch and how much better she had been at magic. The door had opened a wide door to the lovely green rolling hills of home. No city waited there this time since it had already come through, sitting like a malevolent ghost over the real town. However, I found a huge magic wall close by, which had sheltered the fae side of the Edge from notice. This was why no one had realized the odd things goings on here.

I shoved a hole through the second wall, too -- though not a very big one. Then I shaped words by magic. I made them strong.

We need help, we need help, we need help!

I started to send those words through, filed with so much magic they danced with light and flashed with all the panic I could no longer hide.

Adrian yelled something, and I turned in surprise as Aletta launched herself from the horse and straight at me. Adrian had three soldiers he fought already, and he'd taken a bad cut in the side. He was about to go to his knees, and the sword of one of the enemy would kill him.

Aletta reached out and stopped my magic words with a wave of her fingers and a flash of power. I could have tried to stop her.

Instead, I used magic to catch hold of Adrian and threw him into the opening and into the fae lands. He reached back towards me, bleeding, panicked, lost -- but alive.

Mrs. Miniver was trying to pull Cato away, blood covering his side, while Shakespeare and Gaylord swirled and fought and frightened horses away from them. Birds and cats lay everywhere.

I couldn't save the world, but I could save some of my friends.

I shoved Aletta aside with my hands and not magic. She would have countered a spell, but brute force worked for me this time as she slipped on a puddle of melted snow and ice lining the Edge. I used the last of my hoarded magic to grab all of my little allies, and I swept them up in a whirlwind and shoved them through the opening to where Adrian still tried to get to his feet, bleeding and yelling things I couldn't hear about the other sounds. I stepped towards him --

Aletta grabbed me, a gleeful smile on her face.

So I closed the door.

CHAPTER TWENTY-FIVE

Aletta's enraged blow sent me to my knees, my head spinning. Rain, ice and snow fell around us as the storm raged out of control yet again. Maybe the storms these last few days had always portended the end of the world, and I had been too blind to realize until now.

"Open the door again," Tamerlane commanded as he limped towards us.

Aletta scowled his way. There was a match made in hell. "I can't yet." From the look on her face, Aletta hated to say so to this man. "I need to regain magic --"

He slapped her.

She fell to the ground and glared at him with her eyes blazing. I watched with mild interest, knowing this unlikely drama spared my life a little longer. Let them play out their games.

"Never strike me again." Magic crackled in the Edge as she stood, her rage made manifest. Tamerlane had the wisdom not to slap her for ordering him. A man does not conquer all he had without learning to recognize problems.

"If you cannot open the door, why should I not ride off with my men? What difference does this make to me?

Do you think I'm stupid?" He came closer and stared into her face. "The door will bring *you* power. The door is for your kind. I would like to share the power, too, but I will not stay in this winter land any longer. What I want lies close by to the east. Once I have the power, what else will matter?"

"What you want?" Aletta asked, confused.

"The treasures of the Golden Horde," I answered and won a startled look from Timur. "So he can touch them again, things the historical Tamerlane held. Once he does, he will be real in this world."

He gave me an almost regal nod. "Oh yes. You are far wiser than this one. She has never seen past her pride and her personal wants. A shame I had not allied with you, instead."

"It never would have happened . . . because I am far wiser than Aletta."

He gave a little nod of agreement. Aletta, almost hissing with anger, lifted her hands as she snarled.

He slapped her once more. She fell against the wall, surged forward -- and two of the soldiers caught hold of her. Tamerlane brought up a knife and held the blade before her face.

"Open the door or else I have no use for you at all because you are not pretty enough to even throw into the seraglio with my other conquests."

Her face paled as she started to speak, but the knife cut a little path along the side of her neck, almost against the artery. I doubt anyone had ever told her she's wasn't beautiful. Those words struck her harder than the physical viciousness of her ally.

If she had considered anything but herself, she would have reached me with magic and we could have formed a bond to work against him.

But not Aletta. *No.* She turned her rage on me and on the Edge. She shoved me against the magical wall and she began to tear a door open in the surrounding magic, using brute force and anger. the Edge reacted in kind. Magic flicked out, burning and bright. A soldier caught in the power glowed, screamed, and disappeared. Others backed away, but Tamerlane remained with the knife steady in his hand.

I fought her. She snarled in rage and pushed harder; I threw everything I could into the power to stop her, and she chiseled away at my feeble magic, inch by inch --

Power surged through the wall and around me.

I had lost.

No, I hadn't.

Aletta leapt back, startled and then frightened. Close by me an opening flared, huge and wide, and filed with noise and light and movement. Horses and riders rushed through into the human world. They were not Tamerlane's people; these wore the colors of a dozen clans and they shouted as they moved immediately to the attack.

Aletta screamed in rage. Tamerlane's soldiers released her and attacked the new enemy. More warriors from the fae world came through --

Aletta almost stopped them. The power of her rage must have been much akin to the power I often got from fear. She threw the fae back, and I feared she might trap a few in the wall, winning a bigger opening than I would have made.

I heard big wings nearby though I could see nothing in the new snow storm. No time left! Aletta shouted her spell, but I grabbed her leg and she sprawled into the muck and mud. She still grabbed at the Edge and tried to force control through her will. Cago and another of my cousins got caught in the Edge and panicked as they tried to get free. Aletta's magic had begun to work at this crux moment.

No!

I grabbed whatever magic I could and shoved my cousins free. Aletta howled and slashed out at me with magic and physical power. I barely rolled away, almost landing beneath hooves of a horse. I couldn't breathe now, or lift my arms to do more magic.

So much happening! Adrian had arrived and slid off a horse to pull me into his arms and protect me from the others. I held to him, gasping and hoping to live long enough to see what happened. I watched as though through a narrow dark corridor which shifted to nothing beyond Adrian's face. I heard nothing above the roaring in my ears. But we had stopped them; surely I had stopped Aletta in the last battle!

Another set of hands rested on my shoulders. I shuddered at the touch and then felt magic -- healing, warm, welcome. *Father.*

When I had the strength to turn he took me from Adrian's hold and into his own for a moment . . . and then he gave me back. I hadn't expected him to approve of a human --

"You came," I whispered, grateful that something had worked. "I tried get through. I couldn't reach you --"

"Your human is *very* loud," father said with a smile. "And finding a sudden influx of wounded birds and cats meant I knew this trouble came from you and had to be serious. We had other problems, but this . . . this was far worse than what we faced elsewhere. Aletta just kept it well hidden."

"She had allies." I smiled as Cato rubbed against my

legs. Gaylord and Shakespeare arrived a moment later as the others came through behind the fae. I laughed to see them all. The day brightened.

"You did well." My father patted me on the arm as though nothing remained to do.

We still had more work. Tamerlane's soldiers were scattering, while my father's men, on the faster fae bred mounts, followed and overtook them. I saw them battling, grabbing at wrists, tearing off strings -- and the soldiers disappeared, one after another.

Tamerlane and Aletta rode a single horse, riding fast before the others.

"Katlyn?" my father asked drawing back my attention.

"We need to stop them." I stood, though I wouldn't have stayed to my feet without Adrian's help. I waved a trembling arm towards Tamerlane and Aletta. "We need to get them right now."

"We'll get to them soon enough. The trouble here has made the Edge very unstable."

"Now," I said. He turned, startled. "Now. There are *dragons*, father. They want us to deal with Tamerlane or they will. We have little time."

"Dragons? Gods! My horse! We need horses!"

I bent down and grabbed Cato as Adrian picked up his backpack. Someone had healed his wounds though the red of blood still showed on his clothing and I felt a scar beneath Cato's fur. Someone had healed him as well, and he felt whole and good. He purred as I held him close.

"Are we going to ride?" Cato asked, watching the horse someone brought for me.

"Unless you want to grow wings and fly," I replied and held him close.

"A cat flying. Ha!" Gaylord said and came down to my

shoulder.

"Watch what you say, you little feather-brained --" Cato stopped. He looked up, dismayed. "Oh no. I *understand* him."

"And I understand you, too, you big fur ball. So watch what you say." Gaylord snapped his beak at him a few times and then settled smugly against the collar of my jacket.

Cato looked so stricken I barely managed not to laugh . . . well, not too much anyway. Shakespeare settled on Adrian's shoulder when he mounted the horse. My father helped me up in front of Adrian, Cato in front of me and Gaylord still holding tight.

Shakespeare leaned forward and tapped me on the shoulder.

"You are the most thick-headed person I've ever met," the bird said in quite clear parrot. "Why, in the name of all the feathered gods, did *you never look up one of my quotes*? And can we please change my name now? Shakespeare? Come on. At least get the gender right!"

"Oh. Oh." I didn't know what to say.

But we turned to ride anyway, so I didn't need to answer her just yet.

My father and his men fell in around us. None of Tamerlane's army remained, but Tamerlane and Aletta rode full out ahead of us, two shapes nearly lost in the snow storm.

And then a shadow drifted overhead as two dragons sailed beneath the clouds.

We rode with the wind.

CHAPTER TWENTY-SIX

Midnight arrived amid a heavy fall of snow -- no surprise there. We rode along Highway 34, past buildings that were hotels again with only a whisper of the other city still holding to the magic. The ghost city would disappear before daybreak and the humans would awake to find their world normal -- at least if we won this final battle. The fae were already doing their best to counteract the spells and to set things right. My father sent people to take care of the worst problem. I knew when the encircling domes went down and the expanding desert vanished to some other place, though I sometimes still spotted sand in corners, barely covered by the new fall of snow.

We had to find Tamerlane and Aletta. I suspected where they would be and led the group straight there.

The Stanley Hotel still looked like an oriental palace though a little faded along the edges. The grounds held more sand than snow. A few soldiers still camped on the grounds, but they seemed to have lost much of their power and were almost wisps again. They quickly fell to the fae, and we advanced up to the doors without a problem. I saw the horse, abandoned by the Stanley Hotel vans, and glimpsed Aletta and Tamerlane heading inside the ornate doors.

"He will be hard to get out of there," my father admitted as we dismounted. He lifted a hand. "This is damned strong magic, and the power will try to warp everything we do. He's made this his world."

"But we're going in," Adrian said.

"You need not go. You are a human. This isn't your battle to fight."

"I stay with Kat. And last I looked, this was still my world."

My father almost said something. He stopped and nodded instead. I wasn't sure if I was happy that he gave up the fight.

We headed for the door and I sensed the world alter as we pressed forward. Faces stared from the building's gilded windows, and I heard the shouts of people. Oh yes, this place seemed quite real enough this time, though magic still held it here.

A few fae went ahead, and I heard a battle somewhere inside the gilded walls. Cago held the door, battling back one fierce warrior and then another, but they were no match for the fae who knew the secret of the strings.

"Clear!" Cago shouted.

We went inside the building.

"I know the way to the throne room." I took the lead, Adrian standing as my guard, a sword in hand.

We ran the labyrinth of halls, my father's companions sometimes fighting away people who tried to stop us. We reached the room only moments after Tamerlane and Aletta. I saw the ghost of the one Tamerlane dissolve into the reality of the new form. The scribe blinked, frowned and began to write once more.

The tiger stood.

"Be still," I told her. "Be still. This is not your place or your time."

She backed away, tail lashing. Cato, standing at my feet, watched her.

"I am Timur. I am the conqueror and I rule the world of men." He spoke the words and made them true in this place. "Bow before your betters, my subjects! Bow down and accept."

His presence melded with magic of this place and amplified the power of his words.

A mistake to come here: My legs wanted to fold under me, trying to obey his command -- accepting his rule because this was his place and no longer the human world nor the fae one. He ruled here and we could not deny it.

The others fought against the compulsion. Adrian started to bow. I caught his arm and held him to his feet, and in holding him, I gained the strength to stand against Timur. I realized, suddenly, that even here, Tamerlane shouldn't hold the depth of magical power to command us --

Aletta?

I searched until I found my cousin standing just behind Tamerlane, lost in the shadows. Her magic mixed with the power of this myth they'd worked so hard to make real.

But no. She never had so much control. She couldn't have created this --

Another fae here.

"Bow! And accept my place!"

One fae went to his knees. Another followed. Tamerlane smiled and his power grow as the fae accepted him as real.

"No," I said aloud. "No. Magic -- father. Strong -- someone else, helping them --"

My father turned to me, eyes narrowed, face pale. Fighting.

"You have not been given the right to speak, *woman*." Tamerlane crossed and caught hold of my hair, a hand raised --

And Adrian hit him.

Hard.

He stumbled backwards. The tiger growled in wordless rage and yanked at her chain, but I couldn't decide if she meant to come for us or just leap to kill something. She was long past sane.

When Tamerlane stumbled, the power lessened for a few heartbeats. The scribe faded away. Some of the others looked less real. I glanced frantically around. "Magic somewhere. We have to get out."

"Stay!" Tamerlane shouted, the word reverberating through the walls.

I froze.

"Magic," Adrian whispered as he looked at the walls and back to Tamerlane. He moved away from me despite my cry of despair, a slow steady step and closer to the throne where Tamerlane stood. Another. Did Tamerlane think he came to bow to the man? He didn't look worried.

Adrian pulled the backpack from his shoulders and reached inside it.

Oh dear Gods.

Adrian turned on the digital camera and threw the device at Tamerlane and Aletta.

The world shattered, spun, splintered and howled. Winds and vacuum fought each other with the screams of rage and the silence of emptiness: Everything came upon us, the moment when nothing remained real, and the world teetered between the power of reality and technology or myth, and magic.

I folded myself over Cato, holding him tight and grabbing hold of Adrian, dragging him to us to create my reality. All I wanted, I pulled together with my power and made this, for a moment, my place.

I gathered Gaylord and Shakespeare to us, and then my father, and a few more fae, all drawn because my want of something became manifest.

Things calmed.

I lifted my head. Shadows played along the walls as the intricate mosaics melted away. Sand brushed against the floor and disappeared -- but this wasn't the same room. We stood in the lobby of the Stanley Hotel.

Tamerlane staggered to his feet, but his form, too magical and wounded by the technology, wavered, changed, grew misty -- unreal. He became a ghost rider once more though without the horse.

"Catch him!" my father shouted, stumbling to his feet.

Fae swarmed towards him, ready to encircle the mist in magic. Aletta stood, shaken and frightened as the fae came for her. She started frantically for the door and ran --

The mist surged towards her. She saw the movement and screamed.

"No! Not me! Not me!"

She ran, shoving open the door and racing out into the winter storm. If she had stayed, we could have helped her. The ghost followed out into the cold snow and we rushed afterwards, most of us limping and cursing, though a few fae patted Adrian on the shoulder and thanked him. They all looked stunned though.

The night felt colder outside, but the snow had

lessened. Aletta ran down the road, stumbled --

Shakespeare came and settled on my shoulder, watching.

Tamerlane caught Aletta, white smoke sliding into her body. She nearly lost her balance, stumbled, and ran again -- limping now.

"*Till growing bold, he laughed and leapt in the tangles of Love's very hair.*" Shakespeare said, shaking her head.

A dragon glided over the top of the hotel, golden scaled, the sinewy body flowing as though moving through water rather than air. Aletta -- Tamerlane -- turned as the creature came at him and yelled --

The dragon caught her by the shoulder, flapped his wings, lifting upward, upward, gone into the clouds before I could catch my breath.

The other dragon circled around us once, landed and changed into the jade-eyed woman. Fae backed away in haste. Adrian and I did not.

"Have we done this well?" I asked softly.

"Oh yes, my little fae friend. Oh yes. We have him now. Be safe. Be well."

Then she changed, took to the air and sailed to her companion.

Light flashed, and I felt a door open, magic rolling over us for a moment -- a door to somewhere, though not to the land of the fae. They sailed through, taking Tamerlane with them.

And the door closed.

The snow finally stopped falling.

"Done." Adrian said, sighing with relief.

"Almost." I reached into his pocket and pulled out the chain and gem I had hidden there. I handed the necklace to my father. "Aletta had powerful help. She used this to stay in contact."

He held the gem, opened the magic, and traced a line -
- straight to another man whom I almost didn't recognized
since I so seldom saw him: Kalin, Aletta's father. He still
wore the big cape he'd had on when he visited his daughter
at the condo.

"That's him! That's him!" Gaylord snapped his beak at
the man several times as the others took him away.

"Go rest," my father ordered. His rested on hand on
my shoulder gave me a little more magic. "The rest of us
will do what we can to settle everything tonight, before the
humans awake, and clear the signs of the magic and the war
both here and in the park."

"Peripix everywhere," I warned. "Some of the cats got
a few, but they're nesting in places they shouldn't. The cats
can show you where. The Edge though --"

"Already retreating to where it belongs." His hand
rose, measuring the magic. "Damned dangerous stuff,
forcing the Edge to move. Kalin and Aletta had imbued
each of the soldiers with a little door magic, so they could
pass back and forth at will -- at least for a while. They were
not real, so it worked for them, but wouldn't hold the way
open long enough to do what they clearly wanted. Fools."

"The city?" I asked, looking around as the last shadows
of Samarkand faded.

"I haven't fully studied this, but from what I sense,
they used small pieces of the Edge taken from all over the
world and built the mythical city close to the Edge here so
we wouldn't notice, not in the flux time. That's why it could
pass through the Edge. It took them years -- probably
decades, if not a century -- to set this up and put everything
in motion. If I had considered another fae might be
helping, I wouldn't have abandoned you to this." He looked

into my eyes. "You did a good job, Kat. We can do the rest of the work. You need to recover. I would hate to lose you now."

Adrian took my hand, worry in his face. My father smiled and even gave Adrian a pat on the shoulder. That he accepted the human was a wonder all its own.

I let Adrian take me away as we headed towards home. I didn't mind the walk since I still gained magic from the snow. The city was quiet in the darkness of the night and at peace for the first time in days. We had a pleasant walk, despite the cold.

Cato rested on Adrian's shoulders and Gaylord and Shakespeare flew ahead of us. When I glanced back, I saw my father send people out to fix whatever little problems might remain.

We won. The world didn't end.

"Done," I finally said.

Adrian wrapped an arm around my shoulder.

Done and safe.

CHAPTER TWENTY-SEVEN

Three days passed before the road crews got the highways cleared, even with the snow melting in the warm spring days. By then we had power, the phones worked and people had begun to drive out of Estes Park, happy to leave the long adventure behind.

Others had headed to the town and the mountains to ski. Some humans are just crazy.

Adrian and I had breakfast at the Bear Camp the morning he planned to leave. Lily and Jim shared coffee with us as they prepared to go hunt down the creature they'd sought before the snows.

"With luck, the thing has disappeared," Jim said. "I hope so. We have the park open again and even the pass will be cleared within the week. I want nothing dangerous wandering around up there."

I nodded, knowing the gargoyle would no longer be a problem. I gave Adrian a little smile.

He'd already talked to the magazine publisher, confessed everything, and sent scans of preliminary pictures we'd taken on a hike yesterday. The publisher forgave him everything once he saw the work. He even said the pictures of the animals seemed magical.

He was right.

"I'll be back in a few weeks," Adrian promised as we walked out of the cafe. He took my hand and held the fingers tightly in his own. "I will somehow wrangle a way to get settled here, at least for a good amount of time. I want to learn . . . everything. Magic, you, the two worlds. I saw the lands on the other side of the Edge and I want to understand what it all means, Katlyn. I want you to teach me."

I nodded, not trusting my voice at that moment. I didn't want him to go, even for a little while. I turned and tested the Edge, as I did so often these days, while I fought to gain control of my emotions. It had returned to the Terra Tomah area and fallen silent and still. We had calm again though I had trouble accepting the peace.

We still had a few peripix wandering around. Even my father and his men couldn't find them all. The cats continued to do their best, and the clan planned to return to clear them out as soon as they settled things on the other side.

Aletta and her father had set a number of magics in motion there and created considerable chaos to cover what they did at this insignificant little corner of the human world. They had kept everyone running in circles, but they had never expected me to stop them.

I had expected Tiber to replace me. Instead, he had come over and thanked me and Adrian both. He had never come to the human world as far as I knew. I'm not certain Adrian understood the full implications, but it meant a lot to me.

Now I looked at Adrian and gave a little sigh. He had to go deal with things in the human world. His place. I couldn't keep him here with me, without changing him.

When we reached his car I leaned forward and kissed him. We drew whistles and cat calls -- one from a passing cat -- before he drew back.

"I can take you home first --" he offered.

"I would rather walk," I said. "Go and hurry back, Adrian. I'll miss you."

I hadn't said those words to him until now. His eyes brightened and his smile grew. He opened the car door and slid inside, starting the car and closing the door. My heart did a thump of regret. The window rolled down but stuck half way. I reigned in my magic and the car worked again. I leaned forward and kissed him once again. We said nothing more.

He pulled away, the car turning in the parking lot, heading out into the street. Disappearing . . . my heart pounded and tears threatened to blur my vision, but I he would return. His promise gave me something wonderful to look forward to in the near future.

I took a slow walk home, stopping to talk to the pigeons and gathering three peripix I found nesting in the barn. All was well. A couple cats thanked me for the tuna treats they got every time they dropped a peripix into the holding tank. I'd have to send the new batch over to fae before the cell got to full. My real fear, however, was the possibility of peripix dens somewhere in the mountains. I suspected we would be dealing with this problem for a long, long time.

I stopped and talked to Mrs. Miniver, too, while Mrs. Hale bustled around in her garden out back.

"We did all right, we did," she said, all bright-eyed and looking half her age. I wondered if the change came from her short sojourn into the fae lands. "Cato, he showed himself a brave lad, he did."

"You were all brave," I said.

"That we were." She stared into my face. "All of us, Kat."

I smiled, bade a proper farewell, and walked the rest of the way to the house. Trouble, Snow, Smoke and the little black cat I called Shadow lounged under the trees. I'd bring them out food in a few minutes.

As I stepped to the front door I heard Cato and the two birds inside, all three of them laughing.

Cats and birds sharing a joke?

You know that just can't be good.

The End

###

ABOUT THE AUTHOR:

Hello!

I am an eclectic and prolific author whose has published in a number of genres, including Young Adult Mystery, Urban Fantasy, Epic Fantasy, Science Fiction and numerous works on writing. While I started on the outer edges of traditional publication with sales to small press and magazines publishers, I have since moved most of my work to the Indie world and I am madly in love with the new world of publishing and the direct contact with readers.

I live in Nebraska with my husband, my cats and a small but entirely useless dog.

I also own Forward Motion for Writers and the ezine, Vision: A Resource for Writers.

Connect with Zette:

Web Site: http://lazette.net

Twitter: http://twitter.com/lazetteg

Facebook: http://www.facebook.com/lazette.gifford

Joyously Prolific Blog: http://zette.blogspot.com/

Half-fae, genderless and mistrusted by his fae relatives, Skye is unexpectedly drawn into a dangerous magical power-play.

Skye's human half-sister has disappeared, drawing Skye into contact with their bitter mother . . . and into a trap that reaches all the way to the fae world.

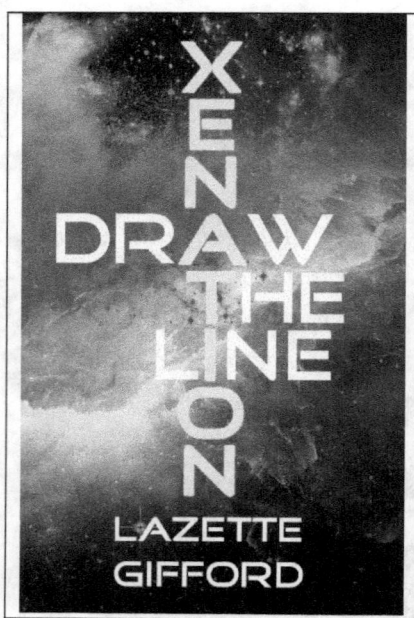

When humans found the abandoned -- and ancient -- space station, they moved in to study the place they called Xeno-Station, and then shortened to Xenation. Following them came three other races, all intent on learning secrets. Only now one of the humans has a dangerous link to the heart and controls of this alien place, and he's learning there are secrets and dangers no one imagined.

FIND WORKS BY

LAZETTE GIFFORD

ON

CREATESPACE

SMASHWORDS

A CONSPIRACY OF AUTHORS

NOOK

AMAZON

AMAZONKINDLE

LAZETTE.NET

www.ingramcontent.com/pod-product-compliance
Lightning Source LLC
Chambersburg PA
CBHW071214250626
47159CB00001B/304